LONDON, BURNING

Anthony Quinn

ABACUS

First published in Great Britain in 2021 by Little, Brown
This paperback edition published in 2022 by Abacus

1 3 5 7 9 10 8 6 4 2

A CIP catalogue record for this book
is available from the British Library.

ISBN 978-0-349-14428-3

Typeset in Palatino by M Rules
Printed and bound in Great Britain by Clays Ltd, Elcograf S.p.A.

Papers used by Abacus are from well-managed forests
and other responsible sources.

Abacus
An imprint of
Little, Brown Book Group
Carmelite House
50 Victoria Embankment
London EC4Y 0DZ

An Hachette UK Company
www.hachette.co.uk

www.littlebrown.co.uk

For Tom Knox

What country, friends, is this?

Viola, *Twelfth Night*

1

The stilted giant of the Westway loomed overhead, the noise of cars swishing across it. Huge pale clouds shouldered over the navy sky. Vicky stepped into the pool of night-shadow, squinting to adjust her sight. She glanced at her watch – coming on for half past ten – and stopped to light a cigarette. The August evening was still warm, and she could feel pinpricks of sweat under her arms. She glanced down, considering her look: thin blouse, leather mini, two silver bangles riding on her wrist; her baseball pumps didn't really go with the fishnet stockings, but they'd be the sensible choice if she had to run. She had a quick rummage through her handbag to check everything was there.

Absorbed in this she didn't notice the tan Escort that had come to a halt alongside her. The driver, face blurred, had leaned over to roll down his window.

'How much, love?' he called out.

She ducked her head to take a look at him. 'I'm busy. Sorry,' she replied, not sure why she'd apologised. She turned away. The car idled along; he asked her again, more coaxingly. This time she hardened her voice. 'I told you, I'm busy. Hop it.'

She caught a muttered oath as he rolled up the window and sped off. The gauntlet of Bramley Road lay before her, illuminated by the cheerless amber glare of the street lights. Up and down she'd walked this road, five nights on the trot: on the look-out. She took a long drag on her Silk Cut, exhaled, and walked on. A whoop made her jump; a couple of kids raced past her on bicycles. Keep your wits about you, don't go out alone if you can help it. That was the advice. You could read it on the warning notices they'd posted in windows and on walls, just below an identikit portrait that was supposed to be his face. To Vicky it wasn't the face of someone – anyone – you might recognise. The dead-fish eyes, the slabbed cheeks and the ungainly shape of the head were like a jigsaw that didn't fit. Who on earth looked like that?

While no one could be certain about his appearance, everyone seemed to know his moniker. The Notting Dale Rapist had been all over the papers, and on telly. Seven women in four months. The attacks followed a pattern, the victims all aged between eighteen and twenty-four, attractive, no taller than five foot seven. Each was approached as she was getting into or leaving her car. The man would ghost up behind and force them at knifepoint into the vehicle. In two instances he forced the victim to drive them to waste ground; then he bound her hands before assaulting her. In the most brutal of the seven attacks the victim had clawed the balaclava from his head, gaining a brief glimpse of his face, for which she was beaten and nearly throttled to death. The intervention of a passing traffic warden saved her.

So it looked pretty bloody silly of her to be out here tonight.

She was now just over halfway down the road. Cars swept past, their tail lights blushing to red as they approached the junction. Up ahead a man was walking purposefully towards her, and she tensed, clutching her handbag in readiness. He glanced at her as they passed one another, but he didn't break his stride. She heard his footsteps fade up the street. On reaching the traffic lights she stopped, and crossed. One of the big housing estates was coming up on the right, with a telephone box standing lone sentry, its pickled yellow light glimmering against the dark. A man was inside, absorbed in conversation. She was so close she could see his leather bomber jacket and the knuckles on his hand holding the receiver. A few moments later she heard the door of the box creak open and he emerged, about twenty yards behind her. She glanced over her shoulder, taking in his tall, athletic figure. He was looking straight at her. Quickening her pace, she recrossed the road, kept moving. When she next threw a backward glance there was no one there. He must have turned into the estate.

To her left was a side road, where the wands of light from the main street lamps didn't reach. Some way along a Mini was parked in the shadow of a towering plane tree. Vicky stopped, and took the handbag from her shoulder to lay on the roof of the car, as if it were her own. She waited a few moments, ears cocked, then took out her Silk Cut and lighter. The night felt stilled, apprehensive. It was taking a risk to deviate from the main drag. She had just fished out a cigarette when she sensed a movement behind her, no more than a disturbance of the air, and before she could shout, a gloved hand was clamped over her mouth. Something cold and steely pressed against her neck. The voice was muffled: 'Scream and I'll fuckin' kill you. Open the door and get in.' She waited a beat, then tried the handle. Locked. He took his hand away from her mouth. 'I said open it.' 'It's not my car,' she said quietly. He stopped jostling her. With his knife hand he tried the door for himself.

She saw this was her moment, and leaned towards her open handbag. Keeping her voice level she said, 'Officer requires assistance.' From inside the bag came the sudden crackle of static. As the man tensed in surprise she donkey-kicked him in the shin – to no apparent effect, as he now spun her round and grabbed her by the throat. It was the phone-box man, only now his face was masked by a dark balaclava. He put his head close to hers. 'A pig, yeah?' he said, the blade gleaming in his hand. 'Well, I'm gonna gut you like the pig you are.' She would have chosen this point to scream for help, but the chokehold he had on her windpipe put paid to that.

A voice in the distance saved her. She felt his grip freeze as he turned his head to where it had come from; now they could both hear hurrying footsteps. She saw his eyes through the slits.

He's going to slash my face just for the hell of it, she thought. He had taken a step back, in a split second of indecision. She was about to say 'You're nicked' – the two most satisfying words in the copper's lexicon – when a lightning bolt slammed her below the eye. She blinked out stars as the punch raced like an electric charge down her body, making her legs wobble. She had seen boxers fall in the ring, but she had never before appreciated the distinct stages of collapse, the way the head rocked back, the shoulders slumped and, after a stunned micro-pause, the knees gave way. The ground rose to meet her with a smack that sounded loud in her ears; the last thing she sensed before blacking out was running feet and shouts.

When she came round she was slumped in the back of a patrol car, parked crosswise on the kerb. 'And she's back,' trilled the gum-chewing paramedic as she stirred and blinked. He was shining a pencil torch in her eyes. His mouth was so close to hers she could smell stale mint. He started by asking her to identify herself. 'Vicky Tress. Police Constable.' He tried a few more memory tests on her before he looked satisfied. 'We're gonna send you to Paddington anyway for a scan. It's probably only a minor concussion, but—'

'Do you really have to?'

'Yes, we do,' came the voice of an older man from the front seat. He leaned round, and now she made out Paul Drewett, the Detective Chief Superintendent in charge of the operation, his firm-jawed, clean-shaven face bathed in blue from the revolving crime-scene lights outside. 'You went down like a sack of spuds just now. We could hear the smack from up the road.'

When the paramedic had gone, Drewett gave her a long, searching look. 'You took some chance, Constable. We had look-outs posted all the way along Bramley Road – and you suddenly decide to go off-piste. Why?'

Vicky tried to order her thoughts. 'I saw him in the phone

box, sir. It was a hunch, so ... I thought if I could make it look like I had a car ...'

'He fell for *that*,' he said, half admiring. 'But things could have turned nasty for you. The knife he had on him, that could have been in your guts, and I'd have had a dead police officer on my conscience.'

'He said something about my guts,' she replied vaguely.

Drewett stared at her. 'How's the eye?'

'It's all right, sir.' It had begun to throb, painfully.

Now he shook his head, and gasped out a short laugh. 'You must be concussed. You haven't asked me yet.'

'Asked you, sir ... ?'

'About the suspect. The man who just decked you? We got him. We got the Notting Dale Rapist. Well done, Constable.'

Next thing she knew PC Lyons had draped a blanket around her shoulders and led her off to his patrol car. He and his partner, Moffat, were taking her to the hospital. On the way they amused themselves with teasing their passenger in the back seat and speculating on next morning's headlines.

'It'll be "Dale Rapist nabbed by have-a-go hero PC – and she's a woman!" Something like that. You ready for your close-up, Vicky?' said Lyons, his eyes flicking to the rear-view mirror.

'Sorry?' she said, not feeling up to their banter.

Moffat turned in his seat to contemplate her. 'Look at that shiner, though. You're gonna be quite a sight on the front pages with a mush like that.'

'Is it terrible?' She hardly dared to look.

He stifled a laugh. 'Put it this way, you can forget about blokes chasin' yer for a while. Even in those fishnets.'

They walked her into the A&E at Paddington just before midnight. The woman at reception told them it was busy this evening, but Lyons, pulling rank, insisted she bump Vicky to the front. 'Police officer, concussed – could be serious.' They would have to wait in any case, it turned out – the doctor on duty was already with patients. That's fine, Vicky cut in, she didn't mind waiting, but could they possibly find her a couple of paracetamol in the meantime? After a brief confab it was decided that Moffat would babysit her. Lyons, as he was leaving, gave Vicky a wink of congratulation.

'Not bad for a junior plonk.'

She laid her head back against the wall and listened, fitfully, to PC Moffat's not quite enthralling commentary on the night's events. *Plonk*. She still didn't know why that was the word for a woman PC. White-clad figures padded up and down the corridor. She must have dozed at some point, because he nudged her awake: an Asian doctor, with serious dark eyes, was enquiring after her condition. On hearing the story he nodded, said he'd take her along to the X-ray department.

She turned to Moffat. 'You'd better go. Looks like I'll be a while.'

'No, no, I can wait.' In his tone she could hear decency struggling with the prospect of a small-hours vigil.

'Just go,' she said. 'I'll be fine.'

With a hesitation that hinted at apology he rose and put on his cap. He'd been spared martyrdom. 'All right, then. Remember what the guvnor said – no coming in tomorrow. Get some rest.'

She watched him disappear down the wide, overlit corridor.

There was no telling how long the scan results would take, and the doctor she'd seen would likely be detained in any case. The nurse who had helped with the X-ray advised her to stay overnight. 'You look dead beat,' she said, with matter-of-fact sympathy.

They even found her a single room. But though her eyes itched with tiredness she lay awake for a long time, the adrenaline still doing its work. *Well done, Constable*. Vicky had joined the Met two years ago, just after she turned twenty. She had done any number of jobs on leaving school – a copy typist for an insurance company in the Gray's Inn Road, a sales assistant in a stationery shop, a barmaid and toilet cleaner in a pub in Kentish Town. Oh, the grinding boredom of all that ... and the rotten pay. The pub was the worst. The landlord once had the gall to accuse her of nicking from the till. 'I've never stolen anything in my life,' she told him, shaking with fury. When he later admitted that he'd miscounted the day's take she said he ought to apologise, and he wouldn't. So she told him to stuff it.

Yet she still wasn't sure what had made her apply to the force. She had asked her dad if he thought it was a good idea. He was a security guard at Truman's Brewery on Brick Lane, so he dealt with the police quite a lot and seemed to respect them. It would be a tough life, a copper's, he'd said, especially for a woman, though he didn't actually advise her not to. She remembered an afternoon when, sitting on a stalled bus in Camden, she'd watched as a WPC directed the traffic around the site of a motorcycle accident, a figure of calm amid the chaos, so at ease with the brisk signals of hand and arm that she seemed to be conducting not just traffic but the very air around her.

She sent off the form without telling anyone. The personnel department of the Met took so long replying that when a letter arrived to acknowledge her application she'd almost forgotten sending it. A woman police officer came to the house to interview her and to meet her parents. Her mother seemed bewildered, though she made no objection. Her father asked some thoughtful questions – the dangers of the job, the chances of promotion – which Vicky noticed the WPC took very seriously. She was proud of him for that. On the morning of her first day she came down to the kitchen to find him polishing her shoes, just as he had done for her and Matthew, her brother, every Sunday night before school. He thought polished shoes somehow conferred an instant advantage on the wearer: they made you look not just smart but capable. The theory stuck, because she too would never set foot outside the house without a parade-ground gleam.

She had just completed her probation period when her father

dropped dead, aged fifty-two. His health had been blameless; he had played football and cricket at school with distinction, had served in an army radio unit in Italy at the end of the war. At Truman's he had never taken a sick day in his life. He drank and smoked his share, but rarely to excess. He was still fit. Then one morning during Jubilee Week he had just stepped into his office with a cup of tea when a massive heart attack felled him. He was dead before the ambulance arrived. The shock of it blindsided her with a near-physical force. She had got back to Harrow Road, her first nick, from a morning patrol to find the DI waiting for her in the corridor; she knew something was up as soon as she saw his face. He drove her home himself, a kindness she was too numb to register at the time. Her mother had already been told, while Matthew was being fetched from school. She had once thought that joining the force was the most grown-up thing she could do; she knew different now. Living without her dad was the most grown-up thing she had done – or would ever do.

In the morning the doctor came in with the results of her scan. No damage to the skull had been sustained, though her headache still hadn't cleared. When she went to the bathroom she recoiled in surprise at her reflection. A bruise glowered on her forehead from the fall; her left eye was a slit beneath a swollen purple golf ball. She looked like some of the women she'd seen at the refuge centre. She wondered if the hospital might lend her a pair of dark glasses. Or maybe a paper bag to put over her head. She checked the *Mail* in the hospital reception, but there was nothing yet about the rapist; it would be in the afternoon edition of the *Standard*. It was quite exciting to think she had played a part in a big news story. The sun was out this morning, and her initial impulse was to walk for a bit, then catch a bus. But as soon as she stepped outside she felt self-conscious about her injuries, and instead she made for the cab rank.

The family home was a neat Victorian semi at the Chalk Farm

end of Harmood Street. Her parents had moved here when they married in 1955, the year before Vicky was born. Her dad had called it a 'decent' road, and it was close enough for Vicky and Matthew to walk to school.

The throbbing engine of the taxi resounded in the morning calm. The front door opened and Irene Tress stepped out. Her mouth made a perfect O of disbelieving horror as she took in her daughter's injuries.

'*Ohmygod*, what's happened to you?'

'Occupational hazard,' said Vicky with a brave smile. 'Can I come in?'

From upstairs drifted the cavernous bass thump of reggae. Matthew was in his bedroom, and probably hadn't heard her arrive. Her mother stood at the foot of the stairs, poised to shout up, but Vicky stopped her. 'I'll go up in a minute. Let's have a cup of tea first.'

As the kettle began shrieking on the stove, her mother continued to stare at her across the kitchen table. 'Why didn't you tell me about this, this – undercover business? And why did they have to pick on you?'

'They didn't *pick on* me. They asked me to do it cos there's not many plonks – women – to choose from on the force. I happened to fit the type of girl he was attacking. And I didn't tell you cos I knew you'd be worried sick.' Her mother shook her head, either at the wickedness of the Notting Dale Rapist or else at the unpleasant surprise of her daughter's involvement in his apprehension. 'It'll be in all the papers, just to warn you.'

'My God,' her mother murmured. 'They won't send anyone here, will they?'

Vicky shook her head. She wanted to explain how this might be a turning point in her career, but her mother had never been a natural at spotting the positives, and since her husband's death had withdrawn further inside her personal bunker of gloom. Life, for her, was something to be got through. Vicky often wondered how her father had put up with it. They talked for a while about Irene's job – she worked at a chemist's on Chalk Farm Road. The number of addicts hanging about the place was on the up, apparently; an awful lot of pilfering went on.

'And the *smell* coming off some of them—'

'How's he been?' said Vicky, eyes flicking in the direction of the music. Matthew, at seventeen, had taken his father's death hard; for the rest of that summer he became withdrawn, almost agoraphobic. When he went back to school his easy-going manner had changed and he started getting into fights. Now he was in the sixth form a different set of problems had become apparent. The fighting had stopped, and in its place had come a lethargy and a sullenness that baffled teachers who had previously known him to be conscientious and personable.

'He's got his mocks coming after Christmas but he doesn't seem interested,' said Irene with a sigh. 'I dunno what to do with him, really I don't.'

Vicky realised that her mother was perhaps not the person best equipped to spring the boy out of his blues.

'He misses his dad, that's all. Give him time.'

Irene's gaze dropped at that. It was Vicky's way of saying that all three of them missed him terribly. Of course they might have shared the burden by talking about it, but she sensed an unwillingness on her mother's part: grief had made her tight-lipped. 'I'll just pop up. Show him the war wounds.'

As she made her way up the carpeted stairs a burnt, ropey smell filled her nostrils. She knocked once on his door and opened it; the deep rumble she had heard at a distance now seemed to flare against her skin. Matthew was lying on his bed reading the *NME*, a tapering joint perched on a tin ashtray at his side. He looked up, his smile abruptly fading as he took in her black eye.

'Hi,' she said, sidling in, hands in her pockets, keeping it casual.

'Where did you get that?' he asked in a single breath.

'Oh, just a fight. Nothing serious.'

Tossing the paper aside, he got to his feet to take a closer look. They stood facing one another. Matthew, skinny as a whippet, wore combat trousers and a ragged T-shirt stencilled with the legend STEN GUNS IN KNIGHTSBRIDGE. His brown hair, whose luxuriant silkiness Vicky had loved when he was fourteen, was now pasted into punkish, antisocial quills. Yet however unnerving his appearance it would always be at odds with the choirboy innocence of his face. This was a relief to her.

'How's things?' she said, plumping herself on his vacant bed. 'Could you turn that down a bit?'

Matthew obediently adjusted a silver knob on his stereo and the dub dropped to an almost bearable volume. He sat down on the floor next to a yard-long row of albums. She asked how the music was going – he was lead guitar in a school band.

He shrugged. 'We haven't played for ages. They're all still on holiday.'

'Mum says you've been talking about jacking in school. Not serious, are you?'

He wrinkled his nose in vague disgust. 'I dunno. I don't see the point.'

'I thought you wanted to try for university?'

Something closed in his expression. He picked up the joint from the ashtray and relit it. Vicky stared at him, then made a show of sniffing the pungent cloud.

'You know I could arrest you for that, don't you?'

He glanced at her, and laughed. She smiled back. They listened to the reggae clanking along. The Clash LP rested on top of the stack, the cover shot an inky negative of the trio blocking an alleyway, moody-eyed. She didn't know what to make of punk at first, or of Matthew's passionate allegiance to it. The sound was raw, loud, right in your face. Her own tastes hadn't much changed over the years: she liked the Bee Gees, Neil Diamond, Fleetwood Mac. She knew every line, almost every note, of *Rumours*. The three-chord thrash of punk seemed so different as to make her wonder if it was actually *music* at all. Then one day while out on the beat she found herself half scatting along to a song she didn't know she knew; the words were unclear, but the rhythm was right inside her skull. It was one that Matthew had been playing, over and over. She wasn't sure she liked it, but she definitely wanted to hear it.

'Put the one I like on,' she said, nodding at the Clash.

In a moment he had cut short the reggae and teed up the record. A crackling pause as the needle dropped, and an urgent drumbeat came hurrying in; 'Janie Jones' sounded like aggression and fear and excitement all rolled into one.

The mood of the song, of all their songs, was violently antagonistic. It was like graffiti set to a beat. One song was called 'Police and Thieves', with the implication that there wasn't much to choose between them. Her old desk sergeant at Harrow Road nick would have described this as 'a problem with authority'. And yet there was no denying the energy in it, or the clenched-jaw conviction. This lot played their songs like they really *meant* them. She looked at Matthew, his head nodding in time to the beat. She was aware of the cautious regard in which he held her – not because she was a copper (they hadn't talked about that much) but because she was her own woman, and carried herself with an authority that never stooped to bullying. When their father died Vicky was the only one he seemed able to talk to.

'What would you do instead?' she asked him, talking over the music. 'I mean, if you don't sit your A levels?'

'Get a job. Like you did.'

'I had to. You know I wasn't bright enough to go to uni. And I did a lot of bloody boring jobs before I found one I liked.' She wondered if he was intimidated by being the first in their family to even think about going to university.

'*Do* you like it – being a copper?' he asked, suddenly serious for a moment. She nodded, and he looked away. 'What happened? To your eye, I mean.' There was a quiver of fear in his voice. She thought perhaps he didn't really want to know.

'I was on a job. You know that bloke who's been attacking women in west London? Well, we got him.'

'He did that?'

'Yeah. But that was all he did. The other women weren't so lucky.'

His head dropped, and when he lifted it again she saw his eyes glistening. She felt a brute stab of love right through her insides. She oughtn't to have told him that; he'd be upset for days.

'I want to make a deal with you,' she said, quickly reverting to the matter in hand. He still wasn't looking at her. 'You do your mocks. You fill in your UCCA form, or whatever it's called. You do your A levels. If you pass them, I'll give you a hundred quid.'

Matthew looked up, startled. 'What? You can't afford a hundred quid.'

'You've no idea what I can afford.'

His expression turned crafty. 'What if I only get Es?'

'Does an E get you an A level?'

He nodded. 'You can pass with Es,' he said, and laughed at his unintended joke. On the stereo 'Hate and War' rang out. 'A hundred quid?'

She held his gaze. 'Deal?'

At the station on Monday morning she was an instant object of attention, in smirking glances or ironic catcalls, or joshing remarks about the shiner, now showing a nicotine tint amid the purple-and-black bruising. A few offered congratulations. Dennis, one of the older constables with whom she'd first done beat work, shook her hand and muttered in an undertone how proud of her they all were. She walked away feeling about ten foot tall. She had just started on a backlog of paperwork when her phone went; someone wanted to see her upstairs.

She recognised DCI Wicks from briefing sessions when she was seconded to the team on the Notting Dale case. He was tall, late thirties, with a sporty gait and thick straw-coloured hair that reminded her of Robert Redford in *The Sting*. He was well known on the force as a tough nut. People feared him. He introduced himself with a handshake and a quick smile.

'David Wicks. I don't think we've spoken before,' he said, gesturing her towards a seat. His voice was light, coaxing. 'How's that eye?'

'Looks worse than it is, sir.'

'You did a fantastic job, Constable Tress. Talked to the Chief Super yet?'

'He phoned me over the weekend, sir. Recommended I should apply for sergeant.'

Wicks inclined his head thoughtfully. 'Sergeant. So you're going to stay in uniform?'

'Sir?'

'How old are you, Constable?'

'Twenty-two, sir.'

'Thinking about what you did on Thursday night, the danger you put yourself in, I'd say you're not afraid of much ... '

She couldn't see where this was going: best to keep it light. 'Well, I'm afraid of a desk job in South Mimms, sir. Or Croydon.'

'I was born in Croydon,' he said, straight-faced, and when she blushed and began stammering out an apology he laughed. 'I know what you mean. You don't wanna get posted there.'

She fell silent, mortified. Wicks rose from his seat, and made a little gesture with his hands, as if to say *Let's talk straight*. 'You'll make sergeant easy, if you want it. Wouldn't be a bad job. Handbag snatches, teenage runaways, domestic affray. But if you're as keen to get on as I think you are, you could go another way. It's tougher, and there's exams you'd have to do. Training school up Hendon way. Worth it, though – and I'll make sure they don't send you to South Mimms. Or Croydon.'

'Sir?' Still no idea.

'I think you should join our mob in West End Central. CID.'

2

The late-afternoon light poured through the library's high windows. Callum, distracted, had found himself reading the same paragraph again. The words on the page would not sit still before his eyes. It was easier to look around, or watch his neighbour out of the corner of his eye – anything to divert him from the book at hand. Another reader might have blamed this on the flat and unattractive style of the prose. In fact, a previous reader had explicitly done so, and in insolent biro, too. The margins were studded with his, or her, complaints, which grew more peevish as the chapter wore on. *No . . . Completely wrong . . . Don't agree with this at all.* And here, on this page, *BORING!* He flicked ahead as the biro-wielder's comments began to thin out, hoping for one more barb. He found it, on an inserted black-and-white photograph of the book's author in conversation with a fellow writer. From their mouths sprouted matching cartoon bubbles: *'Have you read my latest?' 'In a pig's arse, friend.'*

Callum gasped out a laugh, which made a ripple in the library's glazed silence. He lowered his head, embarrassed. On the one hand he was too fair-minded to fault the author, a one-time expert in his field (a time long past). On the other, it felt as hard to ignore these slights from the sideline as it would a fan standing next to you on the terrace hurling abuse at the referee. Even if you were amused by them, it was off-putting. While he had been working the light beneath the low September sky had turned an old gold; autumn was coming. He yawned, and clapped the book shut. He looked around at the heads bowed over the desks. The library's mood of concentration felt rather chastening. He had meant to post up his teaching schedule for the term, due to start in three weeks, but a letter from his publishers that morning had driven him to the desk to resume his research. Diligent by nature, he had lost time this summer when he'd had to go home and look after his mother, who had broken her hip in a fall.

He packed up his things and headed for the exit, the caramel-coloured parquet squeaking beneath his shoes. He crossed the flagged court and checked his pigeonhole for mail. There was a note from Juliet Barwell, the new lecturer, to say that she would be free after all: she'd meet him in the Marquis at six. He looked at his watch and, having assumed her no-show, now realised he'd have to put a spurt on. He had encountered her by chance in the staff common room this lunchtime, and in a reflex of friendliness suggested a drink after work. Yes, friendliness was his thing ... though he couldn't help noticing the outline of her long legs beneath the denim skirt, and the brown leather boots that reached to her knees. He nipped up to his office, had a quick wash and a squirt of deodorant. He rolled up his old college tie, the only one he owned, and crammed it in his pocket for later.

Hurrying along the Strand he had to dodge through a ragged knot of protesters outside the Royal Courts of Justice. Another union, it seemed, with another set of wage demands. STUFF THE 5% read the placards. Protest had become such a feature of life in the last few years you almost didn't notice it any more. Mutiny was in the air you breathed. He found the Marquis already thronged with the office crowd. She was sitting at the bar reading the *Guardian*, oblivious to the steady hum of talk. In profile she looked pointy, the slope of the nose and chin more austere than they looked face-on.

'Sorry I'm late,' he said, edging onto the stool next to her. 'I only just got your message.'

Juliet acknowledged him with an efficient little smile. He

bought drinks, gin and tonic for her, a Coke for him. She gave the room a quick once-over. 'Is this your favourite haunt?'

'In as much as a teetotaller can have haunts.'

She shifted around to look at him, an enquiring gleam in her eye. 'D'you mind my asking you something – where *is* that accent of yours from?'

He laughed. The English. 'Where do you think it's from?'

'Well, it's either Scottish or Irish, at a guess.'

'Northern Irish. I'm one of Her Majesty's subjects, just like you.'

She frowned in apparent alarm at this unsuspected kinship. 'Belfast, then?'

He shook his head. 'Newry. Right on the border. I'm presuming you've never visited.'

'We had a family holiday near Cork once.'

'That's the south. I'm from further up. How about yourself?'

'Oh, Hampshire. Do you know Alton? Jane Austen country. I'm afraid I've gone from one genteel place to another. School in Cheltenham. Then Cambridge for six years.'

'You may not find London so genteel.'

She pulled an apologetic face. 'I'm living in Hampstead.'

'Ah ...' They talked about their departments. Juliet was a classicist, had done a thesis on Latin lyric poetry. She reeled off a list of names he half recognised.

'Can't say I really know the classics people,' admitted Callum. 'Wheeler strikes me as a throwback to Rattigan. Crocker-Harris in his scholar's gown.'

'You get a lot of those,' she conceded. 'He seems all right. I like him because he gave me the job.' She offered him a cigarette, which he declined.

'We were taught Latin at school by a priest. I was so terrible at it I'd learn the English translation off by heart. When it came to the exam I just had to hope I'd recognise the passage. If I didn't I was stuffed. Only thing I can remember now is *nihil expectore in omnibus.*'

She looked at him, puzzled. 'I'm not sure that's . . . '

He blushed as he laughed. '"No spitting on public transport." From *Carry on Cleo*.'

She laughed too, though in a somewhat disapproving way, as if they ought to be above schoolboy jokes. There was an aloofness in her, honed over the years in 'genteel' environments, perhaps, though he conceded it might just be shyness. She dressed more confidently than she behaved.

'And you specialise in – let me guess – Joyce, Yeats, Beckett?'

He gave her a sidelong look. 'None of them, actually. Do I seem such a stereotype to you?'

She considered this. 'Far from it. You don't often meet an Irishman who doesn't drink or smoke.'

He supposed she meant this as a compliment, though it was double-edged, like most compliments. 'Irish writers were the sirens in my teenage years. But I strapped myself to the mast and resisted. The English got me instead – Forster, Lawrence, L. P. Hartley.'

He wondered about this self-mythologising blarney. It sounded to his ears a wee bit rehearsed. But Juliet's mind must have been running on different lines, because she now said, 'Did you never drink at all?'

'Alcohol, you mean? Had a nip of Father Mulcahy's altar wine a few times, when I used to serve Mass. But then I took the pledge, like me ma.'

'Why?'

He sighed inwardly. 'There was a lot of drinking, on both sides of the family. My dad was in and out the drunk tank. She got that sick of the police coming round . . . He died a few years back. I'd grown up with the stink of old booze, so it was no great hardship to give it up.'

Juliet was mid-sip as she heard this, and put her drink down sheepishly. 'Sorry, you don't mind that I . . . ?'

He raised his hand in a disowning gesture. 'You think I'm going to start raging against the demon drink? I'm fine with it. The lads back home used to give me some jaw. Not being a drinker put you in an unloved minority.'

'As a woman in academia I've always felt part of an unloved minority. So, Northern Ireland ... you don't miss it?'

He smiled sadly. 'I couldn't wait to get away. But then I thought that if you were going to be a writer you'd never feel like you belonged anywhere, least of all in your home town. Like you're born in exile, y'know?'

Her gaze had taken on a measuring look. 'And what have you written?'

'Not much,' he admitted. 'The odd paper. Had a contract for years to write a book based on my thesis. It sort of ran into the sand. Or so I thought – now the publishers want to schedule it for next year, so it looks like I'll have to write the bloody thing after all.'

Callum, glancing at his watch, had a sudden inspiration. 'As a matter of fact they've also invited me to a book launch this evening. Not far from here. D'you fancy coming along?'

She pulled a doubtful expression. 'I was going to have a quiet night in ... '

'Come on,' he said, trying not to sound eager. 'It's at one of those big old clubs on Pall Mall.'

Her eyes brightened momentarily. 'I've always wondered what they're like inside.'

'Here's your chance to find out.'

They caught a number 11 along the Strand. Seated together on the upper deck seemed to Callum more intimate than it had been at the pub. It wasn't merely that their bodies brushed against one another; for him it was an unspoken covenant of their future companionability. This was in spite of having to talk to her somewhat haughty profile. It was becoming clear that Juliet didn't know her way around London at all; as the bus joined the stately circuit of Trafalgar Square she gave a little coo of surprise.

'It's because I've been going everywhere by Tube,' she explained. 'I've no idea where anything *is*.'

Callum raised an invisible tour guide's microphone to his mouth and spoke in his best 'English' voice: 'Now if you'd care to look over to your right you can make out Nelson's Column, and beyond *that* the National Gallery.'

In reply to this mockery she gave his arm a light cuff, which he enjoyed. They hopped off the bus and continued on foot along Pall Mall. As they ascended the steps of the Reform Club she asked him what book was being celebrated.

'*The Antrobus Book of Political Speeches*,' he said, and grimaced. 'Sorry.'

In the lobby a porter darted out from his windowed cubicle to remind Callum of the club's dress code, and with a brisk man-of-the-world nod Callum withdrew from his pocket his concertinaed tie, and quickly put it on. They were directed through the atrium and up the staircase, following the babble of voices that reverberated from the wood-panelled library. The party, in full roar, seemed at first glance almost entirely made up of greying middle-aged men in dark suits booming at one another. 'Frightful. Just *frightful*,' he overheard a squat, pudding-faced man say to his companion, who murmured in assent. (Were they talking about the book? Or the company? Or the state of the country?) A white-jacketed waiter stopped in front of them to proffer a salver of drinks. Juliet took a glass of wine, but there was nothing there for Callum to drink so he smiled and walked on.

Having slalomed through the smoke-shrouded press of bodies the two of them found a little pocket of space on the other side of the room. They looked at one another.

'I can see three members of the Cabinet just from here,' said Juliet. 'You didn't say it was going to be starry.'

'I had no idea, to be honest. The only other launch of theirs I've been to was in a bookshop, and about four people showed up.'

Using his height, Callum craned his neck in search of the one person he definitely knew. A few twists of the periscope were required before he spotted her. 'My editor's over there,' he said. 'Would you like to be introduced?'

With another of her minimalist smiles Juliet assented, and followed in his wake. As he approached, Polly Souter caught his eye and – he silently blessed her – excused herself from the conversation she was having to greet him.

'Hello there,' she said, giving him a wry once-over. 'I wasn't sure this would be your kind of thing.'

'Um, Polly, this is Juliet Barwell, a colleague of mine.'

Polly's welcome was all brightness and affability, and reminded Callum why he liked her so much. She had commissioned his book years ago, and had shown patience in not pestering him for it.

'Sorry to have interrupted you,' he began, nodding towards the august-looking couple she had been occupied with.

'Don't be,' Polly said, with a quick glance back at them. 'He's an economic adviser to the PM. Conversation with him is the hardest ten minutes in London.'

'And that's his wife?'

She nodded. 'The hardest ten seconds in London.'

Callum smiled. 'Juliet was just saying what a big deal this is – Cabinet ministers and what have you.'

'Well, it's Westminster giving itself a pat on the back. I don't imagine a book of political speeches getting a reception like this anywhere else.'

'Have you read it?' Juliet asked her.

'*God*, no,' Polly replied. 'Not my area. Mine is arts and literature – civilised stuff, like Callum's impending masterwork.'

'About that,' Callum said, with a grimace. 'Is next year an actual deadline?'

Polly grinned and turned to Juliet. 'He's been promising this book for about three years. He'll do anything not to finish it.'

Finish it? thought Callum, who had barely started it.

'Do you have a title?' asked Juliet.

He nodded absently. '*Go-Betweens: The hidden injuries of class in the English novel.*'

'We're all very excited about it,' said Polly, in such an over-bright tone he couldn't tell if she was teasing him or not. She had taken out a packet of Silk Cut and offered it to them both. At Callum's polite smile she clicked her tongue. 'Sorry, I forgot – you don't.'

'I wouldn't mind a drink, though,' he said. Polly pointed him in the direction of the temporary bar, and he headed off through the scrum, now noisier than ever. Everywhere he looked there seemed a furious multitude of talkers; not so many listeners. Maybe that was the law of the social jungle here – you had to have your say, at all times. Let someone else into the conversational traffic and you risked not being heard again. He asked for water rather than the orange juice, and had just had his glass filled when he felt a hand on his shoulder.

'Pleased to see you sporting the college tie,' said Martin Villiers, beaming. 'How the hell are you?'

Callum had kept up vaguely with Martin since they were students at Trinity, Dublin, four years ago, though in London neither of them had found the time to be in regular touch. Their old intimacy had withered. Something had changed in Martin since he'd last seen him – he looked newly prosperous in his pinstriped three-piece suit and his lacquered helmet of dark hair, like a model's. Even his skin seemed to have acquired a tawny glow.

'Been on holiday?' said Callum.

'I wish! Just the sunbed.'

'How are the corridors of power?' Martin was something in the back rooms at Downing Street, though Callum could not remember exactly what.

'A bit tense, actually. Any day now Jim is going to call an election.'

'For certain?'

'First week of October,' said Martin with quiet authority. 'It will consolidate our base and choke off the Tories. The unions are all for it too.'

'They're not much liking your five per cent wage limit, I notice.'

He scowled, and his voice dropped low. 'They're lucky to get that. If it was up to me they wouldn't get *one* fucking per cent.'

Callum acknowledged this with a twitch of his mouth. 'Which department are you with at the moment?'

'Environment. It's fine,' he added, as if anticipating an objection. 'The usual headaches. Just between us there's a job coming up I'm hoping to get . . . ' He waited for Callum to prompt him, and when he didn't he continued. 'I shouldn't really say, but it's Deputy Press Secretary to the PM.'

'Good luck.'

Martin gazed off, absorbed for a moment in thoughts of his promotion. Then he abruptly turned back to Callum. 'What are you doing here, by the way – still lecturing, right?'

He nodded. 'Antrobus are my publishers. I don't usually get invited to things like this.'

'No, I wouldn't have thought so,' said Martin, deaf to his own condescension. 'Seen any of the old gang – Tom? Sarah?'

Callum shook his head. 'I'm no good at keeping in touch. I barely get to see the people I know in London, let alone the likes of Tom and Sarah.'

While they had been talking the party had closed in around them, and Callum noticed an older man giving him a curious monitoring look. At first he wondered if he knew him, but nothing about his lean face and pale, watchful eyes convinced him he did. It was somewhat disquieting to feel himself being eavesdropped, and he was about to turn his back when the man ghosted to his side. Close up, his bony features lent him a starved, almost cadaverous look.

'An Ulsterman,' he began without preamble. The voice was softly spoken, clipped, patrician. There was no smile, but he evidently meant the overture as friendly.

'I am,' replied Callum, who sensed a fuller reply was expected. 'From Newry. Do you know it?'

'I do indeed. I spent some years in your country.'

The man's presence had had a noticeable effect on Martin, who snapped smartly to attention and thrust his hand forward. 'Mr Middleton. How d'you do – Martin Villiers.'

The smile did come now – small and wintry. 'I know who you are,' he replied, and returned his gaze to Callum. 'So you live here now?'

'Yes, I teach at Holywell. Callum Conlan,' he said, following Martin's lead and offering his hand. A glint – perhaps of wariness – came to Middleton's eye as he heard his name. But still his tone was not unfriendly.

'Some of the finest countryside I know,' he said, returning to his theme. 'I enjoy the shooting over there.'

For a moment Callum wondered if he'd heard him correctly. In his teenage years he had heard the sound of 'shooting' from his bedroom almost every night.

'Sorry . . . ?'

'Grouse, mostly,' Middleton continued, apparently unaware of the confusion. 'Do any yourself?'

Callum would have laughed at the suggestion from someone else. 'No,' he replied, not risking a flippancy. 'I don't often go back there.'

At this point Martin, impatient with occupying the conversation's back seat, cut in. 'I enjoyed your fighting talk in the House the other day, sir. Gave the Republicans something to think about.'

Middleton's tone hardened as he addressed the interrupter. 'The situation in Ulster has drifted for too long.'

'The government's doing all it can. We can't let it descend into war.'

'It already has,' he replied shortly. 'The paramilitaries continue to get away with murder because our security forces aren't properly supported. You don't deal with terrorists by negotiating with them. But I see change ahead.'

'In Ireland?'

'Eventually,' he said. 'But I was thinking of a more immediate change – in government. Perhaps you can confirm when the election is to be called.'

Martin's reply matched the older man's slyness. 'I'll read about it in the papers, sir, just like you.'

Middleton gave an unillusioned nod, and looked at Callum again, the pale eyes shrewd and watchful. 'I was pleased to hear your accent. It's one that I miss.' He withdrew a step and said, 'Gentlemen' – and as suddenly as he'd arrived he was gone.

A puzzled moment passed before Callum said, 'Who was that?'

Martin looked at him aghast. 'You're kidding. Anthony Middleton – the Shadow Home Secretary? Surely you must have seen him on the news?'

'I don't have a telly,' Callum said. 'But I've heard of him. Ex-SAS . . . a war hero, yeah?'

'And a wily old bugger,' Martin muttered. 'He's the man who ran Thatcher's leadership campaign – brilliantly. Enjoys a bit of the old cloak-and-dagger. Woe betide your lot if the Tories get in.'

'What d'you mean, "your lot"?'

'I mean Catholics in Ulster. Middleton's a fervent Unionist, he won't even contemplate power-sharing. If he gets his way, he'll introduce all kinds of anti-terrorist measures against the Provos.'

'Just for your information, mate, not all Catholics belong to the IRA – or even support them.'

Martin nodded vigorously. 'Of course, of course, I didn't mean – actually he seemed rather charmed by you.'

'Yeah, until he heard my name. I felt the smallest dip in temperature.'

'I wish we had him on our side. He's just the sort of back-room operator we could use. Notice the way he tried to get the election date out of me? Ha!' Martin finished his drink with a wince. 'God, *filthy* wine they serve here. Listen, this place is a zoo – how about we nip off for dinner?'

'Don't you want to hobnob with your parliamentary pals?'

'What? I see these people every day – I don't want to spend half my evening with 'em, too.'

Callum raked his gaze over the room. 'I came with a friend. I shouldn't abandon her ...'

'Bring her along,' he said. 'I'll see you in the lobby downstairs in five minutes.'

He slipped away, leaving Callum to go in search of Juliet. After he'd roamed the room he spotted her engrossed in conversation with two dark-suited men, both of them sleek with entitlement. He hovered in her eyeline for a few moments before catching her attention; he smiled and cocked his head as if to say *Shall we get out of here?* But Juliet only returned one of her neutral chin-thrusts and continued talking. It seemed she wasn't going to budge, and Callum, pricked by a sense of his irrelevance, stepped back towards the exit.

In the high-ceilinged lobby Martin had his nose in the late edition of the *Standard*. Callum leaned in to see what he was reading: JUDGE JAILS NOTTING DALE RAPIST FOR TEN YEARS.

'Lenient, I'd say,' Martin sniffed.

Callum peered at the photograph below the police mugshot of the rapist. 'Is that one of the victims?'

'Nope. It's the policewoman who helped catch him. Nice-looking bird, isn't she? Just imagine her in uniform ...'

Callum gave a despairing sigh and turned away.

'What?' said Martin with a snigger, discarding the paper and following him out through the double doors. 'You've never fancied it with a policewoman?'

'How's Christine, by the way?' said Callum, descending the steps. Christine was Martin's wife.

'Oh, fine ... We're still adjusting to living in the sticks. Suffolk's nice enough, but the commute puts a strain on things.'

'Don't you have a place to stay here?'

'Can't afford one,' said Martin gloomily. 'We put everything we had into this bloody rectory. I'm beginning to wonder why.'

They walked down Pall Mall, the sky darkening above the high parapets of clubland. Something plaintive in Martin's tone had touched Callum. It wasn't like him to admit to doubts, personal or otherwise.

'Look, if you ever need somewhere to kip overnight,' he began, 'there's a spare bed at my place. I mean, it's just a wee house in Clerkenwell, but . . . '

'Thanks, nice of you to offer,' said Martin, in a hurried way that suggested he wouldn't dream of taking him up on it. The chugging of a car engine behind them caused him to turn suddenly. He raised his arm and bellowed past Callum, *'Taxi!'*

3

'... I just think we ought to remind ourselves why we started this thing in the first place. We called it the National Music Hall for a good reason – to celebrate music on behalf of the nation. That was our mission statement. We knew there would be sacrifices ahead, and compromises, and setbacks, because that's the way it is with any large publicly funded enterprise. For fifteen years we've taken the knocks and come through stronger. Now we have a rare opportunity to build on our success. The will is there to enlarge this theatre and turn it into a truly outstanding centre of musical performance, one that can rank with the greatest in Europe. But to ensure the government's backing we *must* show a united public front. This is a crucial phase in the fight ahead. We must not be divided by personal issues – I am not pointing the finger, because we're all in this together. No more ammo to the press. Are we agreed?'

Bob Bewley, assistant manager and author of this peroration, looked around the oval table for confirmation. He had been addressing his associates on the board, gathered first thing that morning for emergency talks after the terrible stink kicked up in the papers about the accounts. Reckless overspending was the charge, and Freddie Selves, director of the NMH, was the principal culprit. All eyes turned on him.

Freddie, well aware of this, leaned forward in his chair, rested his chin on steepled fingers and presented his most thoughtful stare. He was a large, bearish man, jowly beneath his dark beard, and dapper in a new navy worsted suit. Nearing fifty, he had gained a fair bit of weight, which he promised himself he would shift once his workload had been whittled to a manageable size. Except that it never would be, since he kept taking on more jobs – directing, promoting, presenting – than he could possibly handle. He justified this industry as the necessary consequence of having a large family to support, which included his ageing parents, a feckless brother in New Zealand, an ex-wife, and two teenage sons by his second. But secretly he knew it was the goad of his own ambition driving him on.

Now he began in his soft, crooning tone, 'Well said, Bob, and thank you, by the way, for not "pointing the finger" – a temptation no one on Fleet Street seems able to resist.'

A murmur of relieved laughter ran around the table. Evasive as he was, the director had just admitted, or at least implied, his own responsibility in the present crisis. Unbeknown to his colleagues, however, Freddie's thoughts were not focused on the accounts scandal, or the possibility of a strike at the theatre, or the ravening hounds of the national press, or the faltering progress of the building work, or even the lavish chaos of his private life. What preoccupied him right at this minute was the single remaining slice of chocolate cake, unclaimed on a plate at the centre of the table. Dawn, his plump, plain, willing-spirited PA, had popped out to buy it before the coffee came round at eleven thirty, and they had fallen on it with grateful *oohs* and *aahs*. Freddie wondered if anyone had noticed he'd already had two pieces. Had everyone had a slice, or had someone held back? Come to think of it, Dawn hadn't taken one before she left the room, and who was more entitled to it than her? But she was otherwise occupied; he could hear her polite, harassed voice on the phone next door.

It wasn't just a matter of wanting to have this last piece. It was that he couldn't properly concentrate on anything else until he did have it. In the meantime, Robin Piddock, head of press, was defending his decision to grant the *London Sketch* an interview with Freddie.

'We thought it would be useful publicity. Unfortunately it coincided with the expenses leak. They jumped on the stuff about the trips to New York.'

'Freddie has to get there somehow.'

'Yes, but by Concorde – on public money?'

'What's the hack's name again?' asked Lord Cadenhead, the NMH chairman.

'Derek Forbuoys,' said Piddock. 'If I'd known he was planning this – this *assassination* – I'd never have put Freddie in the room with him. I mean, he's supposed to be the arts correspondent, not the gossip columnist. Freddie, may I just say I'm terribly sorry about this—'

Eyes half closed, Freddie waved away the apology. He had been incandescent on reading the interview this morning – it had almost ruined his cooked breakfast – but in public he adopted an Olympian detachment from criticism. Never show them you're wounded. He sat up and steered a gaze of urbane confidence around the table.

'The irony of the Concorde story,' he began, then broke off – 'By the way, is that last piece of cake anyone's? . . .' The slice was quickly handed over to him, and he gave an abashed smile. He talked while he ate. 'As I was saying, the irony is that on my last flight from New York, seated three rows back from me was Cecil Monk, proprietor of the *London Sketch*. I haven't noticed *him* being pilloried for extravagance, despite his paper's falling circulation. One might accuse them of hypocrisy, but what would be the point? As a wise man once told me, never get into a fight with people who purchase their ink by the gallon.'

Freddie paused to fork in another mouthful of the chocolate cake. He had been expecting one of the more forthright associates to suggest that some belt-tightening on the expenses might be in order. But either Bob Bewley's call to arms was being heeded or Freddie's show of imperial nonchalance had mesmerised them into submission. Around the table only Dennis – Lord Cadenhead – was his superior in rank, and also the man least likely to challenge him: Freddie had been the chairman's personal appointment as director. Still, this one had been a close call – and the very last time he would allow Piddock to throw him to the dogs. From now on he would handle his relations with the press himself.

Indeed, it was an astonishment to him that he didn't do so already. During his thirty years as theatre director and music impresario Freddie had brought to bear his control on every other aspect of his work. Why not take his PR in hand too? He took a sip of coffee with the last morsel of cake. Well, the fightback started here: bypass the Pillock and secure a friendly ear from among the inky hordes.

A scraping of chair legs roused him from his ruminations: the meeting was breaking up. It had ended in a more congenial mood than it had begun. The faces of the associates, glum as pall bearers when he arrived, had cleared almost to cheerfulness. Nobody had ticked him off; on the contrary, he had received an apology for his trouble. It was what that disobliging profile in the *Sketch* had described as 'the Selves Effect'. Whenever cornered, Freddie would maintain a brooding silence before sidestepping the charge and deflecting the heat onto whoever was trying to take him down. Defence transformed into attack.

As they were filing out of the room Dawn stood at the threshold. Freddie watched as she sidled in and cast her gaze across the boardroom table where she had lately set and sliced the chocolate cake. Her private blink of disappointment pierced him.

'The cake was popular!' she said, catching his eye.

'Went down a storm, dear,' replied Freddie, who looked dismayed. 'Oh, Dawn, did you not have a piece?'

'Not to worry,' she said, with a brave smile; she appeared to be making a calculation. 'I could have sworn there were enough slices for—'

Freddie leaned down to her ear. 'Those *gannets*,' he muttered, and shook his head.

*

He had ten minutes in his office to check the morning's phone messages, noted in Dawn's looping girlish hand. One of them – specified as URGENT!! – came from his older son, Jon, reminding him about this evening, first night of the school play. He was Brutus in *Julius Caesar*. Freddie ripped that note off the pad and stuffed it in his breast pocket. He telephoned down to reception. 'Ask Terry to bring the car round. Back entrance.' He couldn't risk being snapped again today.

He had sweated more than Nixon during the meeting – almost had to peel the shirt off his back. He opened the door of his dressing room, converted from a cupboard, and whipped a fresh one from the rail. Even his dry-cleaning bills were getting out of hand; he wasn't sure he could keep claiming them. He flicked through his rack of ties, and chose the second-most sombre after the black. With the navy suit it seemed to lend him an *homme d'affaires* seriousness. He was making a beeline for the lift when he paused. They would all have read the *Sketch* by now: his staff would see him coming and fix their expressions to face him. He didn't know which he dreaded more, their pity, or their sneaky delight in seeing him under the cosh. He sensed both.

He reversed his steps and instead took the stairs (much quieter) where the picture windows looked down on the excavated site below. Cranes and diggers lolled on a prairie of rubble – not a workman in sight, of course. The National Music Hall had been installed in the shell of a disused Victorian warehouse on Farringdon Road in the early 1960s. Even then it had been thought too small, and for years they had been lobbying the government for funds to extend. The money had come at a trickle, and when the groundwork began two years ago they immediately ran into trouble. Nobody minded them converting a car park, but the prospect of losing a lovely row of almshouses and a pub that had stood since Tudor times had roused the conservationists to action. *Private Eye* and the Victorian Society had got involved and the demolition was halted by court order. The case would be coming up any day, and to Freddie's chagrin the

Save Our Streets campaign seemed to have the momentum. He would soon have to start pulling strings and calling in favours from certain powerful friends in government.

The Daimler's engine was already purring as he climbed in. Terry, his chauffeur, raised his chin in greeting and discarded his *Mirror* on the front passenger seat. Freddie experienced a boost of relief – not everyone read the *Sketch*, thank God.

'The Savoy, please, Terry.'

The late-September sky looked pale with worry. It was dry, though rain was forecast. As they joined the traffic heading south his mind's eye was still on that unpeopled building site at the rear. The whole development had ground to a halt, with the construction company on full pay in the meantime. They were haemorrhaging money at a catastrophic rate. Peace with the union had held so far, but if they decided to go on strike like everyone else, the theatre – his theatre – was done for. The autumn/winter schedule already had a doomed look. The centrepiece of the new year, which he himself was due to direct, now carried a tragicomic air of bad timing. When he had first given the nod to a musical adaptation of *The Ragged Trousered Philanthropists* three years ago he'd felt certain he was on to a winner. As a young man he had loved the Tressell novel, and found a personal meaning in its chronicle of the working man's travails. His own grandfather had been a house-painter who had to walk miles to his job; if it rained, penny-pinching foremen laid him off without pay. Here was a howl of rage against the bosses, the sweated labour, the whole iniquitous system!

In the three years since he had commissioned it things had changed. Not the book, of course – that seemed more pertinent than ever in the era of wage disputes and industrial action. No, it was the perception of Freddie Selves that had shifted. No longer was he the brilliant sorcerer, the theatrical comet who had lit up the 1960s with one blazing production after another. Once appointed director of the NMH, Freddie had become notorious as an operator, a 'modern Machiavelli' who worked all the levers of influence. He was known to spend freely from the public purse while suspected of feathering his own nest. As the headline of the *Sketch* profile had so amusingly summed him up: FROM UNDERDOG TO FAT CAT. How could *he* be entrusted with one of the century's great fables of working-class exploitation?

Someone was calling his name. He looked up to find Terry craning around to face him. 'We're here, sir.'

Freddie peered out at the back entrance of the Savoy. The car journey – Terry's magic-carpet ride – had whizzed by without him even noticing. 'Thanks. Back here at three thirty. No, better make it four.'

Inside, all was carpeted hush and anonymous decorum. He loved hotels, or at least the grand ones like this. People passed him in the corridors without a second glance. He thought how pleasant it would be to live here, waited on hand and foot, everything served on a plate – literally – and nothing demanded of you beyond the price of your bed and board. *Yes, Mr Selves is in the Emperor Suite. He said to go straight up.* That would be the ticket. Nabokov and his missus had lived in a hotel for years, hadn't they? He wondered whether Linda would be amenable to such an arrangement. Separate suites, perhaps. Come to think of it, the way things stood between them at present she'd probably want separate hotels.

He entered the Grill Room and spotted Leo, his agent, at a banquette seat against the wall. As they greeted one another Leo gave him an odd look.

'Have you come from a funeral?'

'No. Why?' asked Freddie.

'Because you're dressed like the chief mourner.'

He bridled, pointing out that his tie was blue, not black. 'Though you're not that wide of the mark. I'm mourning the slow death of my reputation.'

Leo shrugged philosophically. 'I've read the Forbuoys piece, and it's not as bad as all that.'

'*Not as bad as all that*? He made me out to be a tyrant. An establishment toady. A spendthrift. A pincher of others' credits. He might as well have gone the whole hog and called me a wife-beater too'.

'Nice photo of you though. Quite dashing.'

Freddie returned a frown in response. He sometimes wondered if Leo fancied him; gay men often did, at least when he was younger. Leo lived discreetly with a TV producer called Graham, though he would glancingly refer to 'adventures' he had around London's queer scene. In contrast to Freddie he wore a fawn-coloured suit with a flowery, thick-knotted tie. His hair, waved and primped, made him look a right herbert.

'It was the Pillock's fault. He gave the *Sketch* a bloody open goal – like they needed one. All morning I skulked around the building like a whipped dog, not daring to show my face.'

Leo asked the waiter to fetch them menus, then reverted to his grumbling client. 'It'll blow over,' he said evenly.

It was a typical agent's forecast, born of ignorance as much as optimism. Leo would never know what it was like to be a punchbag for the press.

'A counter-attack is what's needed,' Freddie said, thinking aloud. 'A piece that shows me in a sympathetic light. Leader of a great public enterprise. Champion of British talent. The team player, instead of the individualist. There must be someone willing to stick his neck out for me.'

Leo allowed himself a fleeting grimace of doubt. 'I'll have a think. In the meantime—' He signalled the hovering waiter to pour the Burgundy. Freddie took a measuring sniff, and sipped.

'Needs chilling. Put it in a bucket, will you?'

The wine waiter hurried off with the bottle.

'How are the boys? And Linda?'

'The boys are fine. Jon's in the school play tonight. Tim's in the first eleven. Linda ... ' Freddie puckered his mouth ruefully – '... well, if it's not the end, it's probably the beginning of the end.'

'As bad as that?' said Leo. 'Would I be right in assuming, *entre nous*, a certain award-winning actress is involved?'

'How did you—' Freddie stopped himself. Of course Leo would know about Nicola – had he not in fact introduced them? 'I was hoping to keep it on the QT.'

'People talk, Fred. The way of the world. Does Linda know?'

'She suspects. Nothing more. If it comes out you'll probably hear the explosion from the other side of Hampstead Heath.'

'Speaking as your friend, it would be better for all concerned if Linda hears it from you rather than some hack phoning her at home.'

Freddie closed his eyes and began to knead his brow in silence. The fallout from this could be calamitous. Linda would want a divorce, and he would pay for it. Leo looked on, like a kindly doctor with his patient. The approach of the head waiter made a useful distraction. 'I'll have the foie gras to start,' said Freddie, '... and then the tournedos. And would you *please* tell your sommelier to hurry up with that Puligny.'

'I'll have the same, thanks *so much*,' said Leo, with a compensating grace note of charm. He left a pause after the waiter had departed. 'Something to cheer you up – do you know who Castleton are?'

'The wallpaper lot?'

'Right. They run those ads in the Sunday supps, you've probably seen them – photograph of a celebrity in a room decorated with their latest pattern. The tagline goes "Very Roger Moore – or whoever – Very Castleton". Well, they've asked for you.'

Freddie shook his head slowly. 'Did you actually read that *Sketch* piece? "The Babylonian high life of Freddie Selves ... " Putting my mug next to a brand of fancy wallpaper is just *asking* for it.'

'It's hardly extravagant. Everyone uses wallpaper.'

'It'd still look bad. A sympathetic image, remember.' He glanced at Leo, whose meaningful gaze was inviting a question. There existed an almost marital telepathy between them. 'How much?'

Leo took out his fountain pen, uncapped it and wrote a number on the margin of the newspaper he'd been reading before his guest arrived. He passed it across the table. Freddie looked, and tried to stop his eyes bugging. The average salary per annum of an NMH employee – Dawn's, for instance – was smaller than this.

'Are you sure?'

Leo nodded. 'Obviously a bit less after your agent's cut. But pretty good for a couple of afternoons' work. Just think of the kids' school fees. New wine cellar. Winter in the Caribbean. And you might need a bit extra in the event of . . .' *A legal shitstorm with Linda,* thought Freddie. He would need to start up the war chest soon.

'I'll think about it,' he said, which they both knew was code, more or less, for an acceptance.

By now the wine had been poured, just in time for the foie gras. Funny how lunch, and the promise of money, could change the mood. His spirits renewed, Freddie felt able to confess his misgivings about taking charge of *The Ragged Trousered Philanthropists.* First, he had accepted an offer from the BBC to front an arts series, *Compendium,* despite an unseemly set-to with the NMH board. The associates considered the directorship of the Hall a full-time job, amply reflected in his salary. Freddie argued that each programme would take only one day a week, though secretly he thought it more likely to be two. After much back-and-forth, and despite someone's suggestion that he was running the Hall as his 'personal fiefdom', he had won them round. He had just completed the series' pilot. All told, the editing and presenting had taken three and a half days.

Leo, mid-mouthful, only nodded, almost as indifferent to these scruples of loyalty as his client. 'Right. What else?'

'Well, it's the point that Forbuoys made. It's irritating, but my status as the boss, the big chief, doesn't really fit with a musical about poverty and class oppression. It's offering a hostage to fortune.'

'But who else would do it?'

Freddie gave a theatrical shrug. 'We could try out David Bartram. He's hungry and he's smart – and he's done the adaptation after all.'

'Bartram. The one who did *The Cherry Orchard*? Oh, he's *fantastic*. Sign him up.'

Freddie slightly bristled at Leo's enthusiasm. 'Do you think so?'

'That boy's got flair. Rather lefty for my taste, but I've rarely seen Chekhov done better.'

'The "boy" is thirty-five, and the Chekhov was *all right*,' Freddie demurred. 'A bit undernourished.'

'You said he was hungry.'

'Hmm. I wonder if that's why he wears pullovers with holes in the elbows . . . '

'Give him a chance. It would reflect well on you – could be the moment you anoint him as your dauphin.'

But Freddie was already going cold on the idea; he didn't like the prospect of anyone making a better job of it than he could. Give 'em an inch. That was how great men got toppled. 'Maybe I should do it anyway, and to hell with the critics. I could appoint Bartram my assistant director.'

Leo wrinkled his nose in objection. 'Come on, Fred. Either he's good enough to do it alone or he's not. You can't have it all your own way.'

Freddie stared at him. 'I can have it any way I like,' he said coldly. Leo made a face, expressive of one who had had his good counsel rejected but was not going to make a fuss about it. Freddie, having recovered his composure, changed the subject: they had to decide what to drink next.

As four o'clock approached and he got up to leave, Leo raised a hand to stay him. The detritus of lunch was strewn about the table. The dark husk of Freddie's cigar lay buckled in the Grill Room's souvenir ashtray.

'Just had an idea when you were in the gents, about a friendly journo we could tap. I think I've got someone.'

'Who is he?' said Freddie.

'It's a she. Saw her the other night on *What the Papers Say*. Good-looking, thirties, well thought of on the Street. Anna something.'

'Really?' Freddie was doubtful.

'You need a woman for this. The likes of Forbuoys are no good for you – men are too competitive. They resent your power.'

'Ha. And women don't? What paper is she with?'

'Don't recall. But she does a lot of features and op-ed. I could sound her out.'

Freddie sighed. 'What if she hates me?'

Leo drew his chin in sharply. 'Nobody hates you, dear. They just don't trust you. I'll set something up.'

The Daimler was parked outside, in exactly the spot Terry had dropped him a few hours ago. Freddie sat back on the cushioned leather, buoyed by a rare feeling of optimism. Leo had everything in hand, it seemed, and he was too professional to have taken offence at his snappishness over Bartram. *The boy's got flair,* indeed ... Freddie, outwardly self-confident, was prey to the eternal insecurity of age in the face of youth. He would be fifty next year, and dreaded the idea of being usurped. But something else was nagging at him now, some obligation or other ... It would come back to him soon enough.

From the back seat he marvelled at Terry's negotiation of the West End rush hour – the most imperturbable driver he had ever known. He held the steering wheel not with his hands but with the tips of his fingers, and yet he maintained an eerie control, nipping in and out of jams, anticipating the lights with uncanny precision. He seldom used his horn, never swore at other drivers or even clicked his tongue; he was a prince of the road. Freddie almost loved him for his graciousness.

On Brompton Road the shops were turning on their lights against the encroaching gloom. The car glided into Cranley

Gardens and eased to a halt outside one of the tall white mansion blocks.

'Shall I wait, sir?'

'No, thanks, that's all for today, Terry. See you tomorrow morning.'

On the pavement he watched as the car disappeared into the traffic. It occurred to him that Terry might wonder about this drop-off on his weekly itinerary. He had probably guessed by now. Well, no man is a hero to his valet – or to his chauffeur, come to that.

The buzzer on the door admitted him with a peremptory crackle. He climbed the carpeted stairs towards the second floor, hoping to hear her voice. In the early days Nicola would come to the landing to call out a welcome. It used to put a skip in his step. Of late that didn't happen so much. Freddie thought he knew why. Yet her sly grin on opening the door had charm enough.

'Well, if it isn't Signor Machiavelli,' she smirked.

'You read it then?' he said, bending in to kiss her. That *Sketch* profile was going to follow him around for a while.

'Course I read it! Nice plug for the theatre, wasn't it?'

Freddie shot a look at her to check if she was joking. She wasn't. Some people just didn't get it. He followed her into the galley kitchen where she began brewing a pot of tea. He had met Nicola Mayman two years ago at a first-night party, and had been immediately taken by her Bambi eyes and the girlish fringe of her straight blonde hair. He liked her throaty voice, with the little catch in it, familiar from *Unlucky Charms*, the racy adultery drama that had bewitched Friday-night TV audiences the previous summer. This afternoon she was wearing a paisley shirt and faded jeans with a flare so wide they looked like twin tepees on her legs.

She turned suddenly and caught him watching her.

'See anything you like?' she asked him.

He nodded. 'Your bum, for one.'

He knew that would get a laugh. As she handed him a mug of tea she twitched her nose. 'Have you been at a lunch?'

'With Leo. Why – something wrong?'

'Only that pong of cigar. Eww. What did you talk about?'

'Oh, the usual. Money. Work. My reputation. Leo thinks he's got a friendly journalist to give the "other side of Freddie Selves".'

'Is there such a thing?'

Freddie was offended. 'I should *hope* I've another side.'

She shook her head. 'I mean a "friendly journalist". They're not really interested in being pals. They want good quotes.'

'I'll get polishing my *bons mots*, then,' he said, folding himself into an armchair.

They talked about her week. Nicola had just finished filming on a new *Play for Today*. Freddie sensed The Subject circling them, drawing closer. (Was this what he'd been worrying about?) As soon as it was announced that he was to direct a prestigious new musical of *The Ragged Trousered Philanthropists* Nicola had dropped hints, jokey at first, of her availability for the female lead. But it soon turned out she wasn't joking. She wanted an audition. It wasn't as though she were unsuitable, either. She was an accomplished stage actress with a decent singing voice, and her TV fans would ensure the NMH big ticket sales.

Freddie had been evasive on The Subject for two reasons. First, his sense of professionalism would not allow him to play favourites, least of all in casting. Nicola was good, but was she the very best? He felt doubtful. The second reason was more personal and complicated. From the moment they became involved Freddie had wondered if her attraction to him was based on more than his 'legendary charisma' (even Forbuoys had mentioned that). Of course you saw it everywhere, older men squiring attractive young women – older men who might be fat and ugly but were rich and influential. It was your basic *quid pro quo*. And it would have to be a fairly high-minded actress who refused to consider the advantages of intimacy with a director – *the* director. True, she had not asked him for anything, not a single thing, until this.

The Subject would soon be unavoidable, so he decided to back his way in.

'What do you think of David Bartram, incidentally?'

Nicola shrugged. 'I saw a couple of his early ones. Quite powerful. Why?'

'Oh, his name came up at lunch. Leo tried to persuade me that Bartram would be good – no, "fantastic" – for *Ragged Trousers*.'

'You mean to direct it? But I thought *you* were . . .'

'So did I,' said Freddie ruefully. This was good. If he could make it seem that his own involvement in it was precarious it might spike her guns. 'But with all the fuss about me being a fat cat it may not be an auspicious moment to take on a show about the evils of capitalism.'

Nicola narrowed her eyes. 'Why should you care? It's your theatre—'

'It's the nation's, actually—'

'But you run it! People will expect you to do the big show. It's too important to let Bartram take over.'

He inclined his head ambiguously. 'We'll see. But it's something I have to consider. The integrity of the Hall takes precedence over my ambitions as a director.' Did he even believe that? He wasn't sure, but it sounded impressive.

'I'll fix you a drink,' she said, going to the fridge for ice. 'When do you have to decide?'

'Soon. There's also a New York trip to fit in, plus the TV filming. The diary's already full.' He closed his eyes and let his head drop. After some moments of pondering he said, 'The problem . . . the problem is this. I work all the hours God sends earning money for a life I've no time to enjoy.'

He still had his eyes shut as he listened to her movements around the kitchen counter, the rattle of the ice, the gurgle of gin, the hiss of the tonic poured over it. Then a plop as the slice of lemon went in. Her footsteps padded towards him.

'Would you have time to enjoy this?' she said, and something in her tone made him look up. Nicola stood there holding out a tumbler. She had dimmed the lights in the room, so it took him a moment to adjust his sight to her changed appearance. She still wore the paisley shirt; the flared jeans were gone, though, and with them whatever else she had been wearing underneath.

He reached out for the glass. 'I'm sure I could fit it in.'

He had been dozing, and woke with a start. The bedclothes were in amiable disarray; the curtains had been drawn against the evening. Next door he could hear Nicola in the shower. The glowing figures on the digital clock by the bed read 7:27. Whatever had been bothering him was still there, like a thread of meat you couldn't dislodge from a back molar.

The hiss of the shower abruptly ceased, and a moment later Nicola stepped back into the bedroom, towelling her hair. She wore a scarlet kimono that just grazed the tops of her thighs. She peered at him through the curtain of hair; he liked the way it went darker when damp.

'How long have I been asleep?' Freddie asked, propped up on his elbows.

''Bout half an hour. You were sparko right after you . . .' She raised her eyebrows suggestively, and reached over him for her cigarettes. As she did he got a fragrant whiff of her bathroom soap. *Things happen after a Badedas bath* . . . the advert, with its coy photograph of a woman standing in a peek-a-boo robe at an open window, was everywhere.

She plumped herself down next to him and lit a cigarette. Absently, she gave his belly a friendly pat. 'You're padding out a bit, aren't you?'

'Lucky for me I can carry the extra load. *Let me have men about me that are fat.*'

Nicola squinted at him. '*Henry IV . . . Part One*?'

He shook his head. '*Julius Caesar*. Oh *fuck*!' He sat bolt upright. That was it – *Julius Caesar* – his son's play – the thing that had been bugging him. 'Why didn't you wake me?!'

'I tried. You were snoring like a dragon. What's the matter?' she asked, alarm in her eyes.

'Jon. He's Brutus in his school play – tonight. Seven thirty. Fucking hell.'

'How was I to know?'

Freddie was already out of the bed and throwing on his clothes. Could he get to Harrow from here in time for the interval? If only he hadn't dismissed Terry for the night.

'I knew there was something,' he said, frantically buttoning his shirt. 'It's been on my mind all afternoon. Call a cab for me, would you?'

'Darling, you'd be quicker taking the Tube'

He stared at her with horrified incredulity. He hadn't ventured on the Underground in years. 'I'm not about to – would you *please help* me?'

While she telephoned for a cab he worried away at his oversight. He had spent a whole afternoon last week reading *Julius Caesar* aloud with Jon, offering him nuggets of directorial wisdom and encouragement. However rotten he'd been as a husband, he had tried his best as a father, taking the boys to his rehearsals when they were little, and later to his productions abroad whenever school term allowed. Only in the last couple of years had he begun to miss things – parents' evenings, dinners, that football match of Tim's. Missing this would be the worst, a traitor's dagger, the glaring proof that he was a Bad Dad.

As soon as he heard the car outside he bolted down the stairs, Nicola in his wake. He heard her call 'Good luck' as he hurried out to the taxi, and he barely turned to wave her goodnight. It was an abrupt and ungracious end to their tryst. She hadn't been too upset, though, and he knew why. When they had been smooching in bed he had let his guard down and agreed to see her audition for *The Ragged Trousered Philanthropists*. Fool!

4

Hannah was at her desk when she took a phone call from the deputy editor's secretary. Would she mind popping upstairs to see Keith for a moment? She had not had much to do with Keith Carstairs. He was a relative newcomer at the *Ensign*, more involved in the management side than the editorial. When she entered his office he had his feet up on the desk, hands criss-crossed behind as a headrest. Ever since Jason Robards had struck this horizontal pose in *All the President's Men* it had become the in-house power posture of male newspaper executives everywhere.

'Hannah, have a seat,' he said. 'Enjoyed your performance the other night!'

'Sorry?'

'On the box. *What the Papers Say*. You looked very ... authoritative.'

The small hesitation sounded like he'd planned to say something less neutral but swerved away at the last moment. Strange, she thought, that it had taken a TV appearance to prompt a show of approval, given all the articles and stories she'd written without him acknowledging one of them. Carstairs was short, tanned, bulked with muscle (a mean tennis player, it was said). His small dark eyes squinted from a face of disquieting smoothness.

'Some good news,' he continued. 'We've got you an interview with Anthony Middleton. Tomorrow afternoon. His office at the Commons.'

'Gosh,' said Hannah. Middleton was known for his old-fashioned disdain of the press, and made a habit of refusing interviews. 'What's brought this on?'

Carstairs smirked. 'Maybe the prospect of his imminent death. Concentrates the mind and so on. Met him before?'

She shook her head.

'Obviously the thrust of the piece is his provocation of the IRA. What's the deal with his security? Family background, bit of military colour, wartime record. You know . . . '

'Got it,' she said, with a quick nod, forbearing to add that she only had ten years' experience of interviewing politicians. She half rose from her seat before noticing a hesitation in his manner. 'Was there something else?'

'As a matter of fact, there is,' he said. 'Freddie Selves. Know him?'

'I know of him, of course.'

'Yeah . . . They're very eager to get him in the paper. And he wants you to do it.'

'What – he asked for me?'

'Not exactly. His agent did.'

Hannah looked surprised. 'I'd have thought Freddie Selves would be lying low after that profile in the *Sketch*.'

'I presume they want to do some damage repair, plug his other side – the impresario, the director, the born showman.' He waggled his hands, Al Jolson-style, as if she might not know what showmanship was.

'What's it to us? We're not Selves's PR team.'

'No. But he's a public figure, and he's in the news.'

Hannah was silent for a moment, considering. Something felt off. 'I don't really want to write a piece just to help rehabilitate someone. And that *Sketch* profile sounded pretty fair to me. The guy's a creep.'

A frown rippled across Carstairs's smooth forehead. 'I don't think even Derek Forbuoys's close friends would consider him "fair". He's a stitch-up artist.'

'Maybe, but I still don't see any point in us riding to Selves's defence.' She got to her feet. 'And I've bigger fish to fry, in any case.'

'Have a think about it,' he said, as though he hadn't been listening to her. She smiled to hide her irritation, and said of course she would.

Back at her desk she wheeled round on her swivel chair to face the office. It was mid-morning at the *Ensign*, and she could hear the rattle of the tea trolley on its way with elevenses. She reached for her purse. She sometimes wondered how many cups of tea she had bought in the eleven years she had been there. She had joined the paper at twenty-three, almost straight from university, starting out as secretary on the Arts page before moving to the Diary. This had been fun for a while; she liked the party-going and the gossip-wrangling, but sensed very quickly it was no job for somebody with ambition. It would always be the domain of certain raffish ex-public schoolboys who made it a point of honour never to type a word before midday. She managed to transfer to Features, then to News, where she finally made her name by getting the inside story on the IRA siege at Balcombe Street in 1975. She had won a press award for it. In consequence her photo was inserted beneath her byline, and even featured in adverts on the side of buses, until she twigged that some colleagues – men – resented this new-found prestige. She overheard someone referring to her as 'uppity'. When she asked for her picture to be dropped from the page things noticeably improved.

The office was in a lull, so she took her tea and a KitKat along the corridor to Features. Tara Gilbey sat hunched at her desk, so focused upon whatever she was reading that it took her a while to notice her arrival. The two of them had occasionally worked together on stories before Hannah switched to News. Tara was on the short side and dark, a Mancunian, while Hannah was rangy and pale, from London, though in matters of temperament they were of a piece – sceptical, humorous, quietly competitive and scarily efficient. They had become fast friends.

Tara appeared to be working her way through a huge pile of magazines. Parking herself on an adjacent chair, Hannah discarded the KitKat's wrapper and smoothed its foil undercoat flat. Then she drew her nail along the groove separating one segment from another before dislodging the end finger with a snap. It was nearly as satisfying to open the thing as it was to eat.

'Have a break,' she said, as Tara looked up with the blank gaze of interrupted absorption.

'Oh . . . thanks,' she said, taking the proffered biscuit. 'Sorry, I didn't even see you there. How's tricks?'

'Fine. It's so quiet. Where is everyone?'

'Probably at the union meeting. There's talk of the printworkers going on strike.'

'Why weren't we told about it?'

'A memo went round a few days ago. To be honest, I've better things to do,' Tara added, holding up the magazine she'd been poring over. It was *On the Town*, a London listings mag, and Hannah now saw that the stack on the desk were all back issues of the same.

'What's going on – applying for a job?'

Tara sniggered, shaking her head. 'I'm doing a story on personal columns – lonely hearts. And *On the Town*'s are the best, or at least the funniest.'

'Funny?'

'Oh God, you should have a read. Here, listen to this: "Blonde girl on Piccadilly Line, Saturday night, 14 Oct. Please contact guy in specs who mentioned smoky bacon crisps and *Barry Lyndon*. Box 545/2." Or this: "With-it guy, seriously groovy (leather trousers etc), seeks with-it lady for good times. Call Harry. Box 7158."'

They looked at one another and burst out laughing. 'Nice of him to tell us about his leather trousers,' said Hannah.

'Yeah. You wonder about the "etc" he's keeping up his sleeve.'

'Or up his trouser leg . . . May I?' asked Hannah, picking up another issue to scan the back-page columns.

'Be my guest. It's going to be a piece about atomised lives in a big city. All those lonely souls out there wanting, I dunno, companionship, love, whatever. And no way to do it other than by public appeal.'

Hannah soon found herself equally absorbed in the messages. Why had she never looked at them before? She had assumed that personal ads were the preserve of an older generation who sought domestic cleaners, or holiday lets, or second-hand cars. Instead, this treasure trove: humanity in the raw. She and Tara kept breaking off to read the more eccentric ones aloud.

> Kenneth. Sorry about the eggs. And you were so patient. 01-273 7882.
>
> DEE. Please may I have bedroom mirror back? Reward £5. James.
>
> Anyone who remembers removing a harpsichord from 34 Lescott Avenue, SW4, around April 1974 please contact M. Underwood (01-309 6077).

Their attention was riveted as they scoured the columns. A helpless guffaw would peal out now and then, though Hannah discovered that the messages were not exclusively comical.

> Jacky. We don't know where you've gone. Don't punish us. We all love you. Ring Mum.

People looking for a 'soulmate' – that was the popular word – were legion. For all the ones that were creepy or gauche ('with-it'), there were as many who seemed lost and vulnerable, and perhaps more desperate than they wished to appear. Tara was right: it was a lonely city.

> 'Is that concrete all around, or is it in my head?' Formerly Young Dude, loves art galleries, Bowie, dressing up, live music. Interested? I want to relate to you. Box 2047/7.

Hannah smiled at this, absently. 'Would you ever go on one of these – I mean, with a stranger?'

Tara wrinkled her nose. 'I don't think so. Bit of a last resort, isn't it?' A pause followed. 'How did your drink with Jake go, by the way?'

'Hmm? Oh. It was fine.'

Hannah had her admirers on the paper, and Jake Seagrave, from Sports, was the latest to set his cap at her.

'Doesn't sound so great,' said Tara, prying.

Hannah sighed, and pulled a face that would relieve her of further explanation. But Tara's spluttered giggle only made her feel guilty, and she added, quickly, 'He was perfectly nice' – which of course damned him with even fainter praise. She glanced at her watch and made a slight gasp at the hour they had just spent mooching. Before she returned to her desk they made a dinner arrangement for later in the week.

As luck would have it Hannah spotted Jake in the corridor on the way back, and ducked into a side office before he noticed her. Their evening hadn't been so terrible – not really. She had known him for a while, and had provided a sympathetic ear when he was in the throes of his divorce last year. Perhaps that had encouraged him, because eventually he suggested they might have a drink sometime soon, 'just the two of us'. She could think of no reason to refuse. He chose for their meeting not a pub but a wine bar near Temple, an out-of-the-way place which tipped her the wink: this was more than a friendly get-together.

Might there be the faintest temptation? He wasn't bad-looking; his shoulder-length brown hair was groomed, and his wide-lapelled grey flannel suit with mauve tie (raffishly loosened) quite became him. True, he had rather a large backside, and a habit of responding to any light-hearted remark with a long saturnine stare. They got off to a good start, though, with some back-and-forth about the new managing editor – a fool, they decided – and the looming possibility of a print strike. He seemed pleased to see her. But once he got onto the subject of his ex-wife and the bitter fallout over money and kids there was no stopping him. She supplied understanding murmurs and expressions of disbelief as the narrative required, trying in the meantime to steer the talk elsewhere. But Jake wouldn't take the hint, and simply ploughed on with his record of grievances.

When the domestic woes had been exhausted, Hannah tried to brighten the mood. She'd just bought tickets for the new Pinter play coming to the National, and wondered if he'd be interested. Jake pulled a face; he couldn't stand the theatre. They moved on to music, and she drew another blank on mentioning Kate Bush's new album. He shook his head – he was baffled by the fuss over 'Wuthering Heights', he said, which made her want to pay up and leave right then. Heavy rock was his thing, Scorpions, UFO, Judas Priest. Hannah nodded, without remark. They toiled on, picking over scraps of office gossip, but by now it was clear that Jake's repertoire of chat was disconcertingly narrow. What seemed extraordinary to her was that having talked *at length* about his own life he didn't seem inclined or even obliged to repay the compliment. Come to think of it, he hadn't asked her a single question all evening. Except once. Just as they were leaving the bar he tilted his head and said in a low, confiding voice, 'Is there anything in the short-to-medium term I could, er, do for you?' She looked at him. 'What d'you mean?' He blinked, and gave his humourless stare. It appeared he wasn't going to explain.

She was on the bus home when it occurred to her that this had been his attempt at a pass.

A young woman in a navy twinset greeted Hannah in the corridor. She introduced herself as his secretary and said that Mr Middleton was running a little late: would she mind waiting in the Commons bar? Hannah had just settled at a table by the window when a shadow suddenly loomed across her.

'Miss Strode? Anthony Middleton.'

He was tall, with hooded eyes in a bony, angular face; wings of grey hair sloped against an otherwise bald head. Hannah's first impression was of a great famished vulture. A dark pin-striped suit hung on him like armour. He asked her what she wanted to drink, and a tonic water was brought to the table. He drank nothing. While she was setting up her cumbersome tape recorder she felt his gaze fasten upon her.

Unnerved, she tried to break the ice. 'I don't suppose you often talk to people like me.'

'You have no idea what kind of people I talk to', he replied, with a faint trace of a smile. 'I read your reports from Balcombe Street. Surprisingly good, for a left-wing paper.'

She was amused, despite the note of condescension. On television Middleton cut an intimidating figure, hard and impatient, and unwilling to give an inch. In person he seemed to her more human, his manner warily droll. He had done his research, too – he knew that she had been a student at the LSE ('another nest of radicalism'), had once been arrested on a demo, had interviewed the last Tory prime minister, and had won an award for her reporting in 1975.

'I'm flattered you even bothered to find out,' she said. 'I have colleagues who know less than that about me.'

He nodded. 'I have found that it pays to be informed.'

Hannah sensed this as the moment to get to business. She pressed down the RECORD buttons on her machine, and the red light winked on. 'That would certainly be reflected in your career – first SOE during the war, then into the intelligence service as an officer . . . '

She waited for him to continue, but he presented a blank gaze.

'Can you confirm these appointments?'

'No, I cannot,' he replied in a level tone. 'I will tell you that I did voluntary work for the UN High Commission and also chaired a Commons Select Committee on Science and Technology. And I've been an MP for twenty-two years.'

'Right. And it's no secret that you were instrumental in securing the leadership of the party for Mrs Thatcher.'

'I helped with the campaign. I believe my influence was thought useful.'

'Yes, about that influence – did you draw on know-how from your years in intelligence?'

For the first time his pale eyes narrowed. 'What do you mean?'

Hannah swallowed and said, 'Well, I presume in ousting Heath you would have used your experience in the field – spreading disinformation, undermining the enemy and so on. Psy-ops, I believe it's called.'

Middleton stared hard at her for a moment, then leaned across the table. 'Turn that thing off,' he said, pointing to her recorder. Obediently Hannah clicked the button; the red light disappeared. He showed no sign of being nettled, but something had changed in his voice. 'You and I are not going to get along, Miss Strode, if you pursue this line of questioning. You are after a story, like any good journalist, so you pry in the hope your subject will make a mistake and betray himself. Perhaps this has worked for you in the past. But it will not work with me. So I must ask you – tell you – to refrain from any mention of what you have assumed to be my past employment.'

Hannah, chastened, held her silence, until he came back with a sharp 'Is that understood?'

'Understood. D'you mind if I . . . ?'

She nodded at the recorder, and at his signal switched it back on. His headmasterly rebuke briefly lingered in the air.

'Were you surprised that the Prime Minister did not call an autumn election?'

'Nothing he does surprises me. His party is running scared. Putting off the election is merely to delay the inevitable.'

'Do you really think so? I mean, you have an untried leader in Mrs Thatcher. Even with Labour in disarray can you be certain the country would vote for a woman as PM?'

'I would not be serving under her if I didn't believe she could win.'

'Will you continue to serve in her Cabinet should she be elected?'

'I would count it an honour. Though perhaps, if I am asked, in a different role.'

Hannah raised her eyebrows. 'Oh? What appointment would you prefer?'

He gave her a dry, measured look. 'This is off the record – but I would like the office of Secretary of State for Northern Ireland.'

She felt her mouth almost fall open, and she hesitated before saying, 'Isn't that usually a job that's given as a punishment?'

A smile – a genuine one, as far as she could tell – broke over his face. 'Some would think so. I would regard it as a great opportunity.'

'But given the threat to your life from the IRA, wouldn't you be taking an enormous risk in going there – to the front line?'

Middleton reclined in his chair, his mask of enigmatic calm back in place. He waited so long before replying that Hannah prepared to jump into the silence. She was glad she didn't, for he then spoke for twenty minutes, almost without pause, about the state of Northern Ireland. The shootings and bombings in Ulster, he said, had gone beyond a point that any British government ought to tolerate. He was contemptuous of the 'Provos' and their methods ('call it by its real name – gangsterism') and had urged for more resolute military action in the province. The terrorists had to be fought at ground level, and he believed the security forces, correctly deployed, would defeat them. The RUC he considered an 'effective' unit, but they couldn't do the job on their own: ID cards and border passes should be mandatory, new powers of detention instituted, and specially trained troops moved in to 'target suspects'. His conviction was absolute: it would be a dirty war. Photographs of Middleton's home had been found in the possession of the Balcombe Street gang. There could be no doubt they were gunning for him.

Hannah listened with silent glee. She knew him to be a hardliner. But this was something else, something mad, like a crusade. It would make an almighty splash on the front page.

She decided to take advantage of this unexpected volubility and see what else might be coaxed from him. 'As well as Ulster the country faces internal problems – inflation, crippling strikes, social unrest. What's to be done?'

'First, elect a competent government. Second, invest the police with more flexible powers. Arm them, if necessary.'

'So you'd fight the unions as you would the Republican terrorists – a security crackdown?'

A little twitch of irritation came to his cheek, then vanished. 'You're trying to provoke me again, Miss Strode. This country is in the grip of subversive elements, communist many of them. Sedition is on the rise. We see it every night on the news – lawlessness on the streets, intimidation in the workplace. If we allow this to go unchecked, who knows to what depths of violence and anarchy we may descend? If – when – the electorate decides it has had enough and installs a Conservative government, it will be our mission to root out these enemies of liberty and set the country to rights.'

'"Enemies of liberty"? Isn't a democracy founded upon the freedom to protest – to strike if necessary?'

'It's a matter of perspective. As you may know, I was in a POW camp during the war. Until you have known the pain of imprisonment you will never understand the meaning of liberty.'

He turned his head away to stare through the window at the Thames. Above, the late-autumn sky had turned a mauve colour, romantic and menacing at once. Middleton's face looked weary of a sudden. It was strange that she found herself rather admiring him. His politics were repellent and his authoritarian views on civil disobedience clearly something to be feared. Yet there was a mysterious decency in him, too, and aside from the telling-off when she had tried to ambush him with the spook stuff he had behaved in a distantly cordial way. Now the brevity of his answers suggested he was becoming impatient again. But she thought she might be able to squeeze one more quote out of him.

'If you do go to Ulster, is there no possibility of negotiating a peace deal with the Republicans? Couldn't violence be avoided?'

He shook his head. 'If you mean power-sharing between Unionists and nationalists it has already failed once. It is useless to try it again.'

'Is that the politician talking, or the soldier?'

'Both. I know how the IRA should be dealt with.'

'You have a family, Mr Middleton. What does your wife think of the risk you may be undertaking?' The last word unwittingly sounded a knell. He squinted at her sharply.

'My wife understands the nature of public duty. She has supported me in every decision I've made. Should Ulster be my next one I have no doubt she will support me in that, too.'

'So are you prepared for the moment someone points a gun at you?'

His pale gaze drifted away, and then came back to her. 'I will have to take my chances. But if they come for me, the one thing I can be sure of is that they will not face me. They're not soldier enough for that.'

And at that he reached a long bony hand across the table and pressed the STOP button on her recorder.

5

A grey-blue curtain of cigarette smoke hung over the briefing room. Vicky supposed there to be about thirty plain clothes, a few uniforms, all seated at desks, like a classroom. She could see Carol Melvin, the one other plonk there, over by the window taking notes; she would tease her later for being a swot.

The Assistant Commissioner was winding up his address. He had assembled a taskforce here and at Scotland Yard to deal with the renewed threat of violence from the IRA. Vigilance had been his theme. 'These people' weren't just opportunists, they were highly organised and possessed of expertise and cunning. Car bombs had become increasingly sophisticated, and the long-handled mirrors designed to sweep beneath vehicles were no longer sufficient in countering the threat.

'We have to be prepared at all times,' he said. 'It's not enough to thwart them now and then. The terrorists know they only have to get lucky once.'

He had told shocking stories of what had been happening in Ulster, stuff too awful for the newspapers, not just the bombs but the kidnappings and maimings and murders. Even to answer your doorbell was to take a risk; there might be a masked gunman waiting on the step. And they weren't the sort to care about collateral damage – often as not the family were at home and might witness their loved one blasted at close range by a sawn-off, or catch a stray bullet themselves. Vicky had never been to Northern Ireland, but she had learned more than enough about it from the radio and TV. It sounded like the Wild West over there, a place crawling with religious bigots, tribalist politicians, vicious law-enforcers, mad-eyed killers. On the news were pictures of grim terraced streets jagged with rioters and broken glass and burnt-out cars. And they were bringing all this mayhem here, to Britain – to London.

As the meeting broke up and they filed out of the room Vicky craned her neck to look for Carol, but she was busy talking to one of the new detectives. Out in the corridor she moved slowly, preoccupied. What on earth did she know about foiling terrorists? If there were men determined to set bombs and destroy innocent lives by the score what difference could she make? It occurred to her that joining CID might have been foolhardy. She had wanted to fight crime: that was the job. But now it seemed she was being asked to fight a war.

She looked up to see DCI Wicks coming towards her, head down.

'Sir?' she called brightly.

'Vicky. How are you?'

'Just had the briefing on how to combat the IRA. To be honest, I'm none the wiser.'

Wicks laughed. 'You'll be fine.' His gaze lifted beyond her, as though he were scouting the place. He had a tired, distracted air.

'I thought you'd be in the room, too, sir. Aren't we all—?'

'I'm on something else,' he said shortly.

'Oh – something exciting?' She wanted to sound interested without being pushy. The little she knew of Wicks she admired, and hoped to show him she was trustworthy. A couple of senior officers were passing and he lifted his chin in comradely acknowledgement. More bodies crowded the corridor; the din of talk bounced off the walls.

'I'll tell you as and when,' he said, and gave her a wink before moving on.

She was back at her desk and typing up a case report when

Carol stopped by. She was a few years older than Vicky and had shown her the ropes when she first came to West End Central. Carol's blonde permed hair gave a little bounce as she walked; she had startling blue eyes and prominent teeth that seemed too numerous for her mouth.

'What did you make of that?' Vicky asked her.

'Oh . . . He seemed to know what he was talking about.'

'Let's hope. D'you think you took enough notes in there, by the way?'

'Ha ha. Nothing wrong with showing enthusiasm, girl. Got a bit of eye contact from him, too. Talking of which, was that you I spotted talking to Wicks in the corridor?'

Vicky half smiled. 'Yeah. He looked – I dunno – like he had the cares of the world on him.'

Carol squinted shrewdly. 'Oooh. I think someone's got a little bit of a crush on our DCI.'

'Don't be soft. He's much too – anyway, he's married.'

'Separated, actually. They're trying to keep it friendly.'

Trust Carol to know, she thought. Maybe that was why Wicks had looked so distracted – unhappiness at home. Just then her telephone rang, and she leaned over to answer it.

'West End Central.'

'Vicky.' Wicks. The coincidence of it almost caused her to exclaim. 'Don't say anything,' he continued abruptly. 'Don't say my name. Just listen. What you asked me about before, the "something else". I need to tell you, but not here. Walls have ears and all that. Take this down.' He recited the address of a multi-storey car park in Victoria. Third floor. He'd be in his car, and she took down its registration number.

'Can you meet at seven, this evening?'

On hearing her say yes, he rang off. She replaced the receiver. Carol had been watching her. 'Who was that?'

'No one,' she said automatically. 'Just a lead on a case.'

*

Over lunch in the canteen, Carol told her about a new initiative she and other women police officers were trying to launch. Reports of sexual assaults against women were increasing by the year, yet the manner in which they were treated by the force was inadequate and offensive. Rape victims would often be subjected to a grilling by sceptical male police officers, who insinuated that either they had made it all up or else they had 'asked for it'. As for domestics, they weren't even investigated as assault if the couple were married. Carol was pressing for a new approach to the problem – victims should be entitled to understanding and support, and, following a sexual violation, a woman police officer should be present in the interview room. This would be the first step in assuring victims of a sympathetic hearing, and might encourage more women to come forward to report incidents.

'It's pretty certain the number of cases we get is only the tip of the iceberg,' said Carol. 'You know how few plonks there are. We could use some help.'

'Of course. To be honest, after the Bramley Road case I thought it might nudge them to make some changes.'

'It's never going to change unless *we* do something about it.'

Later, on the way out Vicky ran into Paul Drewett, visiting from Scotland Yard. He seemed pleased to see her.

'All well?'

'Pretty well, sir. Nice work, that bust last week. You must have been pleased.'

Drewett had led a raid on a house in Paddington and recovered a huge consignment of dope. It had been all over the papers.

'Thanks. We got lucky, again. You ever been out on a spin?'

'Sir?'

'A spin – a search.'

'Not yet.'

He nodded, thoughtful for a moment. 'Maybe you should come along sometime. See a bit of the action.'

She felt her heart take a bound. 'Yes, sir. You know where to find me.'

He said he would be in touch, and they saluted.

Vicky spent the rest of the afternoon in a muddle of conjecture, pondering the terse phone call from Wicks. It sounded a bit Jack Regan (they all watched *The Sweeney*) except that the DCI wasn't the sort to make a drama out of nothing. Something in his voice had unsettled her. She had been on the verge of mentioning it to Carol, but an intuition warned her not to. *Walls have ears*, he had said, and as much as she trusted Carol you could never tell who might be earwigging their conversation.

She left the station at six thirty and walked across Green Park under lamplight. The trees held their gnarled branches aloft as though they would scare her. She caught sight of other shadowy walkers in the distance. Arriving at the car park she took the lift to the third floor and ventured out into the concrete walkway; a sour whiff of diesel fumes and urine greeted her. Her footsteps sounded a desolate echo as she proceeded along the rows. There appeared to be no one else about. She turned on a right angle, peering at the cars' registration plates. She gave a little jump of fright on being flashed by the headlights of a Peugeot Estate just ahead of her. Through the windscreen she could see Wicks lift his hand in greeting, then lean across to push open the passenger door.

She edged herself inside the car, which was warm, almost stuffy, from the heater. A cassette box lay on top of the dash – *Sinatra at the Sands*, with the Count Basie Orchestra.

'Evening,' he said to her, his smile faintly apologetic, as if he couldn't quite believe his own secretive instincts. He asked her how her day had been, and she told him, though it was hard to know if he was listening or not. 'You're probably wondering why I chose this place to talk,' he said, looking through the windscreen at the cheerless anonymity of parked vehicles.

'Happy to meet wherever, sir.'

He waited a beat before speaking again. 'Do you remember, a few years ago, when the Yard was being investigated? The Drug Squad trials?'

She did remember, though she was still at school at the time. The CID, Wicks went on, was quite a different place in the late sixties. Police came to the underworld knowing that criminals were useful informants and could help you increase your arrests total. They would be mixing socially with men they might one day have to lock up, but for the time being it cut out the sweat, toil and inconvenience of orthodox detective work. Catching small fry set up for you by the big fry (who were your 'friends') was much easier than catching all sizes of fry on your own. Honest but overworked detectives understood the deal. You turned a blind eye now and then to get information you couldn't come by anywhere else.

Vicky couldn't help her own curiosity. 'Is that what you did, sir?'

Wicks nodded slowly. 'In the past. I wasn't proud of it, but we got results. The problem was, it gave coppers too much licence. CID became a firm within a firm. Instead of just trading favours, some of them started taking money, or jewellery, or holidays. The whole system became dependent on backhanders. That's when they brought the new guvnor in. He knew these squads were a law unto themselves, and he decided the only way to reform them was to set up an independent department, A10, that would investigate criminal allegations against the Met.'

'I don't suppose they liked that.'

'Too right. Nor did they like the fact that a uniformed commander was brought in to oversee it. He broke the control of the CID. Widespread corruption eventually came to light, and by seventy-two, seventy-three, cases went to trial. Some detectives were convicted and sent to prison. It sent out a message that coppers weren't above the law – that they wouldn't be allowed to run things as they pleased.'

Vicky wondered where this story was heading. 'So. The bad old days . . . '

Wicks turned to look at her. 'I'm afraid they're not gone. You see, the boys upstairs had let things get out of hand. They had no idea about the scale of the problem. You sling out a few rotten apples, but the barrel's still poisoned. Corruption doesn't just go away.'

'What about this department – A10? Aren't they up to it?'

'They do what they can. But it's not enough. That's what I wanted to talk to you about.'

Vicky, remembering Carol's air of professionalism this morning, reached towards her pocket. 'Shall I take notes?'

Wicks smiled, shook his head. 'No paperwork. This is strictly off the record. The Drug Squad, as you know, have got their own ways of operating. One of them is to arrange deals between themselves and their informants. So a snout might tell the squad about a score, set up their customers for arrest, and get a share of the drugs involved as a reward. It's a scam called recycling, and hard to detect, unless you can get someone on the inside.'

'Have you got someone?'

'I did have. A dealer told me a while back about a bust – a load of LSD tablets had been seized. Now, the official charge sheet recorded about six thousand tablets. But this dealer had been there and knew there was a lot more. He overheard one officer say that they'd got *fifteen* thousand. Somewhere along the line about nine thousand LSD tablets just disappeared from the record. That's recycling.'

'You said *did* have?'

'He's disappeared too. Either abroad or he's been—' He grimaced. 'I could make discreet inquiries but even that's dangerous. You see, some of them involved in this are at our nick. Which is where you come in. I need you to keep alert – to listen out. You're new, so no one will suspect that you're—'

'A snoop?'

'No. A copper who's not bent. Who wants to have clean

hands. It's vital we do this, Vicky, if we're going to be a force that people trust. Be prepared. If there's a chance you can get on the inside, take it.'

Vicky nodded. 'Drewett – I mean, DCS Drewett – said he'd take me on a spin. Don't know if he'll remember.'

'Drewett's a good copper. You can learn from him.' He shifted in his seat to look at her. 'I know all this probably comes as a shock to you. You were expecting to catch criminals. We all do at the start. But bent detectives are criminals – and don't you forget it.'

'I won't, sir. And thanks for this . . . ' – she didn't know exactly what to call it – 'opportunity.'

He held out his hand, and she shook it. Something had changed between them as the gravity of the conversation sank in. Vicky reached over the dash and picked up the cassette of *Sinatra at the Sands.*

'My dad used to play this all the time,' she said.

'Yeah?' Wicks pressed the ON button of the radio cassette player. As he adjusted the volume an MC's voice announced the artists, and the familiar opening bars of 'Come Fly With Me' played out.

His eyes followed her as she got out of the car. She waited there until the sound of his engine faded into the night.

Vicky had for the present moved back to her mum's place in Harmood Street. For one thing, she didn't much care for the flat she'd been renting in Notting Hill – it was noisy, and cold, and she didn't know another soul in the building. For another, she thought it might be an idea to spend more time with her brother. Matthew, mindful of the financial incentive she had offered him, had knuckled under at school again, and he'd talked to her about his choices of university. He had considered applying to colleges in London, but Vicky was encouraging him to go elsewhere.

'I think Mum would like me to be near home,' he said,

with a glance towards the door. They were sitting in his bedroom, smoking.

Vicky nodded. 'Well, I can understand that, but it's not about her. You've lived here all your life – might be time to try somewhere new. Sheffield, maybe, or Manchester . . . '

'The North. That would be weird.'

'You might love it. Think of all the music up there.'

Matthew stared off thoughtfully. His spiked hair had been recently dyed a fierce coppery hue, and his skinny legs were clad in a pair of tartan trousers with bondage straps. They looked complicated, and uncomfortable, but she knew better than to make a funny remark. His expression suddenly brightened.

'Hey, look at this.'

Leaning over the long queue of LPs he plucked one out and handed it to her. Its red, blue and yellow cover was vividly emblazoned with 'The Clash'.

'Oh, the new one,' said Vicky. She flipped to the track listing on the reverse. There was a song on it called 'Julie's Been Working for the Drug Squad'. That sounded a bit close to home. She passed it back to Matthew. 'Let's have a listen, then.'

As they smoked and talked, Vicky's thoughts drifted again to her strange meeting with Wicks earlier that week. She had felt flattered that he'd taken her into his confidence, had spoken to her quite gravely, like he valued her. Even after her commendation on nicking the Notting Dale Rapist she'd had to put up with quite a lot of condescension, daft comments about her appearance, even some physical harassment. Most of it was harmless, throwaway banter, and she was learning to give as good as she got. But underneath she could detect among certain coppers something quite raw, a fear of women, a dislike of them. It wasn't to do with anything you said or did; it was the mere fact of being a woman that riled them. They might try to disguise it, the dislike, but it hung there, unignorably, like body odour.

Wicks had trusted her, though there had been a warning in his tone. Bad apples, even in their own nick: she would have to be careful. His last snout had 'disappeared', perhaps abroad, though the implication was that he might have gone somewhere more permanent. But being relatively inexperienced, and being a plonk, could be turned to advantage, because people would underestimate her. She felt a shiver of exhilaration: she was going to repay Wicks's faith in her. *If there's a chance you can get on the inside, take it.*

'What d'you think?' said Matthew, as the needle lifted from the first side of *Give 'Em Enough Rope.*

Vicky pulled a face. 'Not sure. I liked the opener – the way the end fades out and suddenly comes back in.'

'Yeah, that's cool. But the rest – not as good, is it? I mean, not like the first.'

She shook her head. 'Nothing there like '*E*-don't-*like*-his-*borin'*-job-*no*!' She jabbed her finger at him in time to the beat, and he laughed.

As they listened to the second side Vicky inspected the stack of books on Matthew's bedside table. One of them was *The Mayor of Casterbridge* by Thomas Hardy, which he was doing for A level. It was one of the very few novels she had read and liked. Matthew was revising for his mocks, though school had recently been disrupted by strikes. First it was the dinner ladies; then it was the school caretakers. They had nearly sorted them out when an overtime ban by oil-tanker drivers began. The classrooms couldn't be heated, so the school had to close again. It was a subject on which Irene, their mother, became very exercised. .

'These bloody unions, holding the country to ransom,' she fumed.

'Well, people are entitled to a fair wage,' Vicky replied mildly.

Irene only scowled. She had voted Tory all her life. Six years ago, under Heath's government, she and her husband had bought their council house. This accession to the property-owning classes had brought out her sense of entitlement and sharpened her disgust with the way the country was being run. She had decided that Margaret Thatcher would be their saviour.

'I don't like that voice of hers,' mused Vicky. 'Or the clothes.'

'She's a woman, so she'll get things done,' Irene said firmly. 'Do you know how many are unemployed in this country?'

'Yeah. I've seen the posters.'

'It's a disgrace. The sooner they call an election the better.'

'She may not get in, you know. Remember how close it was last time.'

'Well, if I have anything to do with it she will. I'll canvass for them if needs be – just you wait and see.'

Vicky yawned and got up from the sofa. 'Right, I'm off. Got an early start tomorrow.'

'Earlier than you think,' said her mother, pursing her mouth.

Vicky looked at her, puzzled. 'What d'you mean?'

'It's the unions, I told you. There's a Tube strike on.'

6

Callum was at his local, the Crown on Clerkenwell Green, early doors. The place rarely got full, and on quiet evenings like this he would sit marking his students' essays over a ginger ale. He liked London pubs, with their bevelled mirrors and wooden panelling and air of democratic ease. It was so different from Newry, where you had to be very careful about which places you drank in; such was the strangled atmosphere of suspicion that just to set foot in the 'wrong' one could mean trouble. A hooded look from a stranger would tell you if you had to get out of there.

It had been a good term at Holywell so far. Despite the strikes of maintenance staff and cleaners the college had managed to stay open, and he had been lucky with this year's intake of students – they seemed bright, inquisitive, hard-working. He had also managed to press on with *Go-Betweens*, his book. Even this had been quite enjoyable; he had forgotten how much he liked E. M. Forster. The only slight bump in the road had been his failure with Juliet Barwell. Not that they'd got very far; after the Pall Mall party they'd had a couple of drinks together, and then it had gone quiet. His speculation that she'd already got someone was confirmed when he spotted her leaving college one evening arm in arm with a bloke. Well, useful to get that learned ...

He had been absorbed in his reading when he noticed someone, a woman, stealing a glance at him from her seat over at the bar. He dismissed it as a reflex of curiosity, until she did it again, quite openly this time. Was she on the prowl? He was about to find out, because she was now off the stool and heading towards him. She was tall, and wore a blue belted mac, jeans and black pumps, though what instantly appealed to Callum was her sexy gunslinger's strut. When she got to his table she leaned down, and for an instant he thought he might have seen her face before – but where?

'"Is that concrete all around, or is it in my head?"' Hannah said hopefully, narrowing her eyes.

'Sorry?'

She stared at him for a moment, trying to read his expression. She flinched, as if some error had been made. 'Formerly Young Dude?'

Callum laughed. 'You're a Mott the Hoople fan, I'm guessing.'

Hannah saw friendliness, but no spark of recognition. She swung her gaze around the room, wondering. There were no other likely candidates present. 'Sorry, I think I might have—'

'Don't go,' he said. 'I can quote song lyrics too, if you like.'

He shifted along the table in invitation. She was attractive, though a little older, up close – well into her thirties. Flustered, she was now explaining herself. 'I'm a journalist, following up a story.'

'About Mott the Hoople?'

'No, no, that was just a code – I thought you were a contact.'

'Ah. Sorry to disappoint you ... but you'll have a drink anyway?'

While he went off to the bar Hannah tried to calm herself. Whoever she was meant to be meeting, the young dude who liked 'art galleries, Bowie, live music', had stood her up. Her emergency pretext that she was on a job had sounded fake to her own ears. Well, sod it, this one wasn't bad-looking ...

'I'm Hannah, by the way,' she said on his return.

'Callum. Pleased to meet you.'

She wondered how old he was: she possibly had ten years on him. Still, they had got talking, so she'd play it by ear.

'What's all this stuff?' she asked, nodding at the bundle of papers at his side.

'Student essays. I teach a literature course – at Holywell College. And you?'

'I work for the *Ensign*. Not far from here. Sounds like you're from Ulster.'

He nodded, and explained that he'd lived there with his parents and sister until he was eighteen. 'Just as it was all starting – the struggle. Can't say I was sorry to see the back of it. D'you know the place?'

'Only Belfast. I've been working a lot on the IRA. You remember Balcombe Street? I got my big break on that story.'

The subject occupied them for a while. Callum had known boys at school who'd joined the Republican Army, some of them in prison now. It was odd how quickly you became used to living in a war zone.

Hannah, listening intently, said, 'I was interviewing someone the other week – the Shadow Home Secretary, as a matter of fact – who sounded very pessimistic about them reaching a settlement.'

'Is that your man Middleton? 'Sfunny, I met him too, few weeks back, at a party. Said he'd done a lot of shooting in the North – at first I thought he was talking about the Provos! Turned out he meant grouse.'

Hannah laughed. 'I can see the confusion . . . '

'I liked him, actually.'

'So did I,' she said. 'I mean, his politics are beyond the pale, but he had integrity, and this quiet sense of humour. Not at all like the general run of politicians.'

'Aye. You meet a lot of 'em, then?'

'A fair few. But I do all sorts of profiles – writers, artists, sports people. The odd pop star.'

They talked about music. Hannah was going through a phase of listening mainly to women singer-songwriters – Joni, Carole King, Laura Nyro. She had fallen recently for Kate Bush. 'I don't think I've heard anything like "Wuthering Heights" – ever. What about you?'

'Oh, different stuff. Bowie, of course. Lou Reed. Bit of Roxy, bit of punk. There's a song on the new Clash album called "All the Young Punks". Doesn't sound as cool as "All the Young Dudes", does it?'

'Hardly anything does,' she said, smiling. 'You know Bowie wrote that for Mott when he heard they were going to split up? He sang it himself on *David Live*, but it wasn't half as good as theirs.'

Callum was smiling, too. 'I just love that bit at the end when Ian Hunter starts talking to someone in the audience – "Hey, you there, in the glasses, I want you – I want you at the front – bring him here cos I want him . . ." And then he laughs, like, this *big dirty laugh*.'

'I saw them play,' said Hannah. 'About six years ago, in Croydon – and I was wearing glasses! But he didn't ask me to come down to the front.'

'Still . . . you saw them!' She was tickled at how impressed he seemed. 'I bet you look good in glasses.'

It was a bit early to be paying her a compliment, and his gaze dropped as he did so. But she bought it, with a chuckle, and inwardly he sighed with relief. As they talked and talked it occurred to Hannah that no blind date could have gone as dreamily as this encounter. True, it was a pity his being that much younger than her, and she felt a little unnerved that he didn't drink – he had explained why, about the pledge, but it still made her uneasy. There she was necking lager and yarning away while he sipped ginger ale. Nor did he smoke. Something was lost there in the unspoken compact of strangers meeting. But she liked the way he asked her questions, about her work, about herself, and seemed genuinely interested in her answers. Hannah spent so much of her time interviewing people it felt almost a novelty to be with someone whose focus was on her instead.

'Let me get you another one,' Callum said as the bell rang for last orders.

She smiled her assent, wondering how many she'd had. 'Can you make it a vodka and tonic? I don't think I can take any more lager.'

'Sure. One VAT, comin' right up.'

VAT?! Fuck's sake. Only an eejit would talk like that, and he didn't even have the excuse of being drunk. He was trying to get up the nerve to ask her back to his place – he'd already told her he lived round the corner. Maybe she was hoping he would. There still seemed plenty to talk about.

'I have a confession,' she began as he returned from the bar. She was looking rather sheepish. 'When I came here tonight, it *wasn't* because I was following a story. I made that up.'

'Oh?'

'The real reason is I'd answered an ad in the personals. In *On the Town*. It caught my eye because he quoted that line from "All the Young Dudes". But whoever it was, he didn't show up.'

He stared at her. 'So when you first saw me you thought—'

'You were the "Formerly Young Dude". But then it was clear that you weren't. I should have said straight away, only I was embarrassed. And you were so friendly I thought – you don't mind, do you?'

Callum shook his head, no, of course not – though within he felt a terrible deflation. She'd been stood up, and he had been her rebound option, all unsuspecting. He wished she hadn't told him. Why couldn't she have kept pretending? There was something else, though, and he didn't like to admit it: he regarded the lonely hearts thing as a bit desperate. If she's got to the age of – whatever she is – and has to resort to that, well, there must be something wrong with her. You couldn't go on blind dates and be taken seriously.

She was looking at him intently. 'Do you really not mind?'

He assured her again it was fine, but Hannah was too perceptive not to feel a tiny withdrawal on his part. She tried to restore the mood with a droll account of her most recent dating disaster, and though he laughed along she sensed her mistake in confessing the bluff.

Outside the pub they went through an awkward little minuet of farewell.

'Thanks for saving my night, anyway,' she said, as brightly as she could. It seemed he wasn't even going to ask for her phone number, let alone suggest they continue the evening back at his.

'That's all right. Glad to be of service. Maybe . . . '

'Yes?'

'We should do it again some time.'

It sounded to her half-hearted; she decided to stand on her dignity. 'You can reach me at the paper,' she said with a shrug.

'Oh, right. The *Ensign*, yeah?'

She nodded, and gave him a little wave as she walked off. She couldn't recall another evening that had begun so promisingly and ended in such disappointment. The chances were they wouldn't see one another again. It confirmed something she had often suspected of men: it didn't pay to be too honest with them.

Martin Villiers had looked pleased with himself as he swaggered into Callum's office at Holywell and plumped down on the sofa. *Unusually* pleased, thought Callum, given that self-satisfaction was his friend's customary demeanour. Since they had last met Martin had moved up in the world, had got the job he'd been angling for – Deputy Press Secretary to the PM. He already looked that bit more puffed-up on the oxygen of influence.

'Congratulations,' said Callum, pouring out the tea. 'Two sugars, yeah?'

'Cheers,' said Martin, hands cradling the back of his head as he reclined on a cushion. 'Yeah, we're still just ahead in the polls. Jim's going to sort out the unions and call an election for next year.'

'Last time we met you said he was going to call it in a couple of weeks. What happened to that?'

'He didn't want to take a gamble,' he replied smoothly. 'The Tories might have sneaked in had we called it last month. Now we can consolidate, get inflation down and be ready to crush them in the spring.'

'I hope you're right. These strikes, though . . . '

Martin made a hissing noise. 'We'll get through them. What's the worst they can do? In the end the union leaders will come to heel – it's in their interest to keep us in power.'

The confidence with which he spoke quietly amused Callum, though it impressed him too. He himself was not of a character to feel certain about anything, let alone the country's political future. And yet he sensed something else beyond the need to grandstand had brought Martin to his door today; he didn't flatter himself to think his company alone was sufficient pull. This intuition soon proved correct.

'Anyway, this new job is going to keep me even busier. I'll have to be in London at least two nights a week.' He fixed Callum with a significant look. 'Now, d'you remember making me a very kind offer of a bed for the night?'

'Aye . . . ' said Callum, surprised, 'though I should warn you, it's only a wee room.'

'Clerkenwell, isn't it? I'm not looking for anything fancy—'

'You won't find it. I rent the house from an old couple who live abroad. It's kind of shabby, like the rest of the neighbourhood.'

'But you have the place to yourself, yeah? I just want somewhere quiet I can work and get a night's kip.'

'It's just me. You'd better come round and have a look at it, though. It may not be up to the standard of the PM's Press Secretary.'

Martin waved this off with a laugh. 'Deputy. It'd only be for a few months in any case. If – *when* – we get re-elected, I'll be able to claim for something more permanent. But thanks, mate, it's really good of you.'

'No trouble. Christine all right about this?'

His brow darkened momentarily. 'Yeah. Not that she has much choice. She knows this job is a big deal for me, and commuting back to Suffolk every night of the week would be madness.' He continued his monologue for a while on the 'challenges' ahead for the party, apparently assured that the subject was as urgent for Callum. Among them was Northern Ireland, of course; they were stepping up security in anticipation of a new wave of attacks on the mainland. Suddenly he broke off with a grin.

'Here's one for you. What d'you call an Irishman in a sports car?'

Callum, bracing himself, shook his head.

'A *motorist*, you bigoted bastard!' He roared with laughter.

'Not heard that one,' said Callum, smiling, and privately marvelling at the nonchalance with which Martin would risk offence. But Irish jokes were so ubiquitous it was useless even to think of making an objection.

After he had gone Callum went down to the staff common room to read the papers. He looked through the *Ensign* until he found Hannah Strode's byline on a news story: he read it carefully, trying to match her voice with her writing. He had thought of her quite a lot since their encounter a few days ago, and the realisation had dawned that he had been too hasty about the lonely hearts stuff. Was blind dating really so pitiable? That London could be a lonely city he knew from experience. Perhaps a personal ad, far from being a desperate roll of the dice, was something that showed initiative, willingness, a spirit of optimism. Only – and this was the sticking point – why did someone as smart and good-looking as Hannah have to lower herself? Could there really be such a shortage of decent men?

Through the tall sash window he watched the darkening afternoon. He had no more appointments, and began to pack up for the day. Outside, on the Strand, the crowded buses were lit within by the same pickled light you found in old pubs. As he walked he glanced at the faces of passers-by, stoical, closed, English faces, an endless flow of them, heading home from work, if indeed they'd been at work. It was hard to know these days. He turned up Chancery Lane, past the ancient brick walls of Lincoln's Inn and thence into the Dickensian maze of streets leading to High Holborn. He loved this part of town, with its alternation of gloom and glare, of ghostly old London and the unceasing din of traffic. Outside the Tube he bought a *Standard* and then resumed his walk through Hatton Garden down to Farringdon Road. The evening had descended quickly; street lights had come on, and the shops were closing up for the day.

He felt lucky that home and work were within walking distance. Clerkenwell was an unfancied district, lost between the West End and the City, a place of derelict warehouses, small workshops, dingy pubs. During the week it had a bustle, but at weekends it was almost deserted. Callum had suffered from insomnia for years, and when it became acute he took nocturnal walks about the empty streets. He would encounter the occasional worker from the meat market at Smithfield, or a drunk returning from the West End, or a vagrant, but that was all. One of his favourite daytime haunts was the Italian church on Clerkenwell Road, where he dropped in to light a candle or linger for the weekday Mass. The devotion of the old ladies reminded him of his days as an altar boy, when almost identical old ladies would park themselves in the pews and offer their quavering voices up to the Almighty. Some of them still wore a black veil and worried away at their rosaries. Maybe it was the same the world over.

He had crossed at the junction of Farringdon and Clerkenwell Road when he happened to glance down at the gigantic cratered site where the National Music Hall was being extended. Following a long delay the digging had resumed. The little houses had been flattened, along with an ancient pub, amid a storm of recrimination. Callum saw both sides of the argument; a larger Music Hall had to be a good thing, though he felt sad at the destruction of buildings he had come to love. It was just unfortunate that a change worth making so often involved the sacrifice of something worth keeping. A gang of site workers attired in overalls and hard hats were ambling past him when one of them halted suddenly and called in an unmistakable Ulster brogue:

'Callum Conlan. Is that you?'

He peered at the man's face in the dusk light.

'Sean?' he said uncertainly, and then he did know him. Sean McGlashan had been a couple of years below him at St Cyprian's, their grammar school in Newry. The other workers had drifted on without him.

'Y'all right, big man?' said Sean, vigorously shaking his hand. 'Wasn't sure I knew you behind that beard.'

Callum laughed. 'That tells you how long it's been. I've had this, I dunno, five years. You working here?' He nodded towards the site.

'Aye. On this Music Hall, you know? Casual labour.'

They stood there taking one another in. He hadn't known Sean that well, though they'd played football for the school together. He had bulked in size since then, his face was fleshier and the hand he had just shaken felt as large and coarse as a farmer's. Callum hadn't heard another Ulster accent in a while; he found, to his surprise, that he'd missed it. A surge of friendliness overcame him.

'I live just round the corner. Will you have a cup o' tea?'

The two of them fell into step. Sean laughed grandly.

'Fancy runnin' into you, though. In this city! What are the chances?'

Unlike Callum, Sean had not been eager to leave Newry. He had survived as a builder's mate for a few years before the work dried up. Then he'd done a stint as a barman, a hospital porter and, briefly, an undertaker.

'Can you believe it? Talk about a fuckin' dead end ...'

They turned off Clerkenwell Close into St James's Walk, the

quiet terrace where he lived. The church clock had just chimed five. Inside the house Sean looked around, and Callum was struck anew by its unhomeliness – a few sticks of furniture, an old radio, a two-bar fire. The rest of the poky front room was filled from floor to ceiling with books, racked on the shelves in higgledy-piggledy fashion. His bedroom and the spare room were the same. Books had at first furnished the place; after a couple of years they had engulfed it.

'Jesus. D'you have enough *bukes*?' asked Sean.

Callum gave a laugh. 'I know. They seem to breed independently, so I just leave them to get on with arranging themselves.'

Sean tested the most stuffed of the bookcases with his hand, and it swayed unsteadily. 'You wanna be careful. This thing might come down and bury yer.'

'Yeah. Like Leonard Bast.'

Sean stared at him. 'Bast. Someone you know?'

Callum shook his head, disowningly. 'No. Just read about.'

He led him into the galley kitchen and put the kettle on. From a cupboard he took out a packet of chocolate digestives and opened them.

'So yer all on your own-ee-o?' mused Sean, dunking a biscuit.

'Aye. Rented about three years ago. Cheap neighbourhood – nobody much lives around here. How 'bout yourself?'

'Och, wee room on the Old Kent Road. Bunch of people in this one auld block. Pound a week, though – can't complain.'

The talk turned soon enough to the old school. Callum admitted he'd lost touch with everyone from St Cyprian's; in front of Sean he professed a mild regret, though he didn't feel it. Sean had more recent news of the alumni.

'You remember Tommy Cahill, wee feller?'

'Cahill . . . played in the firsts?'

'Nah, that was his older brother, Liam. Tommy was a bit of a tearaway, always up to somethin'.'

Callum did remember him now, a freckle-faced bantam who

swaggered round the place, a challenging gleam in his eye. 'Yeah … Tommy Cahill. Didn't he join the Republicans?'

'Aye,' said Sean, with a significant look.

'You're gonna tell me he's in prison?'

Sean shook his head. 'Not in prison. Dead. Army shot him down on Chapel Street. He was suspected as a bomb-maker, though they found nothin' on him.'

'He must have been a kid … '

'Twenty-one. Joined at eighteen. Younger than him have died.'

'What a waste,' said Callum quietly.

'Is it? The Cahill family don't think so. But I know what you mean. Seems no end in sight.'

Callum looked away. 'Fuck's sake … I hated seeing soldiers on our street. It made me angry. But I didn't want to stay and see young men and women getting themselves killed either.'

Sean shrugged, and took a swallow of his tea. 'Depends how badly you want a united Ireland. To some it's worth dying for.'

The words were pointed, and Callum felt the weariness of having to defend a position – a pacifist one – he sometimes barely believed in himself. But Sean, alive to the lowering mood, jumped in before him. 'It's all right, Cal, I get it. You and me both. Fuckin' sick to death of all the killin' and maimin'. Let's just leave it.'

His attention had turned to the shelf of cassette tapes above the kitchen sink.

'Got the new Clash, I see. Any good?'

For answer Callum pressed a button on his cassette recorder, which opened its jaws with a half-reluctant motion. He took *Give 'Em Enough Rope* from its box and inserted it. He pressed PLAY. The whipcrack snare of the opening track kicked in and he watched as Sean's head jerked to the beat.

After a minute or so of the music he looked again to Callum. It seemed that something left over from the conversation was still on his mind.

'Safe European home? – that'd be the ticket! So I take it you won't be back there any time soon?'

'To Newry?' He paused, wondering if he should pretend uncertainty – acknowledge the siren call of the auld country. 'Not a chance.'

Sean stared at him, then laughed out loud. 'Don't blame ya. Now what time does that pub on the corner open?'

7

Freddie hurried up the steps of the National Music Hall. In the mirrored lift his suit looked a bit crumpled, and having run the last hundred yards from the car a fine sheen of sweat had moistened his brow. He hated being late, especially on a Monday morning, but not even Terry's expert chauffeuring could elude the traffic on the Euston Road. At this rate he'd have to start taking the Tube. Though of course he never would: quicker than driving it might be, but he wasn't going to be packed like veal into a clanking, stuffy train carriage. If anyone challenged him on the matter he would argue that asthma prevented him – 'doctor's orders'.

He had no sooner stepped out of the lift than Robin Piddock, his fussy clipboard at the ready, darted forward to join him. Had he just been waiting there, to pounce? Freddie immediately quickened his step up the corridor.

'Um, Freddie? Just had a call from the *Ensign* – apparently you've agreed to talk to some journalist there.'

'Yeah. My agent set it up.'

'Right,' said Piddock, his brow knitted. 'It's just that, as head of press, it's my responsibility to oversee press coverage. If it doesn't go through our office it looks like I'm not doing my job.'

Freddie shot him a sidelong look. 'Well, let's not forget, Robin, the last time it went through your office I ended up crucified in the *Sketch*. So forgive me if I'm a bit gun-shy around your arrangements.'

Piddock took the rebuke, though he didn't seem sufficiently cowed to slink away. He was shaping to raise another topic, and Freddie thought he knew what it might be. 'Was there something else?'

'*Sunday Times* and the *Observer* yesterday,' he began. 'I saw the ads in both the magazines.'

The Castleton wallpaper ad campaign had begun, showing Freddie – photographed by Snowdon – lounging regally in a Mayfair club room against a backdrop of burgundy-and-gold fleur-de-lys wallpaper. Beneath it ran the tagline *Very Freddie Selves. Very Castleton*. The stylist had gone to town on the hair and make-up, though his professed intention of making Freddie look more 'natural' had been way off the beam.

'You look like you've been *embalmed*,' Linda had remarked as they passed the magazine around over Sunday lunch. Jon, a sardonic seventeen-year-old, had sniggered appreciatively. Tim, two years younger and his one remaining ally at home, had stared hard at the advert before he looked up and said, thoughtfully: 'You look like Ming the Merciless, Dad.' Hoots of laughter followed.

Freddie joined in, hiding his hurt at their mockery. He would not lower himself to point out that the Castleton fee would help pay for the redecoration of the house, the next summer holiday, and the Chambolle-Musigny they were presently enjoying at the table. It was money, and he couldn't afford to sniff at it even if they could.

'I was just wondering,' continued Piddock, 'will there be *many more* of these ads?'

'Why?' said Freddie, bridling. 'It's all good press for the theatre.' He knew this was disingenuous, but Piddock's tone of sanctimony had needled him.

'With respect, Freddie, I don't think it is. After all the talk of belt-tightening and the five per cent pay policy, the unions will pounce on something like this.'

'If you're that worried, Robin, phone the papers' ad

departments. It's nothing to do with me. I just turned up and had my picture taken next to a wall.'

They had reached his office door, where he dismissed Piddock with a brusquely professional nod. It was true, the unions had been on the warpath for months. Freddie thought he must be an optimist at heart, for the longer they delayed the less likely, he felt, was their commitment to industrial action. On his desk lay a stack of post, which he riffled through distractedly. Most of the dreary stuff Dawn would deal with, but he had to be careful: it would be embarrassing if she chanced upon the Castleton cheque, for instance, with its improbable vapour trail of zeros. She would know in an instant that her boss earned more for two afternoons' 'work' than she did per annum.

His intercom buzzed and, as if summoned by his guilty conscience, Dawn's voice broke in. 'Morning, Freddie. They're expecting you in the auditorium in ten minutes.' It was the final auditions this morning for *The Ragged Trousered Philanthropists*, chief among them the casting of the female lead, Annie, a union organiser and suffragette. It was a part that the adapter had created from scratch, since the novel featured no love interest or, indeed, a woman character of any substance. They had narrowed it down to two – Romilly Sargent, a willowy dancer and singer highly regarded in musical theatre, and Nicola, who'd got this far in the audition process through her TV fame and Freddie's championing. His affair with her was still largely secret, and he intended to keep it that way.

Freddie felt uncommonly nervous as he entered the echoing auditorium, a coffee in one hand, a doughnut in the other. A desert of crimson plush seats stretched before him. 'Over here, Fred,' called Mike Findlay, the assistant director, who occupied a row near the front. A couple of seats along sat Nigel Merryweather, director of music. He squinted as Freddie approached.

'What's that you're eating?'

'Breakfast,' he replied – which, strictly speaking, he'd had two hours ago when the housekeeper, Mrs Jenner, had served him bacon and eggs. He plumped down on a seat just behind the pair.

'I thought we'd see Nicola Mayman first,' said Mike, a lean, floppy-haired Yorkshireman who sat with his knees clasped against his chest, like a kid watching TV.

When she came onto the stage Nicola smiled out at them, her hand shielding her eyes against the stark lighting. She wore denim dungarees over a plain white T-shirt and a spotted rag in her hair, an outfit somehow appropriate to the comradely spirit of *Ragged Trousers*. Freddie raised his hand in welcome: he desperately wanted Nicola to be brilliant, so he could give her the role in good conscience.

'Whenever you're ready, darling,' called Nigel.

The audition consisted of two pieces, the gentle love aria 'Without You I'm Nothing', and then the big audience-pleaser which firebrand Annie delivers to the working men of Mugsborough, 'Don't Let the Bastards Grind You Down'. Nicola's clear alto was touchingly restrained in the aria, and Freddie sensed the others respond to her warmth. The second number, with its aggressive jollity and swoop up and down the scales, proved more of a stretch, though she delivered it gamely enough. After she had exited Mike craned his head round to Freddie and whispered, 'That's the best I've seen from her.' Relieved, Freddie returned a nod and a thumbs up.

His confidence began to falter about thirty seconds into Romilly Sargent's performance. The humble 'who, me?' way she had sidled onto the stage was pure subterfuge. Her version of the aria contained all the feeling of Nicola's but with extra little touches, like the plaintive catch in her voice at the end of the second chorus. Then she took effortless command of the pitch and roll of 'Bastards', nailing the tricky high notes, punching up the witty asides and bringing the song home with a flourish. She was subtle, moving, majestic – and Freddie knew the game was up. He joined the others in thanking Romilly, then watched her as she trotted off into the wings.

Nigel and Mike turned round in their seats to face Freddie.

'Do we even need to talk about this?' Nigel began in a hushed voice, shifting his gaze from one to the other. 'I mean, no one else can do what she just did.'

'You mean Romilly?' said Freddie, bluffing desperately.

'Of course I do. She's sensational. She's gonna make the whole show!'

'I have to agree,' said Mike. 'She's funny, she looks wonderful, and she has an amazing voice. What d'you say, Fred?'

Freddie nodded, pensively resting his chin on his fist. 'Mm, I see it . . . But I do think Nicola's got something too, don't you?'

'Yeah, but it's not a patch on what Romilly's got. Come on, Fred, there's no contest. This one's the brass ring.'

Freddie winced inwardly. He knew he could overrule them. But did he really want to sacrifice Romilly Sargent? Nicola was good, of course she was. But Romilly was great – a true star. They all knew it. He cleared his throat and looked up.

'I'll get back to you by the end of today.'

Nigel and Mike stared at him, nonplussed. 'Fred, honestly, I think we—'

'Don't *hassle* me, Nigel,' he snapped. 'You'll have a decision by the end of the day, all right?'

He rose from his seat and with an air of offended dignity he padded out of the auditorium. Once backstage, he hurried along to the dressing rooms. He needed to organise damage limitation now, his first task being to reassure Nicola of how stoutly he'd been fighting her corner. He was passing the wings when he saw her, sitting alone, deep in thought.

'Ah, there you are!' he cried, aiming for a positive tone that specifically didn't promise anything. He took a folding metal chair from against the wall and sat down next to her.

Nicola looked up, her brown Bambi eyes yearning with appeal. 'What did you think?'

'I couldn't have been more charmed.' It was like going round after a show to pay homage. Freddie had done it often enough to know that, with actors, there was no such thing as overegging it. Whatever the standard of performance, praise had to be instant, extravagant and unconditional.

'Really? I couldn't see any of you for the lights. I gave it my best—'

'Darling, you were *stupendous.* We all thought so.' Something in his voice must have alerted her to what was coming. Her expression tensed as she said:

'But Romilly . . . ?'

Freddie shook his head, solemnly, eyes closed. 'Not for me. Nigel and Mike think she may have the edge. We're going to meet again at the end of the day.'

She put on a brave smile, but her shoulders had slumped. Freddie understood: breaking the bad news was an ordeal, and however much you justified it as a professional decision it always felt to the actor like a personal one. He hadn't wanted to put Nicola through it, but she had begged him to audition her for the part, and he had unwisely succumbed.

He leaned forward in his chair and pressed his hands together, as though about to pray. 'You know if it was up to me, darling, I'd cast you in a heartbeat—'

'But it *is* up to you,' said Nicola, not looking at him. 'You're the boss. You could tell Nigel and Mike to . . . get stuffed.'

Freddie gave a helpless half-laugh, caught in the bind of acknowledging his own authority while refusing to demean himself by playing favourites. 'Mike and Nigel are valued colleagues. I can't just ride roughshod over them to please myself – to please you.'

Nicola stared ahead, not saying anything, and Freddie realised his mistake. He should have kept away from her until this evening. She would have known soon enough anyway; it was tactless of him to have come round offering hope, however slim.

He reached for her hand, and said, almost in a whisper, 'Darling, believe me, you're the last person on earth I'd want to hurt . . .'

Behind him a cough sounded. He turned to find a young woman peering at them interestedly. She wore a belted mac over wide grey slacks.

'Hello,' she said. 'Hannah Strode. From the *Ensign*. I was told I'd find you down here.'

Freddie, flustered, got up from his chair. 'The *Ensign*. Is that today?'

Hannah nodded, keeping her smile in place. 'I checked with your agent – and I've just now talked to Robin Piddock.'

He had forgotten all about Leo's message, so there was nothing in the diary. He was quite unprepared for an interview, but it would be bad form to send her away. He also needed to explain to her the little scene she had just intruded upon, and quickly introduced the two women. Hannah extended her hand to Nicola.

'Pleased to meet you. I thought you were great in *Unlucky Charms*.'

'Thanks,' said Nicola, offering a smile that communicated no delight in the compliment. Freddie now sensed this interruption as a means of escape. He made a show of consulting his watch and sighing with a busy man's exasperation: he told Nicola that he'd get back to her later in the day.

'Miss Strode—'

'Hannah.'

'Hannah, if you'd care to follow me, we can talk in my office.'

He gabbled some flattering nonsense at her while they rode the lift to his floor. She was attractive, tall – taller than he was – and attended to him with an air of scrutiny that put him on guard. He wondered how much of that whispering confab with Nicola she had taken in. He couldn't afford another PR disaster like the last one.

Hannah did a 360-degree turn around Selves's office, with its large picture window facing south towards the Thames. Whereas the NMH itself was looking shabby at the edges Freddie had been determined to keep his own place in it spick and span. His glass-topped desk glinted in the low autumn sun, and the modern Italian furniture, all white leather and chrome, had the covetable aspect of a photo spread in the glossies. Which reminded Hannah—

'Is that wallpaper by Castleton?'

Freddie looked at her sharply. 'Ah, you've seen the ads . . . '

'They're hard to avoid! I presume they made it worth your while.'

Don't rise to the bait, Freddie told himself. 'To answer your question, no, it's not Castleton,' he said evenly. 'My wife chose that wallpaper.'

Hannah nodded and smiled, as though she had asked an innocent question. Freddie pressed the intercom button and asked Dawn to bring them coffee. He gestured to the sofa, where Hannah kicked back, unwinding her striped scarf and setting up her tape recorder. She began the interview with a couple of looseners about his early life, a scholarship boy at a public school so minor he always affected not to remember its name; then Oxford and drama school, his acclaimed versions of Shakespeare and Chekhov, then his switch to opera and musicals at the NMH. Given the chance to talk about his successes Freddie relaxed: his manner became expansive and mildly flirtatious. He had been something of a swordsman in his younger years, and though he didn't delude himself that he turned heads he sensed there was still a sufficient twinkle in his eye to make women wonder.

Hannah, coaxing and disarming, was a patient listener, and instead of interrupting would let her interviewees talk and talk, sometimes to their palpable doom: if you waited long enough they would damn themselves out of their own mouth. She called it Death by Quotation. Freddie had the self-made man's love of his own maker, but he was shrewd, and he knew journalists well enough to keep his flank protected. He was ready for it when she unsheathed the dagger.

'. . . and yet despite the successes the National Music Hall has a reputation for extravagance, for wasting public money. Does that worry you?'

'It would worry me if it were true. It's not all public money anyway. We have private subsidy to shore us up.'

'But doesn't private enterprise mean fewer risks, less creativity?'

'We have to consider the backers – they prefer to play safe.'

'So you put on the umpteenth production of *The Nutcracker*.'

Freddie laughed. 'But we also have a new musical of *The Ragged Trousered Philanthropists*, which we've just finished casting.'

'Ah, yes, and you're directing, of course. Quite ironic, isn't it?'

He paused. 'Ironic?'

'Well, it's a story about the struggle of the working man, and yet here you are, at loggerheads with your own stage staff on the five per cent ruling.'

Freddie took a breath, urging himself to stay calm. 'It's not that black and white. As a publicly funded business we have a duty to get the best deal we can. Actually, I'm not unsympathetic to the working man. My father was a bus conductor, as you probably know.'

'Are your parents proud of you?'

Freddie was wrong-footed by that. 'I hope so. I owe them a great deal.'

She nodded, and paused. 'So will there be industrial action, do you think?'

'I don't know. I gather the staff are debating it this afternoon. We can't break the pay deal, so it's curtains if they decide to strike.'

'I notice quite a lot of anger seems to be directed at you personally. Do you mind being disliked?'

He stared at her for a moment. 'Being director of the NMH I'm used to it. It's like Nelson on his column – you always attract the pigeons.'

Hannah smiled: the analogy was at once self-deprecating and self-regarding. Funny how those different impulses were so closely related. She returned to her emollient line of questioning and got Freddie to talk about his mother, and how she had instilled in him a passion for theatre and music. It was well known how much actors loved him – did he reciprocate the feeling? Of course, he replied, actors were the very lifeblood of the theatre, how could he *not* love them!

Hannah nodded. 'Do you regard them as friends more than colleagues?'

'Well,' he began, 'I think of them as both, really. The theatre is a collegiate enterprise, and the actor–director relationship can become very intense – it's a sort of negotiation – I give you this, you give me that. There are arguments, too, inevitably, but there's also a strong element of trust.'

'Yes, I see. By the way, are you going to be working with Nicola Mayman?'

Freddie paused, sensing danger. 'Erm, I couldn't honestly say. Nicola is a wonderful, mm – I mean, when I talk about intense . . . ' He was stammering, and stopped himself. 'Why d'you ask?'

Hannah heard something off in his tone. 'No particular reason. I like her, that's all. I was glued to *Unlucky Charms* when it was on telly.'

'Yes, she was very good in it,' he said, annoyed with himself. She'd asked him an innocent question and he'd answered as if he were under caution. Fool! He continued with some diversionary blather about the rehearsal process, hoping he'd got away with it. She listened, smiled, made an occasional note. Nicola's name didn't come up again between them.

The telephone rang on his desk. It was Dawn, apologising for the interruption but Bob Bewley, the assistant manager, was on the line. It sounded urgent.

'D'you mind if I take this call?' he asked Hannah, who held up her hands as though to say Go right ahead. As it turned out Bob's call wasn't that urgent, he simply wanted to arrange another associates' meeting to discuss new 'revenues'. Freddie, half listening, thought this might be a good moment to grandstand in front of Hannah – remind her she was in the presence of a *grand fromage*.

'I think such a meeting would be hugely helpful, Bob,' he said in his most authoritative drawl. 'We're facing a moment of crisis in funding, and it really behoves us in the arts to engage with the government – to convince them we need their support. Now's the time to stand up and be counted.' Bob, a little nonplussed, perhaps wondered why Freddie was suddenly addressing him as if they were at a public event. He suggested next Tuesday for the meeting. Freddie hesitated, then said, 'Ah, unfortunately Tuesdays are a bit tricky for me.' The BBC had him booked on Tuesdays for filming the arts series. Bob sounded a bit peeved as he rang off: he would have to get back to the associates to rearrange a date.

Over on the sofa Hannah was laughing silently behind her hand.

'What's funny?'

She shook her head. 'It's nothing.'

'Go on, tell me.'

'Oh, it's just you saying "Now's the time to stand up and be counted", and next minute sitting back down because you can't do Tuesdays. I'm sorry, it made me laugh.'

He gave an irritated laugh of his own. 'Yes, like lining up for the cavalry charge and then crying off with a dental appointment. Oh well. There'll be other meetings, I guarantee it. At times it seems like we do nothing else.'

A few minutes later she clicked off the button on her tape recorder. 'Thanks, that was great.'

'You have what you need?' Freddie hoped he had done enough to charm her. She had been friendly, though with journalists you could never tell: they'd flatter and coddle even while they were looking for the right moment to stab you. 'A pleasure, Hannah, I look forward to your piece.'

'I hope it won't disappoint.'

'If you ever want to come to a show here let me know,' he said, producing a card on which he scribbled his number. 'It's my private line. You can reach me any time.'

'Except Tuesdays,' she said, smiling. 'I'll remember that.'

When she had gone Freddie wandered over to the back window, from where he could see work in progress on the Hall's new extension. The diggers were grinding away; a giant crane bent its long neck peering into a crater. Men in tabards and hard hats loafed about. After months of delay the NMH management had won the case for demolishing the almshouses and the old pub. It had been a wildly unpopular decision, of course, and it had cemented his place as a regular whipping boy in the pages of *Private Eye*. This week, following the Castleton ads, the magazine had reproduced the photo of him seated in the wallpapered salon, with the caption: 'Very Freddie Selves. Very Large Cheque.' Someone must have leaked it to them, though he couldn't imagine who: only Leo and his accountant knew the actual fee he'd got.

Well, he should be used to the stick by now by now.

Hannah Strode's scent – was it Fracas? – still lingered in the air. She was a bright one, personable too. They had got on. But he couldn't help thinking about the way she had tossed out that line, *Do you mind being disliked?* It had been the blithe, matter-of-fact tone that had dismayed him, as if it were something understood between them. He had deflected her with the quip about Nelson and the pigeons, but, truthfully, he *did* mind. Given his public achievements it baffled him. He had been a major force for good in British theatre. Nobody else could have staged productions on the scale he had, nobody else could have promoted the work of so many writers and actors. There had been whispers of a gong for his services. So the Palace seemed to think he was worth honouring.

But the press – they didn't like him, and it was becoming

clear that others felt the same way. His wife, for instance. He had accepted that Linda no longer loved him. More recently, however, he began to sense that she actively *disliked* him. Could he blame her? They had married when he was twenty-seven and freshly divorced, and she was twenty-one, a raven-haired sprite who worked in theatre design; they had first met in Stratford. She was clever, brittle, funny, ambitious – and dazzled by him. Her first pregnancy was a troubled one, and the second wasn't much easier. She gained a fair bit of weight which she never managed to shift, and during the years she raised the boys she somehow lost confidence in her work. Not that she needed to work, what with Freddie's career going gangbusters and the money rolling in. Once they moved to Highpoint, up on the hill, they began entertaining on a baronial scale. The flat was always full of actors, celebrities, the great and good – Freddie's people – and slowly, imperceptibly, Linda was pushed to the side of their life. The loyal wife and mother was now whisperingly referred to as 'poor Linda'. When he began to have affairs the atmosphere at home became fatally poisoned. She never actually caught him at it, but she knew. They muddled through in spite of the rows and flounce-outs and cold silences. Freddie could just about endure it, absorbed as he was with work and the social round. What he couldn't face – what he dreaded – was losing the love of the boys.

He continued to brood over a solitary lunch at Simpson's (pheasant, then apple crumble with custard) which gave way to chewing on another anxiety: the casting of Annie in *Ragged Trousers*. Would it be so bad if he gave it to Nicola? It wasn't as though he'd be the first director to favour his girlfriend, nor would it be risky as a commercial decision. Her stock was still high after *Unlucky Charms*, and people would always pay to see a face 'off the telly'. She would in all probability make a very decent go of it. What's more, in casting her he would be assured of Nicola's unceasing love and gratitude. Powerful reasons.

And yet all of them were trumped by one hard truth – you

had to pick the best, and the best for this was Romilly Sargent. She had proved it this morning onstage. What director in his right mind would pass her over after an audition like that? Even if he could justify doing so to Mike and Nigel, he wasn't sure he could ever live with it himself. The work was the only thing on which you'd be judged in the end.

He didn't want to imagine how Nicola would react.

When he returned to the theatre mid-afternoon he found the place in uproar. The stage staff had delivered an ultimatum: unless management agreed to a ten per cent wage rise they were going on strike the next day. Bob Bewley called him in his office to say a council of war was meeting at 5 p.m.

'What's the use in that?' said Freddie with a groan. 'Our hands are tied – we don't have the sodding money.' And even if we did they can whistle for it, he didn't bother adding.

'I'll see you at five,' replied Bob, and rang off.

Freddie stared at the script of *The Ragged Trousered Philanthropists* on his desk. It was scheduled to start previews the last week in January. He thought of the scene in which the house-painters of Mugsborough agree among themselves to form a union – a pivotal moment, for which the lyricist, Joe Gaughan, had written a great union song ('Our Turn'). It was going to raise the rafters.

He picked up the phone and dialled Mike Findlay's number.

'Mike, it's Freddie. You can tell Sargent – she's about to be major.'

'What? Oh, I see. Ha ha. Great! Romilly's the right choice, Fred.'

'I know she is. Tell Nigel, will you? Oh, and start praying that we'll still have a theatre come January.'

'Eh?'

'The stage staff. They'll be striking from tomorrow.'

He replaced the receiver. The unions. How he loathed them. It was enough to make you vote Tory.

8

One morning at the end of November Vicky was sitting in an observation van alongside three other detective constables. Parked on a quiet street in Pimlico, the van's interior smelt of cigarette smoke, coffee and sweat. She was doing the crossword in the *Mirror* when a double tap came on the rear door and they got to their feet. One of the DCs, Prichard, said 'Set' and pushed open the door. Outside, their breath plumed in the dawn cold. From another obbo van issued more police, these in uniform, with one carrying a battering ram. An unmarked police car was also parked on the kerb and through the windscreen Vicky saw DCS Drewett. He had asked her the day before to join the raid, and she had jumped at the chance.

The house was a grey pebbledashed semi with a scrap of lawn in front. The teams hurried up the path, then stepped aside while the uniform with the battering ram charged the door. Two swings against it and the lock broke with a protesting crash. 'Police!' someone bellowed. Heart beating like a wildcat she piled in through the door with the others, their shouts rebounding off the walls. Two of her plain-clothes colleagues, Prichard and Kenney, were official 'shots', which meant that armed resistance could be expected. Vicky's team burst up the stairs onto the narrow landing and then into the first bedroom, where a man in his twenties was just stirring from bed – she had a glimpse of white flesh before Kenney pounced on him with the cuffs. From the second bedroom came the sounds of a violent scuffle. Moments later another youth was frogmarched out onto the landing.

From downstairs came a shout of 'Clear', and the tense mood began to dissipate. Two arrests, no gunshots. She and the others began to search the first bedroom, tossing out drawers, feeling under mattresses, emptying a wardrobe. She tapped the walls to check for hollows. Downstairs they were tearing the place up. A sniffer dog was eagerly nosing around.

'Anything up there?' Drewett asked her when they met in the kitchen.

''Fraid not, sir.'

'Well, it's here somewhere.'

For the next hour they continued the search, taking up the floorboards in the kitchen, stripping the cupboards of their pitiful contents, emptying every box and container. In the living room they looked inside the fireplace and dismantled the stereo and television. They took down the curtains and felt along the seams, they disembowelled every cushion on the sofa and chairs until the room was a blizzard of feathers. They peeled back the carpet to find the floorboards undisturbed.

Back in the kitchen Vicky found Drewett, hands on hips, slowly steering his gaze about the walls. One of his deputies suggested they should finish up – the place was clean. Drewett didn't seem to be listening.

'We look, but we don't always see.' He squinted at the oven and asked Kenney, 'Have you checked this?'

'Yeah. Nowt there.'

Drewett knelt down and pulled open the oven door. 'Torch?' He was handed a thin flashlight, which he pointed inside. Then he put his head inside.

'Don't do it, skip,' one of them said, to laughter.

He drew back his head, ignoring the quip. 'Anyone got a screwdriver?'

They waited while Drewett patiently unscrewed a blackened panel at the base, lifting it out with a creak. Then, with the satisfaction of a farmer delivering a calf, he gently pulled out a plastic-wrapped package the size of a car cushion – and then another, to murmurs of approval. He hefted one in his hand.

'And there's your two kilos of uncut heroin,' he said, with a coolness that made Vicky almost laugh in admiration.

Later, as forensics arrived, Vicky stood outside the house, stamping her feet against the cold. She was having a smoke with Prichard and a couple of the uniforms. It was still early, the street was waking up.

'Have you ever used that thing?' Vicky said, nodding at the handgun holstered on Prichard's belt.

'Few times,' he said, and, anticipating her next question, 'No, I haven't had to kill anyone yet.'

'Does it make you feel . . . safe?'

Prichard shook his head. 'You feel like a wound-up spring the whole time you're carrying it. I don't feel safe until I've returned it to the armoury.'

At that moment Drewett emerged from the house, and Prichard called as he passed them, 'Well done, skip.' The DCS nodded, and seeing Vicky there checked his stride.

'What d'you make of your first spin, Constable Tress?'

'Tremendous, sir – thanks for including me.' As he was turning away Vicky said, 'Sir, how did you know to look in the oven?'

Drewett paused, considering. 'You get a sixth sense for it. Though if you think about it, the oven's the most obvious place.'

'Sir?'

'Well, where else would they cook skag?' He winked at her in parting as the others broke into laughter.

That evening there was a party at the station's local off Regent Street. A popular DC was leaving for a job up north, and the West End Central team were out to give him a send-off. As soon as she arrived, Vicky got an extra packet of Silk Cut from the cigarette machine: it felt like it might be a long night. Across the table she watched her mate Carol, brooding.

'What's wrong with you?'

Carol shook her head. 'You don't wanna know.'

'Well, you'd better tell me cos I'm not staring at your miserable mug all evening.'

The story came out, grudgingly at first, and then with gathering indignation. Carol and a fellow WPC from the nick at Charing Cross had drawn up plans to establish a sexual assault unit. It would be a first for the Met, and long overdue.

'So we submitted our proposal to her guvnor, Redmond, and waited. And waited. Yesterday he called us in to say they're turning it down – because they can't afford it. "I cannot accept that sexual offences should be given a greater priority than other crimes," he says. Burglaries, muggings, drug offences aren't getting proper attention. He said it would be "irresponsible" to set up a unit and expect the taxpayer to fund it.'

'Irresponsible?' said Vicky.

'I know! As though it's better to spend money defending property than it is to save women from being raped. So there you have it. Back to square one.'

They were still talking about it when David Wicks stopped by their table.

'Vicky, Carol. What are you drinking?'

When he returned with their lagers he looked hesitant. 'Sorry, is there something up?'

'No, no,' said Vicky, 'Carol's just had a hard day.' They proceeded to relate the story of Carol's failed initiative on investigating sex crimes. Wicks listened, silent and impassive, and Vicky wondered if they'd made a mistake in confiding in him. He was a senior copper, after all, and probably held the same prejudices as his peers on the force.

Wicks took out his pack of Senior Service and offered them across the table. He lit them up, and said, 'Why didn't you come to me about this?'

Vicky looked at Carol, both of them taken aback. Carol

stutteringly replied that it was her friend at Charing Cross who'd thought of taking it to her guvnor.

'If you mean Jack Redmond I could have told you he'd throw it out. He's not the sort to make exceptions for women.'

'But you would?'

'I'm not saying that. But if you asked me to look at your plans, and I thought they were workable, who knows? I've seen enough bungled interviews of rape victims to know that male coppers aren't best qualified for the job. There'll be a change in policy sooner or later.'

'More likely to be later,' said Carol, in a hardened undertone, 'if our experience is anything to go by.'

'You have to be canny which allies you pick.'

'You mean which *men*.'

Wicks made a face at that. 'Look, we're not all Neanderthals. Like I said, you want to pitch something to me, I'll consider it – and I'll do it not because you're a woman but because you're a good copper.'

Carol nodded. 'I hope you know what you're letting yourself in for. Once I present this plan I'm gonna pester you for an answer until—'

'—until I'm sick of the sight of you.'

'Yes!' cried Carol.

They got another round of drinks as the gabble in the pub grew louder. When Wicks disappeared to the gents, Carol leaned in towards Vicky and said, 'Want the latest? Old Dave fancies you something rotten.'

'What?'

'Don't act the innocent. He's practically making cow eyes at you.'

Vicky waved this away, though she had noticed that Wicks was more than usually attentive to her this evening. It made her wonder about their hush-hush assignation in the multi-storey a few weeks ago. He couldn't have been more serious when he warned her about what was going on at West End Central. She had felt pleased to be taken into his confidence. But if Carol was right it put a new perspective on the matter: her DCI might also be angling to get his leg over.

And that wouldn't be so bad either, she thought as she watched him dodging his way back through the crush to the table. Their eyes met, and he acknowledged her with a friendly lift of his chin.

Hannah was filing copy when Tara stopped by, holding up the latest issue of *On the Town*. 'D'you want to have a look at this week's?' Following the anticlimactic end to her evening with Callum she had poured it all out to Tara, who had listened in wide-eyed surprise. Having allowed herself to kindle a hope that he would call her, Hannah had felt a tiny buzz of anticipation every time the phone rang. Four weeks passed, but the call never came. They continued to scour the columns, but her enthusiasm had faltered. It was Tara who proposed a change of tack.

'Why not place an ad of your own?'

Hannah stared at her. 'I don't think so. I mean, it'd be . . . weird.'

'Look, we already know how hopeless these "with-it guys" are. Whatever you wrote would knock the socks off theirs.'

'I'm not sure I could,' said Hannah, fearful of being persuaded.

'You're a writer! Of course you could. I'll help you if you want.'

After work they spent an evening in the pub trying to compose a suitable message. It proved harder than it looked, and even harder to stop themselves laughing hysterically. Hannah didn't want to appear needy; she baulked at anything coy. Back in her twenties she'd had no trouble finding boyfriends: she had never really had to think about it. In her mid-thirties the field had narrowed, the game had changed; she felt awkward having to sell herself in three sentences. The very language of the personals was flawed. What self-respecting woman would claim to have a 'bubbly personality'? Tara said she ought at least to describe herself as 'attractive', yet even that was too much for Hannah. The night ended without their agreeing on a message.

In the end she took her inspiration from the ad that had first caught her eye, which was to quote from a song.

> Still I sent up my prayer / Wondering who was there to hear / I said 'Send me somebody/ Who's strong, and somewhat sincere.' Are you that somebody? PO Box 154/W.

She had taken the lines from a song on *Court and Spark* by Joni Mitchell, a record she knew so intimately she could almost imagine it had been addressed to her. The ad ran the next week. On first seeing it she felt a terrible lurching panic, imagining the sort of nutters who might be out there waiting to pounce.

Tara, reading it for the first time, was sternly unimpressed. 'It's just a quote – nothing about you in there at all!'

'That's the way I wanted it.'

'And what the hell's this – "somewhat sincere"? No bloke is going to read that and think *ooh goody*.'

'If he doesn't understand it then we weren't meant for each other anyway.'

Tara shook her head, as though her friend were beyond help.

The first two dates Hannah went on appeared to justify Tara's scepticism. The first was an eager young theology student with ambitions to enter the Anglican Church. He had mistaken the reference to 'my prayer' as Hannah's belief in 'the operation of the divine', as he put it. They parted after a glass of wine. The second was a part-time PE coach who reeked of Hai Karate and sucked on mints. He had no idea Hannah was quoting Joni Mitchell: he just thought she sounded 'desperate'. Apparently that was invitation enough for some.

The third date was different. They met in the upstairs room of the Lamb and Flag in Covent Garden. Christopher Galton was tall, tousle-haired and wore a pinstriped flannel suit that made him look stylish rather than stuffy. He worked for a management consultancy in the City, was well spoken and at ease in company. She felt encouraged by the way he kept eye contact and carved the air with his cigarette hand. It turned out he was exactly Hannah's age – thirty-four – and, being a devoted reader of the *NME*, knew his music.

'Yeah, "The Same Situation" ... the lines just leapt out at me,' he said, and proceeded to sing them in a surprisingly tuneful alto.

'Wow,' said Hannah. 'You really are a fan.'

'She's great, isn't she? I'd put *Court and Spark* just below *Hissing of Summer Lawns* and a few notches above *Blue*. What d'you think of her latest?'

'Er, you mean the double one? I haven't actually heard it.'

'Hmm,' he replied, as though in understanding. 'It has its moments, but probably not enough for a double LP.'

They talked about her work: Christopher was a reader of the *Ensign*, and now he thought about it he'd also seen her on telly. He reckoned she looked much more attractive in person. Hannah laughed off the compliment, and thought *This one's too good to be true.* Yet he continued to be funny, and curious, and even when he admitted that he'd been married and divorced by the age of twenty-five she was already willing to pardon it as a youthful folly. He'd met his wife when they were students at York, where he got a first in Politics. He had considered staying on in academia before deciding to try out 'the real world' – and in any case he didn't think himself clever enough to be a professor.

As she watched him go off to the bar she told herself not to get overexcited. Callum had been tremendous company too, and look how that had ended. 'Strong, and somewhat sincere' couldn't be determined on the basis of a single evening.

'So ... you're a management consultant,' she began. 'To be honest, I don't really know what that *is*.'

'Not many people do. Basically we advise companies on how they should run themselves, where they can improve, inspire the workforce, that sort of thing.'

'Sounds like they could use you at *The Times*. They're about to go on strike.'

'Ha. Them too, eh? I sometimes wonder what might happen if strikers get to be so powerful they begin striking against conditions on their own picket lines. The strike that ate itself.'

'I wouldn't put it past them at this rate,' said Hannah.

'Presumably a strike at a rival is good news for your lot. You'll pick up all the readers *The Times* loses.'

'That's what we're hoping. So what would a management consultant do to save the country from grinding to a standstill?'

He blew out his cheeks, considering. 'Be tougher with the unions. Callaghan was a union man himself, so he'll never bring them to heel – he doesn't know how. The five per cent deal is generous. If the unions won't play, then there has to be a government that will make them. I could see them sending the police in. Or the army! But the whole system has to change – a tighter control on public spending, privatising state industries. Make people understand that there's no such thing as a job for life any more.'

Hannah looked at him curiously. 'Sounds quite draconian. You could live with putting people out of work?'

He put up his hands in a gesture of surrender. 'I couldn't, personally. You asked me what a management consultant would do to save the country – that would make the economy competitive, cut punitive taxes, deal with inflation rather than unemployment. And stuff the unions.'

'What government is going to carry out reforms like that?'

He shrugged. 'Certainly not a Labour one.'

A silence fell between them. Christopher lit a cigarette and took a drag. Through the smoke he met her gaze, which had narrowed. For the first time in the evening he sounded uncertain. 'What would your strategy be anyway?'

'I don't know. Maybe not to go looking for advice from a management consultant.'

He laughed, and another silence built. In their staring contest he blinked first. 'What's that look you're giving me?'

She paused. 'It means you're being silently judged. Another drink?'

Some days later Hannah was absorbed at her typewriter when the phone rang. 'Is that Hannah Strode?' The voice was a woman's, quite posh.

'It is.'

'You're doing a profile of Freddie Selves, aren't you?'

'I'm literally in the middle of writing it. Why?'

'It's just – well – I have certain information about him that might interest you. Compromising information.'

'Really. Who am I speaking to?'

'I can't tell you that, I'm afraid.'

'OK,' said Hannah, wondering if she knew the voice. 'What sort of thing d'you mean?'

The caller began to relate a history of Freddie's extravagance – lunches, dinners, car and chauffeur, flights on Concorde, five-star hotels, suits from Savile Row, needless other expenses all charged to the public account. And despite the enormous salary he was paid at the NMH he frequently took time off to earn extra money in television and advertising. Did she know how much money he made from the Castleton wallpaper campaign? Hannah listened, and noted. The woman ended her aria of denunciation with a pursed, 'So what do you think of that little lot?'

'It's kind of outrageous, I agree. But I know most of this already.'

'How?'

'Well, I read a lot of it in the *Sketch*. Do we know each other?'

The voice, she thought, might have been disguised.

'No, we don't.'

'Right, so you are—'

'I'm not telling you my name. Just trust me. I know about Freddie.'

'Fine. No names. But I need to know why you're telling me this.'

A pause. 'I believe ... I feel wronged.'

'I see. That may be the case, but so far most of what you've told me was in the Forbuoys piece. Is there something about him, maybe, that nobody else knows?'

Now there came a longer pause. Hannah could almost hear the struggle within, and waited. 'All right,' the woman said, with a long-suffering sigh. 'He – Freddie – is having an affair.'

'Ah ... go on.'

'I can't say who—'

'Is it Nicola Mayman?'

A stunned silence followed. *Bingo,* thought Hannah. Now she had to wait it out.

'It might be,' she said cautiously. 'Do you have to use her name?'

'I'm afraid so. And I'll have to check it out, for legal reasons. Can you confirm that it's Nicola Mayman?'

Her voice, when it came, was quieter, more reluctant, as if she regretted phoning at all. 'Yes. That's ... who it is.'

Hannah spent a few minutes going through the details and reassuring her informant that she could remain anonymous, 'though the story would sound more convincing if you did identify yourself'. No, the woman was adamant: she didn't want to be named. Hannah was almost certain that it *was* Nicola at the other end of the line, but there would be no point in pressing her – she might take fright and deny the thing altogether.

'I may need to verify a few details. How can I get in touch with you?'

'You can't. I'm not giving you my number.'

'All right,' Hannah said. 'Call me again if there's anything you need to add.'

She put the phone down, and considered the dynamite that had just been handed to her.

Freddie was making short work of a mid-morning jam tart when the phone went. Dawn told him that Hannah Strode was on the line.

'Hannah,' he said pleasantly. 'What can I do for you?'

'Good morning. You'd better sit down before I tell you this.'

Freddie stopped chewing, put his pastry aside. He licked his fingers. 'Go on.'

'Can you confirm that you've been having an affair with Nicola Mayman?'

Oh Jesus. He felt his insides suddenly start to liquefy. 'Where on earth did you hear that?'

'A tip-off.'

'Who?'

'Come on,' she said. 'I don't reveal my sources. Are you denying it?'

'Of course I deny it. I know Nicola, of course, but the idea of us having – well—'

'Mr Selves, I'm afraid this story will run. The details – where you met, how long it's been going on – it's all very plausible. I'm just putting together the profile of you for next week. Your affair will be the splash. Now you could make it easier on yourself by coming clean. Or else you can make a fuss. Either way, it's going to come out.'

She'd got him, and he knew it. The silence went on for so long she eventually had to prompt him. 'Mr Selves. D'you want to comment?'

'Please don't run it. Not yet.'

'I can't hang on to it, I'm sorry.'

'All right. But can we talk before you – there are things I need to get straight.'

Hannah paused. 'It's going to run next week.'

'OK, let's talk tomorrow, face-to-face.'

'It's Saturday tomorrow.'

'Where d'you live? I'll send a car.'

He must be desperate, she thought. 'I live near London Fields – I don't suppose you know where that is.'

'No, but my driver will. Leave your address and phone number with my PA. Would midday suit you?'

Having made the arrangement, Freddie put the phone down. He had broken out in a sweat. He knew Nicola was upset about not getting the part: they had spoken on the phone, and she had been brusque with him. That was to be expected. But he had not anticipated a reaction like this. Ratting him to the press! Well, hell hath no fury . . . It shocked him, though. Nicola was fiery, for sure, that was one of her attractions – she wouldn't let him get away with things. But she'd never made trouble for the hell of it. Good God (his hand went involuntarily to his brow), he had even imagined a future with her, once he'd got clear of Linda.

Now he was heading straight into a pile-up – a mistress out for his blood, a wife who would take him for everything, and the newspapers ready to sling him on the tumbril.

9

In the first weeks of Martin Villiers's accommodation at St James's Walk it seemed to Callum that the house had taken in a ghost rather than a guest. The arrangement was that Martin would stay Wednesday and Thursday nights, and his promise to keep a low profile had been honoured to the point of virtual invisibility. He would return from Whitehall at such late hours that Callum was usually in bed asleep, and only rarely did he hear Martin's early-morning departure. In the kitchen he would find occasional evidence of a late-night snack or a stubbed cigarette in a saucer, but of the man himself he heard barely a creak on the stair. When Callum refused his offer of rent Martin insisted on paying for the services of a cleaner; perhaps he wondered why his friend didn't have one already.

Recently his presence had become even less palpable. As more strikes broke out the government withdrew into a siege, and Callum assumed that Martin was too busy manning the ramparts at Downing Street to take the option of a night's sleep. He began to think of his resident in the manner of a Henry James story, somehow there but not there, a spectre whose haunting he no longer quite trusted.

But one night Callum did encounter his elusive lodger. Unable to sleep he had gone on one of his noctambulations around the neighbourhood, watching the porters at Smithfield unload their vans and then drinking tea at Mick's on Fleet Street amid the derelicts and the nighthawks. It was nearly two thirty in the morning when he returned to Clerkenwell Green, shivering a little after the smoky fug of the cafe, and saw a taxi come to a halt by the church. He saw Martin get out, still talking to his fellow passenger in the back, and something about his demeanour – the angle of his head as he spoke – put Callum on guard. He overheard a note of coaxing intimacy in his voice that warned him not to approach, and he held back until Martin had said goodnight and the cab pulled away. As it drove past him Callum glimpsed a woman's face through the window.

Martin had his key in the door as Callum hailed him, and he jumped in fright.

'Jesus! I thought you were a mugger.'

'Sorry. I just – was that your cab?'

'Err, yeah. We had our office party this evening – not that there was much Christmas cheer to go round.'

Inside, Martin collected a bottle of Haig and a glass from the kitchen before throwing himself on the sofa. 'Sorry, d'you mind if I have a nightcap?'

'Of course not,' said Callum, wondering if he was going to mention the woman in the cab. 'I've barely seen you since you came here.'

'Work, I'm afraid. It's all hands on deck at Number Ten.' He looked up anxiously at Callum. 'Between us, we're just about hanging on.'

'The Tories don't seem to have any better ideas.'

Martin nodded. 'Yeah, that's the one silver lining. Some opinion polls still put us ahead, but it's tight.' He brooded, sipping at the Scotch, then said quietly, 'It was a mistake, really.'

'What was?'

'Not calling an election. We'd have got in, I'm sure of it. Instead the country's collapsing around our ears, we're being slaughtered by the papers . . . the voters'll be mad as hell by the time we go to the polls.'

Callum recalled Martin praising his boss for not calling an election, but he had too much tact to remark on this volte-face.

He said, consolingly, 'You know what they say – it's always darkest before the dawn.'

The remark seemed to remind Martin of their unlikely meeting on the doorstep. 'What are *you* doing up at this hour?'

'When I can't sleep I go for a walk – sometimes down to Fleet Street – taking in the sights. You see a different sort of place, you know?'

'Yeah ... I expect so,' said Martin absently, then focusing again upon his companion. 'Listen, please don't repeat anything I've just said.' He downed the rest of the Scotch in a gulp and patted Callum on the shoulder. 'It's only the booze talking.'

The first-year poetry class had hit a mid-afternoon slump. Callum took a stick of chalk and wrote on the blackboard:

What country, friends, is this?

'This is a line Viola speaks near the beginning of *Twelfth Night*. Can anyone say what's unusual about Shakespeare's phrasing of her question?'

He looked over the rows of faces in the lecture theatre. Most of them were vacant of expression, indicating either incomprehension or indifference. A few seemed engaged, or at least polite enough not to look bored. He waited for an arm to go up, and eventually one did.

'Yes, Chloe?'

Chloe Nicol, sweetly pale-faced with large brown eyes and a mass of russet hair, reminded Callum of girls he'd known at school in Newry, though Chloe was actually from the Midlands.

'Is it the way he puts "friends" in the middle instead of the end?'

'Yes, good. So why does he do that?'

Silence. Even Chloe wasn't going to risk an explanation.

'Well, if she'd said, "What country is this, friends?" it would sound merely curious. Or if she'd said, "Friends, what country is this?" it's declamatory, like "Friends, Romans, countrymen . . ." But "What country, friends, is this?" shows how the placement of a single word can alter the music of a whole sentence – that "friends" is like a little sob, a catch in the throat. She and her crew have just been washed up on the shores of Illyria. So the question conveys something tender, troubled, almost elegiac. And it demonstrates that Shakespeare was a genius with *cadence* as well as everything else.'

The first-year students gazed on, faces as blank as paper plates. Callum had a lowering sense that his voice was simply a noise to them – that he might as well have been speaking Dutch or Cherokee. He picked up the chalk again.

Only the groom, and the groom's boy,
With bridles in the evening come.

'Here's a more recent example. These are the closing lines of Larkin's poem "At Grass", about two retired racehorses in a meadow. All the fame and excitement of their racing days are gone; now they just crop the grass unnoticed. Look at the syntax of that final line, the way those six words seem to fade into the dusk. The verb "come" might have started the line, but instead it ends it, like a gate being softly shut. It's kind of perfect, isn't it?'

There was a pause, then a hand at the back went up. It was a boy named Simon, who'd never spoken in class before. 'It's not that perfect, Mr Conlan.'

'Oh. Why not?'

'Well, the groom and his boy aren't going to ride these horses, are they?'

'Er, no, I don't think so.'

'In that case they wouldn't put bridles on them. They'd put halters.'

Not very lyrical, Callum thought, but at least it's a reaction.

'Good point. Perhaps you could write to Mr Larkin and tell him. He might be glad to know.'

At the end of the hour he handed out the essays he had marked, offering a comment here and there ('Very lively – though I asked for an essay on slang, Richard, not *in* slang'). He reminded them of their preparation for next week. To mark the sixtieth anniversary of the Armistice they had started on the poets of the First World War, and up next was Wilfred Owen. It had been his anniversary, too, killed on 4 November 1918. He asked them to study four of his poems in particular, and listed them on the board.

'Anthem for Doomed Youth'
'Exposure'
'Strange Meeting'
'The Chances'

Once the class had ambled out he went up to the library in search of a late-Victorian novel he thought might make a useful study. He soon found the book, *Born in Exile* by George Gissing, and glanced at its record slip on the flyleaf. The last time it had been checked out was 8 December 1970 – eight years ago, almost to the day. It occurred to him, more frequently now, that *Go-Betweens: The hidden injuries of class in the English novel* might not even acquire the small readership he had envisaged for it. Who would care a rap about his diligent unpicking of the class system in novels hardly anybody read nowadays? In his bleaker moments Callum fell to wondering why the stuff he wrote should be of significance to *anyone at all*. Maybe every writer worried about that, from time to time. His own students – the intellectual elite of the future – hardly presented compelling evidence of a passion for literature. He sighed to himself. You had to keep on keeping on, as the song went, 'like a bird that flew' – an illustration of the technique of *enjambement*, which probably wouldn't interest them either.

He got the book stamped, then stopped at his office to collect his coat and scarf. Outside the street lamps were on, and he felt a sharp nip in the late-afternoon temperature. On Farringdon Road he passed the building site at the back of the NMH and on a whim he stopped one of the workmen to ask if Sean McGlashan was at the site today. The man returned a puzzled look and said he didn't know anyone by that name. He pointed Callum in the direction of the foreman, who on enquiry also shook his head.

'Dunno any McGlashan, mate. You sure he works here?'

'Definitely. I stopped here once before. He's a casual labourer, from Northern Ireland . . .'

Something cleared in the man's expression. 'Oh, *Norn Irlun*, like yerself. You mean Paddy! End of that block, turn the corner.'

Callum tramped off down the gravel path, through a dreary makeshift scene of skips and scaffolding. Around the next corner he saw a temporary workers' hut, from where Sean at that very minute was emerging. He looked up in surprise on hearing his name called.

'Callum. What brings you here?'

'Just passing. I wondered if you wanted to get a bite to eat?'

Sean grimaced. He looked tired, and his overalls were filthy. 'Och, I got no change of gear with me. I was gonna go straight home and get some tea.'

'Oh, right – another time.'

'Wait, though. Why don't you come back with us? Only a bus ride down to the Old Kent Road.'

Callum paused, wondering if Sean had made the offer out of politeness – and then sensed it would be only friendly to accept. 'You don't mind?'

'Course not. I don't have many visitors.'

As they waited at the bus stop Callum said, 'By the way, nobody on the site seemed to know who you were.'

Sean laughed. 'To the English we're all the same – they call you Paddy, whatever your name is.'

'The foreman seemed decent enough.'

'Aye. He's all right, s'long as you keep your head down, and you can take all the *jokes* . . . Funny, isn't it, how they think we're all either thick or lazy – and yet they hire us to do all the work. Half this fuckin' city's built by the Irish.'

'I've noticed lately, whenever I'm overheard talking in a bank or a shop I get some terrified looks. Do they think I'm gonna take them hostage or something?'

Sean laughed. 'Sure it's the beard – you could pass for a Provo.'

The bus arrived, and Callum followed Sean upstairs, where he could smoke. They fell into conversation about Newry: Sean said he was planning to get home for Christmas, the transport strikes permitting. Callum admitted his family would be expecting him, though in truth he wasn't relishing the prospect. He loved his mother and sister, but the house they lived in, sour with memories of his father's drinking, depressed him, and he preferred to stay away.

'Until you told me I never knew your auld feller was in the drunk tank,' said Sean.

'We didn't talk about it. Wasn't something we *could* talk about. Hey, d'you remember a girl that used to come to the youth club – Karen McAuley?'

'Eh . . . she was a looker, wasn't she?'

'Aye. I hadn't thought of her in years, but seeing one of my students today reminded me. That lovely face she had, with the wee dimple in her chin. Karen McAuley . . . "Star of the County Down"!' He whistled a few bars of the song.

'You seein' anyone at the moment?' asked Sean, dragging on his cigarette.

Callum shook his head. 'I met a woman a few weeks back, just by chance. She was in the pub, waiting for someone who never showed up. I liked her.'

'So you snuck in there?' Sean asked with a leer.

'Nah, I messed up. Turned out the someone she was waiting for was a blind date. She'd put an ad in the personals.'

'So . . . ?'

'I sorta went cold on her. I mean, a blind date? It just seemed, I dunno, a wee bit desperate.'

Sean looked at him. 'Is it? I 'spect people do it all the time. In any case, *youse two* came together by chance, which isn't a blind date at all.'

'No, I suppose not. I should probably have called her.'

'Too right you should've. Honest, for an educated feller you can be a fuckin' eejit.'

The bus was inching around the traffic-choked circuit of the Elephant and Castle. Sean nudged him: they would get off round the next corner. Descending the stairs to the open platform, they waited for a halt before jumping into the middle of the road. Sean, with nonchalant timing, flitted though the rush-hour traffic towards the kerb, leaving Callum dithering in his wake. The narked blare of a car horn and a screech of brakes caused him to raise his hand in apology and then dodge through another honking stream of cars in the next lane.

'Jesus! Couldn't you wait for the bus stop?' he said, shaking.

But Sean just laughed and said, 'Keep up, big man.'

They passed a pub Callum noticed was called the World Turned Upside Down, then into a darkened side road. Sean stopped in front of a huge and ugly Victorian tenement. This was home, apparently. He followed his friend up the tall steps and into a hall lit by a single bulb. It had the familiar atmosphere of a lodging house whose close-packed rooms were never cleaned. Vile odours of cooking hung in the air, mixed in with the emanations from ancient sun-faded wallpaper, plaster and dry rot. Carpeted stairs, trodden thin, led up to the third floor, where Sean admitted him to a single room. Its furnishings were spartan: a bed, an upright chair and an old wardrobe. One of the sash windows, missing half a pane, had been patched up with newspaper, and explained why the room was so cold.

Callum, looking about, asked him where he ate, and was told

there was a kitchen in the basement. There was a single bathroom down there too.

Sean must have caught the twitch of dismay that had ghosted across Callum's face. 'I told you it was a dosshouse,' he said baldly, 'but s'long as you remember to lock yer door it's all right.'

'What d'you mean?'

'Lotta thieving goes on. You have to be careful . . . '

While Sean changed out of his work clothes, Callum considered their accidental reunion – the friendship was an unlikely one, for they had not been close back in Newry. He had never been to Sean's house, but he knew it was in a poor neighbourhood; he also knew that Sean had got a place at their Catholic grammar only because his parents were friendly with one of the Christian Brothers at the school. Callum's family, while not rich, were more comfortable than most. His father had been director of an electronics firm. His mother, a deputy head teacher, had some extra money saved from her own family, and had given him and his sister a decent upbringing in the circumstances. Their slightly aspirational status (there were books in the Conlan house) was never mentioned among his schoolmates, but then nor was the fact that the father was a drunk.

They went back downstairs to the kitchen, where Sean made baked beans on toast, served with tea the colour of brick. They ate at an old kitchen table whose scratched top indicated many years of rough use. There was nobody else about, though from the stairs came the occasional echo of talk.

Callum said, 'You know anyone else here?'

Sean shook his head. 'Not really. There was an auld feller I used to chat with now and then. I think his name was John. Worked as a miner, years ago, somewhere up north. Christ knows how he ended up in this dump.'

'What happened to him?'

'Funny you should ask. Nobody had seen him for a few days. He didn't work or anything, but you'd always see him shuffling about, feeding the birds round the back. So I told the landlord, thought we should check on him. We go up to his room, knocked on the door, called his name – no answer. Landlord got out his keys, opened up. The auld feller's lyin' there. Soon as I saw him I knew.'

'Dead?'

'Aye. I've seen enough in me time to know. Strange thing, when I started at the undertakers, I was that scared of seeing a corpse – like just the word "corpse" put the fear o' God into me. But once I was in the room, looking at one—' he paused, and shrugged – 'I realised there was nothing to fear – I mean, *literally* nothing. Whatever that person had been was gone. It almost made me believe in a soul, cos that thing lying there, that grey lump, it just looked empty of everything that had made 'em human.'

'What d'you mean, "almost"?' said Callum. 'Father Mulcahy would be horrified to think you didn't believe in your immortal soul.'

Sean gave a sceptical half-laugh. 'I can't remember ever believin' in it. And the more they drummed it into yer the more certain I became it was bollocks. But seein' auld John, dead in his bed, it got me thinking . . . '

'About what?'

'He had nothin', Cal. We searched the room, lookin' for a diary or address book, anything that might have told us where he was from – how we could reach his family. If he *had* a family. Not a fuckin' clue. Some auld clothes, a tin watch, some baccy and a pipe. Coupla pawn tickets, though no sign of money. His wee rent book. Then I looked in a drawer and found a rosary. I asked the landlord a few days later if there was a funeral, maybe I'd go if there was. He just sez, no relatives came forward, so there's no funeral. They just packed him off to the mortuary. Prob'ly ended up on some slab, picked apart by a gang of medical students. And that's when I thought, I hope there is a soul, whatever it might be. Cos that poor feller had fuck all else to show for his life.'

'Sufferin' Jesus,' murmured Callum.

'Aye. Where was *he* when he was needed?'

'D'you ever wonder how many people die like that? Just wiped from the face of the earth. Unmissed, unmourned.'

'Thousands ... I imagine,' said Sean.

'But that feller was a kid once, with a mother. Must have had friends and family, just like us. You wonder what happened to him, how he fell through the cracks, lost touch with anyone who ever mattered. Maybe he wanted to cut himself off, and then you get to thinking – could that be me one day?'

'You?' Sean tucked in his chin.

'It can happen. Some random mishap – you lose your job, or your health. Or your mind. Life's hard, Sean; for some people it's too hard to bear. I dread something like that happening to me.'

'Don't worry yerself, Cal, it's not gonna. The likes of auld John – they don't have much luck to start out with. Best to count yer blessings, I'd say, 'stead of worrying about what might happen.'

His tone was pointed, and Callum fell silent, chastened. He had been lucky in most things, he knew, and to make a song and dance about the vicissitudes of fate didn't become him. From somewhere upstairs came raised voices, shouts, the sound of an argument breaking out. Sean gave a sigh.

'This place ... Come on, let's get out of here.'

They walked round the corner to the World Turned Upside Down. Nothing about the pub's interior matched the poetry of its name: tired velour-seated stools, linoleum floor the colour of old blood, the dreary clatter of a fruit machine. They had the Christmas decorations up, which only rendered the room more dismal. Clusters of drinkers sat around, blank-faced, smoking. Callum bought a lager for Sean and a Coke for himself; they sat at the bar like a couple of locals.

Callum looked around before he said, 'This place you're staying ... d'you not think of finding somewhere else? There's a load of rooms to rent if you look in the *Standard*.'

'Too expensive. I wanna save this money to take back home.'

'If I'd known before I could have put you up at my place. Instead I've got a friend stopping there two nights a week . . . '

'Och, you're all right, Cal. I don't mind it. I'm not plannin' on a long stay in any case. This city's not for me.' He lit a cigarette and eyed him through the smoke. 'You think of it as home?'

'London? I 'spose I do,' said Callum. 'I like living in a big city. People let you mind your own business.'

'That's another way of sayin' they don't give a stuff about yer.'

'Aye. I can see why people say it's lonely. But it's not unfriendly.'

'You reckon? My old man talks about getting the boat over here with a few of his mates, back in the fifties. They arrived without anywhere to stay, so they looked around the place.' He smiled, shook his head. 'He said they stopped at one B&B, west London, and saw this wee sign in the window. Know what it said? "No Blacks. No Irish. No Dogs."'

'Nice welcome. I'm not sure you'd get away with that now.'

'Nah. I hear dogs get a pretty good deal here these days.' They both laughed. Sean was warming to his theme. 'You know, I remember watchin' the Prods march through Newry singin' "The Sash Me Father Wore" and I wondered if I really belonged there. But here, on these streets – Jesus – I feel like a fuckin' Martian among the earthlings! Most of 'em don't even understand what you're sayin'.'

'Come on. It's not as bad as all that.'

Sean gave a demurring tilt of his head. 'You don't think so. Fine. All I'm sayin' is watch out. The Irish are the guilty conscience of England. We've been screwed by 'em ever since Cromwell.'

Callum stared at him. 'Are you about to join up or something?'

Sean laughed again. 'No fuckin' chance! All I'm sayin', don't get to thinkin' this lot are yer friends.'

10

They were standing on the westbound platform at Sloane Square as the train barrelled out of the tunnel. Vicky glanced up at DS Kenney, thickset, swarthy, with a dark moustache that reminded her of the *World of Sport* presenter Dickie Davies. The carriage doors slid open, and Kenney gestured with a nod for her to follow him. Inside, they walked down one swaying carriage and into another. He appeared to be looking for someone. The next carriage was less full – they had coincided with a mid-afternoon lull, before rush hour – and when Kenney eventually took a seat Vicky parked herself next to him. Opposite them sat one other passenger, a scrawny, lank-haired fellow in a nondescript anorak and jeans; he stared at Vicky for a moment, then looked away.

Several more stops clacked by; the carriage had almost emptied. The dingy overhead lighting flickered on and off. The lank-haired man suddenly rose to his feet and, with a little twitch of his jaw, flopped himself down next to Kenney.

He nodded in greeting. Then he nodded at Vicky. 'Who's this?'

'Ticket inspector.'

The man, whoever he was, didn't acknowledge her, and said something in an undertone of complaint that Vicky couldn't catch. It had no effect at all on Kenney, who waited a beat before saying, 'What have you got for us?'

A murmuring back-and-forth followed between the men, most of it expressed in an impenetrable slang. Vicky picked up the odd word, but for the most part she might as well have been listening to a couple of foreigners. Occasionally the man would look exasperated, and at one point hissed at Kenney, 'Leave off, will ya?' But the mood between them was familiar, almost friendly, and when the train pulled into Moorgate and he got up to leave, he even deigned to give Vicky a nod in parting. The carriage doors closed, and through the grimy windows they watched him stalking off along the platform.

'Who was that?' asked Vicky.

'George? He's a drug dealer. Quite a successful one.'

He made no effort to elaborate, so she said, hesitantly, 'Shouldn't you, er, arrest him?'

'I *have* arrested him, a few times. I could put him in prison, but he'd be no use to us there. He's me snout instead. He's helped the Drug Squad make more arrests than anyone in the last two years.'

'How?'

'You'll find out soon enough. For now, just remember – banging up every dealer isn't gonna help you in the long run. You need trusted informants out on the street. If you agree to protect them, they can give you the inside track, who's doing what and where, how much it's worth. So instead of wasting time "chasing criminals" all day long, you get straight into the network of smuggling and distribution, and maybe, if you play it right, you catch the people at the top of the pyramid. So listen and learn, DC Tress, cos you're gonna need someone like George one day.'

Kenney opened up about his time with the Drug Squad. He had joined six years before, when the big shake-up of the department was going on. Much of the undercover work during the late 1960s had walked a fine line between pragmatism and outright criminality, a line that eventually 'got stamped all over'. The Home Office got wind of it and took fright. They appointed a new Met Commissioner to tackle the corruption head-on, and the culture began to change, slowly. The best detectives on the squad discovered ways of playing the system – when to support and when to block an application for bail, how to split a group of defendants, soft-pedalling on one to secure a conviction against another. Good judgement was needed in bending the law without breaking it. A fair bit of nerve also helped.

'But what if someone like George tried to play you at this game?' Vicky asked. 'If he went rogue, for instance?'

'George is too smart for that. He knows which side his bread's buttered. But if he did we'd just haul him in.'

'And find yourself another snout?'

'There's always someone ready to turn.'

They continued to sit there as the train made its rumbling circuit, the doors clanking open, clanking shut. Following another long silence Vicky turned to find Kenney squinting at her.

'You're not bad-looking, you know,' he said.

'Oh. Er, thanks.'

'No, I mean it,' he said, continuing his candid review of her. 'You could really make something of yourself.'

Was he coming on to her? She couldn't quite tell, hearing nothing seductive in his voice, and his last comment seemed to suggest there was, if anything, room for improvement.

'Make something of myself?'

'Yeah, if you spent a bit of money. You must be on a decent screw? – for a plonk, I mean. If you bought some nice clothes, for instance . . . '

Vicky was for a moment too shocked to speak. 'What's wrong with my clothes?'

'Well, they're a bit dowdy. Not very feminine. See, you've got a nice figure, you could show it off if you spent a bit of money on yourself.'

She silently considered what she was wearing – a stone-coloured trench coat, scarf, a long woollen skirt, leather boots from Clarks. Not sexy, but not mumsy either. Professional attire. Or so she thought. In truth, she was both surprised by his attention and rather crushed. He had offered his comments in a spirit of helpfulness, it seemed, though it didn't render them any less wounding. It occurred to her now to check what *he* was wearing: a brown leather blouson, a stripy open-necked shirt, Farah slacks with a huge belt buckle. Slip-on shoes. Neutral, unfussy – the plain-clothes default. He also sported, more predictably, a raucous masculine scent. Blue Stratos, was it?

He had stood up and moved towards the doors as the roundel of Edgware Road Tube flashed past the windows. She waited next to him, wondering if she should speak.

'Well ... thanks for the advice.' She kept her tone even, to conceal any hint of hurt.

Kenney glanced at her. 'That's OK,' he said, unsmiling. 'You might do something with your hair, too.'

That same morning, on the other side of London, Hannah was walking back from the corner shop with the papers and a pint of milk. Something was happening, or about to happen, up the road. She saw a police van disgorge a bunch of uniformed officers, and here came trotting a file of mounted police, wearing visors. She called out a question to them, and was told that a march was on its way from Dalston: a demo by the National Front. *In this area?* thought Hannah. In London Fields you would see as many black and Asian faces as white. True, you couldn't ignore the graffiti that sprouted on underpasses, over gable walls, at bus stops: ENOCH WAS RIGHT and NF and KEEP BRITAIN WHITE. But racial tension still existed more as rumour than actuality. Somewhere in the distance she heard the tinny drone of a loudspeaker. There was bound to be a counter-demonstration.

Hannah returned to Lavender Grove and let herself into the house. She had lived here, a pretty but run-down street of late-Victorian terraces, for nine years. The Tube had not yet penetrated as far as E8, despite promises of its extension over the years. For town she took the bus or else walked, less so at night; she had never been mugged, though she knew enough horror stories to put her on guard. It amused and irritated her whenever she let slip that Hackney was her home, and got in response either blank faces or grimacing ones – the Wild East. But she liked living here, its very out-of-the-way-ness was part of the charm; it felt to her like the frontier of something.

Having leafed through the *Mail* she glanced at the kitchen clock. Nearly midday. Freddie Selves had arranged a car for her at eleven thirty. She opened her post, saving the most intriguing package till last. It was a Jiffy bag with her address handwritten on it, postmarked W11. Inside was a note from Christopher Galton, the bloke she'd met a couple of weeks ago, and with it a cassette tape, *Don Juan's Reckless Daughter* by Joni Mitchell – the real thing, too, cellophaned, not a C90 recording. Christopher's hand, in fountain pen, was a responsible cursive:

> I believe I promised you this. Especially recommend 'Paprika Plains', all sixteen minutes of it. If you don't love it we can't go on . . .
>
> Yours, C. G.

He was keen, the mock warning and all. They had had another date since their drink at the Lamb and Flag. Progress was being made. She had just flipped the cassette into the player when she heard a rap on the front door. On the step waited a man – black, straight-backed, dressed in a sombre grey suit and tie.

'Miss Strode? Car here for you.' His voice was inflected with a faint Caribbean twang.

'Ah. You are . . . ?'

'Mr Selves's driver. Terry. My apologies for being late.'

She collected her bag and coat, then stepped out. Terry was holding open the rear door of a shiny black Daimler, its engine running. She got in, and was surprised to find Freddie himself seated there.

'Miss Strode – Hannah – I'm so very sorry we're late. The streets are absolutely chocka with demonstrators! If Terry hadn't been driving I've no idea how we'd have got through.'

The upholstery was tan-coloured leather, butter-soft. The acrid whiff of a recently smoked cigar pinched the air. Freddie looked on edge, she thought, as well he might. He was carefully groomed and dressed in a grey double-breasted suit, with a florid tie.

'You're looking very smart for a Saturday,' she observed lightly. 'Where are we off to – Ascot?'

He gave a nervous half-laugh. 'Just a members' club. Don't worry, they also admit women.'

'I'm honoured,' she deadpanned.

'I suppose you disapprove of gentlemen's clubs.'

'Not really,' she replied pleasantly. 'From what I know of them they're not the sort of place I'd want to spend time in. So I don't feel that excluded.'

'I wish more people felt that way. Elitism is having a very hard time of it at the moment.'

'How's the strike going?'

'Not too bad. We've only lost three days so far. But the atmosphere in the building is terrible – the suspicion on people's faces! It's not exactly conducive to putting on musical theatre.'

The Daimler, heading south, had come to a halt. A thick police cordon lay ahead of them. Terry said, over his shoulder, 'Mr Selves, we'll have to take a diversion.'

'Just get us out of here, Terry,' said Freddie, clicking his tongue in mild exasperation.

The car made another turn. From Queensbridge Road they could hear chanting, whistles, the insect whine of the loudspeaker. A car pulled up behind them and a camera crew got out. This demo was going to be on the news. Terry reached the top of the road just as another cordon was being set up; he reversed the car and took them back the way they had come. It was bad luck to have picked today for a drive, thought Hannah – and worse luck to be in such a conspicuous vehicle.

It seemed that Terry was now lost, and was glancing in the rear-view mirror to ask her if she knew a way out. Before she could answer Freddie leaned forward and pointed at a Black Maria about five hundred yards ahead of them. 'Just follow them,' he said. Thirty seconds later the Black Maria made a U-turn and screeched past them; the road ahead was a dead end, and just as Terry was preparing a three-point turn in the narrow space a loose crowd of about thirty or forty marchers emerged from a side passage. At first Hannah couldn't tell what tribal markings this particular bunch wore; some were skinheads, but that didn't necessarily mean right-wing thugs. They wore what bouncers and football hooligans wore, parkas, black Harringtons, pale jeans, Doc Martens – the motley of the street. More of them poured from the alleyway, and now she could see a grubby white flag of St George proclaiming CHINGFORD NF – PROUD AND WHITE.

Freddie had spotted it, too, and said, 'Terry, keep the engine running. Let's wait for them to pass.' He turned to Hannah. 'Just look straight ahead. Don't catch anyone's eye.'

Terry leaned round to lock the door: he wasn't taking any chances. The mob swarmed along the pavement and onto the road, a ragged chant breaking out from this or that cluster. They appeared not to notice the Daimler idling at the kerb – until one of them did. A donkey-jacketed man, mid-twenties, with an indecipherable tattoo on his neck, had stopped to peer through the windscreen.

'Oi, you seen who's drivin' this car? It's only a bloody nignog!'

Hannah looked away, in a fury of shame, as the man began capering, jutting out his jaw to make ape noises. The performance attracted others, who joined in the mockery. 'Get back to the jungle, ya fuckin' monkey!'

Terry, perhaps embarrassed on their behalf, turned to Hannah and Freddie.

'Would you like to listen to some music?'

'Thanks, Terry, if you wouldn't mind.'

Terry tuned the radio to a station playing light music – a string-laden swirl of Mantovani filled the car – while outside a muffled chorus of irate white men kept up the monkey chants. Freddie had never seen such expressions of hatred at close quarters, not even at football matches. He looked at Hannah, about to say something, but then shook his head despairingly. The first missile, a can, hit the windscreen, squirting a urine-coloured spray of lager over the glass. Cheers followed. The second missile sounded like a bottle, which took one bounce on the roof of the car before smashing on the road. Terry muttered something – he'd clearly waited long enough – and began to turn the car. He hadn't got very far when a third missile smashed against the passenger window and spiderwebbed it.

Terry's front of unperturbed forbearance at last broke. He flicked off the radio and before Freddie could say 'Don't!' he had unlocked his door and stepped out to confront the jeering rabble. Hannah looked on, horrified, as one of the meatier ruffians squared up to Terry, jabbing a porky digit in his chest. *Yew faackin' gollywog!*

'Oh Christ,' said Freddie under his breath, opening the door on his side. He didn't want to, but he had to, and now the terror and the adrenaline had kicked in he felt ready for it. He stepped around the car and interposed himself between Terry and the knot of taunting demonstrators. Perhaps it was because of his well-cut suit and Hermès tie, or because of his unanswerable bulk, but Freddie's sudden appearance caused a hesitation among them – it was a moment of confusion, not fear, yet it allowed him to shield Terry and shepherd back him towards the car. 'Get in and turn the car round,' he said, and when Terry made to object he hissed, 'Just do it.'

The brief hiatus of indecision among the mob ended abruptly as someone shouted, 'Who's that fat bastard?' A few of them laughed. But when one lairy youth in a green bomber made a lunge at him Freddie squared up and threw a jab, flooring him. 'Anyone else?' he snarled, making the come-on-if-you're-hard-enough twin-handed gesture known to all males from the schoolyard onwards. He had a fleeting image of himself as the lone hero up against it – Gary Cooper in *High Noon*, maybe, or Brando in *On the Waterfront*. At his back the car was on the move, which encouraged a tall young skinhead to dart at him. His punch glanced Freddie's ear, which annoyed him; when he came back for a second swing Freddie ducked and threw a haymaker at the kid's face. Something cracked, and his assailant staggered back, moaning.

He heard Hannah scream his name. He turned to find the door flung open, and, with a last baleful glare at his adversaries, he climbed inside. Terry accelerated, causing demonstrators on the road to jump aside. Another hail of missiles bounced off the car. Soon Terry found his bearings, and they were once again in the safety of the open roads.

Freddie, sweating like a racehorse, leaned his head back and exhaled noisily.

'Are you all right, sir?' Terry asked.

After a moment he nodded. *Was* he all right? His body was twitching with hostile electricity. He couldn't tell if he was exhilarated or in the grip of hysteria. He tried to flex his hand, which throbbed.

Hannah was staring at him. 'That was ... scary. I never had you down for a street-fighting man.' She sounded almost impressed.

'A leftover from public school. I learned to box.'

'Those men – they looked ready to murder you,' she said.

'Mm. And I dare say they would have done if I'd stayed a moment longer.' He looked sidelong at her. 'Would have made quite a story for you. "NMH boss beaten to death in street brawl. By our eyewitness correspondent."'

'I'd have styled it more heroically than that. "Theatre impresario dies trying to protect companions from NF thugs." Say how fearless you were. Amp it up a bit. Run a photo of you in all your youthful promise. We'd have the readers weeping into their cornflakes.'

He choked out a laugh. 'Sounds like I'd be more use to you dead than alive.' More use to certain others, too, he thought.

'It's insane,' said Hannah, serious again. 'Those people back there – where on earth do they think they're living?'

'I dunno. South Africa? They don't seem to realise it's too late for them. Race discrimination isn't a policy that's going to win voters, not any more. On our way here I saw more people marching for the Anti-Nazi League than for ... that lot. Terry, am I right?'

'S'true, sir.' Terry had returned to his reticent self: being at the wheel seemed to soothe him.

As they left the East End behind and headed towards the river Freddie's spirits were restored too. The sight of the Tower of London and the pewter-coloured Thames had never been so welcome. This city ... the wondrous place. The close-packed streets, the storeyed buildings, the secretive life of pubs and basements and faces and foggy nights – you could never exhaust its power to bewitch. Of course it had its shabby side, God knows, and he didn't fancy a return to the wilds of Hackney any time soon. But for a civilised man towards the end of the twentieth century there was really no other place to live than London. The view across the city from their living room at Highpoint was one of the sweeteners of his existence ... a vantage likely to be snatched from him once Linda and her lawyers came out swinging. Nemesis was lying in wait, though the exact time of its arrival depended on the person at his side. If Hannah could be persuaded to hold off he might be able to finesse a soft landing; softer, at least, than his long record of marital misbehaviour deserved.

'Just the Way You Are' was floating quietly from the radio.

Freddie leaned forward. 'Turn this up, would you, Terry?' He saw Hannah staring at him dubiously. 'What – you don't like Billy Joel?'

'I like him very well,' she replied. 'I never imagined *you* would.'

'Come on. How could you not love this?' He crooned along for a few bars.

Hannah laughed. 'I just thought you'd be too highfalutin ... directing five-hour operas and all that.'

'I do high, I do low,' he drawled. 'All that matters to me in music is whether it's good. And Billy Joel is *great*.'

By the time they reached his club in Dover Street it was nearly two. They'd had to stop at a chemist on the way for pain-killers. Freddie held open the door for Hannah, then told Terry he should take the rest of the day off once he'd left the car at the repair shop. He wanted to shake his hand, but indicated it was too painful to touch. Installed at a table upstairs, overlooking the street, he asked for a bottle of champagne, with lots of ice. When the bucket arrived he doused his aching hot hand in it, and half expected to see the water sizzle. The waiter poured them each a glass and departed. Hannah raised hers.

'Here's to you – scourge of the racist scum!'

Freddie acknowledged the compliment. 'I felt so disgusted for Terry. I suppose he's had to deal with that stuff all his life, but you can never quite conceive the vileness of it until you hear it for yourself.'

'How long has he been with you?'

'Oh, years. I got to know him through my dad. They met on the buses in the fifties – Terry was a driver.'

'He seems devoted to you,' she said.

'I find that a lot of people are,' he said, and snuffled a laugh.

When the waiter returned to take their order, she chose, on his recommendation, the roast chicken with green beans and mash. Freddie ordered the steak with bone marrow and chips. 'And bring us a bottle of La Tache, would you?'

Hannah eyed him over her glass. 'You do live high on the hog, don't you?'

'I enjoy food and wine,' he said defensively, 'but I wouldn't call myself a *gourmand*.'

'You wouldn't? OK, when was the last time you had a sand-wich for your lunch?'

'What? I don't – I'm not – I eat out at lunch. It's part of the business.'

'So you can't remember when you last ate just a sandwich?'

He stared off into the distance. In truth he really couldn't. Probably before he began as director of the NMH. That would be fifteen years ago – but of course he couldn't say that.

'The precise date escapes me. Though I can imagine returning to sandwich lunches quite soon if my wife decides to take me to the cleaners.'

'Will it come to that?'

'Depends. What can I do to persuade you not to publish this story about me?'

'Nothing at all,' she said crisply. 'The cat's out of the bag.'

'I'd like to throttle that cat,' he muttered.

'If we don't run the story then someone else will. At least you'll get a fair hearing from me.'

He gave her a sidelong look. 'The day I get a "fair hearing" from anyone I'll eat my hat.'

She laughed. 'You see? Always thinking of food.'

Freddie brooded. His hand, which he'd removed from the ice bucket, was pinkly numb. 'I can't believe Nicola's done this.'

'Why did she decide to shop you?'

'Some kind of revenge, I suppose. You remember the day you came to interview me – you saw us together? I'd just auditioned her for the lead in *Ragged Trousers*. It came down to a straight choice between her and Romilly Sargent. Of course I wanted to give it to her, but I couldn't – Romilly was born to play it.'

'So integrity triumphed over favouritism . . . '

Freddie gave a weary shrug, as if to say *Look where it's got me*. Hannah was silent for some moments, digesting this revelation. She took a sip of the champagne.

'I'll wait till after Christmas. First week in January. Will that help?'

He looked at her, surprised, and grateful. 'It would. Thanks.'

'The editor will probably have a fit, but . . . It should give you time to sort things out with your wife.'

'Oh God.' He hid his face behind cupped hands.

'That bad, eh? What happened between you?'

'The job. The ambition. I was often away, working. Linda came to resent it. She'd more or less abandoned her own career to raise the boys while I was . . . having a life.'

'And having affairs.'

Freddie looked up sharply, but had heard nothing judgemental in her tone. She was just being a journalist, getting the facts straight. 'There are temptations, as you can imagine, working in the theatre.'

'How hard did you try to resist?'

This time he did hear a rebuke. He deserved it. He let himself off too lightly, ascribing his misfortunes to temptation. *'We make guilty of our disasters the sun, the moon, and stars . . .'*

'Sorry?'

'*Lear.* On trying to blame fate rather than ourselves.' He examined his hand again. 'So what inclined you to show mercy?'

Hannah shrugged. 'I dunno. Maybe because you're not as disreputable as people say.'

He spluttered out an indignant laugh. 'I must get that inscribed on my gravestone.'

It was evening by the time the cab deposited Freddie at the top of Cranley Gardens. A light fog had turned the street lamps gauzy, and the leaves were damp on the pavement. He had left several messages for Nicola, all of them ignored, so he decided to present himself in person. They would have it out one way or the other. He was rather woozy from lunch, what with the champagne and Burgundy on top of the painkillers.

When he buzzed her on the intercom her voice sounded hard, though she didn't refuse him when he asked to come up. He was sweating again by the time he reached her landing. Nicola was wearing a green roll-neck sweater and a plaid skirt with thigh boots. He liked this sexy Celtic look on her. Like Rod Stewart's dream groupie – an image he thought best to keep to himself.

'Are you all right? You seem done in,' she said.

'I've had quite a day.' He supplied a brief account of his street altercation in Hackney. He showed her his hand, which had swollen up; his fingers looked like raw sausages.

'Why were you having lunch with Hannah what's-her-name? I thought you'd already done the interview.'

Freddie gave her an arch look. 'I was involved in damage limitation. She's about to publish a story about you and me.'

'Really? How did she—'

'Don't act the innocent. Look, I know you must be sore about *Ragged Trousers*, and that you probably blame me for it. But honestly, Nicola, I never thought you'd rat me out to the press.'

Her face was a mask of incredulity. 'What are you talking about?'

He allowed himself a worldly sigh. 'Come on. You made an anonymous call to Hannah Strode and spilt the beans. So now she knows all about my finances, my so-called extravagances – and all about us. She got it from you.'

'She did *not* get it from me! Why would I go to the papers – is that really what you think of me?'

He suddenly found himself in doubt, but pressed on. 'Who the hell else would it be?'

'God knows. Yes, I was upset about not getting the part, and who wouldn't be? It's a great part. But if you think I'd do something spiteful like that out of revenge, you don't know me at all.'

Freddie, perplexed, was silent. When Hannah had phoned him yesterday he was shocked: he hadn't imagined Nicola capable of doing such a thing. And now it seemed that instinct was right – she wasn't and she hadn't. Her expression of aggrieved innocence was no put-on. The audition episode was bad enough. Now he had doubled his trouble by accusing her of treachery.

Nicola, with an air of martyred offence, had sat down on the edge of the sofa, not looking at him.

'Look, I'm sorry,' he began. 'I assumed you had – well, because I couldn't think who else it might be. I still can't.'

She turned to face him. 'Isn't it obvious? It's her. Linda. Your wife.'

Freddie looked disbelieving, and then aghast. 'It couldn't—'

'Ask her,' snapped Nicola. 'And, by the way, would you kindly *fuck off* out of here and not come back?'

11

In the lounge of the Belfast to Birkenhead ferry it seemed to Callum that everybody was smoking. A blue-grey fug hung over all, spiking the miasma of odours – of fried food, damp clothes, engine oil, spilt beer and (a recent addition) baby vomit – already circulating the interior. Children, bored and restless with fatigue, were dashing about the place, whooping, wailing; their parents fixed them with defeated glares. An occasional swell from below tipped the floor one way, then the other.

Eyes itching, Callum slipped away from his bench seat and climbed the metalled stairway to the deck. The rain of earlier in the evening had thinned to a soft drizzle, the sort he had left behind in Ulster – or thought he had. They had been at sea for two hours by his watch: another six before they docked in the Mersey. He walked up and down the clanking deck, the wind blustering in his face, though on balance it was preferable to the sulphurous Hades of the lounge. He leaned on the rail and watched the almighty turbulence of the sea, its dark churn and chop mesmerising him. To think of all those it had swallowed down, arms and legs flailing against the suck of its cold, black maw.

You grew up knowing the *Titanic* had sailed from Belfast, where it had been built, prior to its fateful maiden voyage. 'It was fine when it left here,' went the local quip.

He supposed he ought to feel relieved, having survived a full week in Newry, Christmas Day and all. On returning he had felt the familiar depression settle on him like a heavy overcoat. His mother and his sister Niamh seemed pleased he was home, though their natural reserve never allowed their welcome to be mistaken for enthusiasm. The house didn't change. The surfaces of tables were polished, and yet the heavy old furniture inherited from grandparents anchored the atmosphere in gloom. The small front room, where family photos rested on an upright piano, was hardly ever used. They all either crowded into the back sitting room or remained in the kitchen, where his mother, Eileen, presided glumly over the stove. Their cousins came over on Christmas night, and brought some cheer. But day to day the ghost of his father abided there, and the memory of his terrible moods still infested the walls, the curtains, the food on the table. His shed, where he used to tinker with his vintage MG, had not been touched since his death. Callum had suggested they clear it out, or even knock it down, but Eileen shook her head, saying she'd get round to it one day.

When he couldn't stand to be inside any longer he went out to the local with his cousin Paul. It was he who filled him in on what 'they' – the Provos, the loyalists – had been up to since he'd last visited Newry. This or that pub had been bombed; a taxi driver shot dead in his car; two soldiers ambushed and killed. On the first afternoon Callum ventured into town they passed a funeral cortège, watched from the sidelines by the military. People who had never known the deceased would join the cortège, as if magnetised by the drama. 'Walking behind a hearse is our national pastime,' observed Paul. They talked in the pub about people they used to know from school, from the youth club. When he mentioned Karen McAuley, Paul laughed. 'Sure you'll never forget that one, eh, Call?' No, he hadn't seen her in a while – maybe she'd got out of Newry. Callum could only hope she had.

To Niamh, who had just turned nineteen, he was becoming an object of curiosity. Pale-skinned and tall, like him, she had just finished at the technical college and was considering her options: at the moment she favoured hairdressing. Her own dark hair was cut punkishly short, and her vampire make-up was inspired by Siouxsie, of the Banshees fame. She wanted to know about London, specifically Chelsea and the King's Road.

'You're asking the wrong feller,' said Callum. 'King's Road isn't my manor.'

Niamh looked him up and down, appraisingly. 'Yeah. You wouldn't fit in – not with your clothes.'

Callum laughed: Wrangler cord jacket, check shirt, jeans. Not exactly chic, he supposed, but not square, either.

'You want me to do something with your hair?' Niamh said, squinting.

'What's wrong with it?'

'Well . . . it's a bit, you know, Kenny Loggins. I could make it more Lou Reed.'

It was shrewd of her to bring up Lou Reed, knowing his susceptibility, but he wondered if she had any competence as a stylist. 'I dunno. I could use a trim, maybe.'

She raced off to fetch her scissors and comb, and next thing Callum knew he was sitting on a kitchen chair with a voluminous sheet tucked around his neck. A protective mat of newspapers crackled beneath their feet. He felt encouraged by her frowning look of concentration as she made busy with the electric clippers, but without a large mirror in front of them it was hard to check her progress. Wet hanks of hair fell to the floor, alarming him. When he used to get his hair cut as a boy he always feared the scalp-freezing short back and sides the auld barber gave him – the 'jail crop'.

'You reading anything at the moment?' he asked her.

'Mm? Oh . . . yeah. Just finished *The Fog*. 'Sgood.'

He groaned inwardly. 'There's more to books than James Herbert.'

Niamh raised her eyes heavenwards to suggest how many times they'd had this argument. 'It entertains me. That's all I need from a buke. Why – what are you readin'?' He nodded to the book on the kitchen counter. She put down her scissors and picked it up to read the spine. '*Born in Exile*. By George Gissing. Never heard of him.'

'Victorian. 'Bout a clever young feller who's alienated from the people around him, including his own kin. He pretends to be studying for the Church – he's an atheist – just so he can impress this high-born woman he wants to marry.'

Niamh listened, apparently with interest, and returned to snipping at his hair. After a pause she said, 'Gonna read *The Rats* next.'

Half an hour later, satisfied, she brought out two mirrors from the bathroom and held them at a professional angle for his inspection. The back of his head was shaved close, and she'd managed to layer it to the nape quite well. The reflection from the front gave him a jolt, though: the mid-brown locks that had framed his face had been cropped right back, and his ears suddenly looked huge and exposed. With his beard intact it lent him an oddly disreputable air.

'Jesus. A trim? I look like a friggin' convict.'

'You look *good*,' said Niamh, pleased with her handiwork. 'Like an explorer or somethin'.'

Callum, out on the freezing deck, laughed silently. *An explorer or somethin'*. She'd promised him Lou Reed, and given him Dr Livingstone.

From Liverpool he took the train to Euston, and there caught a bus. It was mid-morning, the day after Boxing Day, and the city felt eerily empty. Not a car could be seen or heard. It was like one of those episodes of *Doctor Who* when the streets have been abandoned to an invasion of Daleks or Cybermen. He humped his bulky ex-army kitbag across Clerkenwell Green, his breath whitening in the air. On letting himself into the house he almost jumped in fright as a woman appeared in the kitchen doorway.

'Oh, hi,' she said with a smile. 'Are you, er, Callum?' She was dark-haired, attractive, about thirty, dressed in a Fair Isle polo neck and jeans.

'Aye. And you are . . . ?'

'Sasha,' she said, raising her hand in greeting. 'Sorry, I wasn't expecting – Martin said you were going to be away for Christmas. I was tidying up a bit before I left.'

Callum nodded, still confused. He thought he'd seen her face before, in the taxi that had dropped off Martin that night, but he couldn't be sure. 'Is Martin here?'

'No, no, he left about an hour ago. Said he had to take the milk in at Number Ten.'

She gave an indulgent laugh, as though the line was a favourite of his. Her voice was tennis-club posh, and her manner so self-assured that Callum felt he was the intruder rather than her. She didn't show any sign of wanting to rush off, so he asked her if she cared for a cup of tea.

'Oh, let me make it. You must be tired after your journey – from Ireland, yeah?'

While she busied herself in the kitchen he lugged his bag upstairs. On his way back down he took a quick peek into Martin's bedroom, where it seemed Sasha had spent the night – her stuff was still on the bed. He was interested to know how Martin would respond should he ask about his overnight guest.

Sasha was sitting at the kitchen table, a cigarette on the go. Instead of dunking tea bags in a mug, house-style, she had made a pot; she'd also put the milk in a small white jug Callum had never used before. A woman's touch.

'Shall I pour?' she said, already pouring it. He wondered if she was going to offer to make him eggs as well.

'Thanks,' he said, reaching for the milk jug. 'So, um, how d'you know Martin?'

It should have been an innocent question, except that Callum already knew her things were upstairs in the bedroom.

'We met a few years ago when he first came to Whitehall. We just got on.' She smiled again, briskly, as if that were all the information he needed. 'And you know him from university, he told me?'

Callum admitted it, and recounted the short history of their friendship. He wasn't sure in the circumstances whether he should mention that he knew Christine, Martin's wife. When her name eventually came up Sasha heard it without a blink; indeed, it transpired that she knew Christine a little, 'though of course we see less of each other now they've moved to the sticks'. But not less of Martin, it would appear. They chatted on quite amiably, though Callum noticed that Sasha was sparing of personal information. When he asked her where she worked, for instance, she said only that she ran her own business and moved the conversation on. He couldn't tell whether she was doing this deliberately or if her character was naturally secretive. She had worked in politics too, which probably instilled in you the habit of caution.

By the time she had got her stuff together and was ready to leave they seemed on very good terms, though Callum sensed that Martin might not be overjoyed to hear of their accidental encounter. When she had gone he washed up the mugs and mooched in the kitchen, grazing absently on a biscuit. He went upstairs and had another look around Martin's room, checking in the wardrobe (no remnants of femininity in there). He was about to leave when he spotted the corner of a book poking from underneath the bed. It was a Penguin paperback, broken-spined, of *Emma* by Jane Austen. He scooped it off the floor and opened it. On the inside page was a name, written in a schoolgirl's hand: Sasha Denning. Perhaps he could use this for his opening gambit when he next saw Martin – Your friend left her book here . . .

Ears ringing, shirt stuck to him with sweat, Callum joined the throng of fans ambling out of the Lyceum on Wellington Street. The Clash had just played their second night there, and the hordes who had been pogoing the whole set now looked wanly exhausted in their tribal plumage – a sea of spiked haircuts dyed green or yellow or black, studded leathers, combat jackets, Doc Martens, some chain-mail vests and dog collars, PVC coats and white jeans, and so much pasty British skin, violently pierced or tattooed. All the young punks. He stopped at a merchandise stall to buy a CLASH CITY ROCKERS T-shirt, which he knew was a bit tame in this company but would do as a memento.

It had been a good gig, if not a great one. The snarling live-wire energy you got from the Clash in performance had to be set against the sacrifice of clarity; the songs he loved from the first LP – 'Hate & War', 'London's Burning', 'Janie Jones', 'Garageland' – came over rather smudged and blunted up onstage. It sounded sometimes like the band would begin a song only to race one another to the end, and Strummer, formidable as he was, too often slurred the lyrics because he couldn't keep up. But nobody cared: it was the Clash, on the Friday after Christmas, and to watch a thousand-plus youths going nuts over 'White Riot' was to understand the meaning of abandon.

Outside, the temperature had taken a nosedive towards freezing. A line of policemen waited as the crowd dispersed, each keeping the other at a wary distance. Sardonic hoots and snatches of drunken song broke on the night air, buses rumbled across Waterloo Bridge, from an open pub door rang the bell for last orders – the urban lullaby. Callum had shrugged on his coat, a second-hand Crombie, and was making brisk strides through Covent Garden in the direction of home. Here and there, in doorways, he noticed a pitiful pale scrap of humankind cowering under blankets, or cardboard, and wondered what terrible mischance had driven them to make their bed on the streets, on a night like this. To have forsaken the ties of kinship and friendship for the random charity of strangers. How had they fallen so far?

He had come to Lincoln's Inn Fields, quiet at this hour. Across the road, under a dim street light, he saw a skinny youth stopping to talk to a trio of his mates. Or else it was a drug deal, and they were his clients. Callum walked on, too far away to hear their muttered exchanges, and was about to turn the corner when he heard a glass smash. He blinked through the gloom. It seemed they were not mates, or buyers: the youth was sprawled on the floor, and the other three were piling in, using his body for target practice with their boots. Callum's instinct was to keep walking, not involve himself, just as if he were back in Newry. No good could come of interfering. But then he heard the youth begging them to stop, and a current of rage leapt in his body, flinging him forwards. He picked up a discarded bottle by the neck and smashed its end off. The oxygen must have cut from his brain because he didn't really know what he was shouting, in fact screaming, as he confronted them, eyes blazing. *You want some, ya fuckin' dogs?!* might have been one of his lines, though in retrospect he thought the bottle he was brandishing was probably instrumental in chasing them off.

One of them seemed to think about putting up a fight, until he too turned on his heel and fled.

He knelt down to check on the stricken kid, who was moaning quietly. He was wearing a Clash T-shirt beneath his leather jacket – he'd obviously come from the gig. His face was bruised, and his head was leaking blood from where they'd glassed him. He would need the hospital. But how to get him there? This corner of old London didn't offer much in the way of passing traffic. Callum looked around; at the end of the street a light glimmered in the lodge at Lincoln's Inn. He asked him if he was able to walk, and managed to get him to his feet. He could smell alcohol on him, one more thing impeding his mobility. When he asked him his name he caught a muttered syllable: Matt. With his arm braced beneath the kid's armpit he somehow stagger-walked them the hundred yards to the lodge, where he knocked on the window. The porter, an old guy, appeared, squinting with suspicion. Callum told him that an ambulance was urgently required. 'I think the ambulance workers are on strike,' the man said dubiously, so they settled on a cab instead that would take him to Barts.

The man went back into his cubbyhole to telephone.

In the faint illumination from the lodge window Callum was alarmed to see how much blood was running from Matt's head. He took out from his pocket the CLASH CITY ROCKERS T-shirt he'd bought and held it against the wound, staunching the flow. 'He looks in a bad way,' observed the porter, who reckoned the cab would be five or ten minutes away. By the time it arrived the kid was shivering, and as he bundled him into the car Callum asked the cabbie to make all haste to the hospital. His efforts to get basic information – Where did he live? What was his phone number? – achieved nothing. He only mumbled, incoherently, and his head kept lolling drunkenly on his chest. They raced past Smithfield Market and into the close fronting the hospital; with some help from the driver he helped his bleeding charge limp through the doors of the A&E. The T-shirt he held against his head looked like a butcher's apron.

Once the nurse had taken him off to surgery, Callum, finding his face and clothes daubed in blood, went in search of a toilet. He considered his ragged appearance in the mirror – like Banquo's ghost in a student production of *Macbeth*. He decided to wait in emergency until they'd contacted the family. His inner ear was still buzzing from the gig. Just after half past midnight he saw a woman consulting someone at reception, then swinging her gaze over the room to land on him. She approached, sombre-faced.

'Mr Conlan? Hi. I'm Detective Constable Vicky Tress.'

Callum swallowed hard. His instant thought was: he's dead, and you're witness to a murder. 'What's happened?'

'He's fine. Lost some blood. Twelve stitches in his head.'

'Thank God. I thought he was—'

She nodded, understanding. 'He's doing fine. He'll have a headache in the morning, that's all. You look a bit shaken up yourself.'

'Aye, it looked pretty nasty.'

'I wanted to thank you – I mean, personally. Matt's my brother, you see.'

'Oh. Right. Well, I'm glad he's OK.'

Vicky returned a smile. 'Can I get you a cup of coffee or something?'

'No, I'm fine. Thanks.'

'The Clash T-shirt. Yours? I'm afraid it's ... ' She grimaced in apology.

'Too bad. I can get another one. Your brother was at the gig?'

'Yeah. The awful thing is I bought him the ticket. Christmas present. I can't imagine how I would have—' She choked off the thought.

'Best not dwell,' said Callum.

'Did they do "Janie Jones"?'

'What?' He was surprised. 'Oh ... yeah, they did, actually. You a fan?'

'Sort of. Matthew plays the records a lot. I'd like to go myself, but, you know ... '

'Might be a bit weird.'

She nodded. They stood facing one another for a few moments, until Callum said he'd better be pushing off. Vicky thrust out her hand.

'Thanks again. Honestly. If you ever need anything, let me know. DC Tress at West End Central.'

'I'll remember,' said Callum with a laugh. 'All right, then. Night.'

Back at reception they told Vicky that her brother had been moved to a ward. They were keeping him in overnight for observation. Irene, their mother, was sitting at Matthew's bedside when she joined her. It was a stroke of good luck that Vicky had been home that evening and taken the call from the hospital. She could only imagine Irene's panicked reaction had she been on her own. Driving to Barts she was almost sick with worry about Matthew; having her mother sobbing into her hanky in the passenger seat did nothing to soothe her nerves. He had gone to the gig with some mates from school. How he'd ended up wandering around Lincoln's Inn Fields on his own she didn't know. He'd been drinking, the doctor said, and she suspected he'd done a lot of weed too.

Matthew, his head turbanned in a bandage, looked very pale – and very young – as he slept against the mound of pillows propping him up. Irene, her eyes red-rimmed from crying, was staring at him intently, as though he might wake at any moment. When Vicky sat down next to her Irene kept herself primly still, refusing to catch her eye. The silent treatment. Vicky could usually tell what was on her mother's mind, and braced herself for what was to come. She waited for a few moments before saying, 'Is something the matter?'

Her mother's eyes slid round at her. 'You can ask that with him lying there?'

'I was asking what's the matter with *you*, not him.'

She made a huffy sound, indicating she was above such fine discriminations. 'I knew no good would come of you giving him that ticket. Of all the stupid things you could encourage him to do!'

'Mum, it was a gig. His favourite band. Thousands of people go to see them. What would be the point in trying to stop him?'

'He's only a boy!'

'He's seventeen. Next year he'll be leaving home. It's good that he wants to get out.'

'You of all people should know how dangerous it is—'

'"Of all people" – you mean because I'm a copper? Yeah, I know it's dangerous out there, but you can't stop someone living their life. In any case, nothing happened to him at the gig, it went fine. It was when he got outside he ran into trouble. So what d'you do – not let him out the house?'

Irene fell into a sullen silence. The argument was lost, and she wasn't prepared to be gracious about it. Vicky knew, of course, that she *would have* blamed herself if something terrible had befallen Matthew – but then you could torment yourself with all kinds of useless speculation. He had been lucky, really, to have escaped with just a head injury; if that Irishman hadn't found him it might have been much worse … On the other hand she couldn't regret giving him a Christmas present he'd loved. The Clash gig had been sold out, and only via a friend of someone at the station had she managed to get her hands on a ticket. It was worth it for the look on Matthew's face. In the end you just had to trust to fate. What else was there to do?

On Christmas Day the Selves family were muffled up and out walking over Hampstead Heath, as tradition ordained. Freddie's aged parents, who always came to Highpoint for Christmas, totteringly brought up the rear. Then Jon and his new girlfriend, Esther, just arrived to stay from some godforsaken part of North Yorkshire, both gabbling away with Tim, who was kitted out in his new team togs (Queens Park Rangers) and juggling a football at his feet. Freddie and Linda were way out ahead. The temperature had plunged to zero. The trees, silvered with frost, struck beseeching postures with their wizened arms. Back at home Mrs Jenner would be cooking lunch for them, though Freddie, for once, felt too distracted to have much of an appetite. He cast a quick look over his shoulder.

'Esther seems nice. Pretty young thing. Hope she won't distract him.'

'No, it'll be fine. They both have Oxbridge to think about.'

Freddie had a thin cigar on the go, and with his butterscotch-coloured sheepskin and homburg he felt like the manager of a football club – or possibly the chairman. Linda was wearing the fur coat he'd bought her, the sort of extravagant Christmas present only a guilty man would give his wife. He had thrown himself into rehearsals for *The Ragged Trousered Philanthropists* with more than his usual gusto; work had become a haven from his worries, about the unions, about ticket receipts, about the impending combustion over his marriage. He still didn't buy Nicola's theory that it was Linda who had ratted on him to the *Ensign*, but like it or not he would have to come clean to her before it got splashed all over the papers.

'Oh fuck,' he muttered. 'I forgot to get the Warninks for Dad.' A snowball was the favourite Christmas cocktail of the eighty-year-old George Selves.

'I'm sure he won't mind,' Linda said leniently.

'Jesus. I sometimes wonder if I'm going senile quicker than he is.'

Linda turned a disapproving frown on him. 'What's wrong with you? You've been in such an odd mood.'

He'd been postponing his confession, and now the moment for it had arrived: she had all but tied it up in a bow for him. Yet still it felt vertiginous, sickening. He glanced over his shoulder again, making sure of the others' distance.

'I should tell you – you should prepare yourself – there's going to be a story about me in the papers.'

'I see. Go on, then.'

He took a fortifying drag on the cigar. 'It's going to reveal an affair I've been having with – someone. An actress. I'm sorry that it's come out like this . . . and on a day like this.' There was a long silence. When he could it stand it no longer he looked at her quickly. 'Did you know?'

She took her time in replying. 'I thought there was someone. I didn't know it was an actress. That's a bit corny, isn't it?' She didn't sound especially upset.

'I suppose it is. Nicola and I—'

'It's not Nicola Mayman, is it? My God, you once told me she couldn't act her way out of a paper bag!'

'Did I?' It must have been a diversionary tactic: if you were harsh about the talent you couldn't be suspected of involvement with them. 'Well, I suppose you'll want me to get out.'

'Is that what you want?' she said, looking straight ahead.

Freddie let out a careworn sigh. 'I'm just trying to be realistic. I know things haven't been great between us for a while.'

Linda walked on, silent again. Now she looked back to check they weren't in hearing range. 'I think we should stick with things as they are for now. If you clear out, the boys are going to be upset – Tim's got O levels next year, Jon's got Oxbridge. We should try to keep up some front of normality, at least until they've got through their exams.'

Freddie nodded. He couldn't believe how calm she sounded. Her tone was almost businesslike. 'Right . . . well, thanks.'

'Thanks for what?'

'For not flying off the handle.'

She emitted a low sardonic huff. 'I've had years to get used to it, Freddie. Years. You've not been here – we'd hardly know the difference if you did move out.'

He winced, his silence acknowledging the justice of her remarks. He had been a negligent husband, and faithless too; he deserved whatever was coming to him. But what was coming? 'So . . . we'll keep up appearances for now,' he said. 'I'll sleep next door, and if they ask I'll say it's because of my asthma.'

After a moment she said, 'Are you still seeing her?'

'Not at present. There's been a falling-out since the – well, we had a fight over who'd told the press and—'

'I don't really want to know,' Linda said shortly. 'Just try to show some discretion – for all our sakes.'

It was fair enough. He could hardly expect a sympathetic ear from the woman he'd been cheating on. He had been too hasty in accusing Nicola, who had gone silent on him. And now there was another anxiety to preoccupy him: if neither his wife nor his mistress had shopped him, who had?

12

'This is the bit I love,' said Hannah. 'D'you mind if I turn it up?'

The virtuoso jazz coda of 'Paprika Plains' abruptly leapt in volume. She hadn't bargained for the decibels Christopher's in-car cassette player could reach, and tweaked the dial back down to an acceptable level.

'Cool, isn't it?' Christopher agreed, with a quick smile before his eyes returned to the road. 'Joni on piano, Wayne Shorter on sax, Jaco Pastorius on fretless bass – that's the funky bubbling sound.'

'Jaco Pastorius? Sounds like a Dutch astronomer. Or a farmer.'

It was great how he knew stuff like 'fretless bass'. She had played *Don Juan's Reckless Daughter* a few times now. It hadn't grabbed her at first, the songs felt a bit shapeless and overlong, and one of them was a straight rip-off of 'Coyote' from *Hejira*. But she had persevered, and even if it wasn't likely to dislodge *Blue* or *Ladies of the Canyon* in her affections she had begun to hear its charm. Yes, definitely growing on her, this one.

She stole a sly glance at Christopher. He was driving them to Kent to stay with friends for the new year – a house party, he called it. She had been surprised by him asking after only three dates ('Is this rather forward of me?' he'd said on the phone) and then surprised herself by accepting. She had intended to go to a party with Tara, but this invitation felt too intriguing to turn down. Christopher had sweetly assured her she would have her own bedroom – he was a gentleman, after all – though she probably wouldn't have objected even if he'd suggested bunking up with him.

She asked him to stop off at a newsagent's, where she dithered for a moment before buying a box of Weekend. When she got back into the car Christopher glanced at her purchase.

'Chocs for our hosts,' she explained.

He twitched his mouth, but made no comment.

Once they were on the motorway he floored the accelerator, and his MG gave a little buck as it began devouring the road. She'd had an inkling he might be the type who wore string-backed driving gloves, but happily this wasn't the case.

'So these friends of yours ... are you going to tell me about them?'

'Oh ... some I know through work, some from the City. Gideon and Julia own this lovely old manor house near Sissinghurst, and they get us all down every new year. They're both great hosts, so we shouldn't lack for a bit of this—' he mimed tipping back a glass – 'and probably a bit of that—' he pinched fingers and thumb into a delicate 'O' and brought them to his mouth with a noisy inhalation.

'Are you implying there'll be *drugs* on the premises?'

Christopher shot her a nervous look. 'Oh dear. D'you disapprove?'

She laughed at his being taken in. 'I'm not that square!'

'Thank heavens. I mean, not to say it's *Easy Rider* or anything down there, but there tends to be weed on offer.'

He drummed his hand on the wheel as Jaco's big elastic bassline did another go-round. He nodded at the packet of Dunhill on the dashboard and asked her to light one for him. As she passed him the lit cigarette she said, 'I wonder what you've told them about me ... '

He laughed quietly. 'Wouldn't you like to know?'

'Did you say I was your new girlfriend?' She wondered if she had gone beyond flirty; this was almost fishing.

'That would be presumptuous of me, he replied evenly. 'All

I said was I'd be bringing a young lady whose acquaintance I'd recently made.'

Now it was her turn to laugh. 'Makes me sound like I'll be wearing a muslin dress and a bonnet. Will you be taking me to the Netherfield ball as well?'

There was a slight hesitation – the allusion had the better of him – but he gamely returned her serve. 'Actually they've got a sprung floor. Their dining room doubles as a ballroom.'

'You're kidding.'

He shook his head. 'Tomorrow night a load of people will be coming from London – it's the New Year's Eve disco! So you'd better have brought your dancing shoes.'

They arrived late in the afternoon. The house, built in the Pugin style, was approached along an avenue of cypresses. A circular forecourt was already half full with parked cars, among them a Range Rover, a Mercedes and a midnight-blue Bristol, a car Hannah had always loved; her father had owned one. A mournful-looking Weimaraner ambled out to meet them as they hefted their luggage to the front door. The dog's master followed hard on his heels. Gideon Casaltine was a short, fair-haired fellow in his late thirties, rosy of face and chunky of build, as content in his own skin as only an ex-public schoolboy knew how to be. He greeted Hannah with warmth, which turned to a sort of confusion as she handed him the Weekend. He took one look at the cheerfully gaudy packaging and said, 'Ah, the kids will love these.'

Hannah laughed, to hide her embarrassment.

'I dare say you're in the mood for a drink,' he said, leading them through the hall into the drawing room, 'especially after two hours of Christopher's driving.'

'He does drive quite fast,' Hannah said, 'but he seemed to know what he was doing.'

'Ye-e-ers, he's very plausible like that', Gideon said archly, taking up a silver cocktail shaker. 'Now, will you try a Stinger?'

Hannah readily assented, though she had no clue what it was.

The gloomy wood-panelling of the room took on the dancing reflections of the open fire, before which the Weimaraner, Mr Chips, had parked himself. Gideon disappeared to tell his wife of their latest guests, which gave Hannah a chance to snoop about the room. The paintings, aside from a few modest landscapes, were of bewhiskered worthies and stern gentlemen of business who Christopher thought were mostly Julia's forebears. It turned out she had inherited the house, while Gideon, who was at Barings, supplied 'the boodle' for its upkeep. The furniture was either heavy, straight-backed chairs of minimum utility and comfort or else vast crumpled sofas loaded with needlepoint cushions. A selection of brass pokers in diminishing size stood watch over the huge stone fireplace. It was not an unfriendly room, though it was stuffy and seemed to belong more to a private country club, or an old hotel, than to a family house. (Hannah gathered that the couple's two young children were in the nursery upstairs.)

'Blimey, what's in this?' she asked, baulking at the strength of the Stinger.

Christopher tested it for himself. 'Brandy, mostly, with a dash of crème de menthe. Pace yourself, is my advice. There's a lot more where this came from.'

A few moments later Julia Casaltine appeared, and made a slightly possessive fuss over Christopher, marking her territory. She was tall, lithe, her blonde hair adorned with an Alice band: she moved with a dancer's quick stride, a remnant of her years with the Royal Ballet before she'd had kids. She turned to Hannah with a smile that glittered as bright as the square-cut diamond on her finger.

'Now I know you're at the *Ensign* but I'm afraid we're terribly set in our ways about the papers – *Telegraph* for Gideon, *Mail* for me.'

'Oh, that's fine,' replied Hannah. 'Actually I was hoping for a complete break from newspapers for a couple of days.'

'Quite right,' said Gideon, 'you're on holiday now. Has

Christopher told you the schedule for the weekend? There's a small gathering here tonight – I think we'll be sixteen – tomorrow morning we're off to Morghew for the shoot. Then it's our New Year's Eve dinner dance, which we're all very excited about.'

Hannah looked to Christopher, who said, 'We might sit out the shoot, Gid.'

'Oh, there's no obligation! Feel free to mooch around here. But I know Banger is most eager to get cracking—' Loud voices from the hallway interrupted Gideon's flow. 'And talk of the devil . . . that'll be him and the others back from their walk.'

There was an animated quiver of hesitation before the door swung open and a large squirish fellow in a Barbour and tweed hat took possession of the room, trailing in his wake a retinue of guests ruddy-cheeked from the cold. In short order Hannah was introduced to each, a flurry of faces and names she tried to hold in her head as they gabbled over one another and called out their drinks order to Gideon. The large man, who had made an instant beeline for the drinks trolley, now approached her, a bumper gin and tonic clamped in his hand.

Christopher was about to make an introduction but the man beat him to it. 'Are you the journo?' he boomed. His eyes, small and incurious, didn't quite meet hers.

'I am. Hannah. And you must be – Banger?'

He nodded sharply. 'So how d'you know the Brigadier?'

She returned a bemused look, until Christopher quietly supplied, 'That's me.'

'Well, we were introduced by friends,' she said, still using the cover story they had agreed upon about their meeting. 'How about you two?'

'The Brig and I first met at school. Then we met up again in the City, in the days when he had a proper job, hur-hur.' He took a swig of his drink and smacked his lips. When Hannah asked what job he did, Banger said, 'Foreign exchange,' as though it required no explanation.

Christopher again stepped in. 'Banger forecasts trends in stockmarkets, commodities, foreign currencies. Stuff like that. Nothing he doesn't know about the value of oil or gold.'

'You ever invest in stocks?' Banger said.

'Er, no, I've never had the—'

'Well, you should,' he insisted, and for the next ten minutes delivered an uninterruptible monologue on the intricacies of the market, the precariousness of this commodity and that, the advantages of having a tipster, and his own triumphs as a technical analyst. By the end of it Hannah felt almost paralysed from lecturitis – a debilitating condition (coined by her) inflicted exclusively by men on women. She was eventually rescued by Julia, though not before vowing to herself never to get trapped on her own by Banger again.

Julia announced to the room that pre-dinner drinks would be served at eight, giving them time for a wash and brush-up. She then gave Christopher instructions on which room Hannah was to have. After some inconsequential chat with a mousy-looking woman named Jill she got the nod from Christopher to follow him.

'You and Banger seemed to be getting on like a house on fire,' he said as they took the stairs.

She looked at him to check that he was joking, but found no trace of irony in his expression.

'He certainly had a lot to say for himself,' she replied, trying to keep her tone nonchalant. Christopher only nodded, as though she might have been praising him. 'Why does he call you the Brigadier, by the way?'

'Oh, it's from school. We'd been watching some war film, and saw from the credits that Somebody Galton played a character called the Brigadier. Banger was tickled by it.'

Hannah's premonition that the evening ahead might be a trial was not wide of the mark. They didn't sit down to dinner until late, by which time Gideon's Stingers and the free flow of wine had got everyone more or less blotto. Even Hannah, hardened by her time on Fleet Street, found it a challenge to keep up with the drinking. She was seated among people who had all worked in the City at one time or another, knew each other well and regarded it as quite natural to talk exclusively of mutual interests in front of an outsider. When it wasn't about themselves the conversation mostly turned to money and shares, and how things might pick up once the country came to its senses and voted the Tories in. In fact she never heard them mention the word 'Tory', it was simply 'Margaret', and what Margaret would do to bring down inflation, and how Margaret would stick it to the unions. They talked of politics without any hint of passion. Conservative was simply the way they voted, and always would be.

Only a jolly-looking woman named Katherine, approximately her own age, asked Hannah questions about herself. She had remembered at least one of her appearances on *What the Papers Say*.

'You were very good, I thought. So confident!'

Hannah laughed. 'It's funny, I don't feel confident at all. I much prefer writing to be honest.'

Katherine worked in the foreign sales office at Christie's. She had been at university with Gideon and Julia, and unlike most of the guests here was still 'a single girl'. Hannah, prompted by feelings of solidarity, said, 'So was I, for ages. I only met Christopher recently.'

'Oh, he's such a lovely man, isn't he?' Katherine said, looking up the table. Her tone was almost wistful. She was plain-faced, plump, with kind eyes, and Hannah felt a stab of compassion that she tried to mask with friendliness.

'I know a few single men at the paper. I could, you know, if you were interested ... '

'Are any of them nice?'

Hannah smiled. 'One or two. I wouldn't set you up if they weren't.'

'All right, then!' said Katherine, and even her hopefulness

made Hannah's heart turn over. She wondered if it was prudent to play matchmaker on so short an acquaintance, but she couldn't help herself.

At the other end of the table Banger's latest monologue had risen almost to a shout, his features puce from the drink he'd been tipping back. Only when the mousy woman, Jill, suggested he might lower his voice – advice he ignored – did Hannah realise that they were man and wife.

She suffered a quiver of dread when Julia brought in the Weekend on the coffee run, and then relief that she made no mention of the donor. She watched the puzzled faces as the opened box progressed around the table, an interloper amid the gleaming candlesticks and the solemn wine decanters. Simon, the man seated next to her, muttered on seeing them 'Good God, what are these?' though he popped a lime candy in his mouth anyway. When the box came round to her she politely passed it on, as though she never had anything to do with cheap confectionery.

At midnight she heard the grandfather clock in the hallway chime, and still the company was in a roar.

On waking the next morning Hannah had almost no memory of when she had got to bed, or how. She pulled back the curtain and felt the light on her eyes as sharp as lemon on a paper cut. The window looked out upon a huge garden, with a paddock and an acreage of green fields beyond. The sight was rendered the more beautiful by a low-lying mist. The quiet of the place astonished her: not even a distant hum of traffic intruded. When she came down to the dining room a couple of young women were clearing up the detritus of breakfast. It was later than she thought. One of the girls informed her that the others had gone off to Morghew for the bird shoot. Hannah asked her if she might have tea and toast – and would there be a couple of aspirin to spare, too?

The Sunday papers were scattered about the room, and she sank onto a sofa, intending to make a start on the *Observer.* A few minutes later Christopher sauntered in, wearing a checked Viyella shirt and chinos but no sign of a hangover.

'Ah, I was wondering when you'd appear. Did you sleep all right?'

'What time did I go to bed?'

'I think you retired about twelve thirty. I'm afraid you missed the games—'

'You played games?'

'Oh yeah. Forfeits was hilarious. I had to brush my teeth with Drambuie!'

Hannah stared at him. 'But when I left you were all absolutely plastered ...'

'Of course we were. But you try stopping Banger when he's in the mood.'

He had finally hit the hay around four, he continued, though at least he didn't have an alarm call this morning. The others were up betimes and ready to drive off to Tenterden. She shook her head, wonderingly. The annoying thing was that he didn't look a bit the worse for wear, unlike the ghoul's-mask she had shrunk from just now in the bathroom mirror.

'Shall we go for a walk?' Christopher asked. 'Might help clear your head.'

In the boot room he found her a musty pair of Hunter wellies. Her stockinged feet felt as cold as ash inside them, but she saw their usefulness once they were out there; the overnight rain had turned the ground soft and mulchy. A feeble sun lolled amid the late-morning clouds. In his long overcoat and silk scarf Christopher looked very raffish, and for the first time since they'd arrived she felt contented. At dinner he had been seated, perhaps deliberately, at the opposite end of the table, and she had snatched longing glimpses of him entertaining his immediate neighbours. He was at ease with women, and charmed them, while he duelled with the men in a spirit of sardonic geniality.

'Your friends seem very fond of you,' she said, as they tramped along the perimeter of an ornamental pond.

He shrugged. 'Aren't friends meant to be?'

'Yes. But in your case it's very noticeable. They seem to gravitate to you.'

He chuckled, began to speak, and then hesitated. 'There's a woman coming to tonight's party who doesn't, well, hold me in very high regard.'

'Oh. Not your ex-wife?'

He shook his head. 'An ex-girlfriend. Name of Devora. We used to work in the City together – went out for a couple of years. Very bright, intense, lives pretty fast. I ended it, four, maybe five years ago, and she didn't like it.'

'I see. Will you be able to avoid her?'

'It's not like that. We've got mutual friends, including this lot, so we see one another from time to time. It's fairly civilised, but I sometimes get this feeling from her . . . '

'What sort of feeling?'

'That she'd like to stab me in the neck.'

'Doesn't sound too civilised. What happened? Did you break her heart?'

He gave a rueful laugh. 'I'm not absolutely certain she has a heart. No . . . it's just that she's the kind of woman who doesn't get dumped. As she explained to me at the time.'

Hannah wasn't liking the sound of this. 'Why? I mean, there must be a reason.'

'Maybe you should meet her first. Some people think she's wonderful.'

'OK,' she said, after a moment, not sure if she was meant to feel intrigued or intimidated.

In the afternoon the gravel forecourt became a car park as the other party guests began to arrive. More staff had been recruited from the local village, and Julia, returned from the shoot, could be heard drilling them in the downstairs kitchen. Upstairs the guests settled about the rooms, drinking and chatting; four of them were playing canasta. Gideon danced attendance as butler and concierge. This place really is like a hotel, thought Hannah, except you don't have to sign for anything. She and Christopher had stopped on their walk at the Victoria Arms and played darts. She beat him 3–1, and felt quite pleased with herself.

Back at the house she had a bath and readied herself for the evening. They had been told to dress 'disco', and she had changed into her white trouser suit with a kick-flare that she knew would look good on the dance floor. Just before seven Christopher knocked at her door and sidled in.

He looked her up and down, apparently beguiled. 'Wow. That's some outfit. You look like—'

'Please don't say John Travolta,' she said.

'I was going to say Diane Keaton, only much better-looking.'

She laughed. 'Well, that's a relief.' His own evening wear was a midnight-blue tuxedo and black tie, which didn't at all answer to disco but looked very dapper. While she brushed her hair he sat down at her dressing table and took out a small white square, which he carefully unfolded. At first Hannah thought he was about to surprise her with a gift – a pair of earrings?! Instead, onto an old-fashioned silver looking-glass he tipped out a dainty half-teaspoonful of white powder which he began chopping very finely with the edge of his Access card.

'Is that what I think it is?' said Hannah.

'You mean my "flexible friend" here? Yeah, comes in handy, I must say.' He laughed, waggling his credit card.

Hannah had never taken cocaine before. Because it was supposed to be expensive she associated it with the spoilt princelings of Hollywood and the cooler fringes of rock – she'd read that Bowie had taken rather a lot. It was for the sort of people who toured the world in private jets rather than attended new year dances in the Home Counties. But maybe that was changing: Christopher appeared to be quite au fait with it.

'Have you got any money on you?' he asked, lining up four neat threads of the powder.

'You want me to pay for it?'

He giggled and shook his head. 'Of course not. I just need a banknote for this.'

She found her purse and got out a fiver, which he rolled into a tight little straw and held out to her. 'You first,' she said, not sure of the etiquette. With a quick smile he bowed his head over the mirror and snorted one line, then another. He reared back, snuffling, and extended the rolled fiver to her. Hesitantly she crouched over the mirror and, like a child at a party game, hoovered up the lines in two long sniffs.

She felt something inside her head clang pure like a bell, and the reverb shuddered all the way down into her chest. She threw her head back, blinking from the shock.

'Oh my—' she gasped, electrified.

He moved his face close to her. 'How does that feel?'

A cold crystalline rush that felt something like love was flooding through her. 'Like nothing on earth,' she said dreamily.

'Good! Shall we go down?'

She held his hand as they descended the staircase, the brittle intimacy of the coke binding them together. She felt ready for anything – even a chat with Banger. In the main living room about thirty guests were already deep in party prattle, and the young servers, dressed in formal black and white, were helping them to drinks. At the other end of the room a buffet supper lay in wait. At once light-headed and focused, Hannah fell into conversation with Gideon and Simon, her neighbour at dinner the night before; they were telling her about the day's shoot, and soon she was doing the most brilliant impersonation of someone hanging on their every word. She took a long swallow of her Old Fashioned (Gideon's cocktail of the evening) and continued to bliss out.

More guests were pouring into the room, and she and Christopher were now separated by the press of bodies. She had just accepted another drink when she found herself being scrutinised, openly, by a sallow-skinned, dark-haired woman in a red halter-necked dress. The woman stepped forward. Hannah, though a good few inches taller than her, had the queer sensation of being looked down upon.

'You must be Hannah,' she said in a languid, throaty drawl.

'And you must be Devora,' she replied in a counter-intuitive flash, for she had imagined the woman Christopher had described as blonde and statuesque.

She nodded in affirmation. 'I heard you were coming. There's been quite a lot of talk about you.'

'Has there?' I'm flattered.'

'Oh, I wouldn't be. It's always the way when Chris brings along his latest.'

Hannah felt the needle in that, but decided to play nice. 'I gather you and Christopher were . . . an item?'

'Yeah, years ago. We lived together. Chris was still pretty shook up from his divorce back then – he had real difficulty trusting people.'

At that moment the subject of their discussion presented himself, his guarded expression flicking from one to the other. 'I presume you've been introduced—'

'Yes, we've done all that,' Devora replied shortly.

Mischief prompted Hannah to add, casually, 'Devora was just saying how you found it difficult to trust people after your divorce.'

The look Christopher trained on Devora was knowing: he had been here before with her. 'Some more than others,' he said drily. 'How's the ad business?'

'Thriving,' said Devora, and turned back to Hannah. 'I'm partner in an advertising agency. I offered Chris a job once and he turned it down, did he tell you?'

Hannah shook her head, and looked at him enquiringly. 'Why was that?'

Christopher gazed off for a moment before saying, 'Personnel issues.'

Behind them Gideon was loudly herding people towards the buffet, an interruption that Christopher seemed to welcome. He steered Hannah away from the crush, away from Devora, and whispered in her ear, 'Something to eat, or would you prefer to powder your nose?'

Hannah looked at him, uncomprehending, until he swiped a meaning finger across the side of his nose. She responded with a smirk, and followed him across the stone-flagged hallway into the loo. Christopher pulled down the polished wooden toilet seat and tapped out another fat white line on it for each of them.

'Is this how you managed to stay up last night?' she said in an undertone.

He nodded. 'And you never get pissed on it either.'

Again, the mighty rush of euphoria bolted through her blood, perhaps even stronger this time than the first. She looked at him, smiling, and without really thinking about it she pulled him towards her and kissed him on the mouth. Their clinch lasted mere moments; but it felt natural, and fun.

'You're really terribly attractive, aren't you?' she said.

He laughed indulgently, then said, 'Was it OK with Devora?'

'I don't know. She seemed rather proprietorial about you.'

He shrugged, and took hold of her hand, pressing it to his lips. With his other hand he tucked the wrap of coke into her breast pocket. 'Mind how you go, and don't let the others see it or they'll all want some.'

Back in the main room they had started on supper. She and Christopher joined a little huddle of people who'd commandeered the two large sofas by the fireplace. The young waiters were offering the daintier items from the buffet – devils-on-horseback, mushroom vol-au-vents, cheese straws – though something, probably the coke, had killed Hannah's appetite. Next to her Katherine, her friend from last night, was hesitating over the quiche.

'I'm meant to be watching my weight,' she said with a guilty glance at Hannah as she shovelled a slice onto her plate.

'I shouldn't worry about watching it, dear,' Banger, overhearing, said, 'it doesn't seem to be going anywhere.'

Someone laughed, and Katherine concealed her mortification under a self-deprecating giggle. Hannah, appalled, looked over to Christopher, hoping he would intervene. He did not let her down.

'That's Banger aspiring to wit. As usual, he is halfway there. Katherine, I think I'll join you – that quiche looks scrumptious.'

When she next got the chance she grasped Christopher's hand tight in gratitude. Meanwhile she and Katherine chatted on, pouring one another huge draughts of white wine that had no apparent effect on either of them. They were suddenly the best of friends. From the next room came a muffled bassline that thrummed along the floorboards: the entertainment had begun.

'Come on,' she said to Katherine, hauling her up from the sofa, 'time to dance yourself dizzy.'

Stopping at the loo for another bump of the coke, she found the dining room transformed into a dark, neon-strobed cavern. 'Everybody Dance' by Chic was booming out, massively, and she felt her heart begin to pound in concert with the beat. A glitter ball spun lights on the groups of dancers who had already ventured forth in twos and threes. Hannah closed her eyes and felt her balance wobble briefly, then strutted her way in, chin held high. She had always been a good dancer, and for once felt no self-consciousness about being taller than most of the men in the room. The music kept on coming, in voluptuous waves, and she surrendered to it – 'Disco Inferno', 'Night Fever', 'I'm Every Woman', 'Got To Be Real', 'Blame it on the Boogie'. She felt invincible, a queen in her own disco palace. At one point she got Katherine and the others to dance the LA Hustle, in a line, with all the claps and turns, and for a few minutes it went like clockwork. Then the rhythm faltered and the line broke up and nobody minded a bit.

But where was Christopher? She checked in the main rooms on the other side of the hall, found no trace of him. The chimes at midnight were getting closer; she couldn't bear the idea of seeing in the new year without him. Someone said that he was out on the terrace smoking. He wasn't there either. By now people were pouring into the hallway where Gideon had taken on MC duties and the grandfather clock was about to come into its own. Julia and her minions were on the move handing out flutes of champagne – and in their wake, through the crush of bodies, came Christopher, bearing a salver of his own. On catching sight of her on the staircase he winked, and she returned a wave, somewhat hysterical with relief. He looked so debonair! Perhaps – she didn't want to jinx it – they could mark the new year together by—

Gideon was leading the countdown as the revelry trembled to the edge of delirium. '... three – two – one – Happy new year!' The hallway rang with whoops and cheers. Hannah knocked back her champagne in two gulps and hugged Katherine. 'I hope nineteen-seventy-nine brings you a nice man!' she yelled over the noise. 'Both of us!' Katherine replied.

Before leaving the dance floor she had parked a request with the epicene youth who was DJing for the night – and now she heard the song's opening bars from the next room. She almost tumbled down the stairs in her haste to get to Christopher.

'*Please* come and dance!' she cried, flinging her arms around his neck. 'They've just put on my song.'

He smiled. 'Well, I *did* have your name on my dance card ...'

She grabbed his hand and hurried them towards the music. Its sequenced beats were gathering in tempo, and Donna Summer's voice was crooning

Ooooooo IfeelloveIfeelloveIfeelloveIfeellove
I feel love

in a trance of ardour. The dance floor had filled up again: it seemed her favourite was everybody else's too. The frenetic throb seized her, so loud it was almost inside her, and she watched as Christopher began to sway. Men in black tie always looked terrible when they danced, but he was doing all right, moving his hips more than his shoulders, still a touch self-conscious. All that mattered was having him there – he could have done the Funky Chicken for all she cared. From the corner of her eye she spotted Devora, eyes fixed hawkishly on them both, which for Hannah was the cherry on the cake.

She had moved her body as close as she dared to him, lip-syncing Donna's dreamy protestations just in case he wasn't getting the message. It seemed too much, because his melting gaze of moments before had dissolved and he was staring at her in – could it be disapproval? Or was it alarm? *What's wrong?* she was about to say when, abruptly, she saw for herself – a fine thread of blood had dripped unignorably down the front of her white jacket. And was persistent in its flow ... from her nose. She was having a nosebleed.

Christopher stopped still, and she heard him say over the thump of the music, 'Let's get you out of here.' He walked her out, his hand at her elbow, while the others danced on oblivious.

'I'm fine,' she whispered, 'I'm fine.' But the blood kept coming, wouldn't stop. The loo was occupied, so they went to a bathroom upstairs. He got her to sit on the edge of the tub and tipped her head back, pressing his handkerchief to her nose. He asked her if she was feeling sick, but she shook her head. She could feel her heart going like a jackhammer, though whether it was from the dancing or the coke or just the excitement of being with him she wasn't sure.

'How much of the stuff did you take?'

'Um, about half of it. Here.' She handed him back the wrap, which he pocketed.

'OK.' His brow was dark with concern. 'It's my fault, I should never have ...'

Her reflection in the bathroom mirror was not pleasing – pale-faced, and sweaty. The bleeding had been staunched at last. His handkerchief was blotchy with blood.

'Don't blame yourself,' she said, in a hoarse voice. That was the coke too. 'Just . . . blame it on the boogie.'

He laughed miserably. 'I think you should rest up for a while.'

He accompanied her back to her bedroom, where she shrugged off her jacket and lay on the bed. She had begun to feel dizzy, and her heart was still doing quick time. Christopher sat on the edge of the bed, his expression preoccupied.

'Can you stay for a while?' she asked, in such a meek voice it almost made her sob. He nodded, and placed a motherly hand on her brow, checking her temperature. She would rather he had checked her heart rate instead.

From downstairs rose the implacable thump of the disco.

Hannah woke, groggily, in the half-light of dawn. Her bedside light was still on. She was tight-throated; but her heart had calmed to steadiness at least. Her invincibility of hours earlier had gone: she felt dull, dried-out, heavy-limbed. She hauled herself off the bed. Across the armchair was draped her white jacket, the spattered blood already turned to brown. She ought to have sponged it out before she crashed.

She drew back one of the curtains and looked out on the garden, glimmering with hoar frost. A few small birds were knocking at the grass. Would a worm answer? In the distance the pleated fields were still sunk in mist. She was about to turn away when, from the far side of the lawn, a couple wandered into view. As they came nearer she saw, with a start, that it was Christopher, still in his dinner jacket, the black tie loosened at his neck. At his side, a man's jacket resting on her shoulders, was Devora. It did not escape Hannah's notice that her arm was tucked, comfortably, through his.

13

One morning in the second week of January Callum came down to breakfast to find Martin seated at the kitchen table, staring dead ahead. He seemed almost in a trance. In front of him lay a tabloid newspaper emblazoned with a grimly sarcastic headline: CRISIS? WHAT CRISIS? Martin, ashen-faced, looked up on hearing his step.

He nodded at the paper. 'They couriered it over first thing this morning.'

Callum had a quick look, though he already knew what it was about. The Prime Minister had left the country last week to attend an international summit in Guadeloupe. The issues discussed there included Britain's nuclear deal with the US, cruise missiles in Europe and the worsening situation in Iran, where the Shah's rule was crumbling. But these high matters of state proved of less interest to the British press than photographs of the PM and his wife Audrey sunning themselves at their next stop, in Barbados. When Callaghan, tanned and rested, arrived at Heathrow, reporters had caught him on the hop. Blinking under the flashbulbs he seemed ill-prepared for questions, and when asked about the 'mounting chaos' in the country he had replied, with fatal blitheness, that he didn't think the world outside shared the view there *was* any chaos.

With a sigh Callum said, 'I suppose it looks bad, stepping off a plane from the Caribbean when your country's up to its neck in strikes.'

'He was *working*, for Christ's sake,' said Martin indignantly. 'Honestly, this is a new low. As if those photos of him in the sea weren't bad enough ... I mean, even the *Financial Times* thinks it's OK to talk about Audrey's sun hat. What happened to honest reporting?'

'It may just blow over,' said Callum with a shrug.

'He should never have talked to them right off the plane. Someone should have told him – go to Downing Street, get briefed, then face them. That's what I would have done.' He picked up the paper, staring at the headline as if it were a personal affront. 'Like we needed another bloody fire to stamp out ...'

Callum had heard it all before. As the union troubles multiplied – now it was the road hauliers, the hospital cleaners, the bin men, the nurses, the traffic wardens, the train drivers – Martin had taken to spending more time in London, and his two-nights-per-week arrangement at St James's Walk had crept up to three or four. He was not the sort to keep his work life separate from home: Callum, recipient of the latest from Whitehall, suspected he was better briefed on Labour's inner turmoil than most of Fleet Street. With Martin's wife Christine in the distant wilds of Suffolk Callum had found the role of chief confidant thrust upon him, *faute de mieux*. He bore it as tolerantly as he was able.

In truth it was not Martin's travails at work that really interested Callum. No mention had been made of Sasha, the overnight visitor whom he had surprised the morning of his return from Ulster, and since Martin was unlikely to volunteer anything Callum sensed it would be up to him to broach the subject. As yet he had not quite mustered the nerve, but now, with his lodger in distracted mood, he saw his moment.

'By the way, forgot to mention, I met your friend the other day,' he said, in a tone of perfect innocence.

'What?' Martin looked at him, puzzled.

'Yeah, er – Sasha, was it? She was here when I got back from Belfast.'

Martin paused for a moment, a fleeting calculation in his eyes. 'Right. She said she'd met you. Old friend of mine – hadn't seen her in a while.'

A lie, he knew, but not wanting to scare him off he kept it light. 'Uh-huh. She said you two met at Whitehall.'

He nodded. 'A few years ago. Really smart girl. She and Christine are very fond of each other,' he added quickly, as if to establish that relations were all above board.

But Callum wouldn't let it go that easily. 'Well, if you ever want to invite her round, for dinner or something, be my guest. It'd be nice to meet her properly.'

Martin squinted at him, unsure of his meaning. 'Actually, Cal, I think she's spoken for. Sorry.'

'Oh, no, that wasn't my – I just thought I'd let you know, it's fine by me if you want to have people round. That's all.'

Now Martin looked uncomfortable as well as confused, which Callum thought, all in all, a satisfying upshot to the conversation. But he also felt pretty certain that Sasha would not be making another appearance at the house.

A knock sounded at the door. On the step Callum found a man from Interflora holding a huge bouquet of cellophaned flowers.

'Callum Conlan?' he asked, consulting a docket. He handed them over to Callum, who said, bemused, 'For me?'

The man told him there was a card attached, and departed. Callum carried his perplexing package back to the kitchen. Martin eyed the flowers suspiciously.

'Don't tell me you've got an admirer.'

'Not that I know of,' he replied, detaching the small square envelope from its pin. The handwritten card inside read:

> These come with thanks from my mum, my brother Matthew and me.
>
> Vicky Tress

Callum gazed at it for a moment. 'It's from the family of a kid I helped out.' Martin demanded to know more, so he told him about the night of the Clash gig, the assault on the boy and the dash to Barts. He hadn't been expecting to hear from them. No one had ever sent him flowers before.

'Well, aren't you the Good Samaritan?' said Martin, failing to hide a note of irritation: he didn't like surprises, and he couldn't understand why Callum hadn't bothered telling him.

'She's a copper – and a Clash fan,' said Callum. 'The woman who sent them. Odd to think, that. Though I suppose coppers need music, like the rest of us.'

Martin, his interest in the subject terminated, stood up. He was off to Downing Street – 'to try and contain the next publicity crisis'.

'Crisis? What crisis?' said Callum, with a grin, but Martin only scowled, as if some things were too serious to joke about.

'It's not ready. It's just not ready,' said Nigel Merryweather, shaking his head.

Freddie puffed out his cheeks. 'It never *is* ready, dear, until you send them out on first night.'

They were in the last stages of rehearsal for *The Ragged Trousered Philanthropists*. The previews were close now. Freddie had never put so much time into a musical before, partly as a distraction from the woes at home and partly in defiance of the strikers threatening to close them down. To think that a tribute to Victorian working men might be undone by their very heirs! The music, which was Nigel's department, was still a bit rough around the edges, but it wasn't the insoluble chaos he was suggesting. He turned to Marie Haynes, his choreographer, a stick-thin former dancer with a crucial and heartening touch of the drill sergeant.

'Marie?'

She narrowed her shrewd, kohl-black eyes. 'We're getting

there. Even the ones who can't actually dance – and we all know who they are – seem to be responding to the whip. I'm pleased with them.'

That's what he liked about Marie – straightforward, encouraging, professional. If she saw a problem she didn't panic, but she didn't let it slide either. There really were members of the cast who couldn't dance ('two left feet, darling') and yet by painstaking effort Marie trained them to a point where it looked like they could. He sometimes wondered at her patience with them.

'But it's not ready.'

'Don't keep saying that, Nigel, it's most unhelpful. We'll do the tech rehearsal on Tuesday, as we agreed, and if there's something really amiss, well, we'll deal with it. I thought Romilly sounded wonderful the last time we ran it.'

Even Nigel, faint-hearted, fusspot Nigel, agreed on that point. Romilly Sargent was as good as Freddie had dared to hope. She inhabited the role of Annie with a poise and a drive that carried all before her. Her example had encouraged the others to up their game, and despite the inconvenience of the strikes at the theatre – or perhaps because of them – it had bonded the actors in a fierce unanimity of purpose. The advance ticket sales had been strong, and the poster for the show – a Victorian brick wall upon which a man on a ladder had just finished painting in bold white caps THE RAGGED TROUSERED PHILANTHROPISTS – expressed both the story's lament (the high prison wall of capitalism) and its revolutionary pluck (the defiant graffiti of socialism). Freddie had almost sung his thanks to the art department.

His good mood was enhanced on returning to his office to read Hannah Strode's profile of him in that morning's *Ensign*. He had telephoned her a few days into the new year, as arranged, to discuss how she would break the news of his affair with Nicola Mayman, though when he told her that he wouldn't be moving out of the family home Hannah had to conceal her disappointment. The affair was over, the marriage was holding steady – which left something of a hole in the piece she had written. 'I'm sorry to dash your hopes of a scoop,' he said, 'though given your decency in holding off for so long I feel I owe you one.' Yes, you bloody do, thought Hannah, who agreed to accept two front-row seats on opening night and a guarantee that she would have first dibs on the story of Freddie's marriage, should it happen to undergo a material change – collapse, for instance. Freddie knew he'd got away with that one, and he could even smile at the occasional feline phrase Hannah had used to scratch him ('While Selves claims to dislike publicity, his alleged shyness has never yet prevented him from retreating into the limelight').

Dawn, who had put her head round the door, asked him what he thought of the piece. 'Not bad at all,' he replied. 'Miss Strode has done me proud.'

'Her interviews are usually much tougher than that,' Dawn remarked. 'She must have fallen for your charm.' Freddie returned a complacent shrug, as if to say *She's only human*.

'Oh, Dawn,' he said, calling her back. 'I wonder if you'd mind slipping out and getting me a sandwich for lunch.'

She stared at him. 'What?'

'A sandwich – you know the sort of thing, made from bread?'

'But . . . you never have a sandwich. Ever.'

'Yes, well, new year, new diet. This photograph here makes me look rather . . .'

'Porky?'

Freddie shot a look at Dawn's moon face, apparently innocent of offence. 'I was going to say "heavyset" . . .'

When she had gone, he considered his reflection in the narrow mirror of his dressing room: the idea of 'working oneself to the bone' had absolutely no application in his case. On the contrary, the harder he worked, the heftier he became. While some drank to relieve pressure, he ate. Food calmed him, that was the long and short of it. The fat and thin of it. His doctor didn't seem to mind his drinking and smoking, but he was stern about watching his cholesterol. Freddie was going to be fifty this year, and the last thing he could afford to do was fall ill. He had too much responsibility and too many people dependent on him. The mood at home had settled, at least. A tense cordiality reigned between Linda and himself, and if the boys noticed the strain they didn't say anything. He didn't even mind the spare room – it reminded him of student digs, and all the *nostalgie de la boue* of sleeping with a girl in a single bed.

What he couldn't put right was his relationship with Nicola. He had offended her grossly with his accusations of treachery, and now she wouldn't return his calls. In his lonelier moments he felt real remorse. Of course he wasn't the first man to have behaved in a cavalier fashion towards his mistress – cancelling dates at the last minute, privileging his own time over hers – but he had always justified it to himself as a mutual convenience. Some of it must have been enjoyable for Nicola, after all, the fancy dinners, the weekends away, the thoughtfully chosen gifts, not to mention the cachet of being squired by the most influential theatre director of his age. But he knew, deep down, he had been guilty of something that no one who claims to love another should be: he had taken her for granted.

Dawn returned to the office half an hour later bearing a cheese and pickle sandwich wrapped in greaseproof paper. He ate it in three mouthfuls. How on earth could something so exiguous properly be called 'lunch'? By mid-afternoon he was starving and had to nip down to the canteen to get a Mars bar and a packet of crisps from the vending machine. 'A Mars a day ...' Not quite what the doctor ordered – but the doctor needn't find out.

Vicky, who had already clocked up four hours' surveillance in the obbo van, was leafing through the *Mirror* when Prichard nudged her.

'Oi oi. I think this is him.'

They were parked outside a pub on Cleveland Street in Fitzrovia. Vicky put her eye to the spyhole and saw a gangly, ill-kempt man ambling up the street. As he got closer something jolted inside her.

'I know this feller. He's a dealer called George Foley.'

'Ah, so Kenney introduced yer. Well, if I'm not mistaken, he's carrying in that rucksack of his a big wodge of cash—'

'How d'you know?'

Prichard fixed her with a disbelieving stare. 'What d'you think we've been waiting for all morning? A deal's about to go down, so look sharp.'

They watched as Foley stopped outside a dingy-looking terrace, knocked, and looked around the street, measuringly, while he waited. His knock was answered, he entered the house, and the door closed. Prichard was immediately on his radio to the station.

'Tell Kenney to bring the hurry-up to Cleveland Street, number 23. Yeah . . . George is there now.'

Ten minutes later an unmarked police car pulled up outside the pub, and two more plain clothes got out. One of them was Kenney. Vicky and Prichard climbed out of the van. The January morning was bitter, and she blew on her hands to warm them up. They crossed the road and stopped outside number 23. Filthy net curtains shielded the windows; the plaster around the door was grey and peeling. Prichard took out a Yale key from his pocket and softly inserted it in the lock. The door opened without a sound. He stood on the threshold, his ear cocked. With a warning finger to his lips he indicated to Vicky to follow him inside.

They sidled into the empty hallway. Voices could be heard from a room upstairs, and Vicky, surprised at the lack of muscle, joined Prichard in his creeping ascent. She could hear a man's laugh through the door at the far end of the landing. Prichard, with a smirk, tapped on the door before pushing it open. Two black men and the one Vicky knew as George sat in a huddle around a low table on which beer cans and loaded ashtrays rested. An old bulldog lay half asleep in front of a floor heater. The rubbery stink of dope curtained the air.

All three looked bemused by their entrance. Vicky realised it was her being there that had thrown them: they had no inkling that a woman might also be a police detective. George, who hadn't recognised her from their brief meeting on the Tube, rose from his chair. 'What's this – you Jehovah's?'

Prichard folded his arms like a schoolteacher and half laughed. 'You wish we were Jehovah's. Drug Squad. We heard a whisper there's cannabis for sale – fetch a nice little tickle.'

One of the black guys was on his feet and opening the window. The other was already moving to the door. Vicky made to stop him but Prichard said, 'Don't bother. He's not going anywhere.' This was soon confirmed by the sound of a scuffle on the stairs: he had collided with Kenney and his partner coming up. The other man had taken a look at the drop outside the window and decided against it. George in the meantime was protesting at their intrusion: 'I've 'ad it up to here with your lot,' he said. 'I know my rights. I'm allowed to pay a visit to a friend's without some bogey hassling me.' He turned to his friend, still standing at the window. ''Ere, Barry, you got any idea what's goin' on? Did you leave the door on the snick?'

Barry shook his head. He wasn't going to say a word.

'What's this one frontin' off about?' asked Kenney, who had appeared in the doorway. At his back the other plain clothes had hold of the fugitive.

'Sez he knows his rights,' Prichard replied sardonically.

Kenney looked at George as though they'd never met before. 'Shall we do this the easy way?'

'What does that mean?'

'It means, are you gonna show me where you've stashed it or do we have to turn this place upside down?' Vicky had her eyes on Barry, so she was well placed to notice the inadvertent glance he cut at the mangy sofa. Underneath her breath she confided this to Kenney, who nodded.

'You won't find nothin' here,' said George.

Prichard sighed, as if the bluff were beneath him. Kenney, now wearing gloves, removed the cushions from the sofa, and taking a Stanley knife from his overcoat, scored an incision along the top of it. He plucked at the stuffing, a cheap foam the colour of custard.

George looked on in disgust. 'You're gonna have to replace that.'

'Mm. Chippendale, is it?' said Kenney, still absorbed in disembowelling the sofa. The blade of his knife was too small, so he was compelled to tear at it with his hands. The foam seemed more plentiful than a single sofa could contain, and the more he pulled out the more comical seemed the effort, as if it were part of some mad challenge on *It's a Knockout*. He'll look a right fool if there's nothing in there, thought Vicky – and he'll blame me for the bad tip-off. George was observing him with scornful nonchalance: maybe he would get his sofa replaced after all. Barry's posture was tense, his expression opaque.

His knee braced against the sofa's back, Kenney had his arm plunged right into its guts, checking for obstacles. Suddenly he stopped, and Vicky wondered for a moment if he'd got his arm stuck. Prichard must have thought the same, because he had bent down to say, 'D'you need some help there, Alan?'

Kenney shook his head. There was a long pause as he tried to adjust his body so as to free himself from the sofa's foam jaws. Finally he disengaged his arm – and there in his grasp was a dun-coloured brick of hash. Vicky, convinced a giant anticlimax was in the offing, felt a sweet relief. In the meantime Prichard had emptied George's rucksack onto the table: four bundles of worn-out tenners were its chief contents.

George looked at it sullenly. 'No law against carrying cash around, is there?'

'No,' Prichard replied, 'but there is one against using it to buy a shitload of cannabis.'

Some minutes later a couple of uniformed officers arrived,

and Kenney directed them to cuff Barry and the other one. They were hauled downstairs without further ado. Once they were gone, the mood in the room changed. George relaxed, his indignation forgotten; he appeared almost cheerful. Prichard offered him a cigarette, and they bantered a while about the destruction of the sofa.

George said to Kenney, 'You shoulda just gone through the back of it, like I told yer, instead of pullin' it inside out.'

And now Vicky realised what was going on. George had helped them set the whole thing up. It was clear he would walk free, and possibly take the drugs with him. When he and the other plain clothes had gone, Kenney sat down at the table and began counting the cash, at bank clerk's speed. Prichard watched, leaning against the door, arms folded. Half of it went back into George's rucksack. The other half he had split into smaller wads, one of which he handed to Prichard. Then he handed one to Vicky, who hesitated.

'What's this for?'

'A perk,' he replied with a wink. 'Buy yourself something nice.'

'But . . . ' She had no clue what to say. This was her initiation test. She didn't want it, but if she objected it would put her at odds with them. The decision had to be instant. She could sense Prichard staring at her. With a little shrug she took the shabby wad. 'Thanks.'

That evening she telephoned Wicks on his private line. She had thought about the bust all day, and felt that a line had been crossed: nothing good could come of this.

'I went into that house a police officer, and I came out of it feeling – well, like a criminal.'

'You did the right thing. If you'd refused it you'd never have won their trust. Now they think you're one of them.'

'What d'you mean – "one of them"?'

Wicks paused a moment. 'Vicky, you know what we talked

about before, A10 and coppers on the take? Well, an investigation is on the go, and like I told you, it concerns the whole of the Met. It's called Operation Bad Apple, and it's serious enough for the Home Secretary to be involved. An outside force, from Somerset, is running it, and I'm one of their liaison officers.'

'Undercover?'

'Of course. I couldn't do it if I wasn't. What you saw at today's bust is exactly the kind of evidence we need. This is the way we get them, the likes of Prichard and Kenney. There'll be others, without question.'

'Why didn't you tell me about this – Bad Apple – before?'

'Because I wanted to make absolutely sure I could trust you. You could have kept shtum about that cash today. But you didn't, and that's why you're gonna be vital to this investigation.'

'Won't they suspect me – of snitching?'

'No. You've got a cool head. Just play along with them, and be prepared. They may want you in on something bigger next time.'

A sudden panic lurched inside her. The responsibility of it – the danger – had become abruptly present.

'Sir, I'm not sure I'm the right person for this . . . '

His voice in reply was steady and assured. 'But you are. I know you are. And by the way, stop calling me "sir" – it makes me feel old.'

14

Freddie stepped out of the lift to find Bob Bewley and Robin Piddock waiting for him, their faces set as if in mourning. *Who's died?* was his first thought.

'Morning, gentlemen,' he said, looking from one to the other. 'All well?'

Bob shook his head sadly. 'You're not going to believe this . . .'

'Tell me.'

'Romilly Sargent has broken her leg. Her agent called, ten minutes ago.'

Freddie stared at him, uncomprehending. 'What?'

'Took a tumble down the stairs. Last night. She's in the hospital – a major fracture, apparently.'

It felt as though a pin had been stuck in him and his entire body was helplessly deflating. Just when he thought they were out of the woods . . . the staff revolt abandoned, the unions kept at bay, rehearsals going like a dream, ticket sales on the up. Romilly in the form of her life. All too good to be true. *Break a leg!* In all his years as a director how many times had he unthinkingly cried those words? He would never say it again.

'The stairs – how – what was she . . . ?' He appeared unable to order his words into a full sentence.

Bob sighed. 'She slipped. She fell. She'll be out for months.'

Robin Piddock said, 'I was wondering if you had any thoughts about the press release. The sooner we get something out . . .'

Freddie looked at him askance. *The Pillock.* 'Robin, please, can you hold your bleeding horses? I'm still in shock. It might take a while before I can collect my "thoughts". Your press release is *not* my priority at this moment.'

'I was only thinking—'

'Thanks, Robin, that'll be all for now,' said Bob firmly. 'We'll get back to you when we've talked it over. Fred, shall we?'

In a near-hallucinatory state of shock Freddie gravitated down the corridor to his office. Bob asked Dawn to round up Marie, Nigel and Mike with all haste, to bring coffee for them all. 'And biscuits, please,' added Freddie absently. He would need them for stress relief. Once they had assembled, and Bob had repeated the inconceivable news of Romilly Sargent's accident, a dismal hush fell on the room. Freddie felt almost too sick to speak, but aware that leadership was required of him he roused himself. Previews were two weeks away. It was too late to postpone the opening, and they couldn't afford to lose the ticket revenues. Romilly's understudy was an able young woman, but she had neither the experience nor the name to carry a major show like *Ragged Trousers*.

'So our only option is to seek a replacement. Annie is a demanding role – singing, dancing, acting, and winning the hearts of the audience to boot. To get the whole thing down inside two weeks, well, we're looking for a miracle worker.'

He looked around the room, waiting. Mike Findlay cleared his throat before saying, 'The obvious candidate is Nicola Mayman, isn't it?'

All eyes turned to Freddie, who gave a slow shake of his head. It pained him just to hear her name spoken. 'Even if she wanted to do it – which I doubt – she's just signed up for a second series of *Unlucky Charms*. I think shooting starts pretty soon.'

'You think, or you know?'

'She won't do it,' said Freddie decisively. 'She was quite sore about being overlooked for it the first time.'

Without much enthusiasm they began batting around other names. The problem, as Freddie perceived it, was that Romilly had made the part of Annie so much her own it was well-nigh impossible to imagine another actress stepping up. Her virtuosity had spoilt it for anyone else.

'Let's think about this,' said Bob. 'Who's the most accomplished stage actress at work today?'

There followed some back-and-forth, until they settled on the name of Isabel Duncannon, beautiful, haughty, mid-thirties – and award-winning. She had made her name with Shaw and Ibsen, but was known to be looking for a new challenge. Nigel reckoned her singing voice was more than passable, and Marie was confident about getting her up to speed with the dancing. It seemed she might also be available at short notice.

Before their excitement ran away with them Freddie decided to pull on the reins. 'Look, I speak as the enemy of typecasting, but Isabel Duncannon is all wrong for this. Annie is a low-born, Mancunian spitfire – a natural rebel. Isabel playing a northern firebrand just won't work. She's the definition of uptight, I mean upright, Englishness. It'd be like casting Celia Johnson as ... Eliza Doolittle.'

'It's only acting, Freddie. You never know, she might surprise us!'

'She might, but in ways too awful to contemplate. I'm sorry – it can't be done.'

Mike and Marie were flicking through the pages of *Spotlight* and its long gallery of headshots in black and white, each with their different expression or smile – cavalier, winsome, hopeful, trustworthy, innocent, affable, wry. And all of them seeming to beg the same thing: *hire me*. Freddie could never bear to look at it for long, he found the pathos of it too upsetting. Some of those faces would make a success of acting, of course; but many more would fall by the wayside, not necessarily because they lacked talent, but because there simply wasn't enough work to go round.

'How about this one?' said Mike, pointing to a sloe-eyed beauty. 'Moira Light.'

Freddie shook his head. 'Belying her name, she's heavy and dull.'

'Stephanie Parish?'

'Can't sing, can't dance, and certainly can't act.'

'Judy Banson?'

'Never done theatre. And she's pregnant. Apart from that, very promising.'

The stream of suggestions became desultory. Whenever a name won support from two of them, someone else would intervene with a persuasive objection. An hour went by, two hours, and still they had nobody.

Freddie said, 'Does anyone know if Edie Greenlaw's available?' That at least made them laugh. Edie Greenlaw, grande dame of the London stage, had just turned eighty-two.

'She's such a trouper she'd probably do it if we asked her,' said Bob.

After another silence Nigel turned to Freddie. 'Are you absolutely one hundred per cent sure Nicola Mayman wouldn't want it? She was keen as mustard when we auditioned her.'

Mike nodded. 'Worth asking her, Fred, surely?'

'I told you, she's due to start filming—'

'Oh, pish! They can film whenever. This is the National Music Hall offering a once-in-a-lifetime shot.'

Freddie sensed that all eyes were upon him. *Mightn't* she do it? It would require an awful lot of wheedling and begging on his part. Time was when he would have backed himself to succeed; if he was in the mood he could bend just about anyone to his will. But Nicola was different: she knew his tricks, and she would probably take vengeful delight in turning him down.

They were waiting for an answer.

'I can only ask her.'

Callum was preparing to leave for work when the phone rang. It was Sean, calling from a public phone box.

'I need a favour, Cal. Going up north for a few days, just to see friends, but I don't wanna leave me stuff here – you know, passport, money an' that. There's break-ins here all the time, think I told you.'

'You want me to mind it?'

'Would ya? Can I bring it round in a bit? You see, I've gotta go this afternoon. Me train ticket's booked and all . . . '

'Well, I'm just about to leave the house – why not bring it to my office? It's just off the Strand.'

'Ah, that's grand of yer, mate. Just let me get a pen and I'll take down the address.'

At the Holywell staff common room Callum made himself a coffee and settled into an armchair. Someone had left a copy of today's *Ensign*, which he began riffling through. There was a long interview with Frederick Selves, director of the National Music Hall, to herald next month's opening of his new musical *The Ragged Trousered Philanthropists*. Callum wouldn't ordinarily have been interested, but the piece was so well written and entertaining that he read it through to the end, at which point he noticed the writer's byline. Hannah Strode. The name jolted him. He hadn't thought of her in a while, or rather, he had managed not to keep thinking about her whenever the memory of their accidental 'date' recurred. He felt another needling of regret. He reread the article, savouring its sly dabs of humour in the changed light of its author's identity, and realised – with a pang – that it was about the missed opportunity.

He was marking essays in the office when a knock came at the door and Sean entered. He flinched. They had not seen one another since Christmas.

'Some haircut you've got there, mate,' he said, shaking hands.

'Aye. My sister thinks she might want to be a hairdresser.'

Sean smiled. 'Made yer look a right desperado, hasn't she?'

As well as a rucksack he handed over an old sports bag.

'What's in there – your porno mags?'

'Ha. All me fuckin' worldlies, more like. Bit of money I've

saved, clothes 'n' that. You'll keep it somewhere safe, yeah?'

'Safe as houses, don't worry. Where are you off to, by the way?'

'Up to the Lakes – some mates are getting the boat over. Just for a wee holiday.'

While Callum made tea Sean wandered over to his office window, with its view onto the Strand. He whistled softly through his teeth.

'Will you look at that mess down there?'

Callum joined him at the window. He was becoming so used to the sight of uncollected rubbish on the street that he passed it by – as he had this morning – almost without noticing. The black bin bags resembled a slimy, lumpy effluent vomited up from doorways and drains. Cardboard boxes and smaller bags of crap mingled with the mounds. He couldn't remember when the bin men had gone on strike. London had always seemed to him untidy and litter-strewn; but this was something else, a towering rubbish dump that choked the pavements and stank to high heaven. Like everyone else, he tried to ignore it.

'The rats'll be havin' a field day on that,' said Sean.

'Just read in the paper the gravediggers have gone on strike, up in Liverpool. They can't even bury their dead.'

'Fuck's sake. This country.'

Callum handed him a mug of tea, and the talk soon turned to other things – work, family, football.

When students began to call at the office Sean took the hint and picked up his rucksack. 'I'll be on me way,' he said, though Callum insisted on walking him to the college's front gate. As they passed through the nineteenth-century stone quadrangle Sean looked about in amused wonder, and made an admiring comment on the quiet of the place – you didn't get that on a building site. They were passing the lodge when Callum was hailed by Juliet Barwell, the classics lecturer he had briefly carried a torch for. As they exchanged hellos he noticed her glance slide enquiringly to Sean, in his donkey jacket and workman's boots.

'Uh, Juliet, this is my friend Sean . . . '

Sean raised his hand in greeting. 'Nice to meet you.'

She squinted at him. 'You sound like you're from the same part of the world as Callum.'

'Aye. We were at school together in Newry. He was the one who won all the prizes.'

Callum, embarrassed, laughed this off. 'Sean's been working down at the National Music Hall.'

Juliet's face lit up with interest. 'Oh, you're a musician?'

Sean sniggered. 'He means I work on the site of the Music Hall – as a labourer. The new extension?'

'Ah, sorry, I thought—'

'I do play the tin whistle.'

Callum, alive to the confusion he had started, traded some inconsequential chat with Juliet before they made their excuses and went on their way. Out on the street, Sean gave a little nod over his shoulder.

'Was that the woman you told me about – the one you fancied?'

'Sort of. We went out to the pub a couple of times.'

'Did you get a ride off her?' He cackled when Callum returned a weary expression of disapproval. 'See you when I get back, big man.'

Freddie stood on the steps of the mansion block at Cranley Gardens, blowing on his raw hands. The January temperature was so bitter it pinched his ears and made his nose run; flakes of snow had begun to whirl about his head. If she refused to answer the door he didn't know what—

The intercom crackled. 'Hello?'

'Nicola. It's Freddie.'

A pause followed. 'What are you doing here?' Her tone was flat, unamused.

'I need to talk to you, and since you won't answer my phone calls I've had to haul my cold carcass all the way down here.'

'You mean Terry has driven you from the office.'

'As a matter of fact I got the bus. There were no cabs and the car's in the repair shop.'

'You never did!'

'Look, I'm freezing my balls off here. Will you *please* let me in?'

'I don't want to hear any more of your apologies. I'm sick of them.'

'You won't. I'm not here to talk about us.'

'What, then?'

'A matter of urgency.'

Another pause came, then the buzzer sounded.

When he got to her landing the door was ajar; she hadn't deigned to welcome him. He walked through, down the hall, and found her sitting cross-legged on the sofa. She stared at him, unblinking, and with a movement indicated the armchair opposite. He unbuttoned his coat and sat down.

'It's nice to see you again,' he said coaxingly.

She returned a small, closed-mouth smile that didn't crease her eyes. It was clear she intended to have exactly nothing to do with charm. All right, he thought, just get it done and then get out.

'I wondered if you'd heard – about Romilly Sargent. She broke her leg, Sunday evening.' Nicola's eyes widened momentarily, before her expression regained its flinty composure. 'Which of course means we need a new Annie. Previews start Monday week, so we have a little under thirteen days' rehearsal. I don't know how anyone might learn the part in that time, but there you are. We've just had a long crisis meeting, and there's only one name we could all agree upon.'

Her face remained poker-straight. 'I see.'

He waited, but there was nothing else. 'So . . . I was wondering if – I'd be grateful if you'd give me an answer.'

'You haven't asked me anything yet.'

She was going to make this awkward. 'All right. We really want you to do this, and not just because you're the best. It would also be a personal favour to me. So, please, will you?'

She narrowed her eyes, coolly appraising him. Then she said, 'Did you *really* get the bus here?'

Freddie clicked his tongue in irritation. '*Yes*. The number 14, if you're going to take notes. That's how important this is – *I took public transport*.'

Nicola shook her head, and he noticed the faintest shadow of a smile. 'Ha. Freddie on a bus ... it's like hearing the Queen has nipped out to buy her own loo roll. You must have been desperate!'

'As you can see,' he said, rising from the chair. She was going to turn him down, he could tell, but first she had to torment him, like a cat playing with a mouse. 'Look, I haven't got time for this. I'm not going to beg. I just want an answer.'

She tucked in her chin, as though surprised at his sudden combative tone. 'All right. Yes. The answer's yes.'

He looked at her, stunned. 'Really?'

'What, did you think I'd turn it down?!'

Freddie, in an onrush of gratitude, sank to his knees. 'Oh thank God. Nicola – thank you. This is – I swear, I will be forever in your debt.'

She laughed delightedly. 'It's not my debt you should worry about, love. I'm contracted to start filming *Unlucky Charms* in three weeks. Second series. They've got the locations scouted and everything. If you want me, you'll have to pay London Weekend for it, I'm afraid.'

'So be it,' he said with a shrug. 'I'll pay 'em whatever they want.' He meant it, too; this unexpected turn of events had almost dizzied him with relief. He described what had happened to Romilly, the panic at the Music Hall, his despair at finding a replacement.

She stared at him. 'You know, if you'd given me the part in the first place I'd probably have done it for free.'

'I don't think so,' he replied. 'In any case, you know I had to give it to her. The others would never have forgiven me.'

'Funny how things turn out,' she mused. 'I can understand why you cast Romilly – I mean, she's wonderful. And I bet she would have given the performance of her life. But a slip on the stairs and everything changes in an instant. It's just all luck, isn't it?'

'Well, luck and talent. Helps to have both.' He looked at his watch. 'Will it take you long to get ready?'

'You want to go now?' Nicola said, taken aback.

'Yes, and with all haste. We'll start rehearsing you this afternoon.'

She rose from the sofa and was making for her bedroom when she stopped. 'By the way, did you ever find out who shopped you to the press?'

He shook his head. 'I have my suspicions about the Pillock – Robin Piddock, our head of PR. He doesn't like me, and he knows I don't like him.'

'All the same, he wouldn't sabotage you, would he?'

He sighed. 'You'd be surprised at what people are capable of. Now, chop-chop. We're out of here in five minutes.'

Before he left for the day Callum went down to the college's basement cloakroom, where he had his own locker. He reckoned this would be the safest place to leave Sean's sports bag. The problem, he soon discovered, was trying to fit it through the locker door. The bag wasn't large, but it had been packed tight, and its bulk proved an agonising inch or so too wide. He tried squeezing it upright, then diagonally; it wouldn't go.

'Having trouble?'

He turned to find Jim Lewin, a college porter, monitoring his efforts. Jim, pouchy-faced, wheezy-chested, was a committed smoker and spy, and would regularly supply Callum with titbits of staff gossip. He couldn't fathom how Jim knew so much, given he was not actually a member of staff – but the information was usually sound.

'Oh, hi, Jim,' he said. 'Just trying to store this bag in here, but it's a wee bit narrow, as you see.'

Jim, sizing up the angles, took hold of the bag and attempted to insert it himself, but the thing was stubbornly refused accommodation.

'If it weren't so bulky you could prob'ly squeeze it in. Maybe take something out of it?'

Callum gave a demurring *hmm*. He didn't care to unzip the bag and delve into Sean's things – it didn't feel right – and in any case he didn't want to let on to Jim that it wasn't his bag anyway.

'Looks like I'll have to take it home, Jim. All well with you?'

Jim puffed out his cheeks. 'Wouldn't say that. They're puttin' the arm on us to go on strike again. It's a disgrace, I'm telling you. None of us want out, but we have to fall in line cos the union's on at us . . . ' He continued in this vein for some minutes, deploring the effect of strikes on 'honest working people'. It was a refrain Callum had heard before. The strikes had become a contagion, a fever, so fast were they spreading; the smallest grievance could trigger a walkout.

By the end of Jim's aria of complaint Callum felt faintly exhausted, but all he said was, 'It must be very frustrating.'

Jim closed his eyes, as if the world's follies were his personal cross to bear. 'I'm telling you . . . This country's going to hell.'

15

Hannah and Tara were queueing for lunch in the staff canteen at the *Ensign*. They pushed their dinner trays along the piped metal rail towards the serving station, where brown meat (was it chicken?) and brown mulch (also unidentified) were being dolloped onto plates. The very odour of the stuff seemed brown. Hannah was in the middle of a story from the weekend when the sight of the food reminded her of something else, and she smiled.

'Hey, I was walking down Brick Lane on Sunday when I saw the funniest thing. There was rubbish all along the pavement, loads of discarded food, too, like everyone had just dumped their lunch there—'

'God, isn't everywhere *filthy* at the moment?'

'Anyway, there are masses of pigeons on patrol round there, and I happen to spot this one scavenging in the gutter. It's poking at this mangy old bagel, obviously dying to eat it. Somehow it gets its beak in there – honestly, I was mesmerised just watching this – and then its entire head slips through the hole. So there's this pigeon strutting about wearing a dirty bagel around its neck!'

Tara shrieked a laugh. 'Maybe it was a kosher pigeon . . .'

'It looked more like the pigeon lord mayor, proudly displaying his mayoral chain. Only now it had the bagel around its neck the stupid creature couldn't reach it with its beak. Like Tantalus.'

'Who?'

'You know, Tantalus. From Greek mythology? He was punished by Zeus or someone by being tied to a spot where he couldn't reach high enough to eat or low enough to drink.'

Tara, flinching slightly at the steaming brown food just deposited on her plate, said, 'Mightn't have felt so bad if he'd seen what we have to eat.'

They carried their loaded trays to a table by the window. Outside the late-January afternoon looked gaunt and grey. The mood in the office, however, was buoyant; the newspaper continued to thrive on the miserable stasis that was throttling the country. The continuous bad news had given a boost to sales, and with *The Times* out of action the *Ensign* was picking up new readers. The only snag in the zipper, as the editor had called it, was the lorry drivers' strike: could they get the paper out to the provinces in time?

'You must be chuffed about the Freddie Selves interview,' said Tara. It had been praised again at morning conference.

'Yeah, but I think it won points mainly for not being about the strikes – there's only so much you can read about a national breakdown.'

'It was good, though,' Tara insisted. 'It had your satirical touch.'

'It doesn't seem to have bothered him unduly. His office sent me two tickets for the opening night next week. D'you want to come?'

Tara wrinkled her nose. 'To a musical?'

'Why not? He knows how to put on a show, old Freddie. Come on, you might enjoy it.'

But Tara was shaking her head, unpersuaded. 'Why don't you ask your feller?'

'What feller?'

'The one you went to stay with at new year.'

Hannah made a face. She hadn't seen Christopher since the Nosebleed Debacle. That morning she would have liked to escape back to London, but there were no trains on New Year's

Day and she was compelled to spend another excruciating twenty-four hours at the Casaltines' house party. Christopher had been somewhat distant with her, either from embarrassment or else because the infamous Devora had got her claws back into him. Hannah couldn't tell, and during the awkward drive back from Kent she convinced herself she didn't care. When he dropped her off at home he parted with the words, 'I'll ring you.' More than three weeks later she'd heard not a dicky bird.

Her feelings about this had fluctuated. On the one hand her pride was piqued, and she fumed at his ill manners. Was his intention simply to disappear? Then good riddance! On the other, she found her thoughts returning to him with dismaying frequency, and began to wonder if she had been at fault. She sensed she'd made a bit of a fool of herself that night, talking too loudly and throwing herself around on the dance floor. She ought to have shown more restraint, maybe. Then again she hadn't *deliberately* had a nosebleed, and the cocaine had been his idea after all.

'I'm not quite sure about him, to tell you the truth.'

Tara looked puzzled. 'Really? I thought you said he was tall, dark and handsome. Sounds all right to me.'

'Yeah, but there's an ex of his hanging round. I can't tell if there's something between them still.'

'Look, he asked you to spend new year with him, right? Meeting all his friends? That's keen, in my book.'

'That's what I thought,' said Hannah, 'so why has he not been in touch?'

Tara narrowed her eyes like a gunfighter. 'He might just need encouragement. He's made all the running so far, now it's your turn. Show him who's boss – men like a bit of that.'

Hannah nodded, though she doubted her friend's insight into male psychology. In her experience men didn't like being told 'who's boss', and they especially didn't like it coming from a woman. In other circumstances she would have written off someone who hadn't bothered to call, but with Christopher she sensed unfinished business: he *had* been keen, and, Nosebleed Debacle aside, she'd done nothing to put him off. Might it be worth another try?

When she returned to the office she found a buff A4 envelope on her desk. She hadn't noticed it when the post had come this morning – and now saw that it had been hand-delivered. Inside she found the current issue of the *Starry Plough*, the newspaper of the Irish Republican Socialist Party. She had seen this paper intermittently in the years since the Balcombe Street siege, though it wasn't easy to come by on the mainland. She checked in the envelope for a sender's note – there was none – and began to flick through it, most of it party news from Derry, Belfast and Dublin. There were interviews with Official Sinn Fein politicians, a long commemoration of the Easter Rising, and an editorial on the continuing war against 'British imperial rule' in Ireland. She was nearly done with it when her eye fell on a photograph of the Shadow Home Secretary, Anthony Middleton. The accompanying piece briefly described his career before focusing on his Unionist politics and his public demands for tougher military action in Northern Ireland. As a one-time POW himself, Middleton was reckoned to have a vital grasp of the 'prisoner mentality', specifically in regard to Republican inmates of the H-Blocks. It emphasised his role as a formidable enemy of 'the struggle', and therefore near the top of the Provisionals' hit list.

The moment she read that Hannah intuited this was the piece she had been meant to notice. But who had sent it? Her writing on Ulster was so well known in political and media circles that it could really have been anyone. She got up and walked over to the deputy editor's office, where she found him in a familiar posture, feet up on the desk, yarning away to a junior reporter. 'Keith, can I have a word?' Keith Carstairs invited her to take a seat, and sent the junior on his way.

'Loved that piece on Freddie Sellers, Hannah.'

'Freddie Selves.'

'Yeah, him. What can I do for you?'

'I just found this on my desk,' she said, setting down the *Starry Plough* open at the page on Anthony Middleton. 'D'you remember, I did that profile of him in the autumn, around the time of the death threats?'

Carstairs gave the thing a cursory glance. 'Yeah. So?'

'This paper is the official organ of the Shinners. If they're making a noise about him it would suggest something's afoot.'

'Mm. But what's the story? A piece about the Shadow Home Secretary in a Sinn Fein propaganda rag isn't gonna stop the press.'

'I think there's something more behind it. You have to ask – why now? My guess is that whoever sent me this knows there's something about to happen. Maybe they've smuggled in some new armaments. The death threats to Middleton were posted months ago, and there's been nothing since. This could be the reminder.'

'Aren't they more likely to target Mason? The Northern Ireland Secretary is a much bigger fish, I'd say.'

'Too much security around him,' Hannah said, 'whereas Middleton doesn't seem to use police protection. Also, his hard-line policy on Ulster will be putting the wind up the Provos. You know, if Thatcher gets in . . . '

'All right then, keep digging. Have you talked to Ian?' Ian Waller was the paper's security correspondent and, in Hannah's view, no use at all.

'There's a copper I know in the Met. But I just wanted to make sure you're prepared to run this once I can confirm.'

'You're that confident?'

She nodded, and scooped up the *Starry Plough* on her way out. Two hours later, fed up with holding the line, Hannah was about to hang up when a voice surprised her at the other end.

'West End Central.' It was a young woman.

'CID? I'm trying to get hold of DCI David Wicks.'

'Sorry, he's not here. Can I help?'

'Maybe. Who am I talking to?'

'Detective Constable Tress. The DCI is in a meeting at the moment.'

Hannah paused. Tress: that name seemed familiar to her. 'This is Hannah Strode calling from the *Ensign*. I'm following up a story about the Shadow Home Secretary. I was wondering if there's been any renewal of that death threat from the IRA?'

'I haven't heard anything. We offered Mr Middleton an armed guard at the time, which he refused.'

'Why did he do that?'

'I'm not sure. Maybe because as a war hero he thinks it's beneath him.'

Hannah was warming to this one – the police were usually tight-lipped when a leftish paper like the *Ensign* began sniffing around. 'DC Tress . . . Aren't you the one who caught the Notting Dale Rapist?'

'Well, I helped with the investigation,' said Vicky. 'I didn't actually apprehend him.'

'When did you join CID?'

'A few months ago. Just after we closed the Notting Dale case. I'm still training, so it's really *Temporary* Detective Constable. Bit of a mouthful.'

'I see . . . ' Hannah began to tell her about the latest issue of the *Starry Plough* and the strong hint of battle stations: it seemed the Republicans were preparing to renew their campaign on the mainland. Senior political figures were sure to be targeted—

'Sorry to interrupt you, Miss, er, Strode—'

'It's Hannah.'

'—but there's another call on the boss's line. We're a bit short-handed here today.'

'Men run the world, and women answer the phone,' said Hannah, with a knowing laugh.

'What?'

'Nothing. Thanks for your help. Will you ask DCI Wicks to call me when he's back in the office?'

It wasn't until the afternoon that Vicky finally caught up with Wicks. He was coming down the corridor with a man she'd never seen before. They stopped, and he introduced her to DCI Alex Goddard, on secondment from Somerset Police. He had short, carroty-brown hair and a vulpine cast to his features. When he shook hands she felt the weight of his gaze on her, and with a nod to Wicks he left them together.

'Vicky, how are you?' Wicks said, laying a friendly hand on her arm.

'Good, thanks, sir,' she began. 'I wanted to say – Carol and I both wanted to thank you for supporting her case. For the sex assault unit.'

'Well, I've recommended it for a review, that's all,' he said.

'But that means a lot. It'll be taken seriously now that it's come from you.'

'I hope it will. Someone told me you left a message?'

'Yes, sir. A reporter from the *Ensign* – Hannah Strode – wanted to talk to you about Anthony Middleton. Said there are rumours about the IRA launching a new campaign over here.'

He brooded on this for a moment, before muttering that he'd get back to her. There were others passing on either side of them as they spoke, and Wicks, with a characteristic sidelong look, waited for the corridor to clear. His voice was low and quick. 'That man you just met, Goddard. He's here with the A10 unit from Somerset, leading Bad Apple. A copper who investigates coppers – so he won't be popular. He's good, and he knows what we're up to. Once he's got what he needs we can start cleaning this place up.'

'Why's he come from Somerset?'

'They needed to recruit a force from outside the Met, near enough for London not to be an inconvenience and far away enough for them not to be tainted. They picked Somerset. Keep your fingers crossed.'

*

Ireland and the Provisionals were back in the news, Callum noticed. It was reported from Belfast that Anthony Middleton had been conferring with the RUC and had let it be known that a security crackdown in Ulster would be top priority in the event of his becoming Secretary of State for Northern Ireland. The Provos had been quick to respond, reaffirming Middleton as a principal enemy of 'the struggle' and a legitimate target of their military operation. The MP continued to decline the offer of a personal security detail.

Callum, lost in thought, closed the newspaper and folded it. Something was bugging him, as persistent as a stone in his shoe. Of course he had lived in London long enough to feel the mood of prejudice against his countrymen. You only had to be overheard in a shop or a pub to realise you were suddenly an object of interest. Of suspicion. Sean's voice, with a carry louder than his, would often turn heads, and his talk, if not openly antagonistic, tended towards the satirical whenever the subject of British rule came up. In his company Callum tried to ensure it didn't, and would sometimes gesture warningly to him that they were being listened to; the faces around them were not always friendly. Sean didn't seem to care.

Callum could not feel as sanguine, however, and he wondered if his friend had ever been tempted to join the struggle, on the sly. As a courier perhaps? He opened his wardrobe and gazed at the sports bag Sean had entrusted to his care. This was what had been bothering him. He hadn't thought of it at the time, but the idea of Sean using his house as a drop had taken a reluctant hold. Could there be something dangerous – incriminating – concealed in it? He didn't really want to know. But what if there *was*? Should it come to light he might be implicated too – aiding and abetting, he supposed.

The longer the bag squatted there in the darkness of his wardrobe the more nagging its presence became. He leaned in and grasped it by the handles. He placed it on the bed and stared at it for some moments. Before he could persuade himself not to he pulled the zipper across, waited, then delved. There were clothes, shirts and jeans – as Sean had said – some balled-up socks and a pair of trainers. There was an envelope stuffed with tenners, his earnings from the building site, with sums scrawled in pencil on the back; a passport; a bunch of keys. The bulkiest object, its hard edges swaddled in an old T-shirt, briefly stirred his suspicion, but once investigated it turned out to be only a cassette player, similar to the one he owned. A C90 tape of the Dubliners was visible in the glassed loader. There was nothing sinister here. In fact the humble innocence of these belongings caused him a surge of shame. He had doubted Sean, betrayed his trust; he was really no better than any Paddy-fearing Brit on the street.

We've got away with it. We've got away with it. This was the line ringing through Freddie's head like a blessed refrain. It was Friday late afternoon, the weekend before the previews, and they had completed the first dress rehearsal of *The Ragged Trousered Philanthropists.* He had cut a couple of the ensemble numbers, shortened a very long middle section and dispensed with the narrator figure who'd been killing the pace. And somehow the whole thing had come together: whatever faults it might have had, it engrossed, it intrigued, it *moved.*

And Nicola – he raised his brimming eyes heavenwards – she had astonished him, astonished them all. When he had auditioned her for the part last year he had sensed the anxiety holding her back: she was game, but she never looked sufficiently at ease to shine, and once Romilly strutted her stuff there could be no doubt as to the winner. Well, that was then . . . Faced with a challenge Nicola had seized the part by the scruff. She took whatever ideas he presented in her stride and used them subtly – and they came back at him a hundred times better. Romilly had done this, too, marrying his suggestions to her own quicksilver instincts, but then he had expected it of her, the darling of the West End stage. Nicola's fame, based on a trashy TV drama, had possibly obscured the true talent beneath. In less than ten days she had not just learned the part of Annie, she had come to inhabit it – humorous, headstrong, vulnerable, persuasive, with a fine streak of oddity that Freddie hadn't bargained for. It was why he adored actors, really. The best gave you something you didn't even know you wanted.

Afterwards, seated halfway back into the stalls, he swapped notes on their progress with Nigel Merryweather and Marie Haynes. A mood of relief was palpable. Nigel was plainly awed, like Freddie, by the speed at which Nicola had immersed herself in the part and the alacrity with which she had mucked in with the rest of the cast. She didn't complain and she didn't ask for favours, in spite of the catching up she had to do. 'Hats off to her,' he said, 'and to you, Fred, for persuading her to do it.' Freddie hadn't told them how little persuasion it had required, but he was perfectly willing to take the credit. Nor did Marie, much tougher than Nigel, stint on her praise. Nicola wasn't a natural dancer, she said, but she had put in 'the effort of ten men' to get the moves down, and her energy had given them all a lift. Now the countdown was on.

Freddie felt a buoyancy lighten his steps as he returned to the office. *We've got away with it!* Improbable but true, and in time to come they would talk of the moment when *Ragged Trousers*, hanging by a thread, as it were, had been yanked to safety by his intervention. He had just exited the lift when along the corridor he saw Robin Piddock coming the other way. Such was the flame of goodwill warming in his chest that he decided to play nice with him. He was by now convinced that Piddock must have orchestrated the campaign of anonymous leaks about his financial and romantic misdemeanours. Time to clear the air, he thought.

'Robin! How are you?' he purred in his most amiable basso profundo.

Piddock checked his step, apparently surprised at this friendly overture. 'Erm, fine, fine. How are the rehearsals going?'

'Staggeringly well,' he beamed. 'The cast have done heroic work. They have cuffed the thing into shape in difficult circumstances – one might say it's a triumph of collaboration.'

'With no little help from yourself, I dare say.'

Freddie offered his most expansive shrug. 'We do what we can. We give what we have. The rest is ... on the knees of the gods!' He sensed that he was misquoting something here, but couldn't quite remember what.

Unaccustomed to such benignity Piddock seemed to relax, allowed himself a smile, and said, 'So we're all set for Monday night.'

'Indeed ... and henceforth we can agree to put our differences aside and pull together for the good of the company.' He fixed Piddock with a significant look on this last sentiment.

'Well, yes, but I think that's what we were—'

'I know we haven't always seen eye to eye, Robin, and that personal resentments perhaps got out of hand. But shall we now let bygones be bygones?'

Piddock stared at him for a moment, and Freddie couldn't tell if the twitch in his face expressed confusion or acknowledged past offences. Or both. But if he knew he had been rumbled he was not going to make an outright confession. 'We're both professionals, Freddie, which means we can agree to differ, so long as we get the job done.'

Freddie, hearing an admission – if not an apology – decided not to push it. 'I think we understand one another,' he said with a beatific nod.

Nicola had told him flatly there was 'no chance' of dinner *à deux* so Freddie had instead organised a late supper at his club with the show's principal collaborators – Bob, Nigel, Mike, Marie, the writer David Bartram, Joe Gaughan, the lyricist, and, on his hunch that she couldn't refuse an ensemble invitation, the leading lady. He had made sure to seat himself next to her. They had gathered in the small upstairs dining room where the hushed candlelight, thickly carpeted floor and smell of roasting meat had forged a convivial shelter from the arctic January evening outside. On the drive from Farringdon Road to Mayfair Freddie had averted his gaze from the city's tottering haystacks of rubbish. He hated the way the streets looked bedraggled: what use in paying your rates if London was going to resemble a Third World shanty town?

The arrival of the *boeuf en daube* put a temporary muffler on these narked ruminations. He looked around the table at his guests, faces animated and aglow with the wine he had considerately provided. '70 Lafite was undoubtedly an extravagance for this lot, and of course they were tipping it back like it was Ribena. Seated on his other side, Mike was raking his gaze about the room in a curious way.

'I think I recognise this place. Was it here they photographed you for those *Very Freddie Selves* adverts?'

'Advert – singular,' he corrected. 'But you're quite right. The wallpaper is from Castleton's popular "Terra Alta" range, I gather.'

'So popular after your endorsement it's given rise to the Reign of Terra,' said Bob, overhearing.

'Oh yes, I remember seeing that peculiar photo of you, Freddie,' said Marie. 'Not hair and make-up's finest hour.'

'Mm, I know,' he said, 'but for the money they were paying I'd have done it as one of the Black and White Minstrels.'

'I bet you would,' said David Bartram quietly, though unmistakably.

Freddie didn't know Bartram well, and had been in two minds about inviting him along. He was an awkward character, known for his truculent leftyism as much as for his intolerance of anything remotely 'la-di-da'. But Freddie liked his adaptation of *Ragged Trousers*, and in the spirit of camaraderie he had thought *Why not*? He was even prepared to overlook Bartram's chosen attire for the evening, a military greatcoat, peaked Lenin cap and a woollen jumper that revealed holes at the elbows. It was perhaps his idea of cocking a snook at moneyed Mayfair. Still, he was young(ish), handsome in a pale, lugubrious way, and would no doubt bring a dash of vinegar to the table talk. He just had, come to think of it.

'I'm afraid we can't all be ideological purists, David,' he said with amused indulgence. 'Sometimes you must take the work where you find it.'

Bartram glanced at him from beneath an unsettled brow, and said in his light Cumbrian burr, 'You misunderstand. It's not a business decision, it's a human one. You don't have to be an ideological purist to regard shilling for the advertisers as contemptible.'

This last word briefly stunned the company into silence.

Nicola spoke up. 'I think Freddie just admitted it was more than a shilling he got for it,' and laughter broke out. He shot her a grateful look for this deflecting drollery, then pressed home his advantage by rising from his seat and calling the table to order.

'I'd like to take a moment to thank you – all of you – for the tremendous work you've done on this great musical. In the face of multiple setbacks – strike action, press harassment, building work, the unfortunate withdrawal of our leading lady – these previews have been a bloody triumph!' He waited for their cheers and *woo-hoos* to die down. 'I want to deliver a particular vote of thanks to someone who joined us only recently, but without whom, I might say, our trousers would have been not merely *ragged* but lost altogether. She has been a trouper, and a saviour, and I'm so happy to have her with us this evening' – he gestured, straight-armed – 'Miss Nicola Mayman.'

She blushed beguilingly at the applause and cries of 'Hear, hear!'

As the plates were being cleared and a cigarette break

intervened, Nicola leaned towards Freddie and murmured, from behind her hand, 'Thanks for that. You really didn't have to.'

'I meant every word,' he replied, also sotto voce. 'Your rescue act, I guarantee, will be talked about for years.'

She looked at him. 'It's funny, you know. Before we ever met I just took for granted what everyone said about you.'

'And what did "everyone" say?' he asked, as if he couldn't guess.

'Oh, you know – arrogant, egotistical, slippery—'

'I see . . .'

'—manipulative, self-serving—'

'You can stop whenever—'

'—and yet while all that isn't necessarily untrue there was one thing I hardly ever heard you credited for – which was your commitment to the work. You'd rather kill yourself than let through something that's not top-drawer, that's second-rate or slipshod. I could tell the moment when Romilly and I were up for the part – I knew you'd choose her, because she's the best. And painful as it was, I sort of admired you for it, for being so single-minded.'

'You're going to be just as good as Romilly—'

She held up her hand to stop him. 'I don't know about that, and it's not the point anyway. I'm just – I'm glad you know how to get the best out of people. It's a talent, really.'

Freddie leaned back, smiling. 'Nice to hear I'm good for something. Now I wonder if we could talk—'

The sentence went uncompleted, his voice overwhelmed by a raucous recital, led by Nigel and Marie, of 'Our Turn', the barnstorming union song that closed Act Two of *Ragged Trousers*.

We've had it up to here with dockin' our wages
Breakin' our backs for lousy money
The powers that be had it their way for ages
It's our turn now for milk and honey

They ran through it once, then did an encore with Marie scrambling to her feet to waltz with Bob as the others sang along. Now we're having fun, thought Freddie, who felt too fat to dance so conducted the singing with his invisible baton. He noticed that David Bartram, alone of them, declined to join in the roistering. He sat there, smoking and watching, his expression impassive. For some reason this irked Freddie more than his disobliging comments had earlier; did the man think himself superior by remaining silent?

More wine arrived, along with a pudding menu. Freddie produced a cigar as hefty as a stick of TNT, and lit it. He offered one to Bartram, who only shook his head and held up the cigarette he had on the go – a roll-up, of course.

Pocketing the cigar Freddie said, 'How goes the struggle, David?'

'What?'

'The struggle – to shake off all the late-capitalist running dogs snapping at your heels.'

Bartram returned a sardonic smirk. 'I'm doing fine, thanks.'

Freddie sensed he should let it go, but goaded by the drink and the unruffled air of his antagonist he found himself up for a fight.

'Was your food all right? You certainly appear to enjoy chewing on the hand that feeds you.'

'Freddie,' said Nicola, who had overheard the needle in his tone, 'we're having such a nice evening. Don't spoil it.'

'Oh, we're having a high old time,' Freddie agreed. 'I just wonder why Big Chief Po-Face over there won't join in.'

Nicola made to interrupt, but Bartram held up his hand. 'Don't worry, love, I'm fine with it. It's the guilt talking – the guilt of a union-basher and a money-grubber who thinks that putting on a socialist musical will endear him to the people.'

'Union-basher?! That's fucking hilarious. The union's had us over a barrel for months – I couldn't bash them if I tried.' *And God knows I'd like to,* he thought. The others had gone quiet, transfixed by this sudden flare-up.

'I read that interview you gave to the *Ensign*. You talk about strike action like it's leprosy or something, but it's not – it's a force for change. Workers want a fair deal, and if you'd ever been a socialist you'd understand the necessity of striking.'

'What you've got out there isn't socialism, it's gangsterism – a small group of powerful men bullying everyone else. And you know the biggest joke? It's a Labour Party – *your* party – that's allowing it to happen!'

Bartram's gaze narrowed with disdain, and he turned to address the whole table. 'Listen to the fat cat. He pisses and moans cos his cream's being taken. He's outmoded, like all his kind, but he's still the loudest at the table.'

'Oh Christ, *vive la revolution*! Can you believe this guy? If I'm outmoded how d'you suppose you're getting your fucking plays staged?'

Bob Bewley had pushed back his chair, palms upraised in a calming gesture. 'Fred, come on, let's cool it. We're meant to be celebrating, aren't we, not having a go at one another—'

'Tell it to the class warrior over there,' Freddie barked, ignoring him. '*We are* celebrating – *he's* just sitting there looking down his nose at me cos I happen to believe the unions are destroying this country and sending our economy back to the dark ages. They're disgusting hypocrites and *he* is their champion.'

He found he was jabbing his finger in Bartram's direction, and that his voice – his fine purring tenor – had curdled into a snarl, like some union rabble-rouser. That was a consequence of the disputatious mood gripping the country at large: everyone sounded so angry. Bartram had stood up, suddenly white with fury. It seemed the charge of hypocrisy was the final straw.

'Maybe you'd like to take this outside,' he said coldly.

'Maybe I would,' Freddie rejoined.

But now Mike and Nigel were also on their feet, preparing to interpose themselves between the pair. Bob was already shouldering Bartram towards the door, muttering in his ear the emollient phrases of a born peacemaker. Mike had placed himself at Freddie's side, like a bouncer ready to deal with a pest.

'Nice evening, thanks. And fuck you,' Bartram said on the threshold.

'Same to you,' Freddie shouted at his retreating figure. 'Try not to come to any harm on your way home.'

The abruptness of his departure had left the room in a state of shock. For some moments nobody said anything; it was as if a death had just been announced. Freddie, his heart pounding, felt the evening had got away from him.

'Er, sorry about that ... Got carried away. Under extreme provocation!' He picked up the decanter and began filling empty glasses.

'No more for me, love,' said Marie, laying a hand over her glass. 'Time to call it a night, I think.' Nigel and Mike both murmured in agreement. Freddie was crestfallen.

'Oh no, this is – I didn't mean to poop the party. Won't you stay for one more?'

It seemed they would not. He looked at Nicola, who was staring straight ahead, her expression unreadable. A few minutes later Bob returned to the room, having seen off David Bartram in a taxi. He puffed out his cheeks in a mixture of weariness and relief.

'I should watch out if I were you, Fred. If that feller ever does get his revolution you'll be first up to the guillotine.'

'I'll take my chances. You'll stay for a nightcap, won't you, Bob?'

Bob looked around at the others preparing their minuet of departure. He looked at his watch, and gave a sad shake of his head. 'Early start tomorrow. Thanks for dinner, though, lovely, great fun – I mean, while it lasted.'

One by one they said their goodnights, and the host, forlornly, waved them off. Nicola had not joined the exodus, however, which offered at least a pale hope of prolonging the night. She had taken out a cigarette, and with quick courtliness he lit it for her. He waited, tensely, for her to speak.

She blew out a meditative cloud of smoke and turned to face him. 'Well, that was a jolly evening,' she began, 'which you managed to ruin.'

'Not on purpose,' he protested. 'I mean, what a sanctimonious prick, with his long face and his lefty rhetoric. The nerve he had lecturing me—'

'Yeah, I know, I was here, remember? You're some piece of work. I asked you not to pick a fight, but you just went ahead anyway. Never mind about your guests, your colleagues – you must have your say, and the rest of us can go to hell. I wonder if you really *see* people at all.'

He gave a sour half-laugh. 'That's confusing. Earlier this evening you told me I got the best out of people. Now I don't "see" them. Which is it?'

A waiter had arrived with Nicola's coat and she smiled at him as he held it open for her. The smile died as she turned back to Freddie. 'You want to know? All right. I think you're a brilliant professional, and probably the best director I've ever worked with. I can understand why actors have said they'd run through a wall for you. Maybe that's all you've ever wanted. But honestly, Freddie, as a human being' – she paused, and he saw no love in her liquid eyes as she searched for the words – 'you're pretty much a disaster.'

He flinched at that, tried to make a reply, but his mouth, instead of articulating sounds, merely gaped like a goldfish. He had so rarely been reduced to silence in his life that at another time he might have found the phenomenon a curiosity. Stupefied, he hadn't even reciprocated her 'goodnight' as she exited the room. He got up from the table and hurried out after her. His progress was briefly impeded by a couple who happened to be coming up the stairs. When he reached the club hall there was no sign of her, and he ran through the lobby and out through the double doors. She was standing on the pavement, arm aloft.

'Nicola! Hang on, would you?' Can't we just – I can drop you home. Terry's parked round the corner.'

'Thanks all the same, but I'll get this—' A taxi had chugged to a halt at the kerb.

'But I've got the car!'

She looked at him pityingly. 'You're going north. It's nearly one o'clock. I don't want to take Terry out of his way.'

'He won't mind driving to South Ken,' Freddie pleaded.

'Probably not, but I'd rather not ask him. And you shouldn't either. Don't you suppose Terry wants to get home too?'

She opened the cab door and got in. Freddie watched as the car drove away. He felt rebuked, and ashamed, and alone.

16

Vicky took a sip of her tea, stewed to the colour of brick-orange. She watched as George the snout chased the final sliver of fried egg around the greasy circuit of his plate. He managed to spear it with his fork and flipped it into his mouth. He and Kenney had spent the last ten minutes chowing down an enormous fried breakfast, eyes glazed, jaws working with bovine steadiness. In between mouthfuls they talked about football, from which Vicky gleaned that Kenney supported Fulham and George Arsenal; neither of them noticed or cared that she hadn't said a thing. Outside the cafe window Hoxton Street market was in a mid-morning drift; the greengrocer cawing his prices had gone quiet for a moment. A winter sun dispensed a thin lemony light.

Kenney, also finished, wiped his mouth and moustache with a balled-up napkin, then quietly belched. He took out a pack of Benson & Hedges and offered one first to George, then to Vicky. As he did so he seemed to wake up to the fact that she was there at all.

'You're quiet,' he said.

'Oh . . . I was just listening. I don't really know anything about football.' She added, in compensation, 'My dad used to go and watch Spurs.'

She saw the men exchange a glance, complicit in their disdain. Vicky had discovered that it was easier if you let men have their say about football, or whatever, without interruption; if you tried to join in they would patronise you or else shoot you a look as if to say *What do you know about it*? Kenney took a drag on his cigarette and said that they should talk business for a moment. Things were a bit jumpy at the nick since the arrival of 'the boys from A10'.

'A10?' said George.

'Anti-corruption. They've sent a crew from the West Country. *Zummerzet*.'

'Oh no – the Wurzels.'

'Yeah, straight from the farm, they are. The guvnor calls 'em The Swedey. So we're gonna have to be a bit careful for a while.'

'How d'you mean?' Vicky asked, feigning ignorance.

Kenney looked at her impatiently. 'I mean we do things by the book. No tampering with the evidence. No recycling. No pension money.'

Pension money was code for the cash they divvied up from drug busts.

'We don't want this lot sniffin' around us any longer than necessary,' he added.

'Sounds like you'll be doin' the sniffin' if they've come up from the farmyard.'

Kenney barked out a laugh, then rose to his feet. He had to slip off to put a bet on – a dead cert for the two thirty at Plumpton. Vicky and George were left facing one another over the tea. George wore a patchy beard and an overcoat that was stained and fraying at the cuffs. His hair was the outgrown feather-cut of an unfancied pub rocker. Whatever he spent his ill-gotten gains on it wasn't personal grooming.

'What news of your mates from Cleveland Street?' she asked. He looked blank, so she prompted him, 'The two black fellers we bust the other week' – and his gaze cleared.

'Oh, that ... I wouldn't call 'em mates.' They were still at Brixton awaiting trial, he said. Plainly he hadn't given them a thought since.

'Ever wonder what'd happen if they found out you set them up?'

George shrugged. 'They never will. That's the beauty of our little arrangement.' He traced a tight circle in front of him with his finger. 'As long as I'm out there you'll keep yer number of arrests up. A favours business, innit?'

'They might decide to lock *you* up one day, George.'

'Not me, love. I know where the bodies are buried.'

He said this with a smirking confidence, and Vicky thought: he probably does, too. He was looking at her now in a changed, appraising way, as if there were something about her he hadn't yet solved.

'You don't see many birds in this game,' he reflected. 'I mean, how did you end up in CID?'

She told him, in a few brief sentences. She didn't mention anything about the Notting Dale Rapist, or how the case had got her name in the papers. An instinct warned her not to get pally with him. George listened, nodding.

'Alan – sorry, Mr Kenney – reckons you're all right. And the guvnor's been impressed too, he says. They thought you might cut up rough, y'know, about the pension money.'

Vicky stared at him. 'You mean – Wicks?'

'No, no, I mean *the* guvnor. The super – Drewett.'

That winded her, though she knew better than to show it. After a pause she said, with seeming indifference, 'I didn't realise you knew Drewett.'

'Course I do,' he said complacently. 'It all goes through him – couldn't work otherwise.'

She felt her heartbeat quicken. George had mistakenly assumed that she was cleared to this level of disclosure. If what he was telling her was true she had just stumbled on dynamite. She knew from Wicks that corruption in the Met went deep, but he had indicated that it was happening in the field, among the likes of Kenney and Prichard, the foot soldiers – not the brass. She was suddenly aware that Kenney would return from the betting shop at any minute. There was something she had to know for certain before he did.

'Wicks isn't involved, is he?' She did her best to make this sound as if she already knew.

George shook his head. 'I think he used to be, years back. But Kenney said he opted out. Didn't want 'em any more.'

'The perks,' Vicky said, holding her breath.

'Yeah. The perks.'

She saw Kenney pass by the window on his way back. It could be dangerous for her if he heard what they'd been talking about. She needed a diversion, quick, and picked up Kenney's *Sun*, left folded on page 3. 'Denise', the young model baring her chest for today's readers, had a sweet, heart-shaped face. Vicky held it up for George's inspection.

'Hasn't she got a lovely smile?'

George, wrong-footed by the change of subject, frowned at her. 'I don't think anyone lookin' at that's interested in her smile.'

At that moment Kenney appeared. 'What's all this?'

George nodded across the table at Vicky. 'This one seems to be missin' the point of page 3.'

Kenney considered Denise with a cursory professional eye. 'Blimey. Don't get many o' them to the pound . . . All right, we'd better be off.'

He went over to the till to pay, and Vicky felt herself breathe again. Of course she had watched all the conspiracy dramas on TV, where 'a trail of corruption' would more often than not lead 'to the very top'. But that was telly, which had to make a big deal of the hero's ingenious unravelling of the clues. Life was different – it hadn't the neatness of drama. Vicky had done no detective work, no truffling in the undergrowth: a name had popped out by chance and fallen into her lap. Revelation had been thrust upon her, and with it a responsibility. That was life, handing you things when you weren't ready.

Christopher Galton picked up on the second ring.

'Um, hello. Christopher?'

'Speaking . . .'

Hannah's spirits dropped through the floor. He hadn't even recognised her voice.

'It's Hannah. Hannah Strode – we spent new year together?'

He laughed, and not nervously. 'As if I'd forgotten! How are you?'

'Fine. I'm fine. I thought – I just wondered how you were. It's been a few weeks.'

'Yes, it *has*,' he said, as if this were somewhat mysterious. 'I thought you would call me.'

'Well . . .' *Actually, you said that you were going to call me* – 'I've been hellishly busy at work, stuff going on . . . and I did sort of wonder . . .'

'Wonder what?'

She took a breath. 'I wondered if you might have gone back to your old girlfriend.'

There was a puzzled pause. 'Devora? No. I mean – no. We're friends, but there's nothing like that between us.'

'Really? Because I had the feeling she'd like to get back with you.'

She heard a light demurring sigh. 'She sometimes imagines that we will, but – believe me – it's not going to happen.'

He sounded quite decided on the point. Encouraged, she asked him if he would like to accompany her to the NMH next Monday, for the first night of a big new musical. Yes, he would, very much, so long as it didn't matter to her that he was no aficionado. 'Nor am I,' she said, and felt doubly pleased: it seemed that he had accepted because of her, not because he wanted to see *The Ragged Trousered Philanthropists*. 'Should I have heard of it?' he asked, and she assured him, no. She named the time, and he rang off with a cheery 'Toodle-pip!'

Halfway down Charlotte Street Callum found the restaurant, an Italian, swankier than the ones he was used to. On entering he caught sight of Polly Souter, his publisher, seated against the long leather banquette. They greeted one another with familiar ease, though in fact this was only the second time they'd ever had lunch together. The first was three years ago, to toast the contract Callum had just signed for *Go-Betweens: The hidden injuries of class in the English novel*. It seemed longer ago to him now. Polly's intelligent blue eyes conducted a humorous once-over of him.

'Something's different. Didn't you used to have long hair?'

He looked at her ruefully. 'I did, until my sister persuaded me to let her at it.'

'Hmm,' said Polly, angling her gaze this way and that. 'Makes you look a bit moody. But it also shows off your finely sculpted head.'

He laughed. 'You always know the right thing to say.'

The smile she returned was somewhat ambiguous. Then the waiter appeared and took their order. Callum noticed the prices on the menu, and wondered why Polly had chosen such a place. He thought a celebration might be in the offing, but when their drinks arrived she only clinked his glass with a casual 'cheers'. She wanted to know what he'd been up to.

'Och, the usual, classes, lecturing. Been to some gigs – saw the Clash! Reading week's coming up so I should get some time to work on the book.'

'And how's *that* going?'

'You know, I feel weirdly optimistic about it. With everything that's going on at the minute – the unrest, people at each other's throats and what have you – a book about English class could be quite timely.'

'You could be right,' said Polly, though her tone sounded thoughtful rather than enthusiastic. He looked at her searchingly.

'You don't sound convinced . . . '

She made a protesting expression. 'Come on. You know I'm a fan. It's been great working with you.'

Callum squinted at her. 'That sounds a wee bit elegiac. Am I missing something here?'

A pause, and Polly's quick glance downwards told him that he was. 'This is partly why I wanted to meet,' she admitted. 'I'm leaving Antrobus. It's been eight years, and I've decided it's time for a change.'

He was, for a moment, dumbstruck. 'I see. What – where will you go?'

'You know Drummond, Walcott – the agents? They've offered me a job. The pay's better and, frankly, the prospects are too.'

Though he felt choked he managed to say, 'Congratulations.'

'Thanks. It's a big opportunity. Lots of famous clients.'

A silence intervened as he pondered the implications of her news. It was ironic that he'd begun to feel 'optimistic' about his book at the very moment Polly announced she was off. He wished now he had been more circumspect.

'Eight years, is it?' He was delaying the inevitable question – he knew it, and so did she. 'So, um, what happens to *Go-Betweens*?'

Polly leaned forward, her expression clouded. 'It'll depend on who they bring in to replace me. If they have any sense they'll want you to deliver it, but . . . You missed the deadline more than a year ago. That didn't matter to me, of course – I didn't care if it was late – but technically you're out of contract.'

'Will they cancel it – the book?'

She winced a little. 'I hope not. I'll make a fuss at editorial before I go. Tell them it's an important work of literary investigation, blah blah—' She stopped herself; it sounded callous. 'I mean, it *is* important, but it's hard sometimes to convince people of the need for a book like this.'

Callum nodded slowly. All that reading, all those hours he'd spent in the library, the research, the doubts . . . all up in smoke. Across the table Polly was eyeing him anxiously.

'It might work out. If not, you could always try somewhere else – OUP, for instance. You're a good writer, Callum, you mustn't be disheartened.'

'Yeah, sure. It's just – I wanted to write the thing for you. It was your encouragement that made me get on with it in the first place.'

'I know. I'm sorry.'

She stretched across the table to squeeze his hand. The next moment their food arrived, though Callum no longer felt much of an appetite.

As he got home that night he was relieved to recall that he would have the house to himself: Martin was at some charity dinner. His moods since the new year had suffered in accordance with the party's continuing downward spiral, and his once doggish loyalty to 'the boss' had curdled into complaint, if not outright dissent. 'He just mooches about his office all day,' he said one evening, shaking his head. 'We give him speeches criticising the unions, criticising Thatcher, but he doesn't deliver them.' To judge from his reports the PM sounded almost as depressed as Martin did. In the months since he had been at St James's Walk Callum had noticed something else about his lodger: he had almost no conversation outside politics. He never showed any interest in books, or the cinema, or music, or anything, in fact, that wasn't connected to his job. He sometimes let slip that he'd been out at a restaurant, but since Callum suspected who his dining companion would be that too was a conversational dead end.

Callum spent the evening reading and then listened to John Peel until midnight. At half past he went to bed, and had just put out his light when he heard the low grumble of a taxi pulling up outside the house. There followed the slam of a car door, a muttered conversation, and after a short delay the taxi departed. Downstairs Martin's voice was low but clear – had he brought a colleague back? Whoever it was had stopped for a drink: noises came from the kitchen, glasses on a table.

He was drifting off when he heard footsteps coming up the stairs, and whispered voices on the landing, one of them, clearly, a woman's. He had left his bedroom door slightly ajar and sensed a shadow stop at the threshold and listen for a moment. He held himself still, mimicking sleep. Then he heard

Martin say in a hushed voice, 'It's all right, he's sparko.' The steps retreated; the door of Martin's bedroom creaked, and closed. An abrupt laugh came from within, and then silence.

The next morning Callum was woken by a scuffle of feet on the staircase. He leaned over to look at his watch: 7.05. The front door was opened, and Callum scrambled out of bed to peek through his bedroom curtain. He was in time to catch sight of a woman emerge from the house and hurry off, heels brisk on the pavement. It was the same woman – Sasha. Martin was getting careless.

'Actually, he sounded quite keen when we were on the phone,' said Hannah, walking down High Holborn with Tara. It was dark, nearly six, and they were among dozens of office workers on their way to the Tube.

'I told you! He just needed a nudge. Did you mention the ex to him?'

'Yeah, and he denied it. Apparently she – Devora – wants to get back with him, but he says there's no chance.'

'Well then,' said Tara, satisfied. They were just passing a restaurant when she grabbed Hannah's arm. 'Oh God, you must have a look at this, I saw it yesterday.' She pointed to a garishly coloured flyer in the window.

COMING SOON
VALENTINE'S DAY
Romantic Dinner for Two, with wine – £19.50
(Extra person – £10.00)

'Extra person!' Hannah shrieked out a laugh. '*Very* romantic.'

Tara said that Rob (her slightly square boyfriend) had asked her where she wanted to go on Valentine's Night. 'I think I might suggest this place – then surprise him when my "extra person" shows up.'

'Who would you invite?'

'Ooh, I dunno. Maybe that new intern with the slim hips.'

'The blond one? Tara, he's about *twelve*!'

'So? That'll save on the wine. I'd do it just to see the look on Rob's face.'

'Poor Rob. You don't deserve him.'

'I know. He'll probably chuck me one day, and then what would I do?'

They glanced at one another simultaneously, and dissolved into giggles.

All morning Vicky had been on the lookout for David Wicks. As soon as she saw him arrive at the station he had instantly disappeared into a meeting, and then another. He seemed always in the company of people – the door of his office was kept open – and she didn't dare draw attention to herself by seeking a quiet word. In the end she became so frantic with waiting that she left the building on the pretext of 'popping out to Boots'. Out on the street she walked for five minutes to a dusty old phone box tucked away in an alley. It stank, inevitably, of piss and cigarettes, and the receiver had the faintly moist warmth of recent use. But needs must. She dialled his office line and slipped in the tenpence on his picking up.

'Sir, it's me – don't say my name' – she had learned that caution from him – 'I've got something to tell you.'

'Right, I see,' he replied, and from his tone she could tell someone was in the room with him. There followed a mumbled exchange as Wicks dismissed whoever he had been talking to. 'Yeah, close the door, thanks.'

When he came back on the line Vicky said, 'I hope you're sitting down. I talked to Kenney's snout yesterday, about recycling, you know – pension money. He said it's all controlled from the top by' – she took a breath – 'by Drewett.'

There was a pause, then a sceptical exhalation of air. 'What?'

'I know, it came as a shock to me 'n' all.'

'You got this from Kenney's snout – you mean George Foley?'

'Yeah, him.'

'Leave off. George is a toerag. A convicted felon. He'd dob his own grandmother in to save himself.'

'I'm not sure, sir. The name came out by chance, he didn't make a big deal out of it.'

'What did Kenney say?'

'He wasn't there. He'd gone off to the bookie's, it was just George and me. So Kenney doesn't know I know.'

Wicks's next pause was longer. She waited, and then came a surprise: he swore, quietly but vehemently, and said, 'All right. I'll talk to you later.'

He hung up. Vicky replaced the receiver and stepped out of the phone box. She felt shaken, anxious. Wicks, far from grateful for the news, had sounded angry. Was that because it was true, or because she'd had the nerve to even suggest it? Back at the nick she happened to pass Goddard, the DCI from Somerset in charge of the anti-corruption investigation. He stopped to hail her.

'DC Tress? I was hoping we could have a chat.'

'Sir?'

'Don't look so worried. I'll be interviewing everyone here at some point.' She felt his gaze on her, fox-like, watchful.

'I'm available whenever you need, sir.'

'Good. I'll be in touch.'

He saluted, and walked on. Vicky looked about her to check if anyone had noticed this encounter. It was quiet, but she felt no reassurance.

17

Freddie had been backstage to congratulate the cast, who looked exhausted, so he was late arriving at the first-night party in the Hall's foyer. As he made his way through the crush a little ripple of 'bravo!'s surged in his wake. He was distracted; his head was still too full of the performance to enjoy himself, but he returned smiles to the well-wishers and waggled his palm when he spotted friends. He stopped first at Lord Cadenhead, the NMH chairman, plump and sleek, his bald pate smooth as an egg.

'Congratulations, dear boy,' he said, pumping Freddie's hand and giving him a sly wink, as if they had just got away with something. Maybe they had. 'First-rate show. Very entertaining.'

'Thanks. I suppose it went pretty well.'

He wondered whether Cadenhead, with his vast wealth and property portfolio, had been truly entertained by a musical that broke a lance against plutocracy and its adherents, but he was happy to accept praise, sincere or not. Freddie had been lurking around the auditorium all evening, spying on the audience, listening to them – when they went quiet, when they laughed, when they *didn't* laugh. There was no end of tweaking to do once you got started.

And now Leo, his agent, hove into view, beaming like a proud parent. He was squiring Edie Greenlaw, octogenarian trouper of the old school whom Freddie had directed years ago in Chekhov. Her eyes glittered in the weathered mosaic of her face.

'Mah-vellous, darling,' she cried, presenting her cheek for him to kiss. 'I couldn't have liked it more.'

'I'm so glad you made it tonight, Edie.' It had been touch and go, travel-wise, after another wildcat strike on the trains.

'My dear nephew drove me here,' she explained, 'otherwise I'd have been stuck.'

Leo made an exclamation of dismay. 'These blasted strikes! Have you ever known anything like it?'

'As a matter of fact I have,' said Edie. 'I lived in London during the General Strike. I had a flat in Spitalfields and a job in the West End, so I cycled everywhere. Had to! No buses, no Tube. Each night we went on at eight thirty just hoping there was an audience in front of us.'

Freddie's heart was touched. Edie had been a grande dame for so long it was sometimes easy to forget that she had been young once. To think of her cycling into town to appear onstage more than fifty years ago!

'That's *exactly* the kind of pluck this country needs now,' said Leo, almost wagging his finger.

'You sound like you're running for Parliament, Leo,' Freddie observed.

'Pluck had very little to do with it,' said Edie. 'Necessity made me get on that bicycle. If we didn't show up for work we didn't get paid – simple as that! Anyway, your girl did awf'ly well tonight, Freddie, eleventh hour and all that.'

'I know, I was proud of her. She sang that finale so beautifully.'

'The evening was perfection,' said Leo, reaching lazily for the agent's shorthand – hyperbole. 'It's a hit, a palpable hit.'

Freddie wasn't sure: to his ears the music tonight had sounded thin and austere, and the story still seemed to drag in the middle, but he knew now wasn't the time to start moaning about it. Waiters were ferrying around salvers of drinks which thirsty guests were downing in double-quick time. Freddie took a sip of the white wine, and almost gagged: it tasted like a cough sweet. He spotted Dawn hovering, and summoned her with a glance.

'Freddie, can I just congrat—'

'Thanks, and would you please fetch me a glass of champagne?'

She pulled a surprised face and hurried off. That was a bit brusque of him, he thought, but Dawn didn't seem to mind, and she always jumped to it. He left Edie and Leo gossiping and made a beeline towards Linda and the boys, who had rather sweetly dressed up for the occasion. Since their truce at Christmas his wife's show of indifference had both relieved and confounded him. He had expected sulks and recriminations, but none had come. She tolerated him as a landlady might, silently counting the days to the moment her troublesome lodger would quit the premises. He had found himself almost tiptoeing around the house.

'Congrats,' Linda said, giving him a peck on the cheek: he was grateful that she still kept up appearances. 'We enjoyed that, didn't we?'

'Yeah, well done, Dad,' said Jon. 'I didn't expect it to be so . . . '

'Entertaining?' Freddie supplied hopefully.

'. . . agitprop,' he said deflatingly, then added, 'I mean that in a good way.'

Linda told him which of the critics had been in the house, and they speculated on who might give it a positive notice. Freddie always felt skittish about the reviews, and would try to hide his nerves behind a front of affable disdain. He knew that success and failure were more exaggerated in his own head than in others', and that most people only read one review of a thing anyway, if that. But for all his pretended unconcern he still pored over them, and the bad ones would fester inside for days, weeks, sometimes years afterwards. He envied those who rose above it, knowing he could never do so himself.

He was about to move on when Tim, quiet up to now, suddenly grabbed his arm. 'Hey, Dad, did you hear about Nottingham Forest?'

'What? Er, no—'

'They just paid Birmingham a million pounds for Trevor Francis!'

His son's football-crazed eyes were round with excitement, and Freddie could only wish that he'd been so enthused about tonight's performance. When he was Tim's age all he ever thought about was the theatre and what Olivier might be doing next.

'Well, some good news about inflation at last,' he commented drily. 'I'll see you all later.' He had just spotted Nicola across the room and knew he must keep her at a distance from Linda – even with the latter's new-found equability he didn't want to risk a scene. He was moving towards her when Hannah Strode loomed in front of him. She too offered her congratulations and introduced him to her companion, Christopher, as tall and rangy as she was: they made quite a striking pair.

'And ticket sales are going well, I hear,' said Hannah.

'Not bad,' Freddie agreed. 'But it's all relative. My younger son's just been telling me about the first ever million-pound footballer.'

'That's a lot of pressure on a young man,' said Christopher. 'I wonder how his teammates will treat him.'

Freddie made a speculative pout. 'I wish someone would pay a million pounds for *me*.'

'You can't put a price on a talent like yours,' drawled Hannah, teasing, and he laughed like a good sport.

'Hmm, I recall a few barbs in that piece you wrote.'

Hannah shrugged. 'Important for contrast. You need a little squeeze of lemon to cut the sweetness.' Her attention was momentarily distracted by something – someone – in her eye-line. 'Is that – what's Anthony Middleton doing here?'

Freddie glanced over his shoulder. 'Ah. His wife is on the board of trustees. I don't suppose tonight's entertainment was much to *his* liking.'

Hannah smiled and said, 'Well, don't let us keep you from your fans. Good luck with the rest of the run.'

When Freddie had moved on, Hannah asked Christopher if he'd mind her buttonholing Middleton for a moment – the Shadow Home Secretary was rarely seen out in public, and this was a chance to meet him in the company of his wife. 'Lead on,' said Christopher.

As she approached him Hannah wondered if Middleton would remember her from their meeting in the autumn. She had been fair to him – more than fair – in writing up the interview, though whether he'd bothered to read it or not she couldn't say. She recalled his way of talking about the *Ensign* as though it were a seditious rag plotting the downfall of democracy. She took a deep breath.

'Mr Middleton, it's Hannah Strode – we met last year?'

His eyes narrowed for a second before a thin smile of recognition crinkled his mouth. 'Ah, yes. Hello again.' He turned to his wife. 'Mary, this lady came to interview me at the House. Do you recall the piece in the *Ensign*?'

Without acknowledging her recall or otherwise, Mary smiled and graciously extended her hand. Hannah introduced Christopher, who asked them if they'd enjoyed the show. 'Very lively,' replied Mary, in a tone of bland diplomacy she was probably well drilled in using. Christopher, keeping his end up, made some agreeable observation about the force of the music, at which the Middletons nodded in wary assent. Eager to ruffle some feathers Hannah said, 'Yes, I was taken by that song "Don't Let the Bastards Grind You Down". Very topical! Did you enjoy that, Mr Middleton?'

The sceptical gaze he trained on her indicated he knew what she was up to. 'I admired the manner in which it was delivered. But I'm afraid I don't share its sentiment, as you undoubtedly anticipated when you asked me the question. I have no sympathy for the unions. They are bent on throttling the life out of this country, and our supine government hasn't the will to stop them.'

'I couldn't agree more, sir,' said Christopher, to Hannah's

surprise. 'May we expect a change of policy under a Conservative administration?'

'You may indeed,' Middleton replied. 'I guarantee Mrs Thatcher will take matters in hand once she's installed at Number Ten. The unions will be among the first to notice the change.' His voice was quiet, undemonstrative; but the glint in his eye looked ominous.

'And the Provisionals too?' asked Hannah. 'You said when we last met that you hoped for the Northern Ireland job.'

'I will undertake whatever office the leader of the party asks me to,' he said crisply and, blocking any further opportunity to pry, bent to whisper something to his wife.

Hannah, seeing that she was about to be dismissed, said, 'One more thing, sir. D'you know a newspaper called the *Starry Plough*?'

Middleton looked at her sharply. 'You keep asking questions to which you already know the answer, Miss Strode. It's a propaganda sheet of the Republicans. I have been profiled in it lately myself – but I'm sure you know that too.' And with that he bid them both a good evening and moved away with his wife.

'He must have thought I was trying to provoke him,' said Hannah.

'Weren't you? He didn't like that last question much.'

'He seems so cavalier about his own safety. I don't understand why he's got no security around him.'

Christopher gave a little shrug. 'Maybe he's just fatalistic. He survived the Nazis and a POW camp, after all. What could the Provos do to him?'

Hannah considered the possible truth of this. She looked at him more closely. 'I didn't know you were such a hardliner on the unions.'

'We actually talked about this before, on our first date,' he said. 'You asked me how the country could stop itself sliding into anarchy and I said the government had to bring the unions to heel.'

'Yes, but you were talking from the point of view of a management consultant, as I recall. In front of Middleton just then you sounded like a dyed-in-the-wool Tory.'

Christopher looked more amused than accused. 'Well, I have voted Conservative before, and given the present mess the country's in I'm inclined to do so again. Would that offend you?'

'No, not really,' said Hannah, who felt astonished at her own obtuseness. Even though she didn't know him that well, wasn't it perfectly obvious that Christopher would be a Conservative? You only had to look at his friends (Banger!). The question was whether it mattered to her. She hadn't been involved with one before – not out of principle, it was simply that the idea had never occurred to her. But she had made assumptions that seemed to rule out the possibility of his being right-wing. He was considerate and funny and well dressed, he didn't patronise women as far as she could tell – and he loved Joni Mitchell. Maybe more important than any of that was his undeniable physical attraction. *Was* there such a thing as a sexy Tory?

'You've got that expression on again,' he said, squinting at her. 'The one that's silently judging me.'

She laughed, and gave him a fond look. But her secret thought was: I am still judging you.

Meanwhile Freddie had been waylaid by some pest from the *Standard* diary canvassing his thoughts on the 'modern relevance' of *Ragged Trousers*. As he yarned away about the dignity of labour he noticed David Bartram hovering – and scowling – close by. They hadn't talked since the night of their altercation. Bob Bewley had gently suggested that Freddie might clear the air with an apology, since they were both 'really on the same side'. Their similar backgrounds – provincial working-class, artistic Labour-voting parents, passion for theatre – might just as easily have made them friends. But their political affiliations, as expressed so heatedly at dinner that night, convinced Freddie there would be no way back. Was their falling out the fault of the Labour Party and the unions? Or an irresolvable conflict of personality? He couldn't say. But there was no use in trying to conciliate someone whose dislike of him felt so visceral.

Dawn came over to say he was required for a photo call, and he allowed himself to be escorted across the foyer to where Nicola was already posing for the photographers. She had changed into a backless silk dress the colour of caramel, so closely fitted you could see she wasn't wearing a bra. As he sidled into the fusillade of flashes she gave him a smile, the public one, not the real one he was hoping for. He leaned towards her and said under his breath, 'You look ravishing.' She brightened the smile in reply, but still he felt no warmth from her. She was drawing away from him, he could feel it almost by the day.

'Can we have a smile, Mr Selves?' one of the snappers called.

Freddie mechanically obliged, baring his teeth, and blinked through another twenty seconds of flashwork before he raised his arm to the attendant pack: 'That's your lot, gentlemen.' Nicola walked off without another word.

He followed her back into the throng, and catching up steered her to one side. 'Is this how it's going to be from now on?' he said in a low voice.

'What d'you mean?'

'This. Your coldness. Your distance with me.'

'Distance? We talk nearly every day. How else could we do the show?'

'Come on, you know what I mean. We used to have such fun – didn't we?'

She looked at him squarely. 'You hurt me, Freddie. You shouldn't behave like that to people you love.'

'I know. And I most humbly and earnestly ask your forgiveness. Can't you give me another chance? This is killing me, Nicola.'

Her expression abruptly changed; she was giving him the public smile again. 'I'm making this face because your wife is over there staring at us right now. You'd better go and be nice to her.'

He felt another downward drag on his spirits. 'I don't think it would make a blind bit of difference to her any more,' he said sadly. He had somehow contrived to lose both his wife and his girlfriend, and no one gave a damn about it. 'Well done tonight.'

She didn't reply, but something softened in her gaze as he backed away. Pity, it looked like.

The party was still in a roar when Freddie decided he'd had enough. He rounded up Linda and the boys and set off for the car park in the NMH basement. They took the staff lift and were heading down a service corridor towards the exit when they saw two uniformed police officers standing guard in the doorway. Freddie, approaching, asked them what was going on.

'I'm afraid you'll have to go back upstairs, sir. The building's being evacuated.'

'Why?'

'We received a bomb warning about ten minutes ago.'

Hearing Linda's sharp intake of breath, Freddie explained who he was – and that their car was in the basement. But the older of the two officers – PC Johnson – said that the car park was exactly where they suspected the bomb had been planted.

Freddie felt his insides flip. 'My chauffeur's in there – he's been in the car all evening.'

'Oh no,' Linda cried. 'Terry!'

Johnson was on his radio in an instant, calling in the problem to an invisible interlocutor. Freddie looked around to Jon and Tim, dumbstruck, and told himself not to panic. After what seemed an agonisingly long exchange the younger police officer was deputed to take Linda and the boys back up to the ground floor and out of the building. PC Johnson announced that a senior officer was coming down to assess the situation. Freddie loosened his tie, as if that might calm his accelerating heartbeat. Why would anyone target an institution like the NMH? What offence could they have caused? A couple of minutes later he heard the lift doors open and a young woman in a short trench coat emerged and stepped hurriedly up the corridor. She took in the PC with a nod and addressed Freddie. 'Mr Selves? Detective Constable Tress. I gather your driver is parked in there, is that correct?'

'Yes. What's going on?' He couldn't believe how young she looked.

'We had a call. A bomb has been set in this building.'

'How do you know it's not a hoax?'

Vicky looked at him levelly. 'They used a code word. That's how we know. It's almost certainly the IRA. One of your guests here is an MP – we believe they're targeting him.'

And Freddie realised who it was: he'd been talking to Middleton and his wife only twenty minutes ago. 'Oh Jesus . . . ' he muttered.

Vicky had her radio on and was talking to Prichard upstairs. The Bomb Squad was on the way; in the meantime she should clear the basement. Vicky finished the call and looked at Freddie.

'Sir – Mr Selves? – would you be able to tell me where your car is parked?'

'Um, yes, of course,' he said, collecting his thoughts. What if it wasn't Middleton they were after, but him? It wasn't impossible. He tried to recall something he might have said in public about the IRA. He was high-profile, a member of the establishment; murdering him would gain them huge publicity.

Vicky pushed down the metal bar of the exit door, which swung open. She stepped into the strip-lit gloom of the car park. Most of the bays were occupied. Their footsteps rang on the concrete. He felt himself shaking as he walked. Could these be the last sounds he ever heard?

They reached the corner, and Freddie pointed down the next aisle.

'There he is.' The Daimler was parked about thirty yards away. He could just make out Terry's profile through the driver's window. He looked at her, hesitating. Which of them should go on? To his relief Vicky took the matter in hand; a quick word into her radio, then she turned to him. 'See that pillar? Stand there – just in case.'

He felt a stab of shame at how readily he took cover. He watched as she walked on. My God, he thought, the bravery! We really do have the best police force in the world. He was a committee man – maybe he should set up some charity to acknowledge the sacrifice of police officers in the line of duty. It was pure displacement on his part, and he knew it. He was too scared to risk his own neck, so a young woman had taken on the responsibility instead. He would have to live with that. But why was he thinking about her as though she were already *dead*? He could see her right there, in plain sight, stepping around the car like someone out for a Sunday stroll.

Vicky was in fact perfectly aware of the risk involved, but a life was in danger and she couldn't wait for the Bomb Squad to show. As she looked through the windscreen she was surprised – for some reason she hadn't expected the driver to be a black man. No more than he was expecting a police detective to be a woman, maybe. She presented her badge to him as she tapped on the glass. His gaze was cautious as he rolled the window down.

'Terry? I'm Detective Constable Tress.' He's probably used to this, she thought. 'There's been a bomb warning and we need to clear the building.'

Terry looked at her, frowning. 'A bomb – here?'

She nodded. 'I've got Mr Selves waiting just along there. Would you mind getting out of the car?'

Terry showed no sign of minding. He climbed out, and closed the car door softly behind him. Vicky gave him a professional nod. 'Let's go.'

Upstairs the last guests were being cleared out of the foyer. Hannah was surprised at how orderly the evacuation had been;

even though the police had announced the bomb warning they had moved to the exits as placidly as cattle. She noticed that a uniformed PC and a plain clothes had taken Middleton and his wife off straight away.

'I should phone this one in,' she said to Christopher. She glanced at her watch. 'They might be able to sneak it into tomorrow's paper.'

He nodded, understanding. His night was done. They had intended to go for dinner after the party, but that plan would have to be shelved.

'Sorry,' she said with a wistful look. 'Can we do dinner another time?'

'Of course,' he said, 'duty calls. Stop the presses!' And he smiled at her so nicely that she half wished she didn't have to go.

'I'll call you,' she said as he waved her off.

Across the foyer she spotted Freddie and his driver emerging from a lift in the company of a young woman. Hannah took her shorthand pad from her coat and hurried towards them, only to have her way blocked by one of the coppers who had swarmed over the building.

'Sorry, miss, can you join that queue of people at the exit—'

'I'm press – I need to talk to Mr Selves over there.'

But the policeman was having none of it. 'I can't let you past, I'm afraid.'

'Freddie!' Hannah called out, and Freddie's head turned sharply in her direction. She was waving at him. He bent to say something to the woman, who nodded and signalled to the copper to let Hannah through.

She gave Freddie a look that said *thank you*. As she approached them she was lining up questions to rattle through, but Freddie, back in control, was not going to forswear the social niceties.

'Detective Constable Tress, this is my friend Hannah Strode, from the *Ensign*.'

The two women nodded at one another, and as Freddie burbled on Hannah thought how odd it was that even in an atmosphere of emergency some people couldn't resist playing the host. She had a sudden image of Freddie on a lifeboat, encumbered by his inflatable jacket, gaily introducing fellow shipwrecks to one another. His conviviality would be the last thing to perish.

She got the story into the next day's paper, with comments from DC Tress and the director of the NMH. Following a search, police had found the device near the wheel of Middleton's car and it was defused. She had phoned the MP's office for a quote, and was rebuffed. His spokesman said that Mr Middleton wouldn't comment on the grounds that he 'didn't believe in giving gangsters free publicity'. Hannah included this phrase, not without a qualm.

18

He stayed a couple of steps behind Sean as they emerged from the auditorium. Neither of them looked at the other or said anything. Callum seemed to be in a daze or a trance, and he didn't trust himself to speak. Outside the cinema Leicester Square was dark, the pavement slick with rain and still heaped with rubbish. They walked around the railings, indifferent to the knots of night-time stragglers and boozers milling about. The West End could be a lonely place at this hour.

He wondered how the mysterious clockwork of his nervous system might be repaired after those three traumatic hours in the dark. He hadn't really known what to expect as they went into *The Deer Hunter,* though Sean had heard it was 'violent'. There had already been talk of Oscars for it. And yet it was slow to work its spell, what with the long opening section amid the dark satanic steel mills of Pennsylvania, the delirious wedding party, and the tough-guy trip into the mountains to shoot deer. He actually felt himself getting restless – wasn't this meant to be a war movie? – when it cut abruptly from a quiet bar-room scene to the noise and horror of Vietnam, and an ordeal in a swamp that he could hardly bear to watch.

They had turned down a side street when Sean stopped outside a pub. 'Fuck sake,' he said, and blew out his cheeks. 'I need a drink.'

Seated in the fuggy warmth of the saloon, they picked over the film in the hushed, disbelieving way of witnesses to a terrible accident – scenes that came back to them, ambiguous meanings, bits of dialogue, moments of shocking pathos. Sean was a devoted admirer of De Niro – the main reason he wanted to see it – and reckoned his performance as Michael, the hero, a cut above stuff like *Taxi Driver* and *Mean Streets*. Callum had been impressed by him, too, and by Meryl Streep, who despite having very few lines in the role of *mater dolorosa*, managed to convey in the movement of her face something poignant and truthful. Yet nothing had prepared him for Christopher Walken, a young actor he had never seen before; his character, Nick, haunted every scene he was in, and his eyes, sunk in that pale martyr's face, seemed to survey not just the agony of Vietnam but the end of American innocence.

It was of course impossible to talk about anything for long without returning to the film's horrific centrepiece, its heart of darkness – the torture of Michael, Nick and their friend Steven by the Vietcong, who force them to play Russian roulette and gamble on who will blow his head off first. Back there in the dark Callum had felt paralysed, sickened, transfixed – he didn't want to watch and he couldn't help watching. The brutality held a dreadful enchantment.

'Did they really do that – the Vietcong?' he said, looking at Sean, who grimaced.

'I dunno ... you never know in a war. But they wouldn't, would they?'

Callum pondered for a moment. 'I suppose the film-makers intended it as a symbolic thing ... '

'Howdya mean?'

'Well, the chances of living or dying were already pretty random for that generation. You remember they had a draft lottery for Vietnam – if you were born on a certain day and your number came up, that was it, you got packed off to fight.'

'Like the bullet with your name on it.'

'Right,' said Callum.

They fell silent again, until Sean said, 'Ach, when he goes back to Saigon at the end, lookin' for him – "One shot, Nicky, one shot!" And Michael thinks he's got through to him, that Nick's remembered, not realising how fucked up he is on them Chinese drugs. And he doesn't remember, he just goes and – ' He leaned back, shaking his head. 'The waste ... the fuckin' *waste* of it.' There was such feeling in his voice he might have been talking about someone they both knew.

They caught a bus back through the midnight streets towards Clerkenwell. Sean would stop at the house to collect his passport and savings. He was about to take off again.

'Not another holiday?' said Callum.

'Nah, this is for a job, on the Costa ... somethin'. They're buildin' a load of holiday homes out there. Money's reckoned to be good.'

'But you're coming back here?'

Sean made a clicking noise that suggested the contrary. 'You know this place isn't for me, Cal. I've had enough at the site over there – thought I might as well try me luck in sunny Spain.'

They had reached the front door at St James's Walk, and Callum said, 'You'll come inside for a drink?'

'Nah, thanks all the same. I'd better be off. Early start tomorrer.'

Callum was nonplussed, but he went up to fetch the bag. He felt a momentary shiver of guilt for having looked inside it that night, and wondered if Sean might suspect that he had. But when he came down and handed it to him there was no searching look from him. Callum only wished he'd had more notice of Sean's departure; they might at least have had a farewell bite to eat.

'Well, looks like goodbye, then,' he said, sounding more cheerful than he felt.

'Aye. So long, big man,' said Sean, extending his hand.

'Look after yourself. Send us a postcard from Spain.'

Sean nodded and sidled onto the pavement. He had gone a few steps when he turned back suddenly. 'Hey, Call.' Grinning, he put his index and middle fingers together and pointed them at his temple. 'One shot.'

Callum laughed at the macabre echo. 'De Niro to the life.'

He waved him off, watching as his figure retreated down the dark street. He wondered at the likelihood of seeing Sean in the next few years – or ever again.

A few nights later Callum was on the sofa reading when Martin arrived from work, looking purposeful. The forlorn aura of doom he had carried through most of January and February seemed to have cleared a little as spring approached. He had stopped railing against the *Daily Mail* and kept his despairing bulletins about 'Jim' to a minimum: the PM seemed to have weathered the crisis of winter strikes and emerged the other side, avuncular as ever, if not exactly girded for the fight to come.

Martin had gone into the kitchen and returned with a bottle of white wine. He poured himself a huge glass and plumped down on the armchair opposite, a gleam in his eye. He clearly had news to relate.

'We think – we're almost certain – there's going to be an election in the summer. So it's battle stations, and the first thing the party needs is a manifesto. Or rather, the first thing we need is a *title* for the manifesto.' At this he leaned over to his briefcase and plucked out a document wallet, which he undid with a little ceremony. He placed a sheet of paper on the coffee table in front of Callum.

'What d'you think of that?'

Callum picked it up. It was one sentence, printed in a headline-sized font: THE LABOUR WAY IS THE BETTER WAY. He looked up at Martin, whose gaze was fixed on him expectantly. He sensed an obligation to be positive.

'Er, is this like, a working title?'

Martin frowned. 'No. It's the actual title.' He held up his

palms and spread them slowly along an imaginary line. *'The Labour way is the better way.'*

To Callum it sounded no more convincing said aloud than it did on the page – in fact rather less. He stared at it intently for a moment, reluctant to pop Martin's bubble of eagerness.

'I wonder if it's possible – d'you think you could tweak it so you didn't repeat the word "way"?'

His frown was deeper this time. 'Repeating a word is effective. What about "Going to a Go-Go"?' He jerked his neck around in a simulation of go-go-ing.

'That's pop music. It's built on repetition. Without music the words just sound . . . ' He didn't want to say *drab* but the implication was there. He could hear when a sentence clunked, just as he could when it sang. It was the kind of thing he debated with his students all day.

'All right, then, what about "no news is good news"? Nobody had to set that to music – it's memorable on its own.'

Callum conceded this with a nod, but he wasn't persuaded. How to explain the difference between a phrase that had acquired through age a patina of truth and wisdom and a phrase that sounded like it had been scribbled down on an envelope? There was no getting out of this.

'It sounds a wee bit flat,' he said, with an apologetic shrug.

Martin narrowed his eyes. 'Don't you want us to win this election?'

Callum stood up and said, 'I'm just going to make some tea. Do you want anything?'

Martin shook his head, brooding. Callum went off to the kitchen, all too aware of his failure as a sounding board for the campaign. He supposed he could try to explain how ill-suited he was for it, having never voted in his life – but *that* admission might just send Martin over the edge. When he'd made the tea he put some biscuits on a plate and took them into the living room, a kind of peace offering. Martin was now leaning back in the armchair, smoking. He took no notice of the biscuits. The piece of paper with the slogan had gone from the coffee table.

Taking a pensive drag of his cigarette he said, 'How long have you lived here?'

Callum considered. 'Coming up for four years.'

'And in all that time you've never thought about getting a telly?'

The question took Callum by surprise. 'Not really. I never used to watch it much when I was at home—'

'Yeah, but that's Irish telly. Who would?'

'Aye ... Maybe that's why I read a lot. There was nothing much else to do.'

He made an airy gesture at the books around them, so many that they had burst the limits of the shelves and were now silting up the floor. Martin took this in with a slow nod. 'The thing is, Callum, you have to accept that we're living in the twentieth century – you can't *survive* without a telly any more.'

Callum made a rueful face, as though to say *Fair cop.* He saw no use in challenging this lofty condescension, could tell that Martin regarded him as impossibly naive. His own expression gave it away: *This bloke knows nothing about politics – he doesn't even have a telly!* It was best to let him think he had won the point; it didn't bother Callum either way.

Martin poured himself another glass of wine and took a swig. 'Incidentally – I've been meaning to tell you – someone at the office has found me a room in Westminster. It'll be handy for when the campaigning starts.'

Callum looked at him. 'Does that mean you'll be ... ?'

'Moving out, yeah. Next couple of weeks.' He was full of surprises this evening.

'I see. So you're splitting up with me?'

'What?' It took Martin a moment to get it. 'Oh, yeah – ha ha! But honestly, I'm so grateful to you for letting me stay. I should really have been paying rent.'

'Away with ya. It's been good having you here,' he said, and realised that he meant it. Martin wasn't a wonderful house guest – he was too moody and self-absorbed to be great company – but Callum had enjoyed having someone to talk to. They'd had some laughs. He'd even learned a few things about the Labour Party. What with Sean gone he already felt bereft; he didn't have enough friends to feel sanguine about losing two in the same week.

Vicky kept looking up from her desk to the glassed office where DCI Goddard could be seen talking. Her interview was scheduled for this morning. Sometimes he flipped down the venetian blinds for privacy, but more often he kept the windows clear, perhaps to lend himself the illusion of transparency. The presence of his team from Somerset Police had made West End Central very tense; the rumour had gone round that evidence of corruption was about to come out and heads would roll. She too had been feeling it, caught between her apparent complicity with the Drug Squad and being Wicks's 'man' on the inside. The strain of the double life was getting to her.

She saw Goddard tapping on his window and beckoning her. She stood up, straightened her skirt and left her desk. She didn't have to glance sideways to know that Prichard was following her with his eyes.

'DC Tress, good morning. Take a seat.'

Goddard unnerved her, in spite of, or maybe because of, his relaxed demeanour – it might be a tactic to trick you into dropping your guard. She didn't trust his thin lips or his dry sardonic voice. But his manner on the face of it was quite friendly, and he conducted their meeting as though it were a casual catch-up rather than a probing inquiry. He asked her how she liked CID, how she was coping with the workload, what improvements she thought might be made in the running of her department. Vicky wondered when he was going to ask her about allegations against the Met; it was why he was here, after all. She wished she had been able to get advice from Wicks, but he'd so been busy fronting the response to the bombing campaign she'd barely seen him. Lately he had appeared on the TV news more often than he had in the office.

Had Wicks told Goddard that she was in the loop? Ought she to admit that she knew about Operation Bad Apple? She was still pondering this when Goddard rose from his chair and stood at the window, so that he had his back to her. He began to talk more specifically about the Drug Squad. His next question was one she had anticipated.

'I wonder, Detective Constable, do you know what I mean by "recycling"?'

'Yes, sir, I do.' She kept her voice low and firm.

'So you'll also know that elements in CID, and the Drug Squad in particular, have been suspected of this practice, for years?'

Vicky was considering her reply when behind her the door opened and Chief Superintendent Drewett entered. She was standing to attention when he said, 'At ease.' Goddard had also turned from the window, and she detected his twitch of puzzlement at Drewett's arrival. The two men exchanged a few mumbled words that she failed to discern. Drewett turned to her and said, 'Good work last week,' a compliment which had the odd effect of excluding Goddard, the outsider new to London and terrorism, 'real' police work as opposed to ratting on your colleagues. He then took a seat in the corner of the office, out of Vicky's sightline. Goddard had returned to his desk and made a note on his office record.

'The Chief Super has asked to sit in on this interview,' he said to Vicky, 'if that's all right.'

Vicky picked up a faint undertone of frustration in his voice. The DCS had pulled rank, muscled in on something that related directly to the investigation of his own department. It was a breach of protocol, and plainly inhibiting, but Goddard, if he did object to Drewett's intrusion, must have known he could do nothing about it.

Clearing his throat he said, 'We were just talking about allegations against the Drug Squad, DC Tress. In your time at West End Central have you been aware of, or been witness to, the practice of recycling?'

It was as if Drewett had known exactly the moment to enter the room. His presence in the corner, like a votive statue in a niche, was silent yet unignorable. Vicky realised how close she had come to telling Goddard what he wanted, and now her chance was gone.

'No,' she replied. 'That's not something I've ever encountered.'

The words came out quite evenly, and Goddard made only a fractional pause before he moved on to another question. But in that pause she could almost hear his train of thought: *This police officer is lying to me, and she's going to be found out.* He wrapped up the rest of the interview quickly, and dismissed her with a curt thank-you. As she left his office she detected in her sidelong glance at Drewett an unmistakable air of satisfaction.

Reviews of *The Ragged Trousered Philanthropists* were still trickling in, three weeks on from the first night. Freddie would arrive at the office each morning to find another one laid on his desk, courtesy of Dawn, who would carefully clip it out of whichever newspaper or magazine for his perusal. This morning's notice, in the *Sketch,* was both late and lacerating: they had always had it in for him. Perhaps in compensation Dawn had kindly left a couple of Danish pastries for him, right next to the offending article. It was strange how she always made a point of buying two at once – custard tarts, chocolate eclairs, iced buns – as if knowing his sweet tooth couldn't possibly be satisfied with one. He sometimes wished it was just the one, but he nevertheless managed to force them both down.

The reviews had been mostly all right. A director friend of his had once opined that you got reviews better than you deserved and reviews worse than you deserved: what you never got were the reviews you actually deserved. Freddie realised that in the end they only mattered to him anyway (the cast didn't read them) and unpleasant or otherwise they didn't appear to have any bearing on the show's success. Ticket sales were flying, thanks to Nicola. He reflected, ruefully, that it wasn't even her brilliant performance that pulled them in – it was because people loved a face off the telly. The fool's gold of celebrity had sold the house out, not talent. As director he felt himself becoming ever more peripheral as the show took on a life of its own. Nicola didn't need his encouragement or advice any longer, although whenever they were together she behaved very politely, which somehow hurt him even more.

Dawn had also left a telephone message from the manager of the Savoy, responding to his enquiry about hiring a function room. Freddie half dreaded his birthday in May – his fiftieth – but he felt that he should take it on the chin and throw a party rather than pretend it wasn't happening. At first he had considered holding a small dinner, somewhere discreet and expensive, just for select friends. He had ditched that idea once the guest list exceeded forty – the selection process was too invidious, and who among his many friends didn't deserve a piece of him? His next plan went wildly in the other direction, a lavish gala that would draw together the great and good from the arts, politics and showbiz, something in the order of Capote's Black and White Ball without all the vulgarity and the Americans. But he soon thought better of this, too, on the Gilbert and Sullivan principle of 'When everyone is somebody then no one's anybody'. For now he had scaled it back to somewhere in the middle, perhaps two hundred guests, lots of champagne, a jazz band, with a dear old pal to give the toast of honour.

He was still mulling on which pal that might be when Bob Bewley sauntered in, with a strange look on his face. He skimmed a copy of the latest *Private Eye* onto the glass-topped desk.

'Something you ought to see. Page five.'

Freddie exhaled a theatrical sigh and picked up the magazine. Another one that had it in for him.

Selves-Promotion

National Music Hall impresario Freddie 'Fat Boy' Selves is up to his old tricks again. No sooner has he been reprimanded by the Board for his expense-account attitude to travel (regular Concorde flights to New York), cosying up to the adman (Castleton wall-paper) and devotion to fancy dining on the public purse (see *Eyes passim*) than he lands himself in another scandal. It started when the Fat Boy's pisspoor musical *The Ragged Trousered Philanthropists* nearly came unstuck owing to the unfortunate Romilly Sargent breaking her leg on the eve of its previews. Of all the hundreds of replacements available to him the Fat Boy decided on Nicola Mayman, not out of any consideration for her talent, mind, merely for her publicity wattage as the star of TV's *Unlucky Charms*. What few realised was that the fragrant Miss Mayman had already signed up for a second series of the adultery drama, and the producers at LWT had budgeted to start filming in the very week the musical would open. Their compensation package for this delay was thought to be close to £10,000. Was the Fat Boy prepared to cough up? But of course, given the money would come out of the much-depleted coffers of the NMH, which, lest we forget, is a publicly funded institution. It seems that Selves will always pay his way out of trouble – so long as it's on someone else's tab!

Freddie discarded the paper and said indignantly, 'Since when have I been known as "Fat Boy"?'

Bob looked at him, disbelieving. 'That's not the part of the story that would be bothering me at this moment.'

'The *Eye* doesn't even check the rubbish they throw at me now.'

'You mean it's not true?'

'Don't sound so surprised. I may have been guilty of

extravagances in the past but I'm not completely irresponsible. That compensation package, as they call it, was actually twelve thousand, and it came out of my pocket – every last penny.'

Bob's mouth bulged open like a goldfish. 'You're *kidding*.'

'Let me remind you of that meeting we had, the one after we heard Romilly had broken her leg. You lot urged me – begged me – to see if Nicola would step in, and I told you right then she'd already signed the TV contract. I knew that even if I did persuade her there would be monster legal fees to get her out of it. But not wishing to let my colleagues down I took the hit, and I paid up.'

'Wow,' said Bob quietly.

'Yes, and this is the thanks I get,' he said, cuffing the copy of *Private Eye*. 'Of course I could write them a letter protesting my innocence but what's the point? The story's already out there, poisoning the well.'

'*I'll* write them a letter,' said Bob firmly.

'Thanks, Bob, but I shouldn't bother. They probably won't print it anyway. What I'd like to know is – who gave them this? Hardly anyone knew about the deal I made with LWT. I didn't tell you, or Mike, or—'

'Piddock?'

'No! That's who I presumed had leaked the other stuff. Looks like I got that wrong.' He lifted his eyes to Bob in a renewed access of outrage. 'Someone is trying to fuck me up.'

19

The voices, bearing the faintest trace of echo, fell silent. George Foley, drug dealer and police snitch, was heard to say 'Is that it?' and the recording ended. David Wicks pressed the STOP button on his clunky reel-to-reel and the tape petered out with an odd fluttering sound. Vicky, seated on the sofa opposite, wore a look of frowning concentration. They had just listened to a long interview with George who, at Wicks's prompting, had given them the goods on the Drug Squad and a history of malpractice within CID going back years. Recycling, bribery, intimidation, deliberate disposal or falsification of evidence were the principal subjects of discussion, as well as a list of names that implicated several senior detectives at West End Central.

'Where did you record this?' Vicky asked.

'Right here,' he replied. 'Right where you're sitting.'

It was the first time Vicky had been to Wicks's place, a flat on a leafy road in Kensal Rise. He had bought it after his divorce, he said, and hadn't lived there long, which possibly explained its impersonal decor and the slightly thwarted atmosphere of a single man's digs, one who hadn't much feel for comfort and did no entertaining. Its bareness jolted Vicky, and made her feel rather protective towards him.

Wicks was smiling at her. 'You've got a very worried look, Vicky.'

'That's cos I *am* very worried,' she said, not returning his smile. 'Are you sure this was the right thing to do?'

'What d'you mean? We've got recorded evidence of corruption from an eyewitness – names, places, dates. You can corroborate at least three of the deals he mentions, including Cleveland Street.'

'Yes, but it's *George* we're talking about here. You said he'd do anything to save his skin. That makes him dangerous, doesn't it?'

'You've met him – he's hardly public enemy number one. If you could see how he crumbled when I told him how long he'd go away for … I mean, you heard him, he sang like a canary. We've got him where we want him.'

Vicky wanted to be reassured, but doubt persisted – it felt like something blocking her throat. She remembered George saying that he knew where the bodies were buried, a phrase that haunted her. In this business its meaning might be literally true. She felt that Wicks had gone too early with his interrogation, had exposed himself to the duplicity of a man whose rascally front hid a ruthlessness – he'd betrayed those two men without a qualm, and they were his associates. What might he do to a copper?

'What about Drewett? When he sat in on my interview with Goddard I sensed – I dunno – that he was watching me. Like he *knows*.'

'He doesn't know. There's no way he could.'

What they needed to secure, he continued, was proof of Drewett's involvement. George's unguarded revelation had been their bit of luck, had opened the door a crack; another push and they might be through. But they would have to be patient: Drewett had been canny up to now, all-powerful but invisible, 'like the Holy Ghost', said Wicks drily. There was nothing with his name on it, nothing that could be traced back to him – yet.

'We just have to wait for him to make a mistake.'

'What if he doesn't?'

'He will,' said Wicks. 'They always do.'

A loud rapping sounded at the front door, and Vicky jumped. Wicks shook his head with a laugh, and rose to answer it.

'It's the takeaway I ordered. Chinese.'

Later, with the smudged foil trays and styrofoam cups strewn across the coffee table, Wicks went out to the kitchen and brought back another couple of beers. He was still laughing about her moment of fright.

'Oh the look on your face when that door went! You were *white*.'

'I know,' she said, with a grimacing smile. 'What a scaredy-cat.'

'Ah, now that's something you're not. After what you did in the Notting Dale case, and this . . . you must have nerves of steel.'

'I really don't, though. I felt frightened when I was on Bramley Road.'

'And that shows why you're brave – you did it anyway.'

It was nice to hear him praise her, but she didn't want to be under his scrutiny. Taking a quick swallow of her beer she looked around the room. 'D'you like living here?' she asked.

He tilted his head, considering. 'It's all right. I haven't done much with it, as you can see. It feels odd, going back to living on your own.'

'Were you married a while?'

'Twelve years. We had some good times, I think. But it was hard for Sandra, the wife – I mean my ex-wife – cos of the hours I was working. You know, pressure of the job. Only another copper could understand it—' He stopped himself, seemed to blush, and Vicky saw where his train of thought was heading.

'It's hard for family in general, isn't it?' she said, tactfully deflecting. 'My mum's always on at me about the job, but I don't really tell her anything. She worries about me being safe.'

'I worry about you too,' blurted Wicks, looking at her earnestly. Vicky was thrown for a moment, not sure of how to reply.

'Er . . . thanks,' she said weakly. Wicks himself looked embarrassed, almost appalled, by the way his spontaneous remark had exposed him, but he seemed to realise it was too late to backtrack.

'I'm sorry if this is – I've thought about you a lot, these last months. It's complicated, because of the case—'

'Yes, I understand,' she said quickly, offering him a way to close the subject down.

'But truthfully, I'd feel this way about you whatever was happening. And I wondered if you . . . I was hoping you might feel something, too.' He had leaned across to take her hand in his. The repressed yearning in his voice was painful to her, and her gaze dropped away. An answer was required.

'I don't know,' she began uncertainly. 'I've noticed the way you look at me, and I do feel – that it's nice. Only it's weird you being my boss.'

'But I'm not just "the boss". I want to be something else to you – someone else. Is that even possible?'

It was strange, she had never imagined him sounding vulnerable. A mask had dropped, and the man she thought she knew looked suddenly quite different.

'I don't know,' she said again. 'Maybe?'

A warm spring wind ruffled the tops of the trees as Hannah and Tara sat eating their sandwiches on a bench in Lincoln's Inn Fields. It was good to be in the open again without huddling in their coats, without all the sniffling and shivering against that murderous cold. Colour was bleeding back into the London grey, the flower beds spangled with snowdrops, crocuses, a few shy daffodils. It felt like a reprieve after what the winter had put them through.

Change was afoot elsewhere. In the Commons that day they were debating a vote of no confidence in the government. Hannah had been put on standby for an interview with the PM, having negotiated on the phone with Martin Villiers.

'Quite bumptious,' Hannah said. 'Making out what a privilege it was to get twenty minutes with his Uncle Jim. Oh yeah, and "can we be assured of a supportive piece?" he asks me.'

Tara snuffled a laugh. 'The twerp. What did you say?'

'I said that I dealt with all my interviewees on a case-by-case basis, and I couldn't promise what view I'd take until I met him.'

'They're getting jumpy, aren't they? Thatcher's making them sweat.'

'It looks that way.' She paused, wondering. 'Maybe it'd be quite exciting to have a woman as prime minister ... wouldn't it?'

Tara returned a doubtful look. 'I think the novelty would soon wear off. She's still a Tory, after all, and she doesn't seem particularly sympathetic to women. The way she talks about the NUPE, for instance. You're not planning to vote for her, are you?'

Hannah shook her head absently. 'Of course not. But I get the feeling that a lot of people will. Even people I like.'

'You mean Christopher?'

'Well, yeah. When we had dinner the other night he was very cheerful about it – he's convinced they're going to get in.'

'How are things with him?'

Hannah pulled a face. 'All right. We still haven't, you know – I'm fed up about him being so pally with the ex. She's really on his case, and I think he enjoys being needed.'

'He'll get over it.'

'But what about this Tory thing?' said Hannah. 'I'm not sure I can be with someone who actually *wants* to vote Conservative. And then I tell myself I'm being too tribal. I mean, he's one of the nice guys – he's funny and clever and he has a good job. Shouldn't that be enough?'

Tara shrugged. 'Rob's a Tory, and I've been with him for years.'

'You never told me that,' said Hannah in surprise.

'Well, he's never told me straight out. But I know he is. Whenever I've asked him how he voted he just says, all hoity-toity, "It's a private ballot." Which is his way of refusing to admit he votes Tory.'

'I feel I should ask Chris exactly what he believes, but it just seems – I dunno – priggish of me.'

'I reckon you should find out what he's like in bed first before you start on the political questionnaire. *That's* the acid test.'

Hannah laughed in spite of herself. She could always trust her old friend for clear-sighted advice.

The no-confidence debate was still going at half past six, and, anticipating something momentous, they went out to the Old Bell on Fleet Street with a few other staff. They would be near at hand for the result when it came through. An odd holiday mood prevailed among them, and they drank as if at a send-off, or a retirement party. Hannah started on lager before switching to vodka and tonic; for dinner it was Silk Cut and crisps. She and Tara talked for a long time to an old hack they both liked, Ray Tewson, who reckoned that Callaghan would survive by a tight margin. No British government had lost a vote of confidence since 1924, he said. His forecast seemed to be confirmed when the news came down from the office that, because of a strike by Commons catering staff, some Tory MPs had gone off to dine at their clubs and hadn't got back in time for the vote. Ray had a good laugh about that. 'There's your story for tomorrow – "The Carlton Club wins it for Labour".'

At half past ten an agitated hum rippled through the bar and reporters began hurrying off to file for the next day. The result was out: 311 to 310. The government had been defeated by one.

The next morning the Prime Minister called a general election. Hannah rang Martin Villiers's office and was put on hold. She kept ringing until, just after lunch, he finally came to the phone – to tell her that the interview with Callaghan was off. 'That's definitive,' he said.

'Is that the same as "definite"?' she asked, irked by his pomposity.

'What?' he said.

The following day Martin appeared to have changed his mind. This time he rang Hannah to say that 'Jim' could give her half an hour that afternoon: it looked like the fightback had begun. She was about to ask him what had happened to 'definitive' but thought better of it; he didn't sound like the sort you could tease.

It had just gone two o'clock when she stepped off the bus in Parliament Square and made her way into the Central Lobby, thronged with MPs, journalists and other flotsam of Westminster life. Villiers had said that he'd meet her there. While she was waiting she spotted through the crowd the gaunt, straight-backed figure of Anthony Middleton walking abreast of two younger colleagues, both of them talking away, eager for his attention. He carried himself with a remote authority, his gaze steady and unsurprisable in the way it switched left and right, though he didn't notice Hannah amid the jostle of bystanders. She was seized by an urge to stop him and say hello, perhaps make up for her impudent provocation of him last time they met – if the Tories did get in he would be a useful contact. But as she hesitated her eyeline was blocked and Middleton disappeared down a corridor.

Ten minutes later a young woman introduced herself as Jeanette, from Martin Villiers's office, and apologised for keeping her waiting. She'd recognised Hannah from her most recent appearance on *What the Papers Say*. 'The Prime Minister is just in a meeting,' Jeanette explained, 'but Martin says he's keen to talk to the *Ensign*.' *Yeah, right*, thought Hannah, who suspected that Callaghan would rather have root-canal work than talk to the press, but needs must. They agreed on a quick cup of tea while they waited, and were just leaving the Lobby when an almighty thunderclap boomed overhead. The echo seemed to crash from wall to wall. Jeanette flinched and looked round at Hannah.

'Was that – ?' The half-question hung in the air.

A silence fell. Everyone in the Lobby was suddenly perfectly still, looking at one another. The Commons chamber, which had been in session, had also gone quiet. Hannah knew from her time in Belfast what the sound was. The gravity of it reverberated, and seemed to anticipate the loss and mourning that would follow in its wake. She thought of what had happened in the basement of the NMH last month, and said to Jeanette, 'Which way to the car park from here?'

Then they were walking quickly down a corridor, past knots of people in murmuring confusion, through a door and along a quieter corridor, this one prohibited to the public. Hannah had no memory of what they talked about on the way, she was too absorbed in guesswork – a member of the security services, perhaps, or a policeman? It couldn't be Middleton because she had only just seen him, minutes ago. Jeanette had pushed open another door that led outside to a narrow walkway overlooking the entrance to the Commons car park. The air was acrid, coated with something, and as they approached the parapet coils of greasy black smoke rose up to meet them. Down below a car, a grey Vauxhall Cavalier, lay mangled and engulfed in flames. Sheets of writing paper fluttered upwards amid the debris. The sight made Jeanette gasp. By the time they got to ground level fire engines and a police car were already inside New Palace Yard. Distant sirens shrilled across the dull afternoon. Ambulance men were crowding around the wrecked vehicle. Half an hour had passed before word came through the police cordon, bearing the name of the victim. Hannah was so shocked she almost felt the ground give way beneath her. She had guessed wrong, after all. She had got her front page for next day, but it wouldn't be about the Prime Minister – 'definitively'.

BOMB KILLS ANTHONY MIDDLETON MP

More attacks feared as IRA launch terror campaign during election

By Hannah Strode

Anthony Middleton, the Shadow Home Secretary, close friend and adviser of Mrs Thatcher, was murdered yesterday. At 2.20

p.m. a terrorist bomb exploded in his car as he drove from the underground car park at the House of Commons. It is thought that he died instantly. Mr Middleton was known for his tough line on Ulster and had long been an assassination target of the Provisional IRA. A war hero and former member of the SAS, he knew the risks involved and had already escaped one attempt on his life when a bomb at the National Music Hall in February failed to detonate. Middleton and his wife had been attending a performance in the building. The IRA has claimed responsibility for yesterday's attack, and questions will be raised about security arrangements. First, how did the bombers manage to penetrate the Palace of Westminster and lay a charge under the MP's car? (continued on page 2, column 1)

INSIDE

Middleton said, 'If they come for me, the one thing I can be sure of is that they will not face me. They're not soldier enough for that.' Hannah Strode recalls her encounter with the controversial MP (pages 3–5)

Late MP crossed swords with the press and regarded the *Ensign* as 'subversive' (page 6)

The terrorists have our security service on the run (editorial)

West End Central was bristling with nerves. Trouble had been anticipated, but this 'spectacular' had caught them on the hop. The authorities were losing the propaganda war now that the IRA had shown they were able to get inside Parliament. An argument had ignited over the language. The terrorists called it an 'execution'. The media reported it as an 'assassination', which supposedly lent the Provos a political status many on the right – including the late MP – had insisted on denying them. 'Murder' seemed the bleakest, and fairest, word for it.

At a press conference Chief Superintendent Drewett promised the Met would do everything in its power to track down the perpetrators. He asked the public to be vigilant. As for the brutal killing of Anthony Middleton they were appealing for information, though it felt as though stable doors were being bolted too late. A mood of anxious reflection overlaid a rising tide of panic. Vicky, watching Drewett's performance, admired the gravely measured tone he had adopted. He gave every appearance of determination and trustworthiness. If only they knew, she thought. A frenzy of flashes went off as the conference ended.

The first week in April saw a flurry of hoax bomb scares in the city. These were a nuisance, though no one would deny they were preferable to actual bombs. The following Thursday Vicky was on her way into the station when she was hailed by David Wicks coming down the steps. He was wearing a stone-coloured mac, quite stylish for a copper. They hadn't spoken privately since the evening she had been at his flat; she feared being alone with him again, and yet looked forward to it.

But today he was in a hurry. 'We've just had a warning. Bomb at a pub near Bayswater Road. Are you ready to go?'

Within minutes he was driving them through Mayfair and then north up Park Lane. The traffic was slowing them, so Wicks told her to put the siren on, and suddenly they were racing past Marble Arch and into Edgware Road. The warning call had indicated a pub on Connaught Street, but when they arrived the Bomb Squad were already there: they'd searched the place and found nothing.

'There's gonna be a lot of this,' said Wicks, as they walked back to the car. 'It's a terrorist trick – spread confusion.'

He bought takeaway coffees which they drank sitting in the car. Wicks recalled the IRA mainland campaign in the early part of the decade, the Birmingham and Guildford pub bombings that marked a turning point in the conflict – when they realised the Republicans were taking the fight to them. He talked on so determinedly that Vicky wondered for a moment if he'd forgotten all about the heart-to-heart they'd had at his place.

But when they were back on the road the professional manner dropped and he reverted to the sweetly uncertain overtures of the previous week.

'I've been wondering if – well, if I'd offended you the other night,' he began, staring through the windscreen.

Vicky, in the passenger seat, turned to look at him. 'Offended me? No ... why would you think that?'

'I dunno. I thought you might be avoiding me.'

She shook her head. 'Not at all. I'd – I'd like to talk, but it's not as though I can drop by your office and say, "I've been thinking about you."'

He laughed unhappily. 'And have you – been thinking about me?' His eyes briefly left the road to glance at her.

'Yeah. I have—' At that moment her radio crackled into life, and she clicked her tongue in annoyance. 'Central 877,' she said, her call sign. It was Prichard on the line: they'd had a second warning, another pub, this time in Marylebone. Vicky told him they were on their way. Wicks did a U-turn and drove east back towards the Edgware Road. She had the *A-Z* open and was giving directions, since neither of them knew Harrowby Street.

On arriving they found a Victorian corner pub, the Duke of York, dusty, unexceptional – and closed for building work. The whole street was quiet, nearly deserted but for a few parked cars. When they knocked at the door nobody answered. Wicks darted a look of disbelief at Vicky. 'What's going on? There's not a soul here.' He called the station to check that a code word had been used. According to Prichard it had.

They went back to the car, a mood of puzzlement hanging over them. Wicks warily surveyed the street, and as he did Vicky thought how handsome he looked; she had never really noticed before. Back inside the car they sat for some moments in silence until she said, 'What you were asking before – about you and me? – I think it could work. I mean, I think we should give it a try.'

For the first time that day he smiled. 'You do? Good. I think we should, too.' He reached with his hand to touch her face, very lightly. 'Oh, and will you call me David? – I've asked you before.'

'All right, sir,' she replied, and they laughed.

He was about to turn the key in the ignition when he squinted at something through the windscreen. She looked too, and spotted twenty yards up the road a car, a blue Austin, parked askew to the kerb. It looked as though it had been abandoned in haste.

'Wait here a minute,' he said, climbing out of the car. It was a copper's sixth sense, and she understood. She watched him approach the Austin, and wondered where their backup had got to – they ought to have arrived by now. Wicks was circling the car, bending down to peer inside. Vicky sat there, gazing through the windscreen. Without warning she felt there was not quite enough oxygen to breathe; the atmosphere about her had thinned, and she found herself gasping for air, hyperventilating. A terrible compression that intimated danger. But what was the danger? – only a foreboding that they had somehow strayed into the wrong place. She was half out of the car, just in time to see Wicks reaching to try the Austin's passenger door.

'David!' she cried out.

He turned on hearing his name and in the next instant the volcanic roar of a detonation ripped away the air from her lungs, the ground bucked and slammed her backwards. She wasn't sure how long it took her to sit up; her ears were keening madly from the blast. As she heaved herself upright her hands touched something sharp – grit and broken glass. Dazed, she saw the blue Austin was now a blackened shell licked about with flames. She could feel the heat of them against her face, and the smoke was causing her eyes to fill.

A siren bleated. An ambulance, it must be. Coming for David, she thought.

20

TERRORIST BOMB KILLS POLICE OFFICER

No claim yet but IRA suspected of second bomb in a week

By Hannah Strode

A senior police detective was murdered on a London street yesterday, six days after the assassination of Anthony Middleton MP at the Palace of Westminster. Police believe the IRA planted the car bomb which exploded near a pub in Marylebone, but so far no organisation has claimed responsibility. A coded warning was received at 12.45 p.m., indicating that the Duke of York public house on Harrowby Street was the target. Two police officers arrived on the scene ten minutes later but found the building unoccupied. One of them, 39-year-old DCI David Wicks, was standing near a car when a bomb detonated, killing him. The other officer, DC Victoria Tress, escaped with minor cuts and abrasions. Buildings were damaged but no one else was hurt; by a miracle the street was almost empty at the time of the attack.

The two officers were called to investigate having earlier left the scene of a bomb hoax on nearby Connaught Street. This follows a recent pattern in the IRA's London campaign. Bomb warnings are delivered apparently to confuse the police and waste resources. (continued on page 2)

INSIDE

Woman police officer who survived bomb blast had worked on Notting Dale Rapist case (pages 3–4)

Silence from the IRA but police are 'almost certain' of their involvement (page 5)

Will London's streets ever be safe again? (editorial)

The cortège, led by David Wicks's parents and sister, was joined by over a hundred police officers in full dress uniform. It made the front page of all the papers next day. Hannah followed at a respectful distance. She and the photographer had caught the train down to Croydon, Wicks's home town, which was just as well – roads had been closed to accommodate the funeral march. The vicar at St John the Baptist, where the service was held, spoke so warmly of the dead man he might almost have known him. The Chief Superintendent, Paul Drewett, delivered a sombre address that commended Wicks's character, his integrity and calm under pressure during his nineteen years with the Met. Then Mickey, an old friend, reminisced about their schooldays, when Dave was a brilliant footballer, about their first holiday abroad together, about their enduring love of Crystal Palace and their competitive nights at the snooker club. He said he'd never known anyone as loyal as Dave, who'd also visited him after Mickey was detained – this coy aside amused many in the congregation – at Her Majesty's Pleasure in Maidstone. 'He was a great copper, see, but an even better friend.'

Afterwards in the church courtyard, as people shuffled around one another, helpless, Hannah saw Vicky talking to another woman police officer. She probably wanted to be left alone, but Hannah's professional instincts overrode her delicacy of feeling.

'DC Tress? We met the night of – at the National Music Hall.'

Vicky nodded. She looked in a state: her face was cut about from fragments of glass and her hands were mummified in bandages. Her eyes were raw from the service. She introduced the officer beside her as Carol.

'I just wanted to say how sorry I was, and I wish I'd known him better. He sounded like a good man.'

'I think he was,' replied Vicky, her emotion brimming close to the surface. She didn't want to give way again, but it was hard.

'I know this isn't really the time—' Hannah went on, awkwardly.

'No, it's not,' interposed Carol sternly. 'This is a funeral, not a press call.'

Vicky touched her friend's arm in a calming gesture: she had remembered Hannah from the bomb scare, and had responded to her warmth, and her toughness. There was an unbiddable spirit in her that she admired.

Carol shot a warning look at Hannah as she withdrew. The two women faced each other.

'How are you doing?' Hannah said, lowering her voice.

'Not so well,' Vicky said, almost in a croak. Then she coughed and seemed to pull herself together, on duty again. 'At least they've claimed it as theirs now – the IRA.'

'Why d'you think they delayed?'

'I dunno. The whole thing ... it doesn't add up. I can't work out why there was no one else around. Just before it happened – this is off the record, yeah? – I had this weird feeling that they'd been waiting for him. For us. And I called out to him, David—' She choked up, and her head dropped as she tried to compose herself. 'I'm sorry, I'm still not ... People have been so nice but they can't understand what it was like to – to be there ... I can't understand it myself.'

Hannah held her lightly by the arm. 'You've had a terrible shock. It's no wonder you feel so raw. Are you taking some time off?'

'I've got to,' she replied absently. 'Orders.'

'Well, if you ever need to talk, you can call me – I don't mean as a journalist, I mean as someone to, you know, have a good cry with ...'

Vicky blinked back tears – any more kindness and she would

break down. It was easier to deal with indifference. She wished she had on dark glasses, her face felt so naked and exposed. Hannah had raised her hand in farewell, turning to leave, when Vicky said, 'One other thing. I've just heard today – it's not official yet – the team investigating the House of Commons bomb, they've got something from the car park. Evidence.'

'What is it?'

'A holdall. Found it in a service bin. Pretty careless of the bombers, unless they were surprised and just dumped it in a hurry. But it may be nothing.'

Hannah nodded. 'Golly. Thanks for letting me know.'

Her interested tone put Vicky on guard. 'You didn't hear that from me, by the way. Like I said, they haven't gone public with it yet.'

'Mum's the word,' said Hannah, who felt a bracing shiver of excitement. A scoop had just fallen into her lap. As soon as she'd said goodbye to Vicky she went off in search of a phone box.

Callum picked up his morning post from the mat, most of it circulars, though there was also something with a Newry postmark, sent second-class. It was a sad reflection on his life, he supposed, that the most interesting item through his door was a letter from his mother. Two sides of news, close-written, unselfconscious in style but entirely self-involved in content. Reading it induced in him a familiar mixture of tenderness, boredom and exasperation.

In one of the buff envelopes he found a mailshot that made him smile. It was a call to arms from the Labour Party outlining their election manifesto, entitled 'THE LABOUR WAY IS THE BETTER WAY'. It appeared that his critical twopenn'orth had been comprehensively ignored. Martin had moved out a fortnight ago, having left a short note and fifty quid in cash – he'd used the phone a lot and payment for the cleaner he had hired was overdue. Callum had heard nothing from his ex-lodger since, hardly surprising given what had been going on in Westminster. On hearing about a bomb at the House of Commons he first thought, for some reason, of Martin. He hoped he was safe; he hoped everyone was safe. When the victim's identity was reported later on the midnight news it jolted him sharply. He well remembered Anthony Middleton from the occasion they'd met, recalled his distant friendliness and his affection for Callum's homeland. By the natural affinities of class, creed and race they might have been bitter enemies, but in the brief minutes they had talked it hadn't seemed like that. Some unspoken kinship had touched him, and he mourned the man, as much as one could ever mourn a stranger.

Freddie was at home finishing a medium-sized fry-up and half listening to the radio when the news of the general election came through. The announcement caused him to halt mid-forkful and unleash a violent oath. Linda, who had just entered the kitchen, looked up in surprise.

'What's the matter?'

'Callaghan. He's called an election for May the third.'

'So?'

'May the third – my fiftieth! The very night of my fiftieth birthday party! Of all the days he could have chosen . . .'

Linda laughed. 'What, and they didn't even consult you?'

'Please don't joke. The invitations have been sent out. I'll be stuck in that huge room at the Savoy and not a friend there to celebrate with.'

'Don't be silly, you'll have loads of people.'

'Like who?' he wailed.

'Well . . . Leo, for sure.' When she saw his crestfallen expression she quickly added, 'And the boys and me, and your parents . . .'

'Right, so my agent and my family are dead certs. Whoopee.'

Linda rolled her eyes and set about making a pot of coffee

while Freddie muttered on. What rotten bad luck, he thought, and considered for a moment whether he should cancel the whole thing. A sparsely attended birthday bash would be too humiliating; he could imagine the guests whispering to one another about the pitiful turnout, all of them knowing that the real party of the night was going on elsewhere. But if he did cancel it would look craven and feeble and, besides, he wanted a big party – he *deserved* one.

He caught Linda training a curious gaze upon him. She looked away abruptly, as though she'd not intended him to notice.

'Something the matter?' he asked.

She hesitated, then said, 'While you're digesting bad news I thought I might as well tell you. I've decided I'm going to introduce my new friend to the boys – I've talked to them and they're fine about it.'

Freddie was nonplussed. 'New friend?'

'Someone I've been seeing for a while. Pam introduced us. You don't know him.'

'You mean – a boyfriend? How – how long have you been . . . ?'

She protruded her bottom lip. 'About six months. He's a designer – Alex – he does up houses.'

Does up a lot more besides, from the sound of it. Six months! No wonder she had taken the news of his affair so nonchalantly, already lolling in the safety net of her own bit on the side. And of course Freddie had had no idea about it, because he was so disengaged from life at home.

'Anyway,' Linda continued, 'he's going to be spending some time here, so it might be a good idea if you—'

'Got the hell out.'

'I was going to say thought about finding a new place. We can do this in a civilised way, you know, like adults.'

'You said you talked to the boys. I thought we were going to maintain the status quo while they were doing their exams.'

'They're doing fine at school. And both of them know what's going on with us. They're more observant than you think. In the end it'll better for everyone if we're open about it instead of you skulking about in this semi-detached way. We can talk to the lawyers when we're ready.'

Freddie made an unhappy plosive sound. 'That's something to look forward to.'

'May I remind you—'

'All right, sorry, I didn't mean – I'm just trying to absorb this ... development. I'll start looking for ... Wouldn't like to hang around where I'm not wanted.'

Linda folded her arms, shook her head, refusing to rise to the bait. She had learned how to play him; there was nothing he could say to hurt her any more. Indeed, so unconcerned was she by his brooding demeanour that she moved the conversation on to work. What was he going to do next?

'Hmm? Oh, something jolly and light. After *Ragged Trousers* I can't face anything with a "message" in it. I'd like to do a crowd-pleaser – *My Fair Lady, Oklahoma, Carousel,* that sort of thing.' He looked round at Linda, who had by now started tidying up in the kitchen, nearly oblivious to his reply. 'Or maybe something that chimes with my current domestic status. There's always *Stop the World – I Want to Get Off.*'

'Many of the Victorian novelists found it hard to resist. It's a useful device for linking a long, multi-character story. Dickens couldn't help himself. Someone wrote of Charlotte Brontë that she "stretched the long arm of coincidence to the point of dislocation". Overuse it and you test the reader's credulity. On the other hand, existence *is* random, as we know, the chance meeting *does* happen. There's no point in denying coincidence. Luck determines a lot.'

Callum slid a hopeful glance at Chloe Nicol, sitting opposite, a first-year student whose company always lifted his spirits. Her bright-eyed diligence and openness would have been endearing enough; that she also reminded him of Karen McAuley, the girl of his youth club dreams in Newry, only sharpened her aura of untouchable loveliness. They were in his office, mid-afternoon, discussing Henry James and wondering whether the coincidental encounter at the climax of *The Ambassadors* was a defect or not.

'So what would you say?' he asked her.

Chloe's pale brow tightened. 'Well, in one way I suppose it's really contrived. The author actually says it was "a chance in a million". And yet, it also seems . . . *like life*. Strether might have just met them on the river like that.'

'Right. So how does James make it like life?'

She paused, her expression doubtful. 'I don't really know . . . '

'Well, let's think about this. Is there coincidence elsewhere in the novel? No, so when it does happen it's all the more effective. The author has earned the right to it, but more than that, he makes it seem, through Strether's perception of the couple in the boat, somehow inevitable. And that perception comes alive through good writing – in other words, the careful, patient, selfless construction of effects by an author on behalf of his readers.'

He read through the passage again, pointing out those effects of timing, of language. In the liquid depths of Chloe's gaze he saw – or perhaps only thought he saw – a glimmer of appreciation. She bent her head to her wire-ringed notebook and jotted something down. For a moment he longed to know what it was.

The clock in the college quad chimed four, but Chloe showed no urge to hurry away and they chatted on as the April light fell through the tall windows. He had just brewed a pot of tea when a knock came at the door. Standing on the threshold, flanked by two uniformed police officers, was an ungainly-looking man in a brown suit. He introduced himself as Detective Inspector Anson.

'Is your name Callum Conlan?'

Callum, mystified, replied that it was. He then confirmed his address. 'Can I ask what this is about?'

Anson's face twitched, and not in sympathy. 'I'm putting you under arrest, and I must warn you that anything you say may be taken down and used in evidence against you . . .' He mentioned something else about having a lawyer present but Callum wasn't listening.

'Is this a – what are you arresting me for?'

'On suspicion of possessing explosives and aiding a known terrorist organisation.'

Callum, momentarily stunned, forced out a single syllable. 'What?' Behind him he heard Chloe's shocked intake of breath. One of the constables stepped forward, asked him to turn round, and handcuffed him. The cuffs felt as cold as death on his wrists.

'This is a joke,' he said to Anson, but saw plainly that it wasn't. 'I've not done anything. What is it I've done?'

'You can talk to a lawyer when we get to the station. Let's go.'

Chloe, all colour drained from her face, was staring at him in open-mouthed astonishment. 'It's all right, it's just a mistake,' he said to her, though he heard no assurance in his own voice.

As they walked him to the college gate, where the squad car was parked, knots of students stopped to watch. It wasn't every day you saw a member of staff being taken away in handcuffs. Callum, aware of the onlookers, did not catch anyone's eye. It wasn't shame that he felt, exactly, more a sense of the absurdity unfolding before him. Arrested! Not even in Newry, where the risk for a young man was high, had he ever been arrested. One of the coppers put his hand on Callum's head as he ducked into the back of the car. They always did this in films; he never knew why.

It was a short drive to Bow Street police station. They hustled him up the steps and into the hall, where he gave his name, age, address. He had to surrender his belt and his shoelaces. He was then fingerprinted. As an officer led him along a gloomy corridor and opened a cell door, Callum said, 'Can you tell me what crime I'm accused of?' The man stared at him for a moment. 'You'll see.'

In the cell he paced around for a few minutes before sitting on the wooden bed. Since arriving he had not been able to engage any of them in a conversation, so he brooded on what DI Anson had said. Presumably the terrorist organisation he was accused of helping was the Provos, but how in the name of God did they imagine he was involved with them? When he'd informed the desk officer that he had no lawyer he was told that one would be appointed. They had taken his watch, so he couldn't tell how long he waited. At some point the lights came on, and a police officer delivered a blanket, and a tray with a sandwich. He ignored everything Callum asked him. The door thunked shut, and he was alone again. He supposed it was coming up to ten or eleven when he called out to his jailers, and banged on the door. Eventually the spyhole opened and a face appeared. He asked if there was a lawyer coming. The officer didn't know.

'Could you bring me something to read at least?'

The spyhole closed. Nobody came. Then the lights went out.

In the morning Callum woke with a start, not knowing where he was. But it came back to him almost immediately. He felt groggy from a fitful night. 'A night in the cells' – the phrase was a commonplace, and yet he had never thought to experience it first-hand. He wondered what other new surprises he should prepare himself for. With any luck someone would clear up the confusion, the police would acknowledge a case of mistaken identity and he would be on his way home with an apology.

From his cell he could hear life going on in its indifferent way, a ringing telephone, passing footsteps, conversation. He banged on his door a few times, and when the spyhole opened he asked for a cup of tea and a newspaper. They brought him a cup of tea. An hour or so later two officers opened his door and took him off down the corridor to an interview room. A man in his mid-forties – sandy-haired with sideburns, bespectacled, harassed-looking – introduced himself as Nicholas Edgerton, who would be his solicitor. They sat down at a table facing one another, and he began taking down Callum's details, where he worked, how long he had been resident in London. Edgerton spoke in a brisk and straightforward manner that gave Callum heart, though he was taken aback when asked if he knew members of Sinn Fein or the Provisional IRA.

'I haven't lived in Northern Ireland for going on eight years, and when I did they weren't the sort of people I used to know.'

'And you've never belonged to any political party?'

Callum shook his head. 'I couldn't even tell you the name of my MP.'

Edgerton made notes of his replies with a Parker biro, nodding frequently and with approval, as if confirming to himself that there was no case here to be answered. Or so Callum imagined. A few minutes later two plain-clothes officers entered, one of them Anson, who had arrested him, the other a keen-eyed, swarthy fellow in a chalk-striped suit and flamboyant tie. He introduced himself to the solicitor as DI Palmer. He crossed his arms and fixed Callum with a hard, unillusioned stare. They went through the preliminaries, most of it apparently for the solicitor's benefit.

Anson held a folder from which he slid three black-and-white mugshots, and laid them in a row on the table.

'Which of these men do you know?'

Callum looked at each face. 'I don't know any of them.'

'Sure about that? All right. Do you know a James Donaghy? Patrick Maloney? Gerard Burns?'

No, he replied. Anson's tone changed slightly when he said, 'How about Sean McGlashan?'

Callum nearly jumped. 'Sean? Aye, I know Sean.'

The two detectives exchanged a quick look, as though

to say *Now we're getting somewhere.* He was asked how long they'd known each other, and he gave a brief account of their schooldays, how they'd lost touch after he left Ulster, and their meeting again by chance in London in the autumn. He described their last meeting at the end of February.

Palmer spoke for the first time. 'And whereabouts is he now?'

Callum said, 'Somewhere in Spain. He said he had a building job in the south.'

Anson produced another photograph, this one in colour, of a green sports bag.

'Recognise this?'

He hesitated. 'It looks like one that belongs to Sean.'

'It's the very one. A porter at the college, Jim Lewin, says he saw you trying to store this bag in one of the lockers. Why?'

'Sean didn't want to leave it in his digs, so I agreed to mind it for him for a few weeks. What's this about?'

Palmer blinked in surprise. 'So you were "minding" it for him? And when you couldn't fit it in the locker you took it home?'

'Aye. He asked me to keep it safe.'

'And you knew what was in the bag?'

'Yeah, it was clothes, money – his passport. Stuff he didn't want to risk being thieved.'

'What else was in there?'

'Oh, a stereo – I mean, a cassette player.'

Palmer stared at him. 'And what else?'

'I dunno. Sean's stuff. I was just minding it.'

Another photograph was produced and set before him. 'You know what they are, don't you?'

Callum stared at it. Now it was beginning to come together. 'They look like detonators.'

'They *are* detonators – as you well know. They were inside the cassette player. The bag was found in a bin at the House of Commons car park. Your fingerprints were all over it. Those detonators were used in the car bomb that killed Anthony Middleton.'

There was a horrible silence as Callum realised what they were implying. 'It looked like what it was – a cassette player. I can't believe Sean's involved in this—'

Palmer slammed his hand on the table. 'Enough of this nonsense. You're an educated man. Consider the evidence from our point of view. A fly man for the IRA needs a safe house in London. He asks his friend to look after a bagful of bomb-making equipment. The friend agrees, keeps the bag while this paramilitary goes off with his cell to plan their next attack. Some weeks later he returns to collect the bag – do you see how this looks? You're right up to your neck in it, son, so you'd better start talking.'

'There's nothing I can tell you—'

'Who else did you meet through McGlashan?' asked Anson. 'Did they come to your house?'

'I didn't meet anyone – Sean didn't *know* anyone. He lived on his own in a dosshouse on the Old Kent Road. He worked on a building site. That's all I can tell you about him.'

'A colleague of yours, Juliet Barwell, said she met you and McGlashan once walking through college. She thought you looked like close friends.'

'If you're accusing me of being his friend, then yeah, guilty—'

'Don't get smart,' Palmer snapped. 'Explain to us how you could be friends with this man and not know he's a paramilitary.'

Edgerton chose this moment to intervene. 'I think that's enough badgering of my client. He's explained his relationship with McGlashan. It's clear he knew nothing of his political allegiances or of his alleged activities. Mr Conlan is a respectable member of society. He's no more guilty of this outrage than I am.'

After more back-and-forth the policemen rose to their feet. Palmer, leaning across the table, said to Callum, 'We're not done with you yet, son. You see, it's not just men in masks with guns and bombs that we're after – it's the people who help them, by providing their cover, by giving them a safe house. It's called conspiracy. Your solicitor will tell you how many years you can do for it.'

When they had gone Edgerton explained that under the Prevention of Terrorism Act the police could keep him in custody for up to seven days. The weakness in his defence was clear – how did he not know that his close friend was an IRA sympathiser? Callum was at a loss. He could argue that Sean wasn't a 'close' friend – they had gone years without seeing one another – but they shared a background and had recently kept company in London. And now he thought back to their accidental encounter on Farringdon Road in the autumn. Had Sean in fact contrived the whole thing, intending to groom him as an unwitting accessory to murder? He baulked at the idea, it was so grotesque. Yet people behaved in grotesque and improbable ways all the time. Before yesterday he would never have conceived of Sean even as a minor criminal. Now he had to get used to his being a cold-blooded killer.

Edgerton had collected his papers in a briefcase when he said, 'There's one bit of good news. When they swabbed your hands the test came back negative.'

'What were they hoping to find?'

'Oh, traces of nitroglycerine. You were clean.'

Callum felt dazed. They had suspected him of handling explosives – as if he would have recognised the stuff.

'I'll come and see you again as soon as I can,' Edgerton continued blithely. 'I'll need a full statement. Go through every detail in your mind of your relationship with McGlashan, where you met, what you said. A character witness would be good. Someone maybe in public office?'

He thought for a moment. 'There's a friend who lodged with me for a while. He's Press Secretary to the Prime Minister.'

Edgerton's eyes widened in candid surprise. 'Well, that would be *very* useful. I'll take his details, if I may.'

'One other thing. What the copper just said – about conspiracy. What would I get if I was . . . ?'

'You shouldn't think about that now.'

'Tell me anyway.'

The solicitor frowned unhappily. 'If it went against you – twenty years?'

21

Vicky's hand shook as she brought the glass to her lips. She was drinking lager with Carol at a pub off Old Bond Street, not one of the force's usual haunts. She was also supposed to be on leave, but life at home and her inability to stop thinking about the case had driven her to seek out her friend on the quiet.

'How's your mum been about all this?' Carol asked.

Vicky shuddered. 'She's doing my head in. Fussin' around me. The one good thing about this election is she's out the house canvassing most of the time. If the Tories don't get in it won't be her fault, I'm telling you.'

Carol sighed. 'I was talking to some of them in the canteen today – they're *all* voting Tory.'

The election was two weeks away. In the wake of the bombings the atmosphere of high alert was almost palpable. In her head Vicky had gone over and over the day of the bomb, piecing each sequence back together in the hope of finding a clue she might have overlooked. She sensed there was some key element hidden within the fragments; one lucky shake and its meaning would fall into place. But it still hadn't come, and wishing it did no good.

In the Middleton case, however, Carol said they had made a breakthrough. They had traced the green sports bag to an Ulsterman, an academic here in London, who at present was denying any involvement with the bombers. She had read the file on the arrest, which included details of the accused.

'Listen to this,' Carol said, stifling a laugh. 'The suspect claims he was minding the bag for a friend – had no idea he was a terrorist!'

'Who is he?'

'Oh, some Irish teacher – think he's called Conlan.'

Vicky started at that. 'Conlan ... oh God ... not Callum Conlan, is it?'

Carol said it was. She said he was about twenty-six, born in Newry.

'I've met him.'

'You're joking. How would you know *him*?'

'You remember over Christmas Matthew got jumped after a gig? This bloke found him, bleeding from his head, and took him to Barts in a taxi.'

'You sure? What was he like?'

'Ordinary. Irish. I only met him once. We sent him flowers as a thank-you.'

Carol was silent for a few moments. 'D'you think – did he look like a terrorist to you?'

'What does a terrorist look like? He seemed ... decent. He looked like someone you'd trust. God knows what might have happened if he hadn't found Matthew.'

'Well, there's good and bad in everyone,' said Carol, and then sighed at her own sententiousness. 'What are you gonna do?'

Vicky shook her head. 'I dunno. I mean ... it isn't beyond the bounds of all possibility, is it?'

'What isn't?'

The expression that Vicky wore seemed to plead for her friend's understanding, or at least her tolerance. 'That he actually *is* innocent.'

Callum had been allowed to take a shower. On his way back to the cell a young policeman walking past had muttered, 'Ya fucking murdering bastard.' That was the first one he had heard. He had been expecting something like it from the start, had braced himself, but still it knocked the wind out of him. He was trembling when they locked him in again – fear, shame, indignation, he couldn't really separate them. Helplessness was his overriding emotion. He had been accused of a crime he was not only innocent of but incapable of, and there wasn't a thing he could do about it. It was his fourth day in custody and he'd heard nothing from his solicitor since their meeting.

They had not given him anything to read, despite his requests, so he passed the dead hours reciting poems he knew by heart. Whenever he made a mistake he would go back and start again. He had just got through 'Ode to a Nightingale', 'Dover Beach' and 'Ulysses' when he heard footsteps and voices outside. The door opened and a young woman stepped through; it took him a moment to recognise her. He swung his legs off the bunk and stood.

'Hello,' said Vicky. 'D'you remember me?'

'Aye. Detective – ?'

'Vicky Tress.' She lifted her bandaged hand in an awkward greeting. He felt heartened to look into the face of a police officer and find no glint of hostility there. He asked her what she'd done to her hands, but she only shook her head, dismissing the question.

She took the chair; he went back to his bunk. After a moment he said, 'How's your brother? Still listening to the Clash?'

She returned a wary smile. 'Oh yeah. Probably while swotting for his A levels. He wants to go to university.'

Callum nodded. 'Good for him.'

A lull, and a silence, ensued. Both of them sensed that the small talk was over.

'I never imagined we'd meet again,' Vicky began, 'least of all in this place.'

'Me neither,' he said, with a rueful lift of his eyes. 'I just passed a copper outside who called me a "murdering bastard". Certainly never imagined that.'

She paused before saying, 'I know you'll have told them this over and over again, but can you go through it for me – from when you first met Sean McGlashan?'

Callum did so, as plainly as he could, wondering if the story sounded any more plausible to her than it had to her colleagues. This woman could confirm that he had at least once in his life been a Good Samaritan. The fact that she was there at all made him almost tearful with gratitude.

'This friend of yours,' she said, 'you must have talked with him about Northern Ireland, about what was happening.'

'A bit. Not much. He knew I wasn't interested – maybe I ought to have been. I remember he once talked about a wee lad we both knew from home – a tearaway. He was shot dead one night, by soldiers. I think it was the only time we talked about . . . the struggle.'

'So why d'you think McGlashan asked *you* to mind his bag?'

He shook his head. 'I've asked myself that. A few times. I don't think he knew many people in London – he didn't like the place. He must have thought it would be safe with me. Someone he trusted.'

'He was taking a risk all the same. What if you'd found the detonators?'

'I've thought about that too. I wish I had.'

Vicky squinted at him. 'If it ever comes to it you're gonna have a hard job convincing a jury you knew nothing. It sounds so . . . unlikely.'

Callum's head dropped. When he looked at her again his expression was desperate. 'But *you* believe me, don't you?'

She held his gaze for a moment, and then nodded. 'Yeah. I do.'

The relief of this caught him off-guard. He felt his eyes prickle. 'There's something else . . . '

She nodded. 'Go on.'

'I've a friend who works at Downing Street, his name's Martin Villiers. He lived with me until recently. We were at a book party, last September, when this feller started talking to me.

No idea who he was. He'd overheard my accent, said he knew Northern Ireland pretty well. Just a friendly chat, lasted a couple of minutes, then he went off. I asked Martin who he was, and he was like, don't you know? It was Anthony Middleton.'

Vicky started. 'You met him?'

'Aye. But like I said, I didn't know who he was at the time. Martin will remember that. So you tell me – how could I go from not knowing this man to wanting him dead six months later?'

'Why didn't you mention this in your statement?'

'Cos I knew it would be dangerous to admit it. But if Martin can testify on my behalf – tell 'em exactly how it went that night – then people will know for sure I had nothing to do with it – that I didn't want to kill Middleton or anyone else.'

'It might help. It sounds like we should interview this friend of yours.'

'I asked my solicitor a few days ago. Heard nothing since. I suppose Martin's busy with the election – he's a press secretary at Number Ten.'

'He can't be too busy for this,' Vicky replied. 'I'll talk to him. In the meantime, sit tight. They've got three more days left to charge you – after that they'll have to let you go.' She rose from the chair. 'Is there anything I can get for you?'

Callum was about to say no when he thought again. 'Can you get me a book?'

'What sort of book?'

'Whatever you've got. Anything to take my mind off being in here.'

One of the office boys stopped by Hannah's desk with a package she had to sign for, delivered by courier a few minutes earlier. She had been expecting it: Vicky Tress had telephoned that morning to say Scotland Yard were about to release details of the suspect in the Middleton murder, and thought Hannah should get an early peek. Opening the envelope she found a note from Vicky with a report on the arrest and a mugshot of the suspect.

Hannah gaped at his face. The hair was much shorter now, but of course it was him. Callum Conlan. The man she had met in the pub that night, months ago. They had talked about Mott the Hoople and the Clash ... and now her hands flew to her mouth as she recalled what else they'd been talking about, her time in Northern Ireland, and the Shadow Home Secretary, Anthony Middleton. She felt the hairs on the back of her neck begin to prickle in horror. This man she had spent an evening with, laughed at his jokes, quietly fancied – this man was a terrorist? She stared at the photo again. It was coming back to her slowly. He – Callum – hadn't he told her he hated Newry and longed to get away from the place? Had he not made clear his utter abhorrence of the paramilitaries, of the violence? She was sure he had. But maybe that was his cover story – the exile who denounced the Provos while secretly plotting destruction for the cause. And if it proved so then this one was a master of deception, because she – award-winning reporter on Northern Ireland and the Troubles – had been thoroughly taken in.

Vicky stood waiting outside an office at the Palace of Westminster, eavesdropping on a conversation through the door pulled half-to. The louder of the two voices was distinctly peevish ('Did you ask her what she wanted?'). She presumed it belonged to the man she had come to interview, a hunch that was confirmed on her being invited to enter.

'Good afternoon, DC Tress. Martin Villiers.' He had put on a smile that didn't reach to his eyes. He was handsome, in a humourless way, his dark hair vainly coiffed and his jaw set at a wary angle. 'Sorry to have kept you waiting,' he continued, 'we're just so busy with the election—'

'Yes, I can see,' said Vicky. 'Can we talk in private?'

Martin looked round at his staffers, seeming to wonder if he should turf them out or not. He gestured towards a door, and conducted her into a windowless side room where box files were stacked on shelves, floor to ceiling. They seated themselves on either side of a table. She took her out her notebook and began.

'Can you tell me how you know Callum Conlan?'

His expression didn't change. They'd met one another at university in Dublin.

'So you're pretty good friends?'

Martin frowned at that. 'Well, I wouldn't say that – I mean we've known each other for a while—'

'I understand that until recently you stayed at his house a couple of nights a week. Is that correct?'

'Yes. I needed a place in London, because we – my wife and I – had moved to Suffolk. Callum offered me his spare room.'

'That sounds to me like you're good friends,' said Vicky.

Martin blustered something to the effect that Callum might have thought so.

'He *does* think so,' she said, 'because his solicitor contacted you on his behalf some days ago. I gather you haven't returned his call.'

Martin shrugged. 'I really have been terribly busy. Can I just say, straight out, I had no idea Callum was involved with … those people?'

Vicky nodded, slowly. So he already knew what trouble Callum was in. 'When you were living at St James's Walk did you meet any of his friends? Friends from Ulster, for instance?'

He shook his head. 'We kept very different hours, though. I work late, so by the time I got back there he'd usually be in bed.'

'So you never saw him in company with anyone who might have aroused your suspicions?'

'No. But that's not to say – look, we kept ourselves to ourselves. Callum's private life was no concern of mine.'

Vicky paused, consulted her notebook. 'Mr Conlan – Callum – said that you met last year after being out of touch for a while. A book party at the Reform Club. Do you remember that evening?'

'Vaguely,' he said, eyes hooded beneath his brow.

'He says that at one point you both had a brief conversation with Anthony Middleton. As he recalls, Middleton approached him first and talked about his time in Ireland . . . Mr Villiers?'

'What?' he said, a petulance in his tone she didn't like.

'Do you remember that conversation?'

Martin nodded reluctantly.

'Do you also remember that Mr Conlan didn't know who Middleton was? He had to ask you afterwards the name of the man you'd been talking to.'

'No,' said Martin firmly, 'I don't remember that. Callum would have known who he was, and in the light of what happened it looks like—'

'Looks like what?'

'He pulled the wool over our eyes. I had no idea he was involved with—'

'You've already said that. Just to get this straight – you lodged with Mr Conlan two nights a week for nearly three months and in that time you never saw him consorting with anyone, Irish or otherwise, who you might have suspected as a paramilitary. And yet you seem to think he deceived you and that he's, well, guilty as charged. Why is that?'

'I don't know if he's guilty but . . . ' He now looked embarrassed, as if he'd rather not continue, but Vicky's expectant air prompted him. 'I do know he used to go out in the small hours – I once got back very late and he surprised me on the doorstep. Gave me the fright of my life.'

'Do you know where he went?'

'No. He said he just went walking around Clerkenwell and Fleet Street.'

'Did he meet anyone?'

'I don't know. But it made me wonder.'

Vicky left another pause. 'Did Mr Conlan ever talk to you about what was happening in Ulster?'

Martin knitted his brow in an effort of recall. 'Not much. I suppose he knew that, given my job, I wouldn't be sympathetic to the idea of a united Ireland.'

'From what I can gather he didn't have strong sympathies in that direction himself.'

He shook his head sorrowfully. 'I didn't think so either until all this came out. It's been a shock. You imagine you know someone . . .'

Vicky stared at him. Either this bloke had the wind up or he else he was pursuing some secret agenda. She felt an abrupt stirring of pity for Callum Conlan. If he had been pinning his hopes on Villiers as a character witness he was woefully mistaken. She got to her feet.

'Thanks for your time. We'll be in touch.'

IRA TERROR SUSPECT IS A UNIVERSITY LECTURER

Academic's house was used to store detonators of bomb that killed MP

By Hannah Strode

A college lecturer in central London has been charged with conspiring to help the IRA bombers who murdered Conservative MP Anthony Middleton in March. Callum Conlan, 26, from Newry in Northern Ireland, was arrested last week and questioned by police at Bow Street station. Though he has admitted to knowing one of the bombers, Conlan claimed that the detonators used in the Parliament bomb were stored at his residence in Clerkenwell without his knowledge. Police found a sports bag used by the terrorists in a bin at the House of Commons. Conlan's fingerprints were on the bag. A police spokesman said that it was unclear whether Conlan knew of the assassination plot. Holywell College, where the accused is a junior lecturer, declined to comment. He has been remanded in custody to Brixton.

INSIDE

Was a university lecturer suborned by the IRA? (pages 2–3)

The scariest part had been the exit from Bow Street inside the Black Maria. Even with the windows blacked out Callum could sense the volatile mood outside, could hear the fists banging on the side of the vehicle and the howls of pure hatred from the waiting crowds. *FUCKIN' MURDERE-E-ER* ... Some of the most savage voices were women's. He supposed his name and photograph were in the papers now; he might as well have had a target painted on his back. They had taken him to the Old Bailey, where he was charged under the Prevention of Terrorism Act. He listened as the judge recited the words – 'unlawfully and maliciously conspired with other persons to cause explosions in the United Kingdom' – and wondered how it could be that his name, Callum Conlan, was attached to them. He pleaded 'Not guilty', and was taken down.

By the time they deposited him at Brixton he was numb, and seemed to have lost the power of speech. After being processed with all the briskness of a supermarket chicken he was handed prison duds and told to change. Two warders led him to the wing for remand prisoners, and put him in a segregated unit. He was locked in his own cell, which came as a weird relief – he had imagined that they would make him share. The smell of the place was instantly overpowering, a vile combination of boiled cabbage, body odour, cigarette smoke, piss and detergent. And something else, which took him a while longer to identify: fear.

As soon as he had been charged his face was on the news and in the papers, and he knew he could hide his ignominy no longer. He had telephoned home after he was arrested. By sheer good fortune Niamh was in the house on her own. Their mother was out with friends. He had haltingly explained to her what had happened.

'But how can they think you'd be involved?' Niamh said, sobbing. 'You'd never do something like that. I know you wouldn't.'

Her teariness gave way to anger. It seemed she intended to prove his innocence in person, and the first thing on her agenda was to visit him in Brixton. He was touched by her determination, and alarmed.

'Please don't do that,' said Callum.

'Why not? Don't you want to see me?'

'Aye, I do, but not in here. I don't want anyone to see me here.'

He asked her a more difficult favour, which was to break it to their mother. He would phone her himself in a few days.

It was strange, he thought, how quickly you adapted to routine – slop-out, exercise, dinner, lights out. The prison officers didn't treat him badly, but his reputation had preceded him. In the yard he heard someone hiss 'Fenian scum' and 'murdering bastard'. At dinner someone spat in his soup. He was aware of being talked about. Later, someone spat in his face. It happened so quickly he didn't have time to flinch before he felt the warm trickle of gob down his cheek. But by and large he was ignored, and he kept his eyes averted whenever he walked among the other prisoners. He felt himself an abject figure. Edgerton, his solicitor, had paid him a visit, though his news wasn't cheering. The press was hostile – nobody could quite understand how he had been taken in, or why he had failed to suspect what McGlashan was up to. Edgerton kept offering Callum cigarettes, forgetting that he didn't smoke. He also expressed his surprise on learning that Callum was teetotal.

'You don't drink, you don't smoke. What kind of an Irishman are you?' the solicitor asked with a nervous laugh.

'An innocent one,' said Callum.

He was loafing about on his own in the yard when a prison officer called him over.

'Conlan. You've got a visitor.'

For an awful moment he thought it might be Niamh, blown in on a righteous fury. He followed the officer to the visiting room, where a woman he didn't know was coming towards him. Only now, up close, he did know her. He remembered that dark-eyed gaze and her confident wide-stepping walk – the journalist. For a moment he couldn't recall her name, but it didn't matter.

'Mr Conlan. We met once – last year? – Hannah Strode. From the *Ensign*.'

'Callum,' he said, offering his hand.

They looked around for an unoccupied table. The surrounding hum of voices was low – and intermittently loud – with complaint, denial, despair. Some of the women visitors had brought their children, and Callum could hardly bear even to glance at their pale, uncomprehending faces. When they sat down Hannah took out her cigarettes and went to offer him one, then stopped.

'You don't, do you?'

He felt obscurely pleased that she had remembered. He watched as she lit up and casually discarded the spent match. Hannah wondered if he too was struck by the contrast with their previous encounter, when a faint but unmistakable frisson of romance had coloured the mood. There was nothing romantic about the present circumstances. He looked shaken to her.

'How are you coping?'

'All right. Not sure about the neighbours, but, you know . . . '

She smiled, eyeing him through a cloud of smoke. 'I had quite a shock when your photo came through. I couldn't believe it, actually.' She hesitated. 'Though our conversation started coming back to me – you'd met Anthony Middleton at a party, and I wondered—'

Callum's face fell. 'Right. You thought I'd been stalking him. Planning the next big hit . . . '

'It crossed my mind,' she admitted. 'The evidence suggests you were at least partly involved. I mean, it doesn't look good.'

He closed his eyes, putting his hands together against his mouth, as though he were about to pray. 'So what are you doing here?'

'Vicky Tress told me about you. Her view, for all the good it'll do – well, she's fairly convinced that you're innocent.'

'Nice to know someone is,' he said drily.

'She said that I should talk to you – about Martin Villiers.'

So he had to tell the story of their friendship again. By the end he felt weary of it. 'If Martin's sticking to that line, I'm stuffed.'

'Vicky said he was quite clear about that night at the Reform. He denied that you asked him who Middleton was. Why d'you think he did that?'

'I dunno. I suppose he doesn't want trouble. He's a high-up in the Prime Minister's office—'

'I know. I've met him a few times. Glad he's not *my* friend . . . '

'There's nothing else I can tell you,' he said, resigned.

'Actually, there is. Vicky said that Villiers also mentioned you sometimes went out at night, for long walks. Is that true?'

He nodded. 'Insomnia. Suffered on and off for years. I find the best thing for it is to go for a walk. Not far – maybe down to the river, or along Fleet Street.'

'You didn't meet anyone while you were out?'

Callum sighed, shook his head. 'Sounds like Martin's determined to make me look like a criminal. Truth is I just sleep badly.'

Hannah was silent for a while, pondering. 'I wonder if there's any way he can be persuaded to . . . cooperate. You've known him for a long time, haven't you?'

'Aye. You think I should appeal to his better nature?'

'Does he have one?'

A desolate laugh escaped him. But then something did occur to Callum, and it was very much not connected with Martin's better nature. Could he do such a thing? His natural sense of loyalty argued against it, but then Martin, who he had always believed a friend, had rejected the chance to save *him*. He looked up at Hannah.

'What if I told you Martin has been – playing away?'

'You mean an affair? I didn't know he was married. Tell me.'

So Callum recounted the story of his accidental encounter with Martin's 'friend' at St James's Walk just after Christmas, and her stopover a few weeks later when Martin untypically flouted discretion. Would that be enough to put him on the spot?

'I should say so,' said Hannah. 'This woman – Sasha? – do you know if he's still seeing her?'

Callum wasn't sure. More pertinently, he didn't know how she might be tracked down. He recalled that she was once a colleague of Martin's before setting up her own business – she had been quite elusive about details.

'All right. What about her surname?'

He closed his eyes in a show of regret, shook his head. 'Sorry.'

There was nothing else. It wasn't much to go on, he could see that. Hannah's expression was doubtful. 'I'll see what I can do, but without a name it's—'

'I know.'

A buzzer had sounded, indicating time was up. Hannah put her notebook away and slung on her shoulder bag. She could sense his creeping mood of defeat. Telling him to keep his chin up seemed to her unhelpful. She had interviewed terrorists before, knew from experience how they talked and behaved. Sometimes it had been vital to her safety to know. Once or twice she had been duped. But nothing about Callum Conlan made her think he was one of them.

She was at the door when he called her back, his voice suddenly urgent. He *had* remembered something else. Sasha had left behind a paperback – a Jane Austen Penguin – in Martin's bedroom, and her full name was written on the flyleaf. He'd put it on a shelf somewhere at home; he was pretty sure it was still there. Hannah scribbled down his address.

'*Emma*, I think it was,' he said, almost beseechingly. 'Can you make a note of that, too?'

This is all getting a bit Nancy Drew, Hannah thought, but his face was flushed with nervous excitement and she didn't dare say anything to dishearten him.

'OK, stay calm. If it's there, I'll find it.'

22

Freddie was browsing *The Letters of Oscar Wilde*. He heard himself sighing a good deal as he read. The dandified wit of the plays and epigrams was not much evident in these pages. 'I put all my genius into my life – I have put only my talent into my works,' Oscar had said; into his correspondence he seemed to have put only his grievances, most of them about money. Towards the end, when he was in exile and bankrupt, nearly every letter included a request (or a demand) for funds, often to friends who appeared just as broke as he was. Unlyrical stuff, and rather charmless. Even his great prison letter, *De Profundis*, which had once moved him, jangled with an obsession over money, as Wilde berated his nemesis, Bosie, for an extravagance to which he himself was hopelessly prey.

And yet the plaintiveness of the letters did suit Freddie's mood. He sat at home in his study, with its huge picture window looking down upon the spires and high-rises of London. It was a view he had cherished from the day they first moved in. Now that Linda had handed him his notice to quit, a valedictory melancholy had taken hold. There had been happy times in this flat, they had hosted some wonderful parties, and in spite of their troubles he and Linda had raised the boys here without noticeable ill effect. To be turned out of the family home this late in the day would be a sad upheaval. All of these books, his records, his mementoes, his awards, the paintings on the wall, these were not merely the chronicle of his life – they *were* his life. Carting them off in a borrowed van seemed like a violation. And where on earth should he go? 'At least you can afford it,' Linda had remarked, which hardly consoled him.

In his more clear-sighted moments he knew this to be so much self-pity. He had made his extramarital bed, plenty of times, and had to lie in it. Only that bed was empty now too. If he were leaving here in the certainty of a life with Nicola all might be well. 'I cannot live without the atmosphere of Love,' Wilde wrote to Robbie Ross. 'I must love and be loved whatever price I pay for it.' Freddie had realised the truth of that too late. Nicola had loved him, he was certain, and if he hadn't been so selfish and puffed-up she might have done still. *I wonder if you really see people at all,* that's what she'd said to him. He had pondered that line quite a lot these last weeks. It was as though all the energy and feeling and shrewdness he had devoted to moving people around a stage had somehow unfitted him to deal with the people he moved among day by day. He had put his talent into his works, but – unlike Wilde – he had no genius for life.

It was a spring day of capricious light, the sudden switches between glare and gloom confounding anyone who cared to look skywards. Terry was driving him into town, and on a whim Freddie decided to get out at Exmouth Market and walk down Farringdon Road. 'Watch yourself out there, sir,' said Terry, a benediction of such rarity from him that he was taken aback. Perhaps it was to do with the public mood at large – the IRA bombs had made people skittish – or else Terry had sensed his boss's low spirits. 'Will do!' Freddie called, and sauntered off. He passed the open door of a newsagent where he spotted the new *Private Eye* on sale. What fresh poison had they been stirring? No doubt someone at the office would be happy to fill him in.

A little further down his eye snagged on a tray of glazed goodies in the window of a cake shop. He walked on, stopped, retraced his steps: he couldn't resist after all. He pushed the door, setting off a jingle, and a young woman behind the counter instantly favoured him with a smile. His gaze shifted greedily along the glassed compartments, from Eccles cakes to iced buns to vanilla slices to chocolate eclairs; he liked the way they wore a film of sweat, as though desperate to be eaten. A separate display held larger cakes on old-fashioned porcelain stands, 'made fresh today' a printed sign declared.

'Can I help you?' asked the young woman, her light brown hair attractively feather-cut. An enamelled staff badge on her jumper read PENNY.

Freddie returned an eager look – his plump jowls told plainly of his appetite. 'Well, they all look delicious . . . ' He nodded at the uncut Victoria sponge on a stand just behind her. 'But *that* looks especially good.'

'Mm,' Penny agreed. 'Shall I pop it in a box for you?'

Freddie blushed, embarrassed. 'Oh, I only want a slice,' he laughed, and almost joked in afterthought 'I need to watch my figure' – but the possibility that she might take it seriously stopped him.

'If you'd like to have a seat I'll bring it over,' she said brightly. He had intended to take his purchase back to the office, but Penny's beaming geniality persuaded him to stay. As he sat at the Formica-topped table he realised that this was the shop where Dawn had been faithfully buying the office pastries all these years – he'd eaten enough of them by now to know. When a few moments later Penny served him his slice of cake he thanked her and said, 'I wonder if you'd put another piece of this in a box for me?' He thought he might surprise Dawn by reversing the routine of giver and taker – she'd appreciate that. 'Actually, better make it two slices – I might want another by teatime.'

Penny laughed at his Bunterish forethought. 'That reminds me of another customer,' she said. 'Nice girl – I think she works round here. Calls in every weekday morning to buy something, usually a Danish or a piece of cake. Whatever it is, she always buys two of 'em, and we get talking a bit. One day I ask her – who's the other one for?' Penny's voice then dropped to a confiding undertone. 'Tells me it's for her boss. Only, he always eats both of 'em.'

'Really?' said Freddie.

'First time it happened she'd bought one for him, one for herself. Without even asking he snaffled them both. The next day he does the same thing. So she made it a kind of test after that – buy two, wait to see if he leaves one for her. And you know what, he *never has*. Not once!'

Freddie made a disapproving face. 'He sounds like—'

'—a right greedy sod, I know! Poor woman . . . Apparently he treats her like a skivvy, fetch this, fetch that. She says he never bothers talking to his staff unless he needs something from them. Honestly, if he was my boss I'd tell him where to shove it – an' his pastries!'

'Why doesn't she, er, hand in her notice?'

'Dunno. Too demoralised? I think she's tried to drop him in it a couple of times – she phoned a newspaper with a story, some bit of gossip. But nothing's ever stuck. That sort always get away with it, don't they?'

'The way of the world,' he said distantly.

Penny returned a smile of rueful complicity, as if that world's wickedness was beyond their fathoming. 'I'd better get on. Enjoy your cake!'

Afterwards Freddie walked on to the NMH, deep in thought. He was recalling an episode of his boyhood, at a school friend's party. There was a cake – a treat during the war, when such things were scarce – and quite a fuss was being made of it. The children gathered, sang Happy Birthday, and one of the adults began to cut the cake. Slices were carefully handed around, until it came to Freddie's turn, by which point it was three-quarters gone. When his small portion was cut, instead of taking that he picked up the remainder of the cake – reasoning that a second piece of it wouldn't be offered. The other kids giggled and pointed, but the lady with the cake knife was outraged and gave him a proper ticking-off. 'Gluttony is a sin, you know,' she said, and in hot-faced shame he had set his piece back down on the plate. He remembered walking home in tears.

The lift doors opened and he ambled into his office. He buzzed the intercom and asked Dawn to come through. When she appeared he considered her, trying to detect some vibration of hostility that had previously eluded him. But Dawn's face was the same as ever – plain, round, as unreadable as a snowman's – and he wondered if she ever played poker. She had brought in her notepad, prepared for his instructions, and he asked her to sit down.

He took a breath and said, 'I fear you've been unhappy in this job, Dawn, and I must own my part of the blame for that.'

She looked startled. 'I'm sorry?'

'You wouldn't be the first person to have been on the wrong end of my brusque manners.' He paused. 'For all that, I don't think such behaviour should warrant an actual campaign against me. I mean, career-wrecking stuff.'

On this last phrase he saw her flinch. 'Erm, is there something the matter?'

'I'm afraid so. Oh, by the way,' he said, nodding at the small square cardboard box on his desk, 'that's for you.'

Dawn stared at it worriedly.

'Go on, open it,' he said with a quick smile.

She leaned over and lifted the lid: on a paper doily sat two slices of Victoria sponge. Her eyes widened in alarm. 'For me?'

He nodded slowly. 'Both of them.'

'Well, that's very—' She made to rise from her chair.

'Sit down, please. Odd, isn't it, that habit we have of confiding intimacies to chance acquaintances? There you are, in a shop, say, and the person behind the counter starts telling you about one of her customers, someone she just chats to ... This customer, though, oh, she's had it up to here with her boss, with his high-handed ways. In fact she's so fed up she's decided to take action – with access to all his letters, cheques, memos and so on she's well placed to hurt him. All it requires is a call to a newspaper ...'

Dawn had gone deathly pale; her lower lip trembled. 'I don't know why you're telling me this.'

'Come on, Dawn. It's too late for that.' For some moments Freddie watched her, and waited. When she still didn't speak he said, in a softer tone, 'May I ask why?'

Her answer came, eventually, in a low, faltering voice. 'I never – I never felt you even noticed me. After all these years. You spoke to me as though I were a ... a stranger. Some anonymous dogsbody.' She dared a glance at him. 'And you always ate the cakes.'

Freddie allowed a chastened silence. Neither accusation was new to him. And neither was unjust.

'Well, *mea culpa*, like I said,' he sighed. 'But, Dawn, you tried to ruin me. I can't keep you on here. You do understand?'

She nodded, tears starting in her eyes, and of a sudden he felt sorry for her. 'You'll clear your desk immediately, but you'll be paid for the rest of the month. I'll get Bob to write you a good reference.'

After some moments composing herself she rose to her feet. She said, dabbing her eye with the back of her hand, 'Actually, I wasn't unhappy in the job. I loved working here.'

He looked at her, puzzled. *So why the hell do that to me?* he wondered. When she had left the room he got up himself and went to the window; he stood there and stared over the jagged line of rooftops and chimneys towards the Thames. Was he such a terrible person?

On the desk lay the open cake box, which Dawn had proudly declined to take. He glanced at his watch, checking how long till teatime.

Hannah was out with Christopher on a dinner date in Soho. They were getting along tremendously. She hadn't realised that as well as rock and jazz he was a devotee of opera; in fact he had a box at Covent Garden and wanted her to accompany him there in a couple of weeks. Hannah had been to the Opera House once, years ago, and found the occasion vaguely alienating – the disengaged audience, the ritualised curtain calls, the thrum of money – but she was impressed by his eclectic taste and thought *Why not?* Though she made sure to establish it would be just the two of them and not an outing with his loud upper-crust friends. He had not mentioned Devora all evening, which she took to be a positive sign.

Talk turned to the election, only a few days away, but what previously had been a source of tension between them was now just a brisk and jolly difference of opinion. It seemed that Christopher didn't mind being teased for his Toryism, and he laughed at her horror of Thatcher's voice and nannyish condescension. His confidence of a victory on 3 May was immovable: Margaret had it in the bag, he reckoned. Yet halfway through April the Tory lead was thinning, and now, into the fourth week, a MORI poll had put the Conservatives only three points ahead. Hannah related what her shrewd old colleague Ray Tewson had said at this morning's conference – that it would no longer be a surprise if Labour squeaked back in. Christopher only shrugged and smiled.

'Shall we have another bottle?' he asked as their plates were being cleared. She returned a mock grimace. Martinis had preceded the bottle of claret they had just finished in double-quick time. He ordered another anyway. The hum of the restaurant played discreetly in the background, and with no apparent self-consciousness he reached out to lay his hand upon hers. He had been at his most charming, and Hannah wondered to herself if this, at last, might be The Night. She tried to remember which knickers she had put on that morning. If they did get back to his place she supposed he would take a lenient view, whatever she was wearing.

He filled her glass from the new bottle.

She raised a constraining hand. 'That's my last. I'm trying to keep a clear head for tomorrow.'

When he asked why, she hesitated, half wishing she had not said so.

'Oh, I'm following up this story about the Middleton murder.'

'Really?' said Christopher, his eyes sparking up. 'God, I'm still spooked by the moment we had with him at the theatre. I shook his hand! Hard to take, a war hero dying like that.'

'I know,' said Hannah, hoping to change the subject. 'So are you—'

'What's your angle on it?'

Again she hesitated. It was too grave a matter to broach on a romantic *à deux*.

But she had trapped herself. 'I'm writing about the man who's been charged – the lecturer.'

He was shaking his head, lip curled in disgust. 'I hope he'll rot in prison. In fact, I'd be pleased to see him hang. Treason's still a capital offence, isn't it?'

'Er, I believe so. Though technically it's conspiracy to aid terrorism rather than treason. And he hasn't been tried yet, either.'

'Oh, but he's guilty, isn't he? All that guff about not knowing what was in the bag ... He'd been friends with the bomber since school.'

'Yeah, I know,' said Hannah, 'it sounds unlikely. And yet ... ' She began to explain how she too had assumed Callum Conlan to be part of the IRA active service unit, how all the evidence at first seemed against him. But a police detective she knew had suggested there was a question about his involvement, and since she had talked to him herself—

'What, you've *met* him?'

I'm a journalist, in case you'd forgotten, she was about to reply, but unwilling to seem combative she only said, 'Yeah, and I think there's room for doubt.'

'You can't be serious.' He sounded incredulous rather than angry.

'Why are you so convinced that he's guilty? How d'you know he wasn't tricked into minding that holdall?'

Christopher's hand, which had rested on hers all this time, was now uncoupled. It seemed he was negotiating with the enemy.

'Has your editor foisted this on you?'

She was offended by the implication. 'No. I've been reporting on Northern Ireland for six years. I've been a journalist for twelve years. I think I've got a decent instinct about whether someone's lying or not.'

He was staring at her now in a narrow, sceptical way, and she cursed herself – she ought never to have brought it up. Whatever line you took on Ireland it was guaranteed to raise hackles and cause ill feeling. She realised it was up to her to get the evening back on track.

'Can we please talk about something else?' she asked nicely.

'I'm not sure. Can we?'

She paused a beat. 'I'm just trying to discover the truth. It's my job. I know you don't much care for the newspaper I write for—'

'Do you blame me? I can put up with most of the cause-mongering, the bleeding-heart stuff. Live and let live, it doesn't bother me. But I draw the line at sympathising with terrorists. These people want to kill and maim us, indiscriminately, and still you think it's OK to rush to the defence of one of them. That to me is inexcusable.'

'Do I have to say it again? I'm not sure he *is* a terrorist, and I'd rather establish the facts before we get down to convicting an innocent man.'

He had poured himself another large glass of wine – petrol on the bonfire. 'Your lot always assume they're innocent,' he said, with a scowl she had not seen from him before.

'"Your lot"? What d'you mean by that?'

'It's the liberal reflex. You always want to understand, to make excuses. Do you suppose Middleton's widow would thank you for taking the side of the man who probably helped destroy her husband?'

'No. But I think she would sooner have a proper investigation into his death than a pitchfork mob looking for a scapegoat.'

At that he fell silent. They had reached an impasse, neither of them prepared to yield. Christopher, still scowling, took out a cigarette; as he lit it she saw his hand was shaking. She had enraged him, it seemed. So much for her anticipation of this being The Night. A sad delusion. They hadn't even managed to get to coffee without daggers drawn.

Callum had been on the phone to his sister again. She had taken on the responsibility after Eileen, their mother, proved incapable of talking to him for more than thirty seconds at a time without breaking down. He preferred the sound of her voice anyway. Niamh, at nineteen, made up for what she lacked in philosophical reasoning with encouragement and an unwavering belief in his innocence. She was also scaldingly honest: Callum was the talk of Newry, his face plastered all over the local news. The press had been camped outside their terraced house for days. When the death threats started coming she and her mother had decamped to their aunt's place a few miles away – 'just till it dies down', she added. He didn't have the heart to tell her that it might be years before it died down.

She wanted to know how far his solicitor had got with the case, and he had assured her that everything was being done to move it forward. In truth he didn't really know: Nicholas Edgerton had gone cold on him, and the police apparently had no clue as to where the bombers had fled. Watching the news on TV (a novel experience for him) Callum felt himself recoil whenever attention focused on the terror campaign. His mugshot came up so often on these items that it seemed that everyone in the country would know him by now – his was the face they would associate with the IRA and the murder of Anthony Middleton, war hero, shadow minister, family man.

As the election drew near the reports dropped further down the order, and slowly began to disappear. But he sensed the respite would be brief. As soon as the trial started his name would be back on the agenda, his involvement debated all over again.

Lying awake in his cell into the small hours, as the distant hoots and bangs and cries of night-time prison faded, he thought of Hannah Strode, and tried to kindle the guttering flame of hope.

Vicky was waiting in her car when Hannah arrived at St James's Walk. The quiet close had been lousy with camera crews for a couple of weeks, and now had gone back to looking deserted. Callum's front door was still criss-crossed with police tape, drooping here and there like forgotten party streamers. DO NOT ENTER it warned. Hannah turned on hearing the car door slam and raised her hand in greeting. Vicky took in her pale complexion, the fatigue around her eyes – the woman looked a bit rough, but then journalists often did in her experience.

'You all right?' she asked.

Hannah returned a wincing smile. 'Had one too many last night.'

Vicky, a jailer's ring of keys in her hand, selected one and unlocked the front door. The police tape fell away at her push, and she entered the hallway, Hannah at her back. The carpet was gritty, and littered. The sight through the next door caused Hannah to gasp in shock: the living room had been turned upside down, as if by vandals or burglars. The floor was deeply strewn with books, perhaps a thousand or more, tossed any old how on their way from the shelves, now denuded. The furniture looked traumatised, a sofa spilling its foam guts onto the floor. A dining chair had been upended, its wooden legs seeming to implore. Pictures and curtains had been torn down; a paper globe lampshade lay forlorn, crushed. She bent down and picked up a hardback book, splayed open with a dirty footprint on its flyleaf. There was everything but graffiti on the walls.

'Did they – the Bomb Squad – find anything?' Hannah asked.

'Not a thing,' replied Vicky, accustomed to the sight. 'And they went through every room with a fine-tooth comb.'

Not that fine, thought Hannah, her gaze wandering around the violated scene. 'Can you help?'

Vicky looked at her watch. 'I can stay for twenty minutes.'

She described what she was looking for, and they set to work, picking through the tumbled piles of books, examining, discarding, pausing now and then to consider a title. Vicky had never seen so many books owned by a single person; she didn't really know people who read a lot. Hannah couldn't help herself dawdling – some were books she recognised from her own student days. You could get such an impression of someone from their reading habits – like this pumpkin-coloured volume she picked at random, *Collected Poems* by Louis MacNeice. *The Shrimp and the Anemone*, L. P. Hartley. *Of Human Bondage*, W. Somerset Maugham. *The Heat of the Day*, Elizabeth Bowen. Just to handle the books, to glimpse the pencilled marginalia, softened her feelings for their absent owner. She could imagine his shock on returning home to find this disarray. He had plainly devoted many hours, and quite a bit of money, to accumulating a library, and to see it so carelessly tossed about saddened her. She was almost tempted to start putting the books back on the shelf.

An exclamation from Vicky broke her train of thought. 'Is this it?'

She held up a paperback of *Emma*, which Hannah examined before shaking her head. 'I think that must be his own copy. The one we're looking for has an orange spine.'

They talked as they continued rummaging on their hands and knees. Hannah asked whether the police had any new leads on the terrorists; Vicky said not, and that in all probability they had been smuggled out of the country within hours of planting the bombs. The sports bag remained the only significant piece of evidence, and Callum was unfortunate in being the last man seen holding it.

'What did you think of him when you met?'

'He seemed, I dunno, a decent bloke,' said Hannah, who hadn't owned up to their chance meeting months before. 'He was happy to have got out of Ireland. I asked around the college. He's popular with the other staff, and the students. None of them could believe what he'd been accused of ... one girl broke down in tears. I think she'd been there when he was arrested.'

Vicky said that if they couldn't get Villiers to change his story then things could go badly for Callum in court. The public mood, stoked by the press, was for a conviction. Hannah, mindful of last night's set-to with Christopher, said quietly, 'I think you're right.'

The book wasn't there. They had turned over many Penguin paperbacks among the piles, a couple by Jane Austen. But none of them *Emma*. Hannah noticed Vicky quickly consult her watch, and said, 'You'd better go. I can get on with this.'

Vicky stood up, looking around. 'Maybe we should check upstairs.'

The first bedroom was evidently the spare, and yielded nothing. The second must have been Callum's, and mirrored the living room, ankle-deep in books, hundreds of them. Vicky cooed, 'It's like a book farm, this place.' With a little sigh she dropped to her knees and resumed the search, with the same desultory talk between them. Every flash of an orange spine would raise their hopes, only to be dashed on taking a closer look. Had Callum in his desperation merely dreamed this book?

As Hannah crouched there she heard Vicky getting to her feet, preparing to go. She had well exceeded her promised twenty minutes. Only she wasn't going. Hannah turned to find her holding a Penguin paperback of *Emma* right in front of her face. 'Oh my God ... at last!' The relief of it forced a laugh from her, which Vicky echoed. She took it from her and looked inside. There, in a student's neat hand, was the name: Sasha Denning.

Martin Villiers's other woman. The hunt was on.

23

Hannah had spent time on missing persons before, but this wasn't like that. Sasha Denning hadn't disappeared, or been abducted, or gone into hiding; in fact she would be quite unaware that anyone was looking for her. The information Callum had provided was scant, but he did know that she had once worked with Martin at the House of Commons. So Hannah started there, careful not to let slip the reason for her search lest Villiers got wind of it and warned his girlfriend to be on her guard. The problem was that election fever was running high and Commons people on the phone were too distracted or harassed to help with an enquiry not related to 'D-Day'. Promises to call back came to nothing. Then she took the more obvious route of consulting the London telephone directory, which listed nine Dennings. She rang all of them, to no avail. Either Sasha had never rented a line in her name or else she had gone ex-directory.

Perseverance at last lifted the edge of the curtain. Someone at the House of Commons did remember Sasha, and was pretty sure that she had left to join an advertising agency. It was a few years ago – she couldn't recall its name. So Hannah phoned around the ad people of her acquaintance, a small but gregarious bunch of networkers who all appeared to know one another, and sure enough the name of her quarry eventually came up. It transpired that she had left the first agency to set up her own public relations business, a place off Devonshire Street in Marylebone. When Hannah phoned SD PR she had to bluff a little – told the assistant she was writing a story about influential women in business: 'Ms Denning's name was recommended.' The assistant came back: yes, she'd be delighted to talk with Hannah, and an appointment was set.

The address was a cobbled mews tucked away from the bustle of traffic at both ends. Hannah knocked at the door of a squat brick house with pretty window boxes on the upper storey. The pretext for her visit had plainly been swallowed; the girl at reception made a fuss of her, brought tea and a promise that Sasha would be with her in a few minutes. When the woman in question did appear looking freshly coiffed and groomed, Hannah felt a stab of guilt that her lie had been so effective: Sasha was expecting a turn in the limelight. She was good-looking, olive-skinned, with dark bobbed hair – a slightly outgrown Purdey. She wore a belted woollen dress and boots not unlike Hannah's own. '*So* nice to meet you,' she said in a refined, low voice that seemed to invite confidences. 'I'm such a fan of the *Ensign*.' Pure blandishment, thought Hannah: she would have bet on her being a *Daily Mail* reader.

She began by bowling Sasha a few gentle questions – how she liked running her own business, what improvements she hoped to make, what she thought of Mrs Thatcher as a role model. This last was her prompt.

'I gather *you* worked in the House of Commons for a while . . .'

Sasha nodded. 'I was a junior civil servant – it taught me a lot about influence and how it works.'

'That must have been where you met Martin Villiers?'

She gave a brief start. This wasn't the line she'd been expecting. 'How d'you know Martin?'

'I don't, really. I've spoken to him a few times. We were supposed to meet on the day of that IRA bomb – I was waiting to be taken to his office when it went off, so . . . it never happened.'

'How awful. You were *there* . . .' She hesitated, perhaps trying to gauge the right level of disclosure. 'I know Martin was very shaken by the whole thing.'

'Of course. You're quite close, aren't you?'

'What – I'm not sure – why would you say that?'

Sasha was trying to maintain her good manners, but a defensive, brittle note had entered her tone.

'Well, I work for a newspaper,' Hannah said, with a friendly laugh. 'You keep your ear to the ground. As a matter of fact, I know Martin's old friend from college. Callum Conlan. The man who's been charged with the murder.'

Now she looked spooked, and something hardened in her expression. 'What's this about – are you really doing a story on me?'

'I might be. But it's not a story you'll want to read.'

Sasha got to her feet. 'I think you should leave. Please leave.'

Hannah didn't move. 'This doesn't have to get unpleasant. But I do need something from you. Please, sit down.'

Fear and hostility were locked in a struggle across her face. 'I don't want to talk to you.'

'I'm afraid you're going to have to. You see, Callum Conlan may be innocent, and his defence would be assisted by a piece of evidence – I won't burden you with the detail – which Martin has chosen to deny. I don't know why. Maybe he got scared. But since he's not prepared to help, we have to persuade him.'

Sasha, arms stiffly folded as she listened, said, 'What's it got to do with me?'

'I happen to know you were having an affair with him. Maybe still are. And that's our leverage.'

'That's rubbish. We're friends, that's all—'

'Right. And I suppose Martin will say the same.'

'Of course he will. We've got nothing to hide.'

Hannah stared at her, disappointed. 'Conlan met you, remember, the morning after you'd stayed the night with Martin. You hadn't been expecting him.'

'So? Doesn't prove anything.'

Hannah reached into the shoulder bag at her feet. She took out the paperback of *Emma* and held it up. 'Yours, I believe.

Has your signature, see? Conlan found it after you left. In Martin's bedroom.'

Sasha, pale with fury, seemed to consider her options. 'He probably stole it. May I have it back?'

Hannah shook her head. 'I was at Conlan's house yesterday, with a police detective. She's got dabs from the bedroom – the one you and Martin slept in. So either you admit it to me, or we bring the law in.'

That silenced her. For some moments she stared off, cornered, sullen. When she spoke her voice was thin with contempt. 'What a way to make a living – snooping on people.'

Hannah laughed. 'That's funny. You just told me you enjoyed learning how influence works. This is how – right here.'

At Scotland Yard Vicky had been introduced to Kevin McDowell, a senior officer with the Bomb Squad. He was putting together his report on the Harrowby Street bomb and had requested a debrief with her. Fiftyish, well built, with shirtsleeves pushed up revealing dark-haired forearms, McDowell spoke to her with a thoughtfulness at odds with the laconic professionalism of most Yard veterans. Perhaps he could see the strain she was still under.

'I'm sorry to make you go through this again. It's just vital that we get as much information as we can – it helps us down the line.'

'I understand, sir. I want to help.'

He asked her to go through the incident step by step, from the time they arrived at the Duke of York pub. As Vicky recounted it McDowell made notes, occasionally pausing to clarify some detail. As she described the moments before the detonation her voice faltered and tears sprang to her eyes. She drank some water, and managed to continue.

'I know you'd rather not dwell on it, Vicky, but I have to ask. Was there any delay at all between Wicks's opening the car door and the explosion?'

'I don't think so,' she replied. Only now she thought about it she seemed to recall David Wicks turning his face to her, after he'd opened the door. 'I'm not sure. There might have been – just a couple of seconds.'

McDowell nodded, as if she had confirmed a private suspicion of his. 'You see, there's something we can't work out. A discrepancy. Even though both attacks were claimed by the IRA, the second bomb was very different. Middleton was killed by a booby-trap device – a mercury-tilt switch. As soon as his car went up the incline, the mercury triggered an electric current that set off the detonator. But the bomb that killed Wicks wasn't like that – from the fragments we've recovered it looks completely rogue, and the explosive came from a different source.'

'Wouldn't that be possible?'

'Possible, but unlikely. The closeness of the attacks – six days – suggests they would adopt the same MO, at least use the same explosive. But they didn't. It inclines me to believe that the Harrowby Street device was planted by someone other than the IRA.'

'Who, then?'

He shook his head. 'We're still trying to trace the explosive. It's not Russian-made, as the Commons bomb was. The theory I'm working on – strictly between us – is that Wicks was deliberately targeted. I have no idea who or why.' He looked at her doubtfully. 'Do you?'

Hannah looked at her watch. Another ten minutes had slipped by since she'd been asked to wait half an hour ago. Jeanette, the young woman she'd met on the day of the Parliament bomb, had greeted her again. With an anxious sideways glance she said that the mood in the office had been 'tense' – the election was two days away and the Tories were inching ahead again in the opinion polls. Hannah took this to mean that Martin's mood was tense, and therefore the entire office would have to suffer. She could hear through the door his querulous, faintly adenoidal voice rise and fall.

She had prepared herself quite carefully for this, and yet a terrible foreboding had ambushed her first thing that morning. What she was about to do – well, 'underhand' hardly covered it. Blackmail was not something she had ever contemplated before, let alone with a government official. She felt she was playing with a strong hand, but then most blackmailers probably thought that, until they got rumbled. Martin Villiers seemed to her such a volatile character it was impossible to guess which way it would go. He might just laugh in her face. Or else have her arrested – suborning a government employee didn't sound too clever as a tactic. *Play it cool,* she told herself. If he senses you're nervous the game's up.

'Hannah Strode – we meet at last!' Martin was standing there, in shirtsleeves, his tie loosened. He had forgotten they had met a couple of times before, and Hannah decided not to correct him. Nor did she complain about the wait.

'It's good of you to see me,' she said. 'I know how busy you are.'

He dismissed the courtesy with a seigneurial waft of his hand. 'Never too busy for the loyalest paper on Fleet Street. We could do with more like you.'

Hannah thought it interesting – too interesting – that he should talk of loyalty so warmly, but again she held her tongue: she would keep her powder dry for the moment. He led her through the office and onto an outdoor terrace overlooking the river; the spring afternoon was mild, and the light benign.

Jeanette brought them coffee, and they settled at a table. Martin offered her a cigarette, and they lit up.

'So how's it looking for Thursday?' Hannah asked. As a journalist she was a dab hand with small talk – the softening up before you went in for the kill. Sasha had been an easy mark. Villiers was a much tougher nut.

'We're cautiously optimistic,' he replied. 'I think the British public still like Jim – they aren't ready to oust him yet.'

'Well, he's a likeable man. It's his politics I'm worried about. The government hasn't looked very inspired these last months – I mean, the way they've handled the strikes . . . '

He gave a worldly shrug. 'It wasn't ideal. But I don't think a Tory government would have handled it any better.'

'I get the feeling people would vote for any party that guaranteed their rubbish would be collected. The bin men strike was the worst of all – and they had a lot of competition.'

'Strikes have changed the whole landscape – they're the new blood sport. Don't quote me on that,' he added with a smirk.

He had noticed that Hannah didn't have a notebook out, and said, 'Was there something specific you wanted to discuss?'

Here we go, thought Hannah, bracing herself. 'Yes. I'd like to talk to you about Callum Conlan.'

Martin gave an impatient sigh. 'Really? I've already talked to the police about this.'

'I know. Vicky Tress told me. We've become quite good pals these last few weeks.'

'I've got nothing to add. Callum – Conlan – had me fooled completely. I had no idea he was involved with the Provos.'

'Yeah, I know. But there's something, something specific, that I think has been overlooked, and it's to do with a conversation you and he—'

'If you mean the night we talked to Anthony Middleton I've already explained to the detective constable. I have no memory of Callum asking me who Middleton was. If he did he was bluffing.'

'"If he did." So you accept that he *might* have asked you?'

'I don't think he did. There's no way he could have been ignorant of the man we'd been talking to.'

'But you're in politics. Conlan hadn't a clue. He doesn't watch telly either. So it's quite plausible that he didn't recognise the Shadow Home Secretary. A lot of people wouldn't.'

Martin shrugged. 'I'm just telling you what I remember.'

Hannah stared at him. 'From talking to him I got the impression that you and Conlan were good friends. You were at college together; until recently you were staying in his spare room, right? And yet now you're doing everything you can to distance yourself from him.'

'Wouldn't you if it came out a friend had been deceiving you? How can I feel the same about someone who's been implicated in a terrorist murder?'

'To be honest, if it were me, I'd want to believe my friend rather than his accusers, whatever the chances of his guilt,' said Hannah.

'Well, that's where we differ,' he replied, and checked his watch. 'Now, if you'll excuse me I've got a campaign to run.'

Hannah watched as he stubbed his cigarette, preparing to go. Well, she had given him a chance to show loyalty, or even mercy, and he had emphatically turned it down. 'One other thing. Can you tell me about your relationship with Sasha Denning?'

'What?' he snapped.

'Sasha. She stayed a couple of times at St James's Walk. I gather you were having an affair.'

Martin froze, narrowed his eyes. She could see him working it out. 'Callum told you that? Well, he'd do anything to save himself. Wrong end of the stick. Sasha and I are good friends, that's all.'

'That was her story, too, until I told her the police had dusted everything in that house. They've got her fingerprints all over your bedroom.'

He was staring at her, his expression mixing disgust with a reluctant admiration of her manoeuvre. 'So . . . this is how he's going to play it.'

'You didn't leave him much option. He thought you'd defend him. When you refused he had to go low – though not as low as you.'

'You realise you could be helping a terrorist walk free?'

Hannah nodded. 'Maybe. But I don't think so. And I'm pretty sure you'd rather not have your private life dragged across the front pages. "PM's aide used suspect's house as love nest." Spare your wife, too.'

They faced one another in silence for some moments. She wasn't sure she had ever seen a lip curl with so much disdain. Such were the perks of the job.

'What d'you expect me to do?' he asked in a flat tone.

She returned an unfriendly smile. The slick veneer of his charm had worn right through. 'You know what you've got to do.'

On Thursday Freddie woke in a mood of ominous agitation. He was aware of it being his fiftieth, but something else nagged at the fringes of his consciousness. It soon came to him: Oh yeah – polling day.

Attired in a silk paisley dressing gown, a birthday present from his parents, he ambled down to the kitchen where Mrs Jenner had cooked him breakfast. Linda gave him a playboy cologne, Eau Sauvage, which he couldn't help thinking of as rather pointed. The boys had called into his bedroom bearing their gifts. Jon presented him with a silver-plated cigar-cutter, bought from the ancient tobacconist's on Charing Cross Road. Tim's gift was wishful – a Queens Park Rangers bobble hat and club scarf. Freddie supported no club in particular, but ever since he had taken Tim to his first football match at Loftus Road his younger son had been aiming to convert him. Their birthday card to him was a sentimental thing dedicated to 'The World's Best Dad', a legend more affecting for its plain untruth. But he had *tried* his best for them.

Terry wished him a happy birthday as he climbed into the car.

'I hope you and the lady wife will be coming to the party this evening,' Freddie said, watching his eyes in the rear-view mirror. Terry assured him that he would be pleased to 'drop in', though he was sorry Winifred wouldn't be joining them. That was a pity: after twelve years in his employ Freddie had been curious to meet Terry's missus, but maybe the feeling was not reciprocated. He knew no one who kept his life as private as Terry.

Leo's treat was lunch at the Connaught Grill. Freddie loved the old-fashioned cooking here, and its discreetly expensive air. His host gave him a flamboyant double-kiss on arriving at the table. 'Dear boy, the happiest of happy birthdays to you!'

'Thanks,' said Freddie, sinking into his chair. Leo had rather selfishly taken the lady's seat on the banquette and was scanning the room over Freddie's shoulder: 'The last time I ate here Dirk Bogarde was sitting over there.'

'And now you've only got me sitting over here,' he replied shortly. 'All set for tonight?'

It had been agreed that Leo would give the toast of honour at the party, a prospect that he seemed to relish. Freddie was secretly mortified that he hadn't been able to secure anyone else for the favour. No one seemed quite right, or else he had to admit that he didn't really have close friends – just famous and successful ones. Leo gave generous speeches, but he was an agent, so they tended to be a lot of gush. Freddie knew he couldn't expect anything wildly original or insightful from him. He had considered asking Bob to do it, which would at least guarantee some laughs. But Bob was a colleague, not a pal, and a fiftieth birthday surely required a speech from somebody outside his professional orbit. In years gone by Linda would have done it – an option no longer available to him.

The pop of a cork roused him from these sad reflections.

'I got us the Krug '59,' Leo said proudly. 'I know it's your favourite.'

They touched glasses, and Freddie took a deep swallow of the champagne. Its yeasty, autumnal flavour always gave him a lift.

'Peculiar atmosphere out there today,' he mused.

'Is there?' Leo asked.

'Mm. There usually is on an election day. A sense of impending . . . something or other.'

'Have you voted?'

Freddie shook his head. In fact he had nipped out early that morning, before Terry picked him up. Even as he stepped into the booth he was uncertain which way he'd go – or so he told himself. He came from stock that had Labour in its blood. His parents would never have dreamed of voting anything else. His dad, thirty-seven years on the buses, mum at the millinery works in Nottingham; they had actually met one another at a Labour fundraiser. Could they have guessed that their son and heir, the boy they had raised for better things, would one day turn his back on the party? Inconceivable treachery – it cried out to heaven for vengeance! He picked up the stubby pencil and took a deep breath, his hand hovering over the voting slip. Look at the mess they were in; the country was at a standstill; there had to be a change.

He placed a firm cross against the Conservative candidate and dropped his card through the slot. First time ever. He felt strangely exultant. Then he sidled out of the polling station, as furtive as a shoplifter.

'I'll start with the oysters,' he told the waiter, 'then we'll both have the roast beef.'

'And you'd better ask the sommelier to stop by,' added Leo, with a glance at the rapidly diminishing Krug. He turned back to Freddie. 'What have you got lined up for the autumn?'

'I have something in mind.' He allowed himself a delectable pause. 'The greatest musical ever written?'

Leo stared at him, open-mouthed. It had been a byword between them for years. 'You're kidding me . . .' A look from Freddie indicated he was not kidding, and Leo, rejoicing, mimicked a shake of the dice in his bunched fist and began whistling 'Luck be a Lady'.

'I thought of keeping it for the thirtieth anniversary next year, but I couldn't resist. There are musicals, and there's *Guys and Dolls*.'

'Let's drink to that,' said Leo, who immediately proclaimed it the highlight of the autumn season and spent the next ten minutes planning it all out. He was good on casting, though Freddie had to be alert to which of his clients he might be pushing. Leo had just launched into 'Fugue for Tinhorns' when their starters arrived and peace was restored.

'So . . . Fifty!'

'Oh for God's sake,' Freddie muttered.

'Tell me, what precious nuggets of wisdom have you accumulated in your half-century?'

Freddie thought it a bit early in the day to be getting expansive, however much Leo's eager tone encouraged him.

'I had to sack someone the other day – did I tell you? My PA. Turned out she was the one passing stories about me to the press.'

'You mean Dawn? Gosh . . . always struck me as such a nice girl.'

'She *was* a nice girl. But it seems she'd had it up to here with me. It was pure chance I rumbled her. I'd never have guessed otherwise.'

Leo puffed out his cheeks. 'She must have been really pissed off to go the papers.'

Freddie nodded sadly. 'I felt bad. Not just about sacking her – I mean, that this awful gittish boss had made her miserable.'

'Come on, I'm sure you weren't that bad,' said Leo. 'Possibly you were a little brusque now and then, but so are we all.'

He tilted his head in thanks for these emollient words. 'Well, you asked me about nuggets of wisdom. I've only got one, but it's been hewn from the rock of long experience. And I think it covers the entire human condition. "Be kind, be gentle." In the end it's all that matters.'

Leo was staring at him with – what? – a reverential seriousness, as if he might have been listening to Spinoza or somebody. Freddie was tempted to laugh, just to defuse the moment, but then another thought occurred to him.

'Please don't mention any of this tonight.'

Leo gaped, and said hurriedly, 'No, of course not, I mean—' And then he looked crestfallen. 'Are you rather disappointed that it's me giving the toast?'

The question, earnest and humble, took Freddie by surprise. Here it was, out of nowhere, a chance to practise the philosophy of kindness, of gentleness, that he had so recently espoused. And he realised that it would sometimes involve nothing more than shielding the truth, or telling a white lie.

'Dear Leo. I'm absolutely *delighted* that you're giving the toast. It's very good of you.'

Leo's face cleared with relief. Freddie beamed at him: he was learning already.

Callum was leaving the exercise yard when a prison officer approached him.

'Conlan. Governor's office – now.'

He had briefly met the Governor on his first day in Brixton but couldn't remember any part of their conversation, so benumbed was he at the time. Now he was standing at his desk and being told to clear his cell. There had been no preamble, no warning, no explanation. All charges against him had been dropped.

'You mean, I'm being released?'

He nodded. 'It appears that there has been some – confusion.' His gaze switched to a letter on his leather-edged blotter. 'A Mr Martin Villiers, press secretary to the Prime Minister, has written an account that completely exonerates you. I had a telephone conversation with him earlier. I gather he lodged with you for some months last year, and is prepared to swear on oath he saw no evidence of any association with paramilitaries. He's also cleared it with the CPS. Why it took Mr Villiers all this time to come forward I have no idea.'

Callum felt suddenly faint, and grasped the edge of the desk.

The Governor asked him if he needed to sit down, but he shook his head. Released. Released!

'It seems the value of friends in high places can never be underestimated.'

Callum might have objected to that, but he didn't want to spend another minute in this man's office, talking.

'Can I go?'

For answer the Governor gestured to the officer, who conducted Callum back to his cell for the last time. Deliverance had arrived as abruptly and as confoundingly as his arrest had.

He collected a cardboard box of his 'valuables' from storage – clothes, wallet, keys, some loose change – and signed for it. Even while he was changing into his civvies he worried that there had been some mistake, a mix-up, and that he wasn't to be released after all. He was nearly holding his breath as they walked him out of the wing, through a succession of clanking doors, past groups of cons he didn't know, and thence into the entrance yard. The officer impassively drew back the bolts, unlocked the lodge gate and swung it open.

'Off you go then,' he said with a sharp jerk of his head.

Callum stepped out into the daylight. It felt weirdly scoured and harsh on his eyes. He had been wondering what to expect – a fusillade of flashbulbs, a scrum of television cameras and reporters, a mob of righteous demonstrators. There was no one. Correction: there was someone, just across the road, a woman leaning on the side of a Mini. She waved at him.

'Welcome back,' Hannah said as he approached, and was surprised when he threw his arms around her. He held her silently in a hug for some moments. When he drew back she saw that his eyes were glistening.

'I don't know what to say,' he croaked.

She smiled. 'You don't have to say anything. I wonder if you'd like me to drive you home?'

He was quiet as she navigated the streets of south London, the traffic slowing and thickening into rush hour. She found herself doing nearly all of the talking. He seemed in a kind of trance, but when in her account of the last few days she reached the interview with Martin, he looked at her.

'Does he still think I'm a terrorist?'

She shrugged. 'I don't know. It doesn't matter, does it? Once he realised we'd got him cold he snapped into action pretty quickly. There was no way he was going to risk a scandal.'

Another long silence followed. Then he said, 'What day is it today?'

'Thursday,' she replied. 'Election Day.'

'So Martin might be out of a job by tomorrow.'

'Yeah. We got to him just in time.'

They crossed Blackfriars Bridge. He glanced out of the window at the commuters on their way to the station, the hesitant tourists, the office people standing outside the pub, doing as they pleased – you only ever thought about freedom when it was being taken away from you. Hannah, interrupting his reverie, said, 'You've been rather unlucky with your friends, haven't you?'

'Hmm?'

'I mean, first with McGlashan landing you in it. Then Villiers doing his St Peter act – you know, denying his friend three times.'

Callum smiled. 'Does that make me Christ? For a while in there I thought I'd been abandoned, that no one was gonna come and help me. Nothing like a prison cell to make you feel lonely. But of course there were people – not even friends of mine – who knew I was innocent and wanted to get me out.'

He was staring at Hannah, who gave him a quick sideways smile. They were approaching the Clerkenwell junction at Farringdon Road. 'You're just off here, aren't you?'

When she drew up outside St James's Walk he invited her in for a cup of tea, and though time was getting on she didn't have the heart to refuse. She had already warned him of the state the house was in. Entering the hallway he picked up an untidy sheaf of letters and circulars from the mat. When he looked into the front room and its chaos of tossed books and furniture he gave a little gasp, but said nothing. She followed him into the kitchen, where every cupboard and drawer had been rifled. The fridge door yawned open.

'I'll go and get some milk,' said Hannah quietly. She had noticed a corner shop as they pulled into the close.

When she returned she found Callum exactly where she had left him, seated at the kitchen table, staring into vacancy. There seemed about him the bewildered air of a convalescent: perhaps prison did that to you. Once the kettle had boiled she made a pot of tea for them.

When he took his first sip his eyes closed in appreciation. 'Nice to get a decent cuppa again. You wouldn't believe the shite they give you to drink in there.'

Listlessly flicking through his post he stopped and held up a card. He skimmed it onto the table: a polling card.

'You voted today?'

Hannah nodded. 'Went out first thing this morning. Labour – though I did it with a heavy heart. Just the tiniest bit of me wouldn't mind seeing her get in. Shake things up at least ... Don't ever tell anyone I said that.'

He smiled absently. 'Your secret's safe with me.'

She took out her cigarettes and was about to light up. 'D'you mind if I smoke?'

He shook his head, thinking of the ubiquity of smokers in Brixton. The idea of one of them asking if you minded! He gazed at her as she struck the match, held it to the tip, inhaled – a pale slim hand waving the match out and discarding it in the ashtray. She looked like a woman who was made to smoke; the languid elegance of the movements suited her.

He hadn't said it yet. He had to say it now. 'Hannah. I can't tell you how – I just want to thank you ... ' He swallowed, his voice breaking. 'I won't forget it.'

She sensed the rawness of his emotion, and patted his hand. 'Yeah, well ... It wasn't entirely selfless of me. I've got an exclusive with you, remember.'

They both laughed, and then his laugh became a sob, and he covered his face. He muttered some inaudible broken words. She touched his shoulder, observing the silence of sympathy. She had watched men break down before, some of them violently, dramatically, as if a central prop had given way inside and brought the entire structure crashing down. Some bayed like a wounded animal. Callum's pale face and bruised eyes seemed to her a different order of suffering, a spiritual crisis quietly borne, like one who had gazed into the abyss and yet found the will to live on.

When he had collected himself he said, 'You'll be wanting to do the interview pretty soon, I reckon?'

'Yeah. Next couple of days. Give you a chance to recover. I could come here, or wherever ... It's up to you.'

'Maybe we could go round the corner to the pub – the one where we first met.'

She laughed again. 'My blind date night. Sure, why not?' She looked at her watch. 'I'd better be off. I've got a party this evening.'

'An election party?'

'Actually, a birthday party. Freddie Selves's fiftieth.'

'Is he a friend of yours?'

'I hardly know him. But I did him a favour once, so he thinks I'm all right – for a *journo*.'

'Seems like you're always doing people favours.'

'Don't worry,' she said, waving away the compliment, 'I usually get something in return.'

She stood up, slung on her shoulder bag. He still looked dazed, and frail.

'Will you be all right?'

'Aye. I'll be fine. Enjoy your party. I'll see you in a couple of days.'

When she had gone he mooched around the house for a while. It would be quite a clear-up job. Upstairs the police had stripped his bed and overturned the mattress. The alarm clock had been taken apart – did they suppose he used it for practice? He went to the airing cupboard and took out fresh linen; he made up his bed and lay on it for a while, dozing. Back in the kitchen he picked up the polling card from the table. Election Day – he would remember this one. He stood there for a few moments, thinking. He checked the address of the polling station – two minutes' walk – and tucked the card in his jacket. He collected his keys and left the house.

Freddie made the mistake of arriving half an hour before his party was scheduled to start. It turned an anxious wait into an ordeal. The room, adorned with white tulips and candles, was situated on the rear side of the Savoy with its blameless view across the Thames. Someone had suggested putting a TV in the room so his guests could follow the close of the polls, an idea he instantly vetoed: this was his night, not theirs. The gauntlet of young waiters and waitresses looked nervously eager as they lined up to greet him, the solitary early-arriver. He exchanged some bantering chit-chat with a group of them before retreating to the bar upstairs – they plainly had no idea who he was.

At the top of the stairs he spotted Edie Greenlaw, his favourite old actress, hovering uncertainly. He almost fell on her neck with gratitude.

'Edie! Thank Christ. I was getting so desperate I started flirting with one of the waitresses.'

Edie was turned out in her inimitable throwback style, wearing a high-collared long black dress with tiny pearl buttons running up the front; perched on her grey head was a dainty tiara. She surveyed him through eyelashes tarred with mascara. 'Happy birthday, dearest. Shall we?'

'No, for God's sake, don't go down yet. No one's here!'

'Well, *I'm* here,' she rejoined, incontrovertibly.

'I do love that tiara, by the way.'

Edie touched it and smiled with the disarming girlishness of an eighty-two-year-old. 'D'you know, I wore this for *my* fiftieth! Or was it my fortieth? At that hotel on Half Moon Street. All my friends were there – Peter, László, Tom, Nina Land . . . poor Nina. And of course Jimmy Erskine. Remember him?'

'I met him once, before he died.'

She looked at him archly. 'Well, I don't suppose you met him *after* he died. Oh, what a time we had. The drink we got through was prodigious!'

'What I wouldn't give to have been there,' sighed Freddie, who loved to hear of Edie's bygone days. He felt he might have fitted right in with London's gay, gregarious 1930s.

Just then a bunch of young men hefting drums, double bass and an assortment of brass ambled past them and down the stairs. 'Ah. At least we'll have music,' said Freddie. 'Perhaps you'll put me down on your dance card for later, Edie.'

'Delighted to, darling, as long as you behave yourself.'

Freddie took Edie off to the bar, where they continued gassing away like a couple of washerwomen. It diverted him from worrying about how few people were likely to attend, despite the RSVPs. The bloody election. It was probably divine judgement on him for voting Tory.

When he next checked his watch it was half past eight and he knew he could delay his entrance no longer.

'I suppose we'd better go down, Edie. Please don't laugh when you see the piteous number of guests I've managed to lasso.'

They downed their drinks and Edie linked her spotted hands around his arm as he led her down the stairs. They could hear the jazz quintet already tootling away as they approached and the lively hum of – surely not? – people. In the half-hour they'd been drinking at the bar a magical transformation had been effected: he couldn't quite take in the faces that had filled up the room. All his NMH colleagues were there, of course, plus the overwhelming company of actors and directors and singers he had worked with down the years. Writers, playwrights, pop stars, a couple of TV dolly birds of sixties vintage, a photographer who'd done his portrait, a few cronies from his club, a trio of theatrical knights – they'd all come out for him!

Edie said, rather crossly, 'I thought you said nobody was here.'

'They must have snuck in while we weren't looking,' he said, as relief flooded his veins like a drug.

A young woman had sidled up on his blind side. 'Happy birthday, Freddie.'

It was Romilly Sargent, his lost star, propped on a walking stick. 'My dear girl, you're a sight for sore eyes. Do you know my friend Edie Greenlaw?'

Romilly's eyes widened with awe. She almost curtseyed as Edie accepted her hand. 'Oh! this is a "dear diary" moment. I'm such a fan of yours! I first saw you in *The Cherry Orchard* and just flipped.'

'So kind of you,' Edie said grandly. 'That was the first time I worked with this fellow, d'you remember, darling?'

'How could I forget? My directorial debut in the West End. I was so nervous I almost cleared the pudding trolley at the Ivy.' He pressed the old lady's hand to his lips. 'Edie carried the whole production. She's a credit to the species.'

Edie gave a little whinnying laugh and turned to Romilly. 'He'll say that about you one day, darling, just wait.'

'Freddie!' 'Darling!' His entrance had by now caught on, and he found himself mobbed by six or seven guests at once, clamouring for his attention. Before moving away he leaned over to Romilly and whispered, 'Let's talk later. I have a dream part for you.' He knew she would jump at the chance of Sarah Brown in *Guys and Dolls.*

As he rode the room's carousel of friends and well-wishers he reflected that fate had been on his side. In his thirty-odd years as a professional he had worked hard, had made a sturdy but unexceptional talent go a long way by surrounding himself with brilliant people – *ergo* the occasional accusation that he nicked personal credit from the collective. He had been ruthless at times, but he had also paid most of them their due, had enabled several notable careers, and had given employment to thousands. They said you made your own luck, which was partly true. But that didn't cover the accident of your birth or your place in the pecking order. He hadn't 'made' the luck of having a kindly father, or an ambitious, artistic mother, or the luck of his opportunities, of his parents' continuing devotion, of the money they gave him in the early years to pay his rent and his debts. That was just luck, period.

He got a wave from Linda; they had talked quite civilly about his departure this morning, now set for a fortnight hence. He was going back to Chelsea, his old stamping ground, a maisonette near Cheyne Walk. Perhaps he would have to be alone for a while, only he couldn't bear life without a woman's company. Without that it wasn't really a life at all. Across the room he spotted Nicola, and felt his heartstrings twang painfully. He had tried to win her back, and been refused. But at least she was here.

A tall, attractive woman was approaching, and for a few seconds he didn't recognise her.

'Happy birthday!'

And then he knew her from the voice. 'Hannah Strode. I was just thinking about the women I loved, and here you are, looking ... divine.' It was true; her hair was fixed in a chignon and she was wearing a long blue silk wraparound dress that accentuated her ranginess. 'The dress!'

Hannah smiled. 'Ossie Clark. He can make anyone look good.'

'Better than good. Sensational. But I'm amazed you're not out there doing the election.'

'My night off. I've been covering the story on the Irish lecturer accused of helping the IRA. You know they've dropped the charges?'

'Really? It did sound to me like he just got duped.'

'And yet a lot of people I know assumed he was in on it – that's the trouble with having an Ulster accent in London.'

Freddie thought about this. 'I once directed a *Hamlet* with a couple of wonderful Northern Irish actors. Did you know, the accent is amazingly close to Elizabethan? It's because of the settlement of English and Scottish Protestants in Northern Ireland in the seventeenth century – the place became a backwater and the accent stayed almost unchanged.'

Hannah returned a sceptical smile. 'I can picture you explaining that to a television camera. Anyway – swell party! And the jazz band is great. But can they do Billy Joel?'

Freddie laughed. 'I'll ask 'em, on condition that you agree to dance with me.'

'Deal.' She looked over his shoulder, where a man in a pink velvet jacket had just edged onto the stage. 'I think you're about to be hip-hip-hoorayed.'

He turned to see Leo politely shushing the crowd and tapping the head of the microphone. Time for Freddie to compose his features in a semblance of modesty, ready to chuckle (not that Leo did jokes) or wave away praise (he could depend on him for little else). The guests fell into a hush, with only the faintest blah from the more determined drones at the back of the room – theatre people, wouldn't you know.

'Ladies and gentlemen, welcome. We are here tonight to celebrate a big event, and a very special person – a formidable operator, a born leader, an irresistible life force and a national treasure in the making.' Leo paused. 'Unfortunately Margaret Thatcher couldn't join us tonight' – a wave of outraged laughter crashed over the room – 'as she's busy elsewhere. But we do have another illustrious personage here instead, your great friend and mine, Freddie Selves. Maestro!' More laughter and applause followed, which Leo rode with a showman's ease. 'I could go on about his greatness, of course, and Freddie often encourages me to, but really I'm just the warm-up act. Let me hand you over to a colleague of his, a wonderful lady at the centre of the birthday boy's most recent triumph and an actress who has been to our TV screens a very *lucky* charm – Miss Nicola Mayman!'

Freddie was astounded: he had assumed Leo the speech-maker incapable of jokes or surprises, and yet here he was doing both. When the clapping subsided Nicola, in a chic cream trouser suit and navy blouse, shyly took up the microphone. 'Um, when Leo asked me if I'd give tonight's toast I felt hugely honoured, and terribly anxious. You see, it's hard enough to describe a legend of musical theatre when you also know him to be the cleverest, funniest, *wickedest* man you've ever worked with. No director could drive you up the wall like Freddie does, and yet there's no wall so high that you wouldn't try and climb it for him – because he loves performance, and he adores actors. He's the best, and he knows it, and he knows that *we* know it. So, my tribute to him on his birthday—' she hesitated, brushing the fringe from her eyes (a tic he had always loved) – 'is this little song we worked on together . . .'

She gave a nod to the band leader, the music started up, and she crooned right through 'Without You I'm Nothing', the love aria from *The Ragged Trousered Philanthropists*. Standing there, as the familiar melody uncoiled, Freddie felt his eyes start to brim, and then hot tears were streaming down his face. He couldn't tell if the song was her way of forgiving him, or thanking him, or bidding him farewell. But no serenade had ever sounded so tender to his ears.

The dancing was still going strong at midnight. As Freddie returned from the gents Bob Bewley waylaid him with a news-flash: the first exit polls were out in the 'barometer seats'. In a constituency up north there had been a swing of 0.7 per cent from the Conservatives to Labour. If this was accurate the fore-cast was for Callaghan, with a tiny majority.

So they've got away with it, he thought. The winds of change might have to hold on. And yet he felt something was coming to an end, taking its leave, and it was not to do with his feeling elegiac about turning fifty. Or not only. He seemed to sense it in the air, like a gun dog, some fugitive spirit of decency, as fine as pollen, going, going. *And that will be England gone* . . . Betjeman, he supposed – or was it Larkin?

He was at the bar a few minutes later when Bob buttonholed him again.

'Correction on that last one. It's a two per cent swing to the Tories.'

'So that would mean . . . '

'She's in. The barbarians are at the gates.'

'Well, they'll need a reservation like everybody else,' said Freddie. 'Don't look so down, Bob. Who knows, the change might do us good.'

'I'll remind you of that in a couple of years' time,' Bob replied gloomily.

The band had just segued into a recent chart hit that was filling up the floor: 'My Life' by Billy Joel. His request. Freddie up-periscoped across the heads of the dancers and spied Hannah doing the cha-cha with some young buck. He'd have to put a stop to that right now.

He turned back to Bob. 'I've just spotted my dance partner. Come on, the night's still young!'

Freddie wiggled his hips, and shimmied off into the press of bodies.

24

Vicky was waiting outside the flat in Kensal Rise when she saw Karen, David Wicks's sister, crossing the road towards her. She was a few years younger than her brother, but with the same brownish-blonde hair, and in the eyes and the shape of her jaw Vicky discerned the ghost of her boss – her friend.

They shook hands, exchanged a tentative smile. They hadn't spoken to one another since the funeral, and would perhaps never have done so if Vicky hadn't telephoned her.

'I haven't been in here since . . . ' said Karen, with a grimace. 'I dunno what sort of state it's in.'

'It's really good of you. I honestly wouldn't have asked if it wasn't important.'

Karen produced the keys, letting them into the hallway, and then into the ground-floor flat. Vicky thought it best not to mention the fact she'd visited here once before; she didn't want to hint that her relationship with Wicks had been anything other than professional. The flat looked unchanged from that night – neat, impersonal, a lonely man's refuge. Its white walls seemed to be awaiting a transfusion of colour, a friendly photo or a picture.

They wandered through the living room and into the kitchen. Karen checked the fridge, which had nothing in it except two cans of Carlsberg and a half-pint of milk. She tipped the lumpy liquid into the sink and ran the tap. The bedroom would have been anonymous but for the framed police diplomas on the wall and a *Rothmans Football Yearbook* by the bedside. The duvet, with a print design familiar from John Lewis, caused Vicky a momentary lurch of pity. The humdrum innocence of it.

'What is it you're looking for exactly?'

'A reel-to-reel tape machine, about so big?'

Karen frowned. 'Wouldn't that be at his office?'

Vicky had wondered about that. The reel-to-reel was police property, which Wicks would have had to sign for. But he would never have risked taking the tapes with George Foley's confession into work; that dynamite required a hiding place. It was clear to her that someone at West End Central suspected Wicks of putting together a case. After she returned from her leave of absence she found the dead man's office stripped bare; when she enquired about it the matter was referred upstairs. Was there something you hoped to find there? Drewett had asked her. His manner was casual, but underneath it she sensed suspicion. She shook her head – I just wanted a memento of him, she explained, I was fond of DCI Wicks. Drewett nodded and apologised: standard procedure to clear the deceased's desk.

'Did David have a safe or a strongbox, d'you know?'

Karen shook her head uncertainly. 'None that I know of. But we could look for one.'

So they went from room to room, checking the drawers, looking under carpets, rummaging in cupboards. On returning to the bedroom Karen opened one wardrobe door: a row of startling white shirts waited there, ghosts of all the days he would never have. The sight of it caused her an involuntary gasp, and she looked away. Tears had sprung to her eyes. Vicky stepped up and put her arms around her.

'Sorry … seeing these. Brings him back.'

'I know,' said Vicky. 'It's hard, isn't it? When I'm at the nick I keep thinking he's just gonna walk in.'

They stood together for some minutes, lost in their thoughts.

On the wardrobe's other side were shelves of his clothes, a rack of ties, several pairs of highly polished shoes, expensive-looking sweaters.

'He was always smart,' Karen observed absently.

In the bottom compartment was his sports gear, football boots, tennis whites, a squash racquet. A shoebox emblazoned with a sportswear logo had been gathering dust, though it looked new. Without knowing why Vicky took it out and opened the lid; inside was a pair of pristine white trainers. She removed them from the folds of white tissue, and tested the weight of the box; not quite right. She lifted up the polystyrene moulds on which the shoes had rested to disclose a set of four reel-to-reel audio tapes. Karen stared at them.

'These what you were looking for?'

Vicky nodded, and smiled. 'Your smart brother.'

After Karen had locked up the place again they lingered for a few moments on the pavement. It was a cheerful spring day, with clouds loitering on a pale blue horizon. Traffic flowed along the avenue, unceasing, uncaring. Vicky touched the handbag in which she'd put the tapes.

'If anyone should happen to ask – this is important – you never saw these. And I never came here.'

Karen nodded. Her expression changed, became wary. 'You let Conlan go, I heard . . . '

'We had to. He had nothing to do with it.'

'So what now – will they ever be caught?'

Vicky pursed her mouth in doubt. 'I dunno. But I'm going to do whatever I can to find them. You have to believe that.'

At the *Ensign* the editors were deciding the headline to accompany the full-length photograph of Mrs Thatcher for Saturday's front page.

Hannah could hear them at it from the other end of the room. She had got home at just after four o'clock that morning, drunk as an owl. The Tories had won with a majority of forty-three. She had expected the office to be subdued but in fact the mood was jolly. The country's first woman PM was news, after all, however unwelcome her politics. Tara had just arrived with coffee and chocolate for both of them.

'Are you feeling a bit fragile?'

Hannah heard this as code for *You look rough as a meths dosser.* 'I've felt better. But all things considered . . . My abiding memory of last night is dancing with Freddie Selves, shirt unbuttoned to his navel.'

Tara grimaced. 'Eww. Enough to make anyone queasy.'

'What did you do?'

'Oh, we were with friends. As the results came in I could tell Rob was loving every minute of it. Awkward, cos the rest of us were Labour.'

'Old Freddie thought it was a good thing, too – said a new government would help a fractured country come together, or something. He was absolutely pie-eyed by this point.'

'How about your Tory boy? Any word?'

She shook her head sadly. 'After that night it felt pretty much over. It's funny, I'd never have thought an opinion about a man's innocence could put the kibosh on the way you felt about someone. I think Christopher liked me, and possibly fancied me, but he just couldn't take it that I had, well, a different view of the world.'

'For a certain type it really matters – I mean, it's life and death to some. But if he couldn't see that you're lovely and amazing, and a brilliant journalist, then it's his loss. Here, have a KitKat.'

Having negotiated a leave of absence from college Callum took a short holiday, walking in Sussex and Kent. He stayed in B&Bs along the coast, at Brighton, Eastbourne, Hastings, Folkestone. In the evenings he wrote a journal, mostly about his experience of prison: he found an odd absorption in putting it down on paper. And he didn't have anything else to write. As he anticipated, Antrobus had not renewed his contract on *Go-Betweens*;

he sensed that the book had gone cold on him in any case. It would join the phantom library of so many others out there in the world, half finished, neglected, abandoned. Before he was due back in London he visited Newry to see his mother and sister for a few days. Niamh gave him another haircut, less severe than the one at Christmas; he thought it made him look friendlier, though he wasn't sure.

Back at St James's Walk one evening, a little before midnight the telephone rang. When he picked up he heard a sound like wind in a tunnel, and in the eerie pause before a voice came on the line he knew who it would be.

'Callum. Is that you?'

'Sean . . . I was wondering if you'd call.'

The lag of a long-distance call dislocated the rhythm of their talk.

'. . . I'm sorry – can you hear me? – Cal, I wanted to say I'm sorry. I never meant to land you in trouble. Honest to God.'

'You didn't leave me with much of a chance, did you? Carting around a bag with fucking detonators inside it. Why me?'

'. . . I needed a safe place for them. That dosshouse was too risky, with all the thievin' an' that. I just didn't know anyone else to ask.'

Callum felt more bewildered than angry. 'But – how did you know I wouldn't find them?'

The pause seemed to lengthen. 'Cos I knew you, Cal. I knew you weren't one to go rootin' about in a mate's stuff.' Callum felt a pricking of remorse at that, but he wasn't about to concede the moral high ground on a technicality.

'You nearly got me sent down, Sean, d'you realise? I could be doing time now if it hadn't been for a coupla people who helped me.'

'It was a mistake. One of us tossed the bag. It should never have been traced to you.'

'But it was. And by the way, one of those people was a copper. She was the mate of that detective you killed.'

'No no no, that second bomb wasn't us. Middleton had it coming, he was a legitimate target, but we had nothing to do with that copper dying.'

For some reason this enraged Callum. 'You're a fuckin' murderer, Sean – why should I believe a word you say? The Provos claimed the one of that copper, or hadn't you heard?'

'Yeah, they did, but I swear to you, Cal, it wasn't us. When nobody came forward I reckon someone in the Council said we might as well claim it for ours. But it wasn't. Check it with someone who knows – the explosives used, the timers, none of it was ours.'

He heard the agitation in Sean's voice: it seemed to matter to him that he was innocent of the policeman's murder. But if it wasn't the Provos, who could it have been? Sean didn't know, but he suspected from the bomber's method that the victim had been deliberately targeted. Some rogue operative who'd slipped under the radar.

'And what exactly have you achieved by killing Middleton? There's a whole government gonna prop up the union now.'

'We're in a war against a military occupation, Cal. Wars are dirty. There's gonna be casualties. Maybe you'll understand one day.'

'I don't think so. Murder will never sit right with me.'

Another long pause intervened. 'Sorry to hear that.'

'You sound far away. Where are you calling from?'

He heard the ghost of a laugh. 'You know I can't tell you that. In any case, I reckon you're not planning to visit.'

He'd got that right. Callum didn't know what else to say. Should he wish good luck to a man who had nearly destroyed his life?

'Cal . . . You still there?'

'Aye.'

'Christ, I'm sorry about . . . Those months in London, you were the only real mate I had. I'll miss that.'

It was simply said. Sean would spend the rest of his life on the run; this might be the last time they would ever talk. 'I'd better be away. Take care of yourself, Sean. Watch your back.'

He paused, then placed the receiver in the cradle.

'And – cut! Thanks, everyone.'

It was an early Friday evening at the end of May. In the drawing room of a country estate in Surrey they had just wrapped for the day on set. Slowly the crew began to melt away and pack up. Freddie, lurking in the wings, watched as Nicola had a quick word with the director, a bright fellow he recalled once interviewing for a job. They were deep into filming on the second series of the popular TV drama *Unlucky Charms.*

The rapprochement which began on election night had been slow going, but he didn't mind. It was nice to be wooing her again. He had stayed that night at Cranley Gardens for the first time in months, and recovering from the colossal hangover of the next morning he had worried that this might be a one-off, an unrepeatable birthday treat. He tried not to act the whipped cur when he wondered aloud if the two of them could start over again. 'We'll see,' she had replied. Funny, that was what his mother used to say when he pleaded with her for some boyish indulgence or other. The words held forth a tantalising possibility while retaining the right to withdraw it at any time.

The heavy make-up Nicola wore for the camera lent her face an extra vivacity, like a cartoon version of her good looks. It was strangely stirring.

'When did you get here?' They kissed.

'Twenty minutes ago. I was watching you on the monitor. *I never knew it could be like this, Trev. We've got a special connection.*'

'Oh, don't,' she groaned. 'I had to say that line about fourteen times.'

'Who writes this stuff? Not exactly Stoppard, is it . . . ?'

'No, but he wouldn't get us an audience of twelve million on a Friday night.'

Freddie sighed: true enough. They wandered out onto the mansion terrace where a few of the cast were having drinks. The weekend had started. He briefly put his arm around her waist.

'You look wonderful, by the way. I took the liberty of booking us a table at that place down the road.'

She looked at him with a half-smile. 'That *is* quite a liberty, actually. I agreed to have dinner with a few of the cast tonight.'

He must have looked crestfallen, because she then tilted her head and said, 'I'm sure they won't mind if I pull out.'

She asked him about his week. Freddie, installed at last in the Chelsea maisonette, had been culling the overflow of books and records – the collection he had begun as a teenager had grown wildly out of control. He had packed up whole boxes for the charity shop. A bed had arrived from Heal's but still no curtains for the windows.

'Just hang a sheet up there for now,' Nicola suggested.

'Not in Chelsea. Sheets across a window make it look like a squat. The neighbours would have conniptions.'

'Please yourself.'

'The place needs a woman's touch,' he said, offering her a feed.

'Well, once I get clear of this maybe I'll come round and give it the once-over.'

That took him by surprise: he had expected a rebuke, or a dismissive laugh. Was she responding in some way to the kinder, gentler Freddie Selves? He wondered how long he could keep it up. Maybe virtue was social. When you behaved decently and put others before yourself people liked you. And when you behaved like a prick people resented you. It wasn't such a difficult principle. But it seemed to have taken him most of his life to grasp it.

They had arranged to meet at Valoti's on Shaftesbury Avenue. Callum had discovered the cafe when he first came to London; he liked the friendly Italian staff, and the non-aggressive prices. He had taken a table facing the window, so that he could spot her arriving. He was alarmed to see that she had brought someone along, a young bloke – but then he recognised him.

Vicky smiled as she shook his hand. Matthew loitered behind her. 'I brought him along just to say hello. Hope you don't mind.'

'You've dyed your hair,' Callum said to him. The colour had changed from the peroxide yob-blond to an inky blue-black. 'Suits you.'

'Cheers,' mumbled Matthew. The T-shirt under his leather jacket carried the legend RUDE BOY.

They settled at the table and ordered tea. Callum noticed Vicky give her brother an encouraging nudge. He barely caught his eye as he spoke.

'Um, I just wanted to say thanks for, er, looking after me . . .' More a shy boy than a rude boy, thought Callum.

'Well, I couldn't ignore a Clash fan in need, you know?' They talked about the new EP the band had just released, called 'The Cost of Living', and when they might be touring again. Matthew played guitar himself, but was busy revising for his A levels at the moment.

'You're gonna go to university, I hear,' said Callum.

He blushed, and muttered about offers from Liverpool and Sheffield. Callum wished him luck with the exams; moments later, at Vicky's signal, the boy was allowed to leave. As he watched him slouch out of the cafe, Callum wondered what might have happened – to both of them – if their paths hadn't crossed that night. What luck had been on his side. In the end there was only one law in life, and that was its randomness.

'I saw your story in the paper,' said Vicky, lighting a Silk Cut.

'Aye. Hannah did me proud. Without you and her . . . I'd probably be in a cell right now getting my head kicked in by some sixteen-stoner.'

A silence settled between them. He had told her on the phone that he had news for her, so she waited.

'I had a call a few nights ago,' he began. 'Sean McGlashan. Believe it or not, he wanted to apologise.'

'Where was he calling from?'

He shook his head. 'I asked him that too. Spain? Somewhere he won't be found. Anyway, he swore to me the bomb that – the one that killed your friend – it wasn't IRA. They claimed it, but it wasn't theirs.'

Vicky stared at him. That would confirm what McDowell from the Bomb Squad had told her. 'D'you think he's on the level?'

Callum nodded. 'He didn't have any reason to lie. He admitted to the Middleton bomb – seemed proud of it. But maybe even killers want to be thought discriminating. The Provos use a coded warning, right? Did you get one for the Harrowby Street bomb?'

'Yeah, it was called through from the station.'

'Then you should check who took the call – Sean said if anyone had phoned it in for the IRA it would have been him. And he didn't call your station that morning.'

Prichard, thought Vicky. It was Prichard who had radioed her that day. But how could he have made a mistake like that? Unless ... Vicky realised her mind had been playing a trick of omission on her. There are moments when you conceive a suspicion before you actually express it to yourself. Life seems to have gone on, unnoticing, but the suspicion has just lain in wait, ready to rise up, from implicit to explicit. This was one of those moments. The quietness of the street when David Wicks approached the car, and her terrible intuition that something was wrong – she had suppressed that feeling, because it didn't seem possible that someone was deliberately plotting to kill him. Someone close to home – a policeman, in fact.

Callum was staring at her across the table. 'Sorry. D'you not believe me?'

'No, I believe you,' she replied. 'The Bomb Squad told me the same thing. The method, the materials. Something doesn't check out. I've an idea—' She halted. No, she had to keep this absolutely to herself; if what she suspected was true then it would be endangering anyone else she told. 'But listen to me – don't tell anyone about McGlashan's call. Not yet. There may come a time when you have to, but not yet. Will you promise me?'

'Aye. Of course.'

They shook hands on it.

Having returned to the station Vicky checked the telephone records from the day of the Harrowby Street bomb. All of the calls Prichard had taken that morning were recorded there in black and white; not one of them was from a London phone box. She could ask him about this, only that would be to draw attention to herself. The Anti-Corruption Unit had found no evidence of recycling or collusion with the underworld. But they were mistaken. David Wicks had pursued his own investigation and uncovered a chain of corruption and bribery that implicated police officers including DC Prichard and DS Kenney, and DCS Paul Drewett. Somebody – almost certainly George Foley – had tipped off one or all of these. From that moment Wicks was a dead man walking. It was a stroke of diabolical cleverness to have killed him by a booby-trap bomb right after the Middleton assassination, thus making it look like part of the IRA terror campaign.

She had promised Karen she would do her best to bring the killers to justice. That job started right now. But she would have to be so careful. If Drewett and the others suspected that she was on to them her life was in danger. Maybe it already was.

That afternoon she took the reel-to-reel tapes she had recovered at Wicks's flat to a bank, and left them in a safe deposit box. She took a copy of the key and put it in an envelope with a letter addressed to DC Carol Melvin. The next day she would go to her solicitor with instructions to forward the letter in the event of her death.

Dear Carol

This key unlocks a safe deposit box at my bank (address below). The tapes were made by David Wicks in interview with a police snout, George Foley. The information he gave about bent coppers – as you'll hear – got Wicks killed.

If you're reading this you'll know what's happened to me. I trust you as my good friend and an honest copper to finish the job I couldn't manage.

Good luck and God bless.

Vicky

The day after he met Vicky, Callum turned up at the offices of literary agents Drummond, Walcott, at the behest of his one-time editor Polly Souter. He had made the mistake of telling her about the journal he'd kept on his time in prison, and now she was dead keen to have him develop it as a book. His initial impulse was to refuse: he had not meant it for publication. And he wasn't sure how he could write a plausible ending, either. (Martin Villiers would have his lawyers all over it.) Polly soon got to work on him, however, presenting it as a chance to expose post-imperial scapegoating, and a stick with which to beat the criminal justice system. He would only admit to himself that these noble motives carried rather less clout than the potential fee Polly reckoned she could get for the book – roughly ten times what his study of class in the English novel had commanded. Such was the age.

Polly was walking him out when she was hailed by her senior colleague Leo in the company of his most famous client. Introductions were made, and Callum found himself suddenly chatting with Freddie Selves, a friendlier – and larger – character than he'd assumed from his public profile. He had a great deal to say for himself, some of it quite entertaining. Polly asked him what his next project would be.

'Ah, Leo and I were just discussing it. The BBC wants me to do a series about Shakespeare. Placing the man in the context of his time. I intend to try out my theory that the Elizabethans spoke in a very specific accent, close to the Ulster one today.'

He looked at Callum. 'Like yours, in fact. It's remained more or less pure because the Protestant settlers from England in the seventeenth century were so isolated.'

'Interesting theory,' said Callum. 'I'd not thought of that before.'

Freddie clicked his fingers delightedly, as if his point had been proven. 'That's the accent, the music of it, right there. *"I'd not thought of that before."*' It was a decent imitation, and they all laughed.

Polly leaned in to say, 'Well, my client here happens to be an English lecturer and would certainly be available as an expert witness on the subject.'

Freddie smiled, and looked at Callum more closely. He had a presentable face. 'That's not a bad idea. Do you have a card?'

Again Polly stepped in, scenting opportunity. 'I'll send over his details to your office, Mr Selves.'

'It's Freddie, please,' he replied grandly. 'We should all have lunch.'

'His favourite sentence,' said Leo with a wink. 'Come along, Freddie, the car's waiting for you.' He hurried him off towards the lift.

Polly turned a rather pleased expression on Callum. 'That's two deals I've made for you in one morning. And while we were talking I thought of a title for your book – *Not to Yield*. You know, from "Ulysses", the Tennyson poem?'

Callum smiled at her and said he'd think it over. She would make a success of him if he wasn't careful.

On his way back home through Covent Garden he stopped at a record shop, having noticed the new David Bowie LP in the window. He did love a gatefold sleeve, though the cover of *Lodger* was faintly repellent. Bowie was photographed full-length in the broken posture of one who had just crash-landed on a bathroom floor, his black-suited body twisted and his face askew, like an Egon Schiele reimagined on a Polaroid. He had to think twice before buying it.

He had turned down Fleet Street when he realised he was close to the offices of the *Ensign*. He must have passed the building hundreds of times before on his perambulations. It was mid-afternoon. He knew how busy she was; she would probably dread persons from Porlock dropping by as the evening deadline approached. He hesitated on the step, caught in two minds, before he entered. He asked for her by name, and had just arranged his features in an expression of hopeful enquiry when the man at reception informed him that Miss Strode wasn't in the building. He nodded his thanks and was quickly back on the street again. Then he began to wonder if she was in fact up there and had told reception to fob him off. Unsolicited visitors *were* a pest.

He was in a kind of waking dream when he heard his name spoken and flinched in surprise.

'Sorry, I didn't mean to give you a fright!' It was Hannah, coming the other way, smiling at him.

'S'funny, I just called at your office a second ago—'

'Oh, I went out for a sandwich. It's nice to see you again. I thought you'd gone back to Ireland or something.'

'I did, for a few days. Leave of absence. I've been meaning to say thanks for that piece you did about me. I should have written.'

She beamed at him. 'No need. It went down well. Gold star and a tick from the editor. Maybe I should be thanking you instead.'

She wanted to know what he was up to, so he told her about Polly's book proposal, and his chance meeting with Freddie Selves. He'd had quite a day.

'What have you bought?' she said, indicating the record-shop bag.

A spontaneous idea jabbed at him. 'Actually, it's for you,' he replied, handing it over.

She pulled the record out and gave a gasp of delight. 'Oh, the new one!' Then she frowned as she examined the bizarre cover art of *Lodger*, apparently as bemused by it as he was. They agreed that the reviews had been sniffy, and that the video of 'Boys Keep Swinging' was wonderfully daft.

'You remember we talked about Bowie that first time we met?' he said hopefully.

'Of course I do. "Is that concrete all around, or is it in my head?"'

As they laughed their eyes met, and Hannah sensed in him that shy tenderness that had been there, flickering away, since she had visited him in Brixton. At first she had supposed it to be mere gratitude, the neediness of an accused man. But it had persisted, become weightier with meaning. So she was ready for the next thing he said.

'I – I was wondering, maybe we could meet for a drink sometime. I mean, if you're not too busy . . . '

'I'm not too busy – not for you. Just pick up the phone and call me.'

He took her hand in his and raised it to his lips – he supposed the gesture might seem old-fashioned, but he didn't care. She gave a half-laugh. In the spring-afternoon light her hair had changed colour, the brown now had amber streaks of light in it. He thought of remarking on it – how beautiful it was – but stopped himself. Next time. He would save it for next time.

Acknowledgements

Thanks to Richard Beswick, Zoe Hood, David Bamford, Peter Straus, Jon Wood, Katherine Fry, Doug Taylor, Jenny McCartney, Mike McCarthy.

Among the books I read, Andy Beckett's *When the Lights Went Out: Britain in the Seventies* (2009) was the most useful, and a hugely enjoyable *tour d'horizon* besides. I also found valuable material in *Central 822* (1998) by Carol Bristow, *Public Servant, Secret Agent* (2002) by Paul Routledge and *The Fall of Scotland Yard* (1977) by Barry Cox, John Shirley and Martin Short.

Writing this book made me nostalgic for my fourteen-year-old self, though I would never wish to live the time again. Of all the music referenced here, the one record that meant most to me was *The Clash* (1977), formative then, inspirational now. I would like to thank the band – Mick Jones, Paul Simonon, Nicky Headon and the late Joe Strummer.

My thanks as ever to my first and best reader, Rachel Cooke, whose love and support are unfailing.